"Evocative, vivid, and enchanting: Historical fantasy at its best."
—Belinda Alexandra, bestselling author of *The French Agent*

"*After the Forest* is full of enchanting references to various folktales and truly feels like a children's storybook come to life, albeit one with delightfully wicked and haunting twists. With its cookbooks that speak (and bite!) and enchanted gingerbread, *After the Forest* is a tantalizing treat." —*BookPage* (starred review)

"This utterly captivating novel blends folklore and European history with themes of family discord, trauma, and self-discovery. . . . Dark as molasses and dripping with witchcraft, love, and magic gingerbread, *After the Forest* is the fairy-tale retelling of the year."
—Lauren Chater, bestselling author of *The Winter Dress*

"Clever . . . Her mingling of the historical setting with the magical—shape-shifters, forest magic, unnaturally long lives—works beautifully. This is a worthy addition to the world of fairy-tale continuations." —*Locus*

"Offer this lyrical, character-rich fantasy to fans of Mary McMyne's *The Book of Gothel* and Genevieve Gornichec's *The Weaver and the Witch Queen*." —*Booklist* (starred review)

"With one foot in history, the other in folklore, *After the Forest* is a love song to fairy tales. Replete with secrets, magic, witches, wolves, bears, and whispering books, Greta's world is one where enchantment can become a curse on the turn of a tongue. At once sweet as gingerbread and bitterly dark as heart's blood, *After the Forest* is reminiscent of Juliet Marillier at her finest."
—Angela Slatter, award-winning author of *The Path of Thorns*

"This enthralling debut novel by the appropriately named Kell Woods is a skillful combination of fantasy, historical fiction, and fairy-tale retelling." —Chicago Public Library

"Kell Woods has a historian's eye for detail, a born storyteller's understanding of tropes, and a poet's gift for description. Woods's debut offers readers a fresh take on fairy-tale reimaginings, exploring women's agency through a convergence of myth, magic, and history. A sophisticated and intricately plotted debut with a compelling heroine."     —Jo Riccioni, award-winning author of
*The Branded* and *The Rising*

"An enchanting (sometimes tear-jerking) concoction spiced with shape-shifting wolves, a cursed bear, green witches, and gorgeous fairy-tale symbolism, and I devoured every word. If you're looking for a wondrous and terrifying fairy tale, Kell Woods has the secret ingredient. Magic, love, loss, and adventure; *After the Forest* has it all."
—*The Fairy Tale Magazine*

# AFTER the FOREST

## KELL WOODS

**TOR**

TOR PUBLISHING GROUP
New York

AFTER THE FOREST

Copyright © 2023 by Kell Woods

A Tor Book
Published by Tom Doherty Associates / Tor Publishing Group
120 Broadway
New York, NY 10271

www.torpublishinggroup.com

Tor® is a registered trademark of Macmillan Publishing Group, LLC.

The Library of Congress has cataloged the hardcover edition as follows:

Names: Woods, Kell, author.
Title: After the forest / Kell Woods.
Identifiers: LCCN 2023033313 (print) | LCCN 2023033314 (ebook) |
    ISBN 9781250852489 (hardcover) | ISBN 9781250852502 (ebook)
Subjects: LCGFT: Fantasy fiction. | Novels.
Classification: LCC PR9619.4.W67 A68 2023 (print) | LCC PR9619.4.W67
    (ebook) | DDC 823/.92—dc23/eng/20230804
LC record available at https://lccn.loc.gov/2023033313
LC ebook record available at https://lccn.loc.gov/2023033314

ISBN 978-1-250-85249-6 (trade paperback)

Our books may be purchased in bulk for promotional,
educational, or business use. Please contact your local bookseller or
the Macmillan Corporate and Premium Sales Department
at 1-800-221-7945, extension 5442, or by email at
MacmillanSpecialMarkets@macmillan.com.

First Tor Trade Paperback Edition: 2024

Printed in the United States of America

0  9  8  7  6  5  4  3  2  1

*For Ellen Josephine (Nan)*
*who was always kind to lost children—*
*and who always knew*

*A child lost in a village draws kindness like a swarm of bees: mothers young and old flock and fluster, their wombs tightening in sympathy. Cries are taken up and the child kept in safety until the mother arrives, face ashen, arms reaching.*

*The cries of a child lost in a vast forest are very different. There is no one there to hear, and the threat of the wild is there in every old tree's creak, every scratch and scurry in the undergrowth. Alone in the forest there is real fear. Once felt, it is never forgotten.*

# AFTER the FOREST

# 1

## Forest Fair

**Lindenfeld, the Black Forest**
**April 1650**

*Once upon a time, in a land where the winter snows fall thick
and deep, a young viscountess sat sewing by her window. She
was content. She carried a child, her first, and her husband was
home again after long years away at war. As she sewed, the lady
pricked her finger with her needle. Three bright drops of blood, a
deep and startling crimson, fell upon the snow lining the ebony
window ledge. The three together—black, white, red—were such a
pretty sight that the viscountess smiled and whispered a little spell
to herself. A daughter, she charmed. With hair as black as the ebony
frame, lips as red as blood, and skin as fair as winter snow.*

It is a delicate thing, the smoking of a wild-bee hive. There is a
rhythm to it that cannot be rushed, a knowing: of the bees themselves, of flame and air, of the seasons. Greta Rosenthal had done it
so often she had ceased to think upon it. She merely pressed a hand
to the old beech tree in greeting—it was always wise to respect the
elders of the forest—knotted her skirts, checked the satchel hanging at her shoulder and began to climb, her bare toes slipping easily
into the notches cut into the smooth, silver-grey bark.

The hive nestled high in the tree's heart. Greta propped herself
between two branches and listened. The murmur of moving leaves,
the ceaseless hum that signaled the bees' contentedness. Satisfied,
she drew a handful of green pine needles and an ember encased in
river-damp moss from the satchel, breathed gentle life back into the

latter, and lit the needles. The tang of burning pine filled her nose as she tucked the ember away and carefully, carefully, slid aside the board covering the hive's entrance. Within, hundreds of bees coated swaths of golden comb in a warm, moving mass. Greta held the burning needles close. The spring air was warm and gentle and it was not long before the bees succumbed to the smoke's sleepy spell. She drew her knife from her belt and cut away a slab of comb, tucking it into her satchel. She raised the knife to cut more, then faltered as a wave of sudden faintness washed over her. Greta fumbled for the tree, balance lost, breath hissing as the blade sliced her hand.

Three bright drops of blood, a deep and startling crimson, fell onto her apron.

She stared at it, removed from the pain, fascinated by the sight of the blood mingling with honey and the remnants of the morning's baking—ginger and cinnamon, rose water and cloves—upon the pale linen. A bitter taste rose in her mouth. Her throat burned and her gaze blurred, until it was not an apron she was seeing, but a spreading of winter snow. Not *her* blood, but someone else's. Three drops, and more.

Much, much more.

She removed the coif from her hair and used it to bind her hand, then forced herself to cut the honeycomb she had come for, clumsily thrusting the sticky chunks into the satchel along with her knife. For a heart's beat her eyes cleared and she glimpsed a shadow through the trees below.

A shadow in the shape of a woman.

Greta gasped, lost her footing, and fell. The powdery crunch of snow beneath her, a surge of cold, the breath pushed from her lungs. Black branches above, and a winter-grey sky. Then nothing.

Spring-green leaves sharpened slowly against a blue sky. The scent of crushed larkspurs and the drowsy hum of the bees. Greta sat up gingerly, tested each of her limbs. Nothing damaged. Her satchel lay nearby. She slipped its strap over her shoulder and got to her feet, brushing the forest from her skirt.

When had the birds stopped singing? Greta had the distinct sensation that she was not alone. That someone, or something, was watching her. The air at the back of her neck turned to ice. Slow as winter, she turned.

The bear was enormous. Larger, surely, than any of God's creatures had a right to be. The mound of muscle atop its sloping shoulders meant it reared tall as a common man. Its black fur gleamed. It gave a long, dusky breath, then, horribly, swung toward her, enormous paws strangely silent on the forest floor. Closer and closer it came, until Greta felt its warm breath and smelled its earthy, animal scent. Her heart crashed against her ribs. Her body screamed at her to run, to get down the mountain and behind the safety of her own door. But she remembered tales from the hunt. Wolves, boars . . . any predator will attack when its prey flees. It is instinct; a command surging in the blood, nameless and ancient.

To run is to die.

The bear nosed Greta's sticky-sweet hand, licking the honey away. It was gentle as a lamb. And yet one strike was all it would take. A single blow with one huge paw to kill her where she stood.

Fear crushed her in its claws. The world filled with muscle and fur as the bear shunted yet closer. Would it devour her now or drag her, half dead, into the woods? Wisdom failed. She staggered backward, tripped, and sprawled on her rump in the ferns. Curled herself up and cowered against the earth. Words came to her, unbidden, tumbling from her mouth.

> *"Leaf that's green, earth and air,*
> *Protect me, forest fair."*

She took a rasping breath.

> *"Darkness, devil, death and fear*
> *Get thee gone from here."*

They were old words, and strange, springing forth from the depths of her memory like startled birds, but they were *good*. Her mother had taught them to her, of that much she was certain, though Greta could not say when. She said the words again, faster.

> *"Leaf that's green, earth and air,*
> *Protect me, forest fair.*
> *Darkness, devil, death and fear*
> *Get thee gone from here."*

Again and again, each time waiting for the bear's claws to rake her body, for its teeth to tear into the back of her neck. Hours passed, it seemed. Days, months, years. At last, when the flood of mother-prayer finally faded, Greta opened her eyes. She saw her own hand—a beetle crawling merrily across one knuckle—and strands of her hair, copper-bright. She raised her head. But for the lingering scent of pine smoke and the humming of the bees above, all was still. The bear was gone.

Greta did not wait for the beast's return. Down the mountain she tore, bare feet slapping on pine needles and moss, satchel thudding against her hip. She scrabbled over a bank of twisted roots. Fell. Rose. Fell again. Thought fleetingly of her shoes, back at the base of the tree. There would be no returning for them now. With every step she heard the bear behind her, felt its hot breath between her shoulder blades. Vaulting over the mossy flank of a fallen oak she glimpsed—in the timeless, weightless eternity of flight—a child, tucked between wood and earth, its upturned eyes a violent blue. Then she was falling.

"*Oomph.*"

The angle of the world was all wrong: uphill was down, the sky was not in its accustomed place, and there was dirt where air should have been. Greta coughed and wheezed, vaguely aware that the child was screaming.

"S-stop," she spluttered into the dirt. "Be quiet."

The child shrieked on. Greta shoved herself up. "Stop it, or you will bring the very Devil down upon us both!"

The girl's mouth snapped shut.

"Thank you." Greta took in the child's face, the angry-looking scars marring her cheek and neck. This was Jochem Winter's youngest daughter, Brigitta, her scars the result of a hearthside accident when she was little more than a babe. Greta raised a warning hand in the child's direction, then rose unsteadily. The mountainside was peaceful in her wake, fir and spruce, pine and beech standing to calm attention. A wren tittered and its mate answered. A child's inquisitive voice drifted up from the fields far below, followed by a woman's faint reply.

There was no sign of the black bear.

"By all the stars." Greta slumped back against the tree. Her jaw trembled and her words jumped and stuttered, but she felt an unreasonable urge to laugh. Brigitta Winter looked on, blue eyes wide with fear. Greta did laugh then, a wild, incongruous cackle that, when echoed back to her by the forest, sounded unsettlingly like a sob. She glanced at the child and forced herself to calm.

"What are you doing so far from the village, Brigitta? Are you lost?"

"Yes. My father is down in his fields," the girl said, hugging herself. "He'll miss me, soon enough, and come to find me."

Brigitta was not the sort of child to wander the forest alone. Her family lived in a fine house near the Marktplatz, with two servants and a cook. At the same age, Greta could have skimmed lightly up a tree to see the shape of the land. She could build a fire and find water. She would never have left the house without her tinderbox and knife, and a cautionary store of nuts or berries in her pocket. You learn to be careful when you have been lost.

"Your father may not come for you," she said gently. "No doubt he's busy with the planting. I can take you to him, though." She offered her hand. "Here, let me help you up—"

"*Don't touch me!*" Brigitta cried.

Greta drew back as though she had been burned. She had known Brigitta her whole life. Could recall her as a baby, sweet and plump, eager for gingerbread on market days. Now her face was hard with mistrust.

"I know it can be frightening here when you're alone," Greta said warily. "But I promise you, Brigitta, no harm shall come to you." She glanced back up the slope, half expecting the bear to loom once more into sight. "That is, if you do exactly as I say."

The child made no reply. She simply laid her head upon her knees and began to cry, great wretched sobs that shook her entire body.

"Did you know, Brigitta," Greta said, casting another careful glance up the mountain, "that when I was a girl—not much younger than you are now—I became lost in the woods. I was so frightened. I would have given anything for someone kind to come along and help me."

Brigitta stilled. She raised her head slightly, peeking at Greta over her tear-dampened skirt. "Is that—is that when you found the little house? Made of gingerbread?"

*"Brigitta? Where are you?"*

"That's my sister," Brigitta said, scrambling to her feet and wiping her cheeks. "Papa must have sent her to look for me. *I'm here, Ingrid!"*

Part of Greta wanted to tell both Ingrid and Brigitta to quiet themselves, lest the bear hear. The rest of her was lost, adrift in memory. *I will eat a piece of the roof, and you can eat the window . . .*

Ingrid Winter appeared between the trees, her skirts held carefully off the ground, her golden hair neat beneath a spotless coif. Behind her, glimpses of the valley dozing below, the shining river, the tiny reddish blobs that were grazing cattle. And above them, the steep, forested face of the opposing mountain. "What are you doing up here, Brigitta? Papa said he told you not to leave the river!"

Brigitta hung her head. "I was looking for blue stars."

"Whatever were you thinking? You know it's not safe."

"Not safe?" Greta echoed, rising.

"You haven't heard, then?" Ingrid's sharp blue gaze flicked over

Greta's bare head and disheveled clothes. "Everyone's been talking about it. Two cutters were found dead in the forest near Hornberg, their chests laid open, their . . ." She glanced at Brigitta. "There are soldiers about. On their way back to France, Papa says, or perhaps Bavaria. Brigitta knows better than to wander off."

Greta could not help but throw another nervous glance over the slope. A year and a half had passed since the war finally ended. For thirty long years Württemberg had suffered along with the rest of the Empire. Armies had passed back and forth across the Black Forest from France and Bavaria, marauding, burning and looting. They were just one claw of the great armed beast wielded by the Catholic emperor as he warred against the Protestant allies, Württemberg among them. Lindenfeld, at the farthest corner of Württemberg, tucked away in the mountains, had avoided the worst of the chaos. Even so, bands of foraging soldiers had still found their way into the valley. Ragged and starving, they had attacked the villages, taking what they could carry and hurting or burning what they could not. Taxes had been raised and raised again to pay the war tax, to buy safety from the closest army or the French garrison in the next valley. The promised peace had been a blessing, but its coming was slow. Bands of soldiers, lone deserters, and those who had lost their own homes in the war were still known to raid villages like Lindenfeld.

"I *told* you," Brigitta was saying, "I was looking for blue stars!"

"All the way up here?"

"I got lost," Brigitta admitted. "Fräulein Rosenthal found me."

"Luckily for you. But why were you shouting at her? I could hear you clear as day."

"I thought . . ." Brigitta twisted one leather-clad toe in the pine needles.

"Yes?"

"I thought . . . she was going to eat me."

"*What?*" Greta and Ingrid said, as one.

"You frightened me so, when you flew over the log like that," Brigitta told Greta in a rush. "Your hair was wild and your face was white, and you said the Devil was coming. . . ."

Ingrid sneered. "What a thing to say, Brigitta!"

"What? Everyone knows witches eat children."

*Witch.* The word betokened many things, none of them good.

"They can change their shape, too," Brigitta said. "Bats, cats, owls, foxes . . . I don't know why you're laughing, Ingrid. It was *you* who said Fräulein Rosenthal cursed Herr Drescher's field. And that—"

"Hush, Brigitta!"

"—she brought down a storm once, and ruined the harvest."

"*Brigitta!*" Ingrid's cheeks burned.

"I heard you speaking to Frau Lutz of it just last week," the girl continued. "She said that when Fräulein Rosenthal was a little girl, she killed an old woman." Brigitta squinted up at Greta, the scars on her cheek shining with the memory of long-ago flame. "Frau Lutz said you pushed that old woman into an oven full of fire and burnt her up. She said it made you strange."

Greta had always suspected that the village women spoke of her when she was not there to hear them. Gathered together like that, the shreds of her past were . . . worrying. Especially when the only real link to that time was at this moment laid open on her workbench, in plain sight of anyone who happened to peer through the window. The witch's book, Hans called it, among other troubling names. Thoughtless to leave it lying there like that. She had seen women—good, kind women—accused of witchery for possessing far less.

"Is it true?" Brigitta asked.

Greta forced herself to meet the girl's eyes. *In truth, I cannot remember. It was a long time ago and I was very young.* These were the words she would have uttered, were she a braver soul. The temptation to defend herself, to dispel the lies the village women shared like eggs and cabbages, burned her tongue. But there was nothing she could say. For all she knew she *had* killed the old woman. No, not just killed. *Burned.*

"And was the house made of gingerbread?" Brigitta asked. "Frau Lutz said the house was made of gingerbread."

*No. It was made of wood and stone, like any other.*

"I thought you were a sensible girl, Brigitta," Greta managed. "All this talk of storms and gingerbread houses, and eating children. I didn't know you believed in such nonsense."

"Everyone knows there are witches," Ingrid said, sharp. "And you cannot blame the child for saying such things when you roam the forest as you do, Greta, all alone and wild. You aren't even wearing shoes."

Greta scrunched her bare toes beneath her skirts.

"Perhaps Greta's hair frightened you, Brigitta," Ingrid said. "Red *is* the Devil's color, after all."

Greta raised a hand to her hair. It had come loose from its pins, rambling down her back.

"My hair isn't red," she said, poking ineffectually at it. It had always been a curse, her hair. If she stood in the shade it seemed plain enough, innocent and brownish. But in the light russet and bronze conspired to be noticed.

"Yes, it is," Brigitta said, not unkindly.

Greta did not trust herself to speak. She had realized, with a sinking heart, that her hair ribbon, a fine strip of lavender linen embroidered with a trail of ivy, was also lost. It had belonged to her mother.

Ingrid led her sister away. "Come, Brigitta. We'd best get back to Papa."

"That wasn't very kind." Brigitta's voice floated back. "Especially when she'll be leaving Lindenfeld soon."

"Leaving? Whatever do you mean?"

"I heard Father say Hans Rosenthal lost all his money throwing bones. He will not be able to repay what he borrowed from Herr Hueber and will have to give up his holding. Look! Blue stars!" She scampered through the trees, stopping before a carpet of violet-blue flowers, their petals bowed like wives at prayer. "Aren't they lovely?"

Greta hurried after the sisters. "Wait . . . what did your father say, Brigitta?"

"He said he will rent your land once your brother loses it."

"When did you hear this?" Ingrid, too, was frowning. "There must be some mistake."

"See how upset my sister is?" Brigitta smirked. "She thinks your brother very handsome, you know. She sits in wait for him in the Marktplatz, so he can happen upon her *unexpectedly*."

"*Brigitta!*"

Ordinarily Greta would have smiled at this; women had always admired Hans's golden curls. "Did your father say anything else?"

"Only that it's to be settled on May Day."

The tale had the clear shine of truth to it. It was no secret that others coveted the Rosenthals' holding, and that of them all Jochem Winter had ever been the most persistent. And debts were often reckoned on May Day, struck over a cup of beer and a merry dance with another man's wife. But May Day fell after Walpurgis Night—in three days' time.

"You're certain it was May Day, Brigitta?"

"Yes. That's when Herr Hueber wants his money." Brigitta grasped a handful of blue stars and prepared to yank.

"Don't do it like that," Greta warned, distracted. "The juice is poisonous."

"Poisonous? But they're so beautiful!"

"That doesn't mean they won't hurt you." Greta sliced the stalks neatly with her knife, wincing at the pain in her wounded hand. "Some of the loveliest flowers in the forest are the most dangerous. Here; try not to touch the stems."

"What about those white ones there?"

"They're just snowdrops. How much does Hans owe Herr Hueber, Brigitta? Did your father say?"

"No. Can you cut me some snowdrops, please?"

Ingrid stamped her foot. "Brigitta, come along!"

Greta cut the snowdrops, her mind already back at the house, counting the baskets of gingerbread stacked neatly for Walpurgis. She hated the festival, always had. There had been years during the war when the festivities had not gone ahead, and though she had pretended disappointment she had secretly been relieved. The crowds, the noise, the costumed witches hideous in the alleyways, and everywhere fire. But there was no avoiding it—not with the coin her gingerbread made there. She had hoped the festival would earn enough to pay her taxes and part of the year's rent, with a little left over. She had planned to buy linen for a new shift; both of hers were wearing thin. Hans needed a new coat, too, despite Greta's careful patching.

"Brigitta? Are you sure your father didn't say how much?"

"Yes. But he *did* say it will be for the best. He's going to run pigs on your land, he says, when the baron signs the holding over to him. Better that than wasting like it is now." She plucked the snow-drops from Greta's grasp and stroked one sad, white petal. "Perhaps it would be different if you had a husband, but he says you'll never have one because you have no dowry. Not that it matters. After all, no one wants to marry a witch."

# 2

## The Witch's Book

*It was an innocent enough spell, a harmless cast to bestow beauty upon a longed-for child. But the viscountess was young and innocent. She did not see that the wind that day was ill-omened, or that the moon was deep into its waning turn. No sooner had the words left her lips than the little spell twisted and thrummed in her bloodred womb.*

Witches always have red hair. It's the Devil's color.

Greta's coif was ruined, the linen stained a watery crimson as though her hair had seeped into the cloth. Dirt smeared her bodice. Her overskirt had ripped during her flight down the mountain, and there was blood on her apron. She knelt in the shallows near the falls in her shift and petticoat, scrubbing at her clothes with crushed soapwort until her fingers were red with cold. It was only when the cut on her hand began to bleed again, threatening to undo her hard work, that she stopped to hang her clothes on the rocks.

The Wolf River fell no less than seven times as it cascaded down to join the Schnee. Water grumbled and rushed above and below, the heavy roar of it reverberating through the forest. There were pools tucked beneath pools, secret places where one could float on one's back and watch the clouds, or wash one's hair with only the birds for company. Greta had done just that countless times and yet now, as she regarded her reflection in the pool, she felt far from peaceful. Or clean. She unlaced her stays and threw them onto the rocks, then seized the soapy leaves and plunged into the water, skin goosing with cold, shift and petticoat foaming around her. She scoured the last of the blood and dirt from her skin, soaped her hair and rinsed it clean. Soaped it again and again, combing the lengths with her fingers until she was out of breath. Still, her reflection wavered back at her, unchanged.

Blood. Dirt. Tears. If only other things could scrub away as easily.

At last she waded back to the bank, reaching it in time to see her stays slip from their rocky moorings and—buoyed by the stiffened reeds giving them their shape—sail gracefully over the falls.

"For the stars' sake . . ."

She slid down the steep path, only to see the stays reach the edge of the pool below and drop tantalizingly out of sight. Greta slipped after them, soaking and shivering, damp ferns tugging at her ankles. She twisted through a narrow fall of rocks—and slithered to an abrupt halt.

There was a man climbing the path from the pool below.

A glance was all it took for Greta to know that he was not of Lindenfeld, nor any other village in the valley. Ingrid Winter's talk of passing soldiers flared in her mind. She had lived through the war. Had seen what careless violence soldiers could inflict when they had a mind to. She wondered how far she would get were she to run. There was an old hut not far from where she stood. Her father had used to shelter there when he was out cutting and caught in bad weather. It was rough, but it had a door.

The man saw her, stopped. "Don't be afraid," he said, raising a palm. "I mean you no harm."

His voice hinted of Tyrol, the land of mountains to the south. No soldier she had ever known had hailed from there. Even so she scanned the forest, the rocks below, the water. He might not be alone. Soldiers, even those whose regiments had been disbanded, rarely were. She saw nothing but a puddle of belongings in the ferns: some clothes, a bow and a sword, a rolled blanket. A little cook pot, pitted and scratched with age, and a hunting horn of gleaming bone. No telltale soldier's buffcoat, no bandolier or musket.

"You see?" the man said. "No harm, I swear. I came only to give you this."

He was holding her stays.

A burst of heat rose in Greta's cheeks. She hugged herself, horribly aware of her dripping hair, her damp skin beneath clinging linen. He was aware of them, too. She knew it by the way he did *not* look at her.

"I—thank you." She took the sodden garment from him, wondering if it was possible to die of shame. The *whit whit* of a wood lark was loud against the mutter of the falls.

"Forgive me," he said. "It was not my intention to . . ." He gestured vaguely, encompassing the awkwardness of the moment, and his lamentable part in it. Water gleamed in his dark hair. His feet, beneath damp black hose, were bare. Like her, he had been bathing. Like her, he had thought himself alone.

Greta risked a longer glance. He was taller than most; as tall as her uncle, Rob Mueller. His complexion was the bronze of one who spends much of his time out of doors, and his jaw looked as though it had not felt a razor for many days. But he was straight of nose, and his eyes, beneath rather heavy black brows, were blue. Or green. They were creased with worry. Despite her embarrassment, Greta was sorry for him.

"I won't speak of this to anyone," she said, "if you will do the same."

The corner of his mouth rose. "Agreed." His shirt was torn beneath his ribs, the edges of the cloth washed through with pinkish blood.

"You're hurt," she said, pointing.

His gaze flicked over the cut on her hand, bleeding again after her scrabble down the falls, and back to her face. "So are you."

She should turn, go, be away. Instead she lingered, her stays dripping mournfully on the path.

"Wait here," he said, and slipped lithely down the path to where his belongings lay. He returned a moment later with a cloak. "Please take it."

"I couldn't—"

"Please."

Grateful, Greta bundled herself into the thick, greenish-grey wool. "My brother's house lies along that path," she said, gesturing to the slope above. "I will keep it for you there."

He nodded. "Good day, then."

Were they green, or blue, his eyes?

"Good day."

When he was gone, Greta collected her wet clothes and sopped her way homeward. The stranger's cloak was thick and fine. It carried his scent: pine needles, woodsmoke and the not-unpleasant saltiness of his skin. She wondered where he had come from. Not Freiburg or Tübingen, surely; he was of the woods: he carried it with him, moss and water and earth.

He was still in her thoughts when she arrived at the house. Unlike the dwellings in the village, which stood in ordered rows, the Rosenthal home was a settling of centuries-old oak that seemed to have sprouted into existence, then rambled across the clearing like ground ivy. In winter, snow coated the quirks in the sloping shingled roof, while in the spring the ancient apple tree near the garden frothed with blossoms. Greta hung her wet clothes from the tree's gnarled branches. Could it really be true? Could Hans have gambled, lost, and borrowed so much that he had risked their home?

Inside, she hung the stranger's cloak and her satchel near the door and set the honeycomb to drain, then gazed around the open room, trying to see it as her brother might. It was furnished sparsely: her father's old chair, two long benches at the table. A scuffed clothes chest, a wide workbench lined with resting dough, baking trays and gingerbread molds. Aside from the molds, there was nothing of particular worth there. But Greta's mother had woven the rugs covering the floor, and her father had crafted the workbench. Generations of Rosenthal women had scrubbed the table to a comforting gloss, while the squat stone oven—the heart of the house—had delivered hundreds, no, *thousands* of pieces of gingerbread over the years. Many times, the sweet golden bread had been all that stood between Hans and Greta, and starvation.

Was it all truly lost on the roll of a carved knucklebone?

*. . . you took your time.*

The voice was the barest whisper in the back of Greta's mind, lisping and female, so soft she might have missed hearing it altogether had she not expected it. She crossed the room. The book lay where she had left it that morning on the workbench, surrounded by the debris of a half-finished bake.

*. . . how long does it take to cut honeycomb?* it asked.

"I'm sorry," Greta said. She thought of the strange sickness that had come over her in the beech tree. The bear, and the old rhyme her fear had awoken. How to explain it all?

"I had some trouble," she said simply. The book would ask questions—it always did—and there was no time for that. The possibility that Brigitta's final words were true—that Hans had indeed gone and lost their home, as she had always feared he would—filled her with a hurrying fear. She needed to speak to her brother.

*. . . I can see that,* the book said. *Fall in the river, did you?*

"You could say that."

*. . . no shoes? You look like a hedge whore, dearie.*

Ordinarily, Greta paid no mind to the book when it said such things. But today, with the memory of her meeting with Ingrid and Brigitta still fresh in her mind, the barb stung.

"At least I have feet," she said, passing beneath the ladder leading to the sleeping loft. Hans had draped a shirt carelessly over a rung and its sleeve brushed her cheek. She swiped it irritably away and pushed aside the curtain separating her own small space from the rest of the house. A cracked washbasin, a little pot filled with wilting snowdrops, a bunch of dried lavender hanging above the narrow bed.

She shrugged out of her wet things and reached for the fresh clothes—dry shift and stays, nut-brown skirt and undyed bodice and sleeves—hanging neatly on a row of hooks. She dressed quickly, coiling up her wet hair and pinning it beneath a clean coif.

Less like a hedge whore, though still shoeless. She would have to take small steps and hope her skirts hid her bare feet.

*. . . you're not going out again, are you?* the book asked peevishly as Greta emerged.

"I have to go down to the mill."

*. . . we've work to do. Or did you fail to notice the mess you've left?* Pages fluttered as though touched by a breeze.

"We'll finish when I get back," Greta told it. "I'm sorry. Something has happened. I have to find Hans—"

*. . . ah, Hans, is it? What's the useless fool done now, then?*

"I'll explain everything when I get back." She bit her lip. "I'm afraid I'll have to put you away before I go. We can't risk anyone seeing you."

*. . . you've just realized?* The book cackled, and for an instant Greta saw the forest crone bent low over its pages, her face harsh with oven-glow as she bickered with someone who was not there. At the memory the scrawling and ink splotches covering the book's open pages—*take a quart of honey and sethe it and skime it clene . . . beat finely also the whitest Sugar you can get . . . strewe fine ginger both above and beneathe*—took on a more sinister cast.

She closed the book with a floury *whump;* she had learned long ago not to think upon its origins, or of the person who had taught her to decipher its pages. After all, the book could not help who had once owned it, could it? It was just a book: bound in the usual way, in soft leather, greyish-smooth with age. It was, however, slightly warm, in the way a person is warm: a disconcerting quality in a book, and one Greta managed, with much practice, to ignore. On this day, however—*everyone knows there are witches*—she could not help but shiver with distaste as she slid it into an empty garner.

*. . . no need to be so rough!*

"I'm sorry," she said guiltily. "It's just . . . we can't be too careful." She slapped the lid into place and left the house, the book's indignant voice—*. . . after all I've done for you!*—trailing behind her. There would be a reckoning later, she had no doubt—the book hated to be shut away—but she couldn't help that. She *had* to find Hans. And, she knew from experience, it was not likely to be easy.

Ordinarily, there were no bears in the Black Forest. They had been hunted away long ago, banished to higher mountains and deeper forests than the ones surrounding Lindenfeld. Before the black bear Greta had seen only one other, or its head at least, mounted beside the hearth in the Rose and Thorn. A brown she-bear, fur greased by years of fire smoke and the fug—tinged with sweat or snow, depending on the season—that came always with drinking men.

The she-bear looked on as Greta hovered in the pothouse's doorway, hoping for a glimpse of her brother in the Thorn's murky innards. The beast's mouth had been forced into a snarl that should have been fearsome, but instead seemed pained. Not for the first time Greta wondered which long-ago hunter had killed it and basked in its deathly glory. Had it fought for its life before the end?

There was a shout of surprise and spluttered laughter from a nearby table: someone had spilled their drink. Greta watched the man's companions serve him a ribbing and merrily order more beer. What would these cheery men say if they knew another bear had come to the valley, far larger and grander than the poor, scrawny beast above their heads? One word from her would see them guzzle their drinks and rush out to kill it. Would they nail its head beside the she-bear's?

Two merchants had settled at a table beneath the bear. Herr Tritten, the taverner, was serving them.

"They say the new wife is young," one of the merchants said with a smirk. "Young enough to be his granddaughter."

"And uncommonly beautiful," his companion added.

They could only be speaking of old Baron von Hornberg and his bride, Elisabeth. Greta had seen the baroness but once, in Hornberg. The young woman had been in an open carriage and heavily veiled, her shoulders wrapped with furs against the winter chill. A glimpse of dark lashes against one smooth cheek. A fall of ringlets, shining black.

Herr Tritten poured beer smoothly. "Mayhap she is."

"Someone so young and beautiful will long to surround herself with pretty things," the first merchant continued. "We passed a trader on the Waldtrasse. He told us the lady bought everything in his wagon when he called at Schloss Hornberg. And for a goodly sum, too." He clapped his companion's shoulder. "I told you, Friedrich! We shall make our fortunes here. Embroidered velvet, Venetian lace and silver-gilt thread . . . The baron's bride will buy it all!"

"No doubt she will," Herr Tritten said. "With the baron so very ill the Lady Elisabeth may do as she pleases."

"Ill?"

"He is weak, they say, and failing."

"Well, of course he is," the first merchant brayed. "That filly of his must be exhausting!" Both men laughed, but Herr Tritten frowned as he wiped a splash of beer from the merchants' table. The baron was a kindly lord, as far as lords went, and his ill health begat real sorrow among the people. He had done his best to heal his lands in the months since the fighting had ended, supporting the villagers in their efforts to restore fields that had lain neglected and rebuild what had been destroyed. Now, however, it was whispered that the young baroness had taken charge. There were already rumors of raised taxes. No doubt Herr Tritten wondered who would *really* pay for the lady's embroidered velvet, Venetian lace and silver-gilt thread. His frown deepened when he noticed Greta.

"Can I help you, fräulein?" He bunched his polishing rag in his fist and strode across the greasy boards, glaring at Greta as he would a rat come to nibble his customers' boots.

Greta set her chin. "Is my brother here?"

"Maybe he is and maybe he isn't."

Rob Mueller's sawmill, where Hans worked, had been empty when she passed it. No water sluiced down the channel to feed the wheel, no saw knocked and clattered. If Hans was not at the mill he would be at the Thorn. Herr Tritten knew it as well as she.

"I must speak with him."

"In here? Not likely."

"Perhaps you can fetch him for me . . . ?"

"You think I have time for that?"

"Then let me in and I shall find him."

"A woman, alone, in my tavern? I think not. Come back when you have a husband to accompany you, fräulein. I won't have any trouble here."

Greta narrowed her eyes. "Trouble?"

"Trouble." His gaze scraped over Greta's bare toes, peeping out from beneath her skirts, then flicked to an old horseshoe beaten into the tavern door. "And more, besides."

Hans had once laughingly told Greta there were more horseshoes hidden beneath the doormat. *Witches cannot step over iron, Greta. I thought everyone knew that!* They had both forced an uneasy laugh, aware that Herr Tritten's wife, Barbara, who was born in Bamberg, had been a young girl during its infamous witch trials. Hundreds of people had burned in a terrifying wave of suspicion that had lasted years, only stopping when Swedish troops had marched on the town. Barbara Tritten had fled southward with her family and started a new life in the Black Forest. But judgment and suspicion had come with her. Indeed, Greta's father used to wryly say that when Barbara Tritten married she had given mistrust to her husband as a wedding gift.

Greta considered stepping boldly across the threshold and past Herr Tritten, or pressing her palm against one of the horseshoes, then raising it, unscathed, for him to behold. It would almost be worth it to see the look on his face. Almost. The zealous judgments of the Trittens were one thing; the whisperings of witchery and fire divulged by Ingrid and Brigitta that morning quite another. Bamberg was not the only place that innocent women had been arrested and burned. Greta had seen it herself, right there in the now-peaceful Marktplatz. And so, instead of doing what she very much wanted, Greta turned away and hurried down the street, dodging rough stones and puddles of muck, silently cursing her brother with every step. Why couldn't he, just this once, be where he was supposed to?

She crossed one of the village's three stone bridges and entered the heart of Lindenfeld, the Marktplatz, a large, cobbled square bordered by the Rathaus—where the Council had their brightly polished rooms and the watchmen their shadowy dungeon— Lindenfeld's only inn, and the steeply roofed, half-timbered homes of the wealthiest villagers. Behind them, the church's spire rose against the blue sky and the mountains.

An ancient linden tree, the village's namesake, stood guard before the Rathaus, its branches spring green.

Greta trailed her fingertips through the lowest leaves as she passed beneath it. Three children played in the fountain nearby, scooping cool water from old stone and flicking it, shining, into the air. They laughed as it rained down on them, skidding and sliding on the wet cobbles. She and Hans had used to do the same when they were children. Before . . .

She shifted, flicked her eyes to the church, surrounded by its congregation of yew trees. There was, of course, another person who could tell her how much her brother owed. Herr Hueber, as the village's bürgermeister, would doubtless be aware of not only every pfennig that Hans was yet to pay, but every coin that was owed in Lindenfeld, down to the poorest laborer. He had managed the village's assets and accounts, including its lands, for over thirty years. It was Herr Hueber who would, when the time came, collect the village taxes for the baron, as well as for the baron's lord, the Duke of Württemberg himself. When it came to numbers there was no one who could match Herr Hueber's scythe-like mind. Surely, then, a man with such knowledge and experience, would know better than to lend coin to Hans?

The bürgermeister's house lay on the far side of the square, its shutters freshly painted, its timber embellishments standing stark against whitewashed wattle-and-daub. It was a perfectly respectable, even welcoming, home. And yet Greta hesitated, unwilling to leave the linden's shade. When it came to it she would very much rather not speak to Herr Hueber, and not only because she dreaded to learn the true depth of her brother's poor choices. Keen-minded and esteemed Herr Hueber might be, but where others saw wisdom and generosity,

Greta saw only greed. He also had a way of looking at a woman that was not entirely different from the way Herr Kalbfleisch, the butcher, regarded a cow on slaughter day: from every angle, top to bottom.

Curse Hans. It had been so long since he had owed anyone money. Not since he had sold their father's axes, and he had promised her then—he had *promised* her—it would not happen again. *And then to seek help from Herr Hueber, of all people . . .*

There was nothing for it. She *must* know the truth. Greta took a deep breath, marched across the square, and knocked upon Herr Hueber's finely made door.

"Good day, Anna," she said as the door swung open and a thin, anxious-looking maidservant peered out. "I need to speak with your master. Is he here?"

The girl smiled wearily as she swung wide the door. "I'm afraid not, Greta. He went to Hornberg this morning."

"Do you know when he will be back?"

"I couldn't say." Anna's gaze flicked over Greta with interest. "Is anything amiss?"

"Not at all," Greta muttered, forcing a weary smile of her own. "Not at all."

# 3

## Winter Apples

*The viscount was soon after blessed with not one daughter, but two. One was fair as snow, her hair black as the ebony window frame, while the other's hair was red as blood. The first was named Liliane for the pale flower, and the second Rosabell, the rose.*

G*inger. Honey. Cinnamon. Flour.*
     The words kept rhythm with Greta's feet on the road home, a litany against the dread that had seized her heart the moment Brigitta Winter first spoke of Hans's debt. Her brother was fickle and, she thought regretfully, rather selfish. But with ginger, honey, cinnamon and flour she could bake, and protect herself from fickleness and selfishness alike.

*Ginger. Honey. Cinnamon. Flour.*

It was clear what must be done. What Greta had *always* done to solve a problem.

Bake.

It had begun with hunger. The years directly after the battle at Nördlingen, when Württemberg was occupied by Imperial armies, had been the hardest. There had never been enough to eat. She had foraged for acorns and beechnuts, mushrooms and berries, and climbed trees to find nests. How sorry she had been to steal the birds' babies away. But hunger, gnawing and relentless, had her in its thrall. She had resolved to bring her mother's vegetable garden back to life, clearing the weeds and tending the tired earth. One market day she pilfered a handful of her father's pfennigs from beneath a loose hearthstone and stole down to the village to buy seed.

The smell of freshly baked bread had smacked into her as she stepped through the village gates, leading her, a donkey with a carrot dangled cruelly before its nose, to the Marktplatz. She had stood before the baker's stall, inhaling and inhaling and inhaling, near losing balance with the beauty and the hunger of it. Those loaves, plump and golden against the worn linen covering the board, were all but magical; a reminder of a time before the brutal defeat at Nördlingen, before raids and war taxes and neglected fields. A time when butter cakes and apple cakes and biscuits sprinkled with sugar as fine as new-fallen snow would lie thick on the baker's board. A time before her mother had died. But then Greta spied the three gingerbread hearts, precious beyond measure in that season of wanting. And everything changed.

She had known exactly how those hearts would taste. Soft with honey, rich with spices. In the witch's house Greta had tasted gingerbread to make the heavens sigh and the heart sing. It was not until that moment, as she stood starving before the baker's stall, that she realized how her soul had longed for it.

She had considered thieving one. Snatching it from right under the baker's soft, floury hands. Stealing away to the old churchyard, where she might savor every crumble of spice, every sprinkle of cinnamon. But she realized, then, that she *knew* gingerbread. She had made it before, and even more beautiful than the hearts on the baker's table. And if she went even farther into her memories—the ones she tried her best to forget—she could picture other things, too. A tiny house made entirely of gingerbread and set in its own pretty glade. An oven, fiery hot. A cage.

And a book.

The shingled rooftops of Rob Mueller's mill and outbuildings came into view across the meadow, half hidden by the lindens lining the road. Greta barely saw them. She was thinking of the village's erstwhile healer, Frau Elma, who had not seemed to notice Greta's poorly hemmed skirt or her bare feet as she stood before her market board that long-ago morning, thoughts hungry and ginger-blazed. Frau Elma did not treat her as though she were too young to understand, or too poor to matter. She had listened carefully to

Greta's plans for the garden, her lovely, wrinkly hands tying the little packs of seeds with string, and had not stopped listening when Greta asked about the cost of her board. Perceiving it was too great for a ten-year-old to manage, she had offered up terms for sharing it—a pfennig for a third—and smiled as Greta nodded solemnly in agreement. A pfennig was well within the generosity of the jar beneath the hearthstones.

"We'll do fine together, I think," Frau Elma had said. "Do you mind me asking what it is you'll sell?"

Greta took a breath, unable to believe that the tiny beginnings of her plan, as small and insignificant as the seeds in her apron pocket, were beginning to unfurl.

"Gingerbread."

Greta left the road and veered onto the bridge, distracting herself from the pain that always came with thoughts of Frau Elma by looking over the supplies back at the house with her mind's eye. The sacks of flour and garners of spices were, thankfully, nearly full. She had replenished her stocks the last time she had sold at the market at Hornberg, loading the little cart Rob Mueller had lent her with enough ingredients to see her through till autumn. It had seemed foolish at the time, to hoard so much away; the war was over, after all. Now she was grateful for her caution.

"Täubchen!"

Greta, halfway over the bridge, paused and peered over the railing. Christoph Mueller stood thigh-deep in the river, a stalk of grass between his teeth and a fishing pole in his hands.

"Will you fish with me?" he called.

Christoph's father, Rob Mueller, had been Greta's father's truest friend. His mill perched prettily on the bank of a smaller channel adjoining the Schnee, surrounded by a modest house and outbuildings, including the sawmill where Hans (occasionally) found employ. Greta loved the mill—the haze of willows along its banks, the old waterwheel and the steady flow of its industry. She had grown up playing in Rob's fields, holding his large, dusty hand when she was very small, then doing the same for his son.

"You do realize that some of us must work, don't you, Christie?" She smiled as he clambered up the bank, breeches dripping, grass sticking to his bare feet.

"Of course. Haven't I been out in the fields all day?" He pulled himself up onto the bridge, dripping and grinning. "But you know what they say: if you're too busy to fish, you're too busy."

At eighteen, Christoph still bore traces of youth: a smattering of spots on his forehead, a loping awkwardness to his long limbs. He had widened through the shoulders of late and gained his father's prodigious height, but even so he still seemed the sweet little boy who once toddled in Greta's wake.

"Walpurgis is two days away," she said, flicking at a piece of grass stuck to his shoulder. "Believe me, I'm too busy."

"Nonsense." He drew a kerchief from his pocket and unwrapped it, revealing three dried apples. "I found these in the cellar. Last of the winter. Sit down a moment and share them."

He held the apples out to her. They were small and rather wrinkled, their skins red against the whiteness of the kerchief. At once Greta was back in the beech tree. The slice of the knife and three drops of crimson blood. Snow, and a wash of sickness and fear.

"Are you not well, Täubchen?"

The name—as a child Christoph had stumbled over *Margareta*, adopting instead Peter's sweet-name for Greta, *little dove*, as his father had—brought her back to herself. "I'm fine, Christie. It's been a long day, that's all."

"All the more reason to rest, then."

The fruit did look tempting. Remarkable, really, that they had lasted so well. Greta's own small store had dwindled weeks ago. And she *was* hungry. Tired, too. Tired of her own thoughts, which burbled on, insistent as the river, and at the thought of baking all night alone with nothing to still them.

"Very well." She followed Christoph onto the bridge and sank down beside him, their feet dangling companionably over the water.

"It's not like you to leave your oven so close to Walpurgis," Christoph observed, cracking an apple between his teeth and handing her the rest. "Where have you been?"

"Looking for Hans." She took a careful bite and found the flesh still firm and juicy.

"Aye? What's he done now, then?"

Greta gave him a pointed look.

"Da always says he keeps Hans on for your father's sake. And for yours. If not for that he would have seized your brother by the seat of his britches and thrown him into the river long ago." Christoph took another smacking bite and grin-chewed. "What's he done?"

Greta found she was tired, too, of hiding her brother's mistakes. "He owes Herr Hueber money."

"How much?"

"I don't yet know," she said miserably. "But I'm hoping I can bake enough to pay it back."

He gave her a playful nudge. "Chin up, Täubchen. Your baking's the best in Württemberg, after all."

Greta looked out over the river. "Perhaps I should do nothing. Let Hans give up the holding and leave."

"Nonsense. This is your home."

"Is it, though? I found Brigitta Winter in the woods this morning. She was afraid of me, Christie. *Afraid.* She's heard the stories about the storm and Herr Drescher's spelt. Ingrid said Brigitta's fear was entirely reasonable, on account of my hair being red."

Christoph managed not to laugh. "Your hair's not really red." He held what remained of his apple against her hair. "I'd say it's more brown. . . ."

She shoved him away. "It's red enough. I was a fool to think they would forget. Even after all these years . . . I should have left after Papa died. There was no reason to stay. I have no family but Hans and I never shall—"

"That's a little dire, don't you think?"

She looked sideways at him. "I'm twenty-two, Christie, and I have no dowry. Even a child like Brigitta understands no one is ever going to ask for me."

"Then why did you stay?"

"Because . . . because the mountain is the only home I know. Sometimes I feel it is all that holds my feet to the earth."

Christoph finished the apple and tossed the core into the river. It bobbed sadly away.

"Well, if we're being all dreary and hopeless," he said, "I suppose I should tell you that things aren't so pleasant on the other side of the river, either."

Greta frowned. "What do you mean?"

"It's Da," he said gloomily. "He's not himself at all. Just yesterday I overheard him arguing with some men at the mill."

"Arguing? *Rob?*" Greta tried to imagine the man she called "uncle," who smelled comfortingly of linseed oil and clean linen and who was quite possibly the calmest person she had ever met, arguing like a laborer at harvest time. "Who were the men?"

"I've never seen them before. They were soldiers, though, that much was plain. Rough. The leader's name was Conran. He's a Scot, like Da. I think some of the others are too—they wore plaids."

Greta had glimpsed Rob's plaid once, a length of strong-patterned weave tucked away in a chest with a musket, a pair of pistols, a powder horn and a moldering bandolier: remnants of his days as a sell-sword during the war.

"I asked Da how he knew them—seems to me they must have fought together once—but he wouldn't tell me."

Greta was not surprised. Rob never spoke of his years as a merce-nary, other than to say it was how he had met Greta's father, Peter, when they had both fought with the Protestant alliance against the Catholic Habsburg emperor during the war: Peter for the Duke of Württemberg, and Rob for the duke's ally, the King of Swe-den. Chance had thrown the pair together on the field at Nördlin-gen, and when the battle was lost it was Rob who ensured that the wounded Peter made it back to Lindenfeld alive. His fighting days over, Rob had settled in the valley, taking on the mill. He had remained her father's truest friend, and when Peter had died seven years ago, had taken to watching over Greta and Hans. When the roof had needed mending last winter, Rob had slogged through the snow to repair it. He kept Greta's stack of firewood high and full, and he charged her far less than he should for flour, often delivering it himself to save her the walk and bringing a blutwurst or a cut of smoked ham as well. He had given Hans steady work at the sawmill, despite her brother's fickleness. And when Herr Drescher had blamed Greta for his failed spelt all those years ago, it was Rob who had defended her. He was, in all, the best and kindest of men.

"But it wasn't just that they argued," Christoph went on slowly. "It was . . . there was a very bad feeling between my father and these men. They spoke of duty and blood, and other things I did not understand. Da told them to leave the valley and not return. I've never heard him speak like that."

"Was he terribly angry?"

"Worse." Christoph glanced at her, then away. "He sounded scared."

The air cooled as a breeze slid along the river, rustling the trees. Christoph took his leave and cut homeward across the meadow, his hair butter-bright, his long legs crushing clusters of gooseflowers and marsh marigolds. Watching him, Greta felt a chill as though a storm cloud had passed suddenly across the sun. She searched the sky and found it clear and cloudless. When she looked back the meadow was empty.

# 4
## Wolf at the Door

*The viscount's joy was equaled only by his sadness, for soon after the birth his dear wife died. His grief was deep but short-lived, for his lady's spell had rung true. Her tiny daughters were so lovely that none could look upon them without smiling.*

*. . . add a drop of your blood to the mix, my dearie,* the book whispered in Greta's mind. *Then you can bind any man you want to your will.*

Greta looked up from the cinnamon she was measuring. "I'll do no such thing," she said mildly. "As I've told you before. Many times."

All through the afternoon she had lost herself to the familiar, measured movements of the bake: the sweet scents of cinnamon and cloves, the delicious golden bubbling of melting honey, the satisfying sight of rows and rows of gingerbread cooling on the bench. Every heart that emerged from Greta's oven meant a copper coin in her pocket, for the people *would* buy her gingerbread at Walpurgis—every last piece of it. They always did.

They could not help themselves.

She ignored the book's grumbling and added nutmeg and cardamom, measuring the amounts with practiced smoothness. She knew the recipe by heart, could recite it in her sleep, and yet she was always careful to work with the book beside her, open at the same dusty page, the ink worn with long use. To not do so would result in an altogether different kind of gingerbread—no less sweet, but somehow . . . lacking. It would serve, of course. But it would not smell the way the book's baking smelled—enticing and heady, full of rapture and delight, as though to not eat of it would be your very ruin.

Greta knew how it felt. She had known the sweetness of the witch's gingerbread, could recall its hold upon her still. The little gingerbread house that had so entranced her and her brother all those years ago had been crafted with more than just cinnamon and cloves, honey and eggs and ginger; there was magic in it too, seeping from the book's pages, working its way into the dough. It was not only hunger that had driven them to eat it.

. . . *I don't know why I stay here, when you've no intention of heeding my advice,* the book said sullenly.

"Because you'd miss me?" Greta deftly rolled out the dough. "And I *do* listen to you."

. . . *then why not let me help you? There's so much we could do together, you and I. Why waste your life slaving away in a poky kitchen, when—*

A rap at the door broke the stillness. Greta glanced at the window. The sun was sinking behind the ancient spruces that ringed the clearing, the shadows at their feet lengthening into dusk.

. . . *look out, look out!* the book sang gleefully. *A visitor at this hour! I wonder who it might be?*

"Hush." Greta scooped it into its garner, wiped her hands on her apron, and opened the door. Her heart sank at the sight of the bürgermeister, resplendent in a feathered hat, a new jacket and a set of petticoat breeches gathered fashionably above the knee.

"Good evening, Margareta." He paused, allowing her to bask in his presence. With his skinny legs sticking out of a pair of heeled boots beneath those billowing breeches, he resembled nothing so much as an aging rooster.

Greta forced a smile. "Hello, Herr Hueber."

"My maidservant told me you came to see me today." He doffed his feathered hat with a flourish. "I came as soon as I could."

"That was very kind of you." Kindness? She very much doubted it. It was a long way to come, especially so late in the day. And in heeled boots, no less.

"Indeed." He smiled indulgently, revealing a set of yellowing teeth.

"The fact is, Herr Hueber, I wanted to speak to you about my brother. Is it true that you lent him money? And that he promised to pay it back by May Day?"

Herr Hueber sighed. "I suspected it might come to this." He drew a piece of paper from within his coat. Neat figures scored the page: Hans's name, and beside it an amount so large it sucked the air violently from Greta's lungs.

"Surely . . . surely there has been some mistake?"

"You underestimate my tallying abilities, fräulein. Not to mention your brother's throwing hand."

"But—so much?"

"It is a weighty sum, I'll warrant."

"How could you do this?" Greta asked bitterly, thrusting the paper back at him. "How could you not refuse him? Clearly, he cannot help himself!"

"It is not my place to refuse those who ask me for help, my dear. I am sorry."

*No, you are not.* He loved the glint of gold more than any man had a right to.

"If you could but give us more time . . ."

He shook his head. "I have given it, my dear. I have my own interests to mind, you understand."

"But we will lose our home!"

"Yes. But we both know it was only ever a matter of time, don't we?" He cast his eye over the worn doorway with obvious distaste. "The true marvel is that your brother has managed to hold on to it this long."

A low pallet leaned against the wall beside Greta. Her father had lain there when he had become too weak to climb to the loft. *The mountain is yours.* Peter's last words, his thin hands clutching at her brother's. *It is all that I can give you. Hold to it always. Keep it, and your sister, safe.* And Hans, nodding. Promising.

"There must be another way," Greta whispered.

"I'm afraid there is none." Herr Hueber clacked his tongue against his teeth. "At least, not for your brother. But I believe *you* were meant for a different fate. What would you say if I told you I have need of a new maidservant? And that I think you would be—in all ways—suited to the task?"

Deep in its garner, the book snickered.

"I'm afraid I have no experience in service," Greta said, forcing another smile.

"That is no matter. You would soon learn what pleases me, my dear." There was an oiliness to his tone that Greta liked not at all. For years Herr Hueber had contrived to lay his hands upon her when he bought her gingerbread at the market or passed her in the square. Now, as he tucked the paper into her apron pocket and let his fingers brush against her waist, Greta knew exactly how he meant to be pleased.

"Sometimes, we must accept the path God chooses for us." His breath was sour against her cheek. "*You* cannot afford to pay your brother's debts. *I* am in need of a serving maid. Is there anything simpler?"

A breeze riffled through Greta's garden, staining the air with apple blossom and lavender. How long would it last if she were to give up and let Herr Winter claim it? He wanted the land, not the house. How long would it stand before it fell to ruin, reclaimed by the forest and the weather? Fifty years? A hundred? Besides the old apple tree there would be no sign that she, or any of her kin, had ever been there. No sign that a family had lived and worked and loved there, and cut a small space out of the wild wood for themselves.

*The mountain is yours.*

Greta jerked away. "It is a kind offer. And you are most generous. But I'm afraid I must decline."

"But my dear—"

"I am certain my brother will pay what he owes by May Day. And if he cannot, then I will." She gestured at the baskets of gingerbread behind her.

Herr Hueber's brows soared. "You intend to pay his debt with *gingerbread hearts?*"

"Not just hearts. It is Walpurgis; I am baking witches, too."

"It cannot be done," he laughed incredulously. "Any fool could see that!"

"Good evening, Herr Hueber." Greta went to close the door, but one shining boot, perfectly placed, prevented it.

"You are making a mistake." His eyes glinted at Greta through the cracked door. Beneath them, curled fingers gripped the wood. "Let me help you, Margareta. You are all alone in this. You really have no choice."

Greta bristled. She had learned long ago how to take care of herself. To not rely on anyone, for anything. "I don't need your help," she hissed, trying once more to close the door upon him. Herr Hueber, however, pushed back with surprising force. Greta's heart quickened. There was a good chance he would open it, ridiculous boots or no. For the first time in her life she regretted living so far from Lindenfeld, with its closeness and its night watchmen. There would be no one to hear her now, should she cry for help. Unless . . . Behind Herr Hueber, the forest gloomed. Was the black bear out there still? Part of her wished it would appear. One beast, it seemed, could easily eradicate the other.

And the *idea* of a beast could do much the same.

"Do be careful, Herr Hueber," Greta said sweetly. "There is an *enormous* bear out there."

"What?" Panicked, Herr Hueber spun toward the trees. Greta gave him a neat poke with one finger. He overbalanced on his ridiculous heels, toppling off her step, and she slammed the door and turned the key. Leaned hard against it, listening.

"Foolish girl!" the bürgermeister bellowed. He beat his fists upon the sturdy timber. "You'll regret this!" He kicked the door once, twice. "Do you hear me? When you are ruined and put out of this place, and gazing at the stars for your living, you will think of me! *And you will be sorry!*"

And after one final, petulant kick Herr Hueber tottered down the mountain, curses dwindling in his wake.

The night passed slowly, as nights filled with worry are wont to do. Greta struggled through long hours of wakefulness, imagining all manner of sounds: footsteps, the rattle of a door handle. The slow bulk of the bear's body brushing against the house. In the deep of the night it rained and she thought of her shoes and her mother's ribbon lying sodden on the mountain. What little sleep she managed was embittered by fearful dreams: Blood in the snow. The shape of a woman at her window, blacking out the moon, watching her sleep. She was a child again, cowering in her bed as her stepmother, a poor sleeper, moved restlessly about the house. And she was lost again, roaming the forest with Hans as they had all those years before.

"It's gone, Greta." Such despair in her brother's eyes. "The path has gone. There is no way back now. We are lost and will die from cold and hunger soon enough."

Greta wanted to comfort him. *That is not how our story will end,* she tried to say. *I will find a way to get us home again.* But her voice would not come. It caught in her throat, and struggle as she might, she remained silent. When Hans trudged on, Greta's feet sank in the snow, as heavy as stones. She tried to call to him, to follow him, and could only watch uselessly as he stumbled through the trees. He did not look back. Somewhere in the snowy night a wolf howled.

It was only when she padded through the house to retrieve the book from its place in the kitchen that Greta finally slept.

. . . *poor child,* it whispered, in the quietening dark. Before she drifted Greta could have sworn she felt the touch of gentle fingers in her hair. . . . *sleep now.*

She woke too soon to daylight and the soft scuff of footsteps on the hearthstones.

"Hans? Is that you?"

"Who else would it be?"

She rose, rubbing at her aching eyes, and began to dress. Birdsong floated in from the woods. And another sound: the rasp of shifting stone beyond the curtain.

Greta paused, fingers halfway through lacing her bodice. "Hans? What are you doing?"

No answer. She plaited her hair and pinned it up beneath her coif, then buckled on her belt with its knife, so sharp and sure, and her tinderbox.

Her brother was on his knees, back to her, narrow shoulders straining as he pulled up hearthstones.

"What are you doing, Hans?"

"Looking."

"For what?"

She knew, though. He remembered, as she did, the jar of coins her father had once kept. "You won't find anything there."

Hans heaved himself to his feet and wiped his hands on his breeches. "I thought there might be something left."

He turned and Greta saw his face.

"By all the stars, Hans, what happened?"

It was a comely face ordinarily, all sharp angles beneath the brilliant gold of his hair, but now half of it was purpled and swollen. One eye peeked warily out from a mound of mashed flesh.

Hans sighed. "I got into a disagreement at the Thorn."

"A disagreement?" Greta could not keep the disbelief from her voice.

"It is nothing."

"I hardly think so. Sit down and let me look at you."

"Don't fuss, Greta, please!" He warded her off, wincing at the pain in his face. "Listen. Do you have any money laid away?"

"Hans—"

"I owe a little, you see. Nothing to fret about. A man acquires a debt here and there in his life, you know." One by one he replaced the mess of stones that had been the hearth.

"I know of your dealings with Herr Hueber, Hans."

He stilled.

"Why didn't you tell me sooner? Herr Hueber said—"

Hans was on his feet. "You *spoke* to him?"

"Yes. I could not find you yesterday, so I went to see him."

"You went to . . . ?" He clutched at his hair, horrified. "When?"

"Near midday."

"And how was he?"

She frowned.

"Did he seem angry, Greta?"

"Not then, no, but—"

"What do you mean, *not then*?" His voice was rising alarmingly. "You saw him more than once?"

"No. Yes. He came here, later."

"He was *here*?" Hans strode away from her, turned, came back. "What happened, Greta? Did you grieve him?" His eyes widened. "Did he hurt you?"

"No." Greta folded her arms. "Who did that to your face, Hans?"

"Never mind my face. Tell me what happened."

She did. Hans listened, pacing all the while.

"Is that true? Did he offer you a place?"

"Yes. But, Hans . . ." She struggled for the right words. "It was not honorable."

"I see." He blew out a breath. "Well. I'm glad you said no, then. Even though part of me wants to shake you for doing it. One does not simply refuse men like Herr Hueber."

"I have no need of men like him. I can make my own living, as you well know."

He sat heavily at the table. "What, with magic gingerbread?"

Greta flinched. "You've never complained about my baking before." She lowered her voice. "And you mustn't call it that."

From the bedroom: . . . *why not? It's the truth, isn't it?*

Greta poured water into a bowl and wet a wad of clean linen, half an eye on her brother all the while. He was eyeing the baskets of baking assembled near the workbench with distaste. It was laughable, really: every man, woman and child in Lindenfeld—and beyond—adored Greta's gingerbread, while her own brother refused to so much as touch it. He had never said as much, but she knew why—the scent of it, the taste, took him straight back to that dank little house in the woods.

"It was Herr Hueber, wasn't it?" She tilted his face and dabbed at the worst of the cuts. "He did this to you."

"No." Hans winced. "He has others to do such work for him."

"Because of the debt."

"Yes. And it would seem my foolish sister played a part as well."

"You cannot blame *me* for this. You promised me you would stop dicing. You *promised*—"

"I know, I know." Hans scraped back his bench, got to his feet. "I've got us both into a proper bind. I only hope I can see a way out of it." He smiled ruefully and kissed Greta's cheek, then opened the door, stumbling over something on the step. "You should have a care with your shoes, sister. That's twice I've nearly fallen over them."

"What did you say?" Greta hurried to examine the step. There, just as Hans had said, lay her shoes. Dry and unmarked, they looked no different from the day before, when she had taken them off to climb the beech tree.

"But how did they get here?" She raised her voice so that Hans, already halfway across the clearing, would hear her. "Did you see anyone on the path this morning?"

"No," he called back. "Wait, yes. An old woman."

"Which old woman?"

"How the Devil should I know?"

Greta sighed. "Well, what did she look like?"

Hans shrugged so hard his shoulders near brushed his ears. "Old. Womanish."

"Hans!" Greta called in frustration, but he had already disappeared between the trees.

. . . *let me see, dearie,* said the book. Greta scooped up her shoes and brought them inside, then freed the book from its hiding place in the garner.

. . . *someone brought them back to you?*

"Yes. But who?"

*. . . who indeed?*

One of the shoes felt heavier than the other. Greta turned it over. Several coins, alarmingly large and silver, clattered onto the table.

*. . . how do you suppose they got there?*

"They must belong to whoever brought my shoes back." Greta raised one of the coins. It was the size of a gulden, as round and as heavy. On one side, a mounted knight. On the other an eagle, wings outstretched. "I've not seen their like before."

*. . . nor have I.*

So beautiful. So silver and rich and weighty . . .

"Heavens save us." She shook herself. "I'll have to find whoever left them here. Return them."

*. . . yes, I suppose you must.* The book flicked a page idly. *Although, you could always . . . keep them?*

Greta gave it a level look. "We're not thieves."

*. . . I speak of luck, not thievery. For all we know this person meant for you to have those coins.*

"Meant it?"

*. . . where I come from, someone leaves a coin in a woman's shoe, they have a good reason.*

"What reason?" Greta asked, curious.

*. . . desire,* the book drawled. *Intention.*

"Don't be absurd." Greta tipped the glistening pile into her pocket and drew tight the strings. "In any case, we can't think of keeping them."

*. . . of course, of course,* the book soothed. *After all, we've no need of those lovely shiny coins.*

"We've not?"

*. . . of course not. We have all we need right here, don't we? I take care of you and you take care of me. That's the way it's always been and how it always will be.*

The words put Greta sharply in mind of the long-ago moment when—her nose still filled with the scent of Marktplatz gingerbread—she had first taken the book from its hiding place beneath her bed. For three years it had lain there, silent, undisturbed, in the exact place she had thrust it when she and Hans had returned. It had shuddered like a live thing when Greta slid it free, and she had dropped it with a cry and scooted back in fear. Heard, very faintly, a woman's voice whispering in her mind.

*. . . poor child. No need to be frightened. I shall take care of you and you shall take care of me.*

"You're right," Greta told the book, patting the now-heavy pocket beneath her skirts. "We shall be fine as long as we have each other."

*. . . although, if you wanted more . . .* The book hesitated, weighing its words carefully. *. . . . a few drops of your blood is all it would take—a small cut, say, on your hand—*

"We've discussed this," Greta reminded it. "You know I'll have no part of such doings." She knew, of course, that the book was privy to darker knowledge. It knew far, far more than Greta had ever asked—or wanted to ask—of it. It had to. After all, it had belonged to the crone in the woods. Who knew what despicable dealings it had witnessed?

*. . . of course, of course. It was just a thought, dearie. But . . . you know there could be more for you, don't you? A little blood, a little pain and you could be free from this place. Haven't you ever wondered what's beyond those mountains? Don't you want to know?*

"I want to begin baking." Greta busied herself arranging spoons and trays, her precious baking molds. "You are a recipe book, are you not? Time to behave like one."

# 5

## A Little Blood, a Little Pain

*Liliane was so fair that she enchanted everyone around her. She smiled sweetly, she danced prettily, and she wove wildflowers into her black hair.*

Night was descending when Greta closed the oven down and wiped the bench for the final time.

*. . . those baskets will burst if you're not careful,* the book grumbled from its place on the workbench. *And we've run out of straw to line them.*

"I know." Greta stretched her back and went to the window, where the trees stood black against the twilight. She frowned, leaning closer to the gloomy glass. "There's someone outside."

*. . . Herr Hueber, back for more?*

"I don't think so." Greta grasped her knife and, after a moment's thought, her rolling pin. She opened the door. Peered out into the yard.

"Hello?"

Nothing there but the old apple tree, the crooked fence surrounding the garden.

"Is someone there?" The forest seemed thicker and closer than usual. Quieter, too. Not a breath of breeze, not a scuttle or squeak. Then, the unmistakable sound of stacked wood toppling. Greta ran around the side of the house, and drew up short.

There was a soldier by her woodpile.

It took less than a breath for her to register the musket leaning against the timber, the dull woolen cloak over the figure's buffcoat and worn breeches.

A musketeer.

In the fading light his eyes were two grim holes in his thin face, his dark beard long and scruffy. Two powder horns hung over his right shoulder, and a bandolier sat across his chest, hung with the small wooden vessels that her father had once told her held single rounds. In the crook of his left arm he cradled several pieces of Greta's firewood.

"Put that back," she snapped, "and be on your way. My brother is inside; even now he has a musket trained on you."

"Does he?" The soldier's eyes glittered. "That's impressive. It wasn't so long ago that I saw him drinking at the Thorn."

Greta frowned. "What did you say?"

"I said—"

He took a step closer and the rest of his words were lost, swallowed by an instinct born of long years of fear and dread. She plunged forward and swung the rolling pin at the musketeer's head. It connected with a cracking *whump*.

"Ugh!" He staggered, dropped the firewood.

Greta raised the pin again.

"No!" the soldier cried, in a voice that was vaguely familiar. "Leave off, Greta, for God's sake!"

She hesitated. Saw, by the light trickling through the shutters, the soldier's eyes above his ragged beard. The skin around them had aged, creasing into folds belonging to a far older man. And yet . . .

"Christ, Greta, don't you recognize me?"

Greta blinked. "*Jacob?*"

The wordless terror she had felt at seeing a soldier in her yard dissipated, and was replaced with a sense of relief so strong she threw her arms around his neck.

"You're home!"

"And you're shaking like a leaf." He chuckled against her hair. "Are you quite well?"

"No! What were you thinking, creeping about the yard like that?" The rough wool of his cloak scraped against her cheek, but she held on.

"I thought you might need wood."

"I thought you were—"

"I know. I'm sorry." Ever so gently he detached himself and looked into her face. "Has it been bad here, then? Have you—"

"No." She shook her head. "No, we're all fine. The fields are ruined, of course, after being so long neglected; too many men went off to join the Protestants and never came back. But we survived."

He nodded. "The village looks good. Almost untouched. I saw too many razed to the ground, or burnt out when the plague came through . . ."

"We were spared that." Thanks to Rob's quick thinking. No sooner had word reached them of plague than he had built a series of large straw crosses, the common sign for plague, and erected them at the village boundaries. Anyone passing by, including soldiers, had given Lindenfeld a wide berth.

"I'm glad to hear that. You have no idea how often I thought of you and hoped that you were safe. I'm sorry I frightened you so." His lips twitched. "Though I must say, the look on your face was almost worth it."

She crossed her arms. "Was it worth a hit with a rolling pin, too?"

"You have quite an arm. I'd forgotten." He probed gingerly at his head, then fumbled in the shadows near the woodpile for his pack. "I bought us a blutwurst and a loaf of weissbrot for our supper. I was hoping to warm my toes on your oven while you tell me everything that's happened while I've been away."

Greta could not help but smile. "Sounds fair. Perhaps I'll throw some gingerbread into the bargain, too."

"Don't tell me you've baked!" He rolled his eyes heavenward and pretended to swoon. "Thank God I'm home!"

Once Jacob had removed the promised bread and wurst from his pack, he placed them—along with a flagon of beer—on the table and roved about the room. "You've not changed a thing, Greta. It is just as I remember it."

Greta could not say the same for him. After almost five years away Jacob seemed taller, with a new, wiry strength. Only that grin of his was unchanged, all mischief and twinkle.

"Is it?" Greta and lit an extra candle, then set a pot of water to boil for the blutwurst.

"Can we be expecting a starving army to arrive for Walpurgis?" Jacob asked, regarding the rows of gingerbread-filled baskets with interest.

"One never really knows what Walpurgis will bring," Greta said airily, placing the bread on the table with bowls, cups, spoons and a knife. She would not betray Hans by speaking of the debt. To her relief, Jacob did not ask further.

"I brought you these, too," he said, handing her a small parcel. Inside, a cluster of silk ribbons. Pink, cream, scarlet and blue. Greta ran her fingers over them, thinking of her mother's ribbon, lost on the mountain. Her throat tightened and she tucked them away.

"They're lovely, Jacob. Thank you."

When the blutwurst was warmed through she brought it to the table, adding dishes of greens and sauerkraut. The bread was soft and white, much finer than the bauernbrot she and Hans usually ate.

"I had hoped Hans would be here by now," Jacob said, after Greta had taken her seat and he had said a simple prayer. "I was with him in the Thorn this afternoon."

"We will save some food for him." Greta had learned long ago not to wait for her brother at suppertime.

"Do you remember the tree house we built?" Jacob asked, attacking his supper with vigor. Without his buffcoat and cloak he was leaner than Greta had realized.

"Of course. It's still there, you know."

They had spent hours playing there as children: chopping wood and cooking over an imaginary fire. Later, Jacob had slept there, too, far from his father's cruel fists.

It had been almost five years since the old man—heavy with drink—had drowned in the filthy river water lapping his own tannery. No sooner was he in the ground than Jacob was on the

Waldstrasse, his mind set upon joining the nearest Protestant soldiers. *I will return,* he had told Greta, *when I have made my fortune.* She had watched him on the road, a figure growing smaller and smaller with each step, until the forest stole him from sight.

"Did you get any of my letters?" Jacob asked.

"Just one. You were in Swabia for the winter, with the Swedes."

"A miserable winter it was, too. The French had joined us by then. The plan was to invade Bavaria together . . ." He trailed off, his gaze fixing on something distant only he could see.

"And did you?"

He met her eyes, smiled thinly. "Greta. I know I'm the one who brought it up, but would you mind very much if we didn't talk about that? At least, not now? It's just so good to be home."

"Of course." But she watched him as he turned back to his food. She had heard enough over the years to know that it was not only the common people in a war-torn land who struggled. Soldiers had their own trials to bear. Starvation, disease, wounds and exhaustion. Long marches, meager lodgings, dead companions, the stresses of battle itself. Looting and stealing were a soldier's right, or so they said; an accepted part of war, which meant that violence and destruction were never far away. Her father had spoken little of his time with the army of Württemberg, but on one thing he had been clear: war changes a man.

"You told me you wanted to hear about Lindenfeld," she said. "What is it you want to know?"

Jacob smiled. "Everything."

He listened attentively as Greta spoke, occasionally spooning himself more sauerkraut, or cutting another slice of bread. She was describing the celebrations in Hornberg when the peace agreement in Westphalia had been announced two autumns ago—there had been music and dancing, tumblers and jugglers, men who swallowed fire and spat it out again—when a soft knock on the door interrupted her.

"That'll be Hans," Jacob said, rising. "About time, too." He opened the door, then tensed, all traces of ease and good cheer fading. Greta, leaning back on her bench, made out a tall shape against the night. It was not, she realized, her brother, but the man from the falls.

"Can I help you?" Jacob asked warily. He turned his head ever so slightly toward his musket, out of reach against the wall.

"It's fine, Jacob," Greta said quickly, getting to her feet.

In the soft light thrown from the house, the bow on his back carving a half-moon, the stranger appeared uncommonly wild, as if he had spent long days afoot in the woods and would like nothing more than to return there. "I take it you've come for your cloak?"

He nodded. "Forgive me for disturbing you, fräulein."

"I'm sorry, who are you?" The Jacob Greta knew was long gone. He had been replaced by another man, cold and watchful.

"My name is Mathias Schmidt," the stranger said.

"And you met Fräulein Rosenthal when?"

"Yesterday," Greta put in, feeling oddly defensive. "At the falls. He . . . helped me."

The stranger—Mathias—did not look at Greta, though his mouth twitched slightly. She felt herself flush.

"You are not of this valley," Jacob said. "From where have you traveled?"

"I was born in Tyrol."

"You're Catholic?"

"I am."

Greta's heart sank. Tyrol was part of the Catholic League, the very center of the Habsburg emperor's lands. There was every chance Mathias Schmidt had fought in the war—on the Catholic side. She glanced sideways at Jacob. The fighting was over, but would he still regard this man as his enemy?

"Jacob," she said, placatingly, at the same moment Mathias raised one palm.

"I don't want any trouble," he said. "I came only for my cloak. The nights are chill; I have need of it, else I would not have disturbed you."

The thought of him alone in the night, cold and friendless, pulled at Greta's heart.

"Please join us," she found herself saying. "There's a warm fire and plenty of food. You'd be welcome."

She felt Jacob's eyes on her, accusing.

"I would not want to intrude," Mathias said.

"You wouldn't be," Greta said firmly. She threw Jacob a meaningful glance. "Would he, Jacob?"

"Of course," Jacob said, surprising her. "Please join us. It would be the right—no, the *Christian*—thing to do." It lay there unspoken on the cold night air: *even if you* are *a Catholic.*

Greta smiled at him. Whatever he had seen, whatever he had done, he was still the same Jacob after all.

"I assure you, my cloak is all I need." Unlike Jacob, the Tyroler was not smiling.

"Nonsense," Jacob said. "The road is a lonely place; I have only just stepped off it myself. Come inside. Eat with us."

"It really is no trouble," Greta added.

"Did we mention Greta's baking?" Jacob said proudly. "Five years I was away and I never found gingerbread to match it."

Mathias was quiet so long Greta was sure he would refuse. At last he inclined his head with surprising grace. "In that case, I would be honored."

Jacob returned to his seat. "Just leave your weapons outside," he threw back with a wink. "Nothing personal, eh?"

Greta waited while her guest shed his bow and hunting sword, then led him inside. He wore a knee-length tunic of greyish green over the hose she had glimpsed at the falls. It was much behind the fashion but looked so well on him Greta wondered why men preferred coats and petticoat breeches at all. His belt was wide and slung low on his hips, hung with all manner of pouches and implements: a flint and steel, an eating knife, a waterskin.

*Here,* she thought, as he folded himself into a seat, *is a man who could disappear into the forest for days and days, and never become lost or hungry.*

She fetched a third bowl and filled it with wurst, as well as sauerkraut and greens. Jacob cut a generous hunk of bread and handed it across the table.

"Tell us, Mathias Schmidt of Tyrol," he said, as their visitor began to eat. "What do you do for your daily bread?"

Mathias did not look up from his food. "I do whatever is needed, wherever my feet lead me."

It was not uncommon for men to ramble into the valley seeking work. Many had lost everything during the war, their homes destroyed, their livelihoods lost. The fighting, which had stretched across the Circles of the Empire, from the Black Forest to Bohemia to Pomerania, had not reached so far south as Tyrol, but Greta did not doubt it had shared Württemberg's fate at one time or another.

"And what of your home? Your family?" she asked.

Many such men brought their families with them, while others left wives and children behind. Greta took in her guest—the broad sweep of his shoulder, the ends of his black hair curling against his collar. *A wife, for certain.*

"I've no home," he said simply. "No family."

"I'm so sorry."

"Do not be." He looked at her. A smile, small and sad, flickered at the corner of his mouth. "I lost them long ago."

Were his eyes green, or blue? Impossible to tell in such light.

"How long will you stay in Lindenfeld?" Jacob asked, pouring beer into three cups.

"I've not yet decided," Mathias said, turning back to him. As they talked Greta scooped up her empty bowl and took it to the washtub. A treacherous blush stained her cheeks. What in Heaven's name was the matter with her? She opened the window above the tub, allowing the cool night air to drift inside, then filled a plate with gingerbread and took it back to the table.

"At last!" Jacob cried, delighted. He breathed deeply of the hearts' sweet scent, then slid a handful of pfennigs toward Greta. "Payment for the baker," he said with a wink.

"You don't have to do that," she said.

"Of course I do."

He took a heart for himself and tossed another to Mathias. Greta watched with interest as her guest finished his first bite.

"What devilry is this?" he said, staring at the heart as though he had never seen gingerbread before.

"I told you," Jacob said, chuckling. "Five years and I never tasted anything like it."

Mathias took another bite, closed his eyes reverently. "In *all* my years I have never tasted anything like it."

"The gingerbread in Nuremberg came close," Jacob said thoughtfully. "I passed through there on my way home. The markets are enormous. Rows and rows of stalls selling anything you can imagine. Ribbons, chickens, hot pies, gingerbread, cheese, shoes. I even saw a bear led on a chain. It performed for the crowd, standing on its hind legs and dancing."

"That poor creature," Greta said. Mathias looked at her in surprise.

"Nonsense, Greta," Jacob said good-naturedly. "Why, you speak as if the beast had feelings!"

"Perhaps it does. Or did. No doubt it is dead, now. I know I would be, were I forced from the forest and made to parade through city after filthy city."

"Dear Greta." Jacob laughed. "I forgot how strange you are."

Greta dipped her head, her blush returning.

"Where were you when the peace was agreed?" Mathias asked.

"Prague," Jacob said.

"I heard the Swedes looted Prague to the ground."

"We did, at that," Jacob said. "A man must make his fortune somehow."

Greta touched the silk ribbons he had given her. They had all heard of what had befallen Prague. Its citizens and soldiers had fought bravely to defend their beloved city, but even so the Swedes had looted it viciously. Perhaps, she thought with a sideways glance, Jacob was not as unchanged as she had first thought.

"And after that you went north?" Mathias took another heart.

"Yes, with the rest of the Swedish army. Queen Christina couldn't afford to bring her men home. They grew restless, unpaid and undisciplined, and so they were ordered north, closer to Swedish territory, while they waited for their 'compensation.' You'd know all about that, Greta. I'm sure Württemberg paid its share."

She opened her mouth to wryly agree, but Mathias spoke first.

"And what of all the towns and villages you passed on your way north?" he asked politely. "Did you treat them all as courteously as you treated Prague?"

Another silence, heavy with misgiving. Greta tensed, waiting for the inevitable conflict.

It did not come. Jacob went still, his eyes fixed on the table, his fingers tracing a curling shape upon the worn wood over and over again. "What happened in Prague . . . was as nothing compared to what I saw in other places. In towns and villages just like Lindenfeld." Back and forth his finger went, trailing into memory. "At night I see them burning all over again. I hear the people's screams. I took food from them. Coin, too, and clothing; whatever I could. But others did far worse. The things they did to the women. . . . Women like you, Greta—" He looked up at her, broken. "I've seen a soldier beat his failing horse to death with a hammer and starving folk butcher the poor beast where it fell. I've seen women cooking cats and mice. Lining their pots with moss. A boy crying over the stripped bones of his dog . . ."

Greta looked at Mathias and saw her own pity and horror mirrored in his face.

Jacob sniffed, wiped his nose with his sleeve. "It was easy to push it all aside when I was still with my company. When we marched and had purpose. But now . . . Worse and worse my shame has grown; it is as though a storm and a fury is beating constantly at my mind. I did not try to help those people. I let the men do what they would. I see their faces, hear their screams, constantly. I have no peace."

Greta searched for words that might comfort him and found none. But Mathias leaned forward.

"One man cannot turn the tide of such violence once it has begun," he told Jacob quietly. "I doubt there was anything you could have done, besides get yourself killed. Believe me, looking to the past will bring you neither comfort nor joy. Better to turn your mind to what is in front of you. To those small things too often overlooked. A warm fire, say. Or the kindness of strangers. A piece of gingerbread."

"Wise words," Jacob said with a shaky smile. He brushed at his wet eyes.

"War changes men," Mathias said. Greta, hearing her father's words in his mouth, wondered what he had seen to make him speak so. "It is a violent teacher. Once its lessons are bestowed it seems as though peace will never return. But it will, Jacob. It will."

The world was wrapped in darkness when Mathias got to his feet. "I should go. Thank you both for your generosity."

Jacob stood, clasping Mathias's hand in farewell. Greta followed her guest outside, his cloak folded neatly in her hands. She waited while he slipped his bow over his shoulder and strapped his sword around his waist. Inside, Jacob had taken up his gingerbread once more. He looked tired, but calm.

"Thank you," she said. "For what you said to him. I am glad that you were here."

Mathias smiled. "It is the least I can do for the baker of such fine gingerbread."

A wolf howled, sudden, close, and Greta cringed, dropping the cloak.

"They are not so very near," Mathias said, retrieving it.

"Forgive me." Greta struggled to calm herself. She peered into the forest, imagined what might be skulking there.

*Blood on snow. Snow on blood.*

Another howl shattered the night. She seized Mathias's arm instinctively, apologized, released it.

"There is no shame in fear," he said, gentle.

"It is more than fear for me." She hesitated. "My mother was killed by wolves."

It had happened in the winter, when the snows were deep. A pack of wolves, displaced by war, desperate for food in a starving land, had pushed closer to the villages. It was Greta who found her mother, cold and still on a bed of red snow.

Horror. Curiosity. Pity. This was what she usually met, when she spoke of Lena's death.

"I see," was all Mathias said.

The wolf howled again and another answered.

"The wind makes them seem nearer." He shrugged his cloak over his shoulders, settled it in place.

"Why do they do it?"

"Howl? Many reasons. They could be claiming land, or hunting."

"Hunting," she repeated with a shudder. "Two men have died in these woods of late. They are blaming soldiers."

"But you think it could have been the wolves?"

"Perhaps. I saw a bear yesterday, too. Up on the mountain."

He fastened his cloak, fingers sure on the leather ties. "A bear is a rare sight in these parts."

"Yes. This one was huge. And black as the sky, there." She pointed to a patch of icy stars between the pines.

"You think the bear killed the men?"

"No."

"But surely you told the council . . . ?"

She swallowed. Duty and common sense both dictated she should warn others. But the council would only alert the forest warden, Herr Auer. And Herr Auer . . .

"Fräulein?" Mathias had stepped closer; she could almost feel his warmth through her sleeve.

"I have not. I'm only telling you now because you were on the mountain yesterday. You should know the danger."

"Why would you not go to the council?"

How to explain? She hardly knew herself what had caused her to protect the bear. It had not harmed her, it was true, but there was something more. Its eyes? The low, sad tilt of its head? The thought of its beautiful fur struck through with shot?

"Greta?" Her name in his mouth was warmth and gold. Springtime and sunlight. "Why would you not speak of this in the village?"

She hesitated. How could she tell this man, who bore a bow and sword with such ease, whose clothes were dyed in huntsman's hues, that pity for the beast had stayed her tongue?

"Greta?" Jacob's voice carried through the open doorway, saving her. "Is everything well?"

"I should go in," she said, stepping back. "Good night."

"Good night." He turned to leave, stopped. "And thank you for your kindness, Fräulein Rosenthal. I shall not forget it."

Before Greta could reply he was gone, pushing out into the darkness.

Jacob, it seemed, was recovering from his melancholy. "What took you so long?"

He was rummaging through his pack, spreading its contents across the table. Greta counted three new-looking shirts, two pairs of breeches and a coat of good broadcloth embroidered at collar and cuff.

"We heard wolves."

"Wolves? Really?" He cocked his head, listening, but the wolves had quietened. Whatever wild game they had played was their secret once more.

"How strange Herr Schmidt is," Greta said, closing the door. "He didn't carry a lantern, or seem at all concerned that there are wolves about. I hope he gets to the village safely."

"He isn't staying there," Jacob said, brushing at one of the shirts. "Were you not listening? He said there's an old cutter's hut near the falls. It's rough, but that won't worry him. He's a hunter, after all. Is there somewhere I can hang my shirts?"

She looked at him blankly. "The cutter's hut?"

"Yes. Near the falls. He told us all of this just now. Did you not hear him?"

*No. I was wondering if his eyes were green like the forest, or blue.* She pointed to some empty hooks on the wall, and began to stack the men's bowls. "He will be cold and miserable in the cutter's hut."

Jacob hung his shirts neatly on the hooks. "I'm sure the thought of you will keep him warm."

"I beg your pardon?"

"What? You didn't think him comely?" He grinned. "Don't look at me like that. There's no harm in it. And I can't blame you. In truth, I don't think I've ever come across a finer example of a man." He frowned. "Is it odd, do you think, for me to say that?"

"You have cabbage in your beard."

"Do I? Good thing I plan to shave it off in the morning." He followed her as she carried the bowls to the washtub. "Come now, Greta. Don't be angry. One day we'll all laugh about this. You and Mathias can drink to me at your wedding and thank me for bringing you together."

"Don't be ridiculous."

"Why is it ridiculous?"

"Because even if I did regard him in that way—which I do not— and if he returned such feelings—which he does not—the question of my worth would soon come into it."

Land and gold were more important than feelings when it came to settling marriages, and she knew it. "I've no dowry, Jacob. And there's never been a man so in love that he would disregard that." She looked at the pile of baking things already heaped in the washtub and sighed. "Can we speak of something else?"

"Of course. But I know you liked him. And I think your interest was returned, dowry or no." Jacob popped the last of the bread in his mouth. "Here, I'll help you with that."

He cleared the remaining mess from the workbench, chattering easily. Greta, filling the tub with water she had left warming on the oven's stone top, barely heard him. Had her regard for Mathias been so obvious? Had *he* noticed?

She opened her mouth to ask, then closed it again, afraid her questions would only make things worse. Jacob, however, had fallen silent. He was staring at something on the workbench. Something dusted with flour, though the scrawls and swirls of faded ink were clear to see.

Greta's heart gave a sick little twist.

He had found the book.

# 6
## Fire and Ice

*Unlike her sister, Rosabell was shy. She was often out of doors, helping in the kitchen garden, learning the names of the herbs and flowers. She asked for little, which was fortunate, because her sister asked for much.*

You kept it, then." All trace of Jacob's good cheer was gone.

"Of course I did." Greta added a sliver of soap to the tub. "You think I could do all this baking by myself?"

"You promised me you would be rid of it, Greta. You told me you would burn it."

It was the last thing he had asked of her before he had left Lindenfeld. And fool that she was, she had agreed.

"That was years ago. Besides, it is only a book." Looking at it there on the bench, one could almost believe it.

"It's witchcraft," Jacob said, eyeing the book mistrustfully. "No good can come from using it."

"Something good *does* come from using it." Greta turned her back on him and plunged her hands into the hot water. "It's called money."

He leaned himself against the bench beside her, arms folded, tilting back slightly so he could see her face. "Money has its uses, I'll admit. But there are less dangerous ways of getting it."

"Such as?"

"Well, you could find work in the village."

"As what? A servant?" Greta scrubbed so hard at a bowl that soapy water rolled dangerously close to the washtub's edge. "And live in a cramped room with one Sunday a month to myself? No, thank you. I'll stay here and tend my own hearth, and walk the woods when I please."

"You could sew, then."

"Not well enough."

"You could—"

She faced him, hands on hips, suds dripping. "Do you think I haven't thought of all the things I cannot do, Jacob? Do you think I have not wondered, and worried at it? My baking has kept food on that table for years. It has made all the difference to us. So I ask you again—what would you have me do? Chop wood? Raise pigs? Serve ale in the Rose and Thorn?"

"Certainly not!"

"Well then. I'm glad that's settled." Greta sloshed her hands back into the washtub.

"It's not settled, not by any means." He watched her, intent. "I'll do it for you, if you'd like. I'll burn it now."

. . . *he wouldn't dare.* The book's furious hiss was so vicious, so thick with loathing that Greta glanced at Jacob, wondering how he could not hear it. . . . *I'll curse him through and through. I'll burst his bladder and singe his snitch—*

"You will do no such thing," Greta said to them both.

"It's a witch's book," Jacob reasoned. "Full of curses and spells!"

. . . *and he'd do well to remember it!*

Greta scoured a baking tray in silence.

"But surely by now you know the recipe by heart?" Jacob tried a different approach. "You can hardly have forgotten it. Not after so long."

"It doesn't work that way. The gingerbread is always better with the book."

"Greta, listen to me." Jacob shifted against the bench, leaned close, so that Greta could not help but meet his eyes. "It's dangerous. They've burned women for less. You remember what happened to Frau Elma."

Her hands stilled in the water. "Of course I remember." She would never forget the trial, the fever of fear and hatred in the crowded Rathaus that day.

"She did less than what you are doing now," Jacob said quietly. "And look what they did to her."

Greta pulled away from him sharply, barely noticing the hot water splashing her floor. "Frau Elma was *not* a witch. She was a good, kind woman."

"Yes, she was. But that didn't save Frau Wildenstein's baby."

"The child was sick! Frau Elma tried to help—"

"But that did not help *her*, in the end. Did it? And you shared a board with her at the market. The people will never forget that. They remember, even now, how you cried for her and begged them to put out the fire." Jacob's voice rose, the illusion of calm and good sense he had crafted beginning to slip from his grasp. Beneath it, Greta glimpsed real fear. "They might have accused you then if Rob Mueller had not stepped in. And if they find you with this book, even *he* will not be able to save you!"

Despite the kitchen's heat, Greta was suddenly cold. "I'm a baker, not a healer. No one ever died from eating gingerbread."

"You and Hans almost did." He took in her stricken face and sighed. "What I *mean* is, your gingerbread is different. We've both seen what it does. Folk are drawn to it like a bear to honey. Didn't it lure you when you and Hans were lost in the forest?"

"That was different," Greta said stubbornly. "The crone *was* evil. She *did* lure us. It's ridiculous to say that I am anything like her."

Jacob cast his eye over the remaining gingerbread witches, their clawed hands and lumpen backs. They would be the most popular treat at Walpurgis. They always were. The villagers would devour them greedily while they danced around the Hexen fire, never guessing the quaint gingerbread witches they so enjoyed were graven in the image of a real woman. That a carpenter of considerable skill had managed, with Greta's guidance, to perfectly capture the features of the witch who had stolen her and Hans away all those years ago.

But Jacob knew.

"I can't stand by while you endanger yourself, Greta," he said. And he pushed away from the bench, seizing the book.

*. . . tell him to take his filthy hands off me . . .*

Jacob threw open the oven door. Within, the embers burned fierce and hot.

"No!" Greta cried, the book's shrieks harsh in her ears. "You mustn't!"

Hans's debt, the raised tithes, Herr Winter's plans for the mountain danced across the glowering embers. She clutched at the book, but Jacob held her easily away. He angled his wrist, ready to throw, then gave a great howl.

The book clattered to the floor.

"It bit me!" he cried, clutching his fingers. "It *bit me*, Greta!"

Greta stared at the book. It looked as it always did, an innocent binding of paper and thread. But for the briefest moment she had seen the cover gather itself into a leathery mouth with thin, puckered lips. She had seen those lips crack open, revealing row upon row of pointed teeth.

It was disgusting.

It was utterly fascinating.

Jacob sucked his fingers. "You see? As if we needed more proof than that!"

And before Greta could move he bent down, snatched up the book and hurled it into the fire.

"*No!*"

*. . . no!*

Greta thrust her hand into the oven. Pain gripped her fingers, but she tore the book from the embers and dashed it to the floor, beating at it with her apron.

*. . . I'm dying!* The book moaned. *Dying, I tell you!*

"You're not dying. Here, let me look at you." She flicked it open. The witch's secrets—the scrawled recipes and charms; the longer spells Greta had never been able, or willing, to untangle—were unscathed. There was only one page that truly mattered, though. She ran her scorched fingertips over the familiar words. *Gyngerbrede that Calls Unto the Heart and Maketh It Sing.*

*. . . murderer,* the book sobbed. *Cold, callous, cruel . . .*

"He doesn't understand," Greta told it. "He wants to help."

Jacob was staring at her in horror. "It *speaks* to you?" he whispered hoarsely. "And . . . you *hear it?*"

The door crashed open and Hans scuffed in, brandishing a jug.

"I'm late," he announced, the bruises on his face gleaming. His gaze drifted about the room, then settled unsteadily on Greta. "God's britches. What's happened here?"

"It's nothing, Hans," Greta said as Jacob, grimacing, helped her to her feet. "I burnt my hand, that's all."

"Nothing a drink won't fix, sister dear." Hans set the jug on the table with a merry thump and tottered across the room. "After all," he said, throwing a ghastly, swollen wink over one shoulder, "we need to celebrate!"

"And just what are we celebrating?" Jacob asked tersely.

"You, of course!" Hans gathered three fresh cups in a clumsy embrace and brought them back to the table. "Come, Greta! Let's drink to the great man's return!"

"I am hardly that," Jacob said quietly as Hans slopped beer into the cups. "Just the same Jacob, your friend."

"Nonsense." Hans took a cup and drank deeply, then wiped his lip with his sleeve. His gaze, loose and heedless, came to rest on the clothing spread on the table. "Why, look at that coat!" There was a bitterness to his grin that Greta liked not at all. "Has he told you why he's come back to us, Greta?"

*. . . aside from trying to burn other people's books?*

"No." Greta tucked the book in her apron pocket and assembled sauerkraut and the remaining blutwurst in a bowl, ignoring the pain in her burnt hand. "Here, Hans. Supper."

"Tell her," Hans urged Jacob, ignoring the food. "Tell her about Ingrid!"

"Ingrid?" Greta looked between them. "You don't mean Ingrid Winter?"

Jacob sighed. "Yes, Ingrid Winter. I'm going to ask her to be my wife."

*. . . and a fine match it will be, too!* The book guffawed in Greta's apron pocket. *Those two fopdoodles deserve each other!*

"Ingrid Winter?" Greta said carefully. "But Jacob, she was so *cruel* to you . . ."

"Yes. She was. They all of them were. And why not? I was nothing, then. Skinny and poor. The tanner's son. But no more."

Hans snorted and drank deeply.

"I asked about in the village today." Jacob fiddled with his cuffs. "I know Ingrid is not yet spoken for. I'll call on Herr Winter in the morning. And on May Day I'll ask Ingrid to marry me." He looked from Hans to Greta and back again. "Is it really such a surprise? You always knew I loved her."

"Yes," Greta said. "Yes, of course. But it has been years since you last met. Things change, and so do people." *Or rather, they do not, more's the pity.* Ingrid was widely regarded as the loveliest young woman in the valley. But her beauty was matched only by her coldness.

"I thought of her every day I was gone," Jacob said. "Everything I did, I did because I knew that one day I would have my own land and Ingrid as my wife." He looked bewildered. "I thought you would be happy for me."

"I am happy for you," Greta said hastily. "We both are. Aren't we, Hans?"

Hans raised the jug. "Of course. Ingrid is very beautiful."

The tension drained out of Jacob. "Well, then. That's good." He excused himself and slipped outside.

"Gallant, isn't he?" Hans remarked languidly, pouring himself more beer. "The hero returned."

"What is wrong with you?" Greta hissed. "He's your oldest friend. You could have tried to be happy for him."

"She'll break his heart, sister. We both know it." He dragged the food Greta had prepared for him across the table, rumpling Jacob's new coat. "That girl is made of ice."

Jacob soon returned, bringing the freshness of the night with him. "And what of you, Hans? I half expected to find you married with a family of your own."

"Not likely."

"No? Forgive me for saying so—but I'm sorry to hear that."

"Why's that?" Hans made a great show of eating.

"Well, I suppose it's because I can see that things haven't been easy for you. Or for Greta."

There was a pointed silence. For the first time since Jacob's return Greta wondered how she and Hans must look to *him*. Her brother in his faded coat, his face a swollen mess as he downed beer after beer. Greta herself, drowning in worry and gingerbread dough. Jacob had admired the house and its unchanged state. But did he secretly pity them?

"I am in a position to help you, should you need it," Jacob said. "If it's a matter of money . . ."

Hans glowered at Greta. "You told him."

"What? No!"

"Told me what?"

"About the debt," Hans snarled. "About Hueber." He stabbed a finger at his injured face. "About *this*."

"I didn't say a word, Hans, I swear!"

"I take it you owe Herr Hueber money?" Jacob asked. "Why did you not tell me? If you and Greta need help—"

"We don't need help," Hans snapped. "Between my work and Greta's baking we manage well enough."

"Ah," Jacob said, in a tone Greta greatly disliked. "Greta's baking. I wanted to talk to you about that, Hans. Indeed, I was shocked to see you have allowed her to keep that accursed book."

*Stars preserve us.* Hans would lose his temper now, and they would all be the sorrier for it.

But her brother answered calmly enough. "The book belongs to Greta. I'll not make her give it up."

"Perhaps you should."

Hans narrowed his eyes. "I don't see how my sister's affairs are any concern of yours."

"She is like my sister, too." Jacob paused as though wondering whether he should speak on. "She told me there's no money for her, should she wish to wed. I'd be happy to help with that."

"Well, of course you would," Hans said bitterly. "Seeing as you've made so much of yourself."

There it was. Hans's jealousy, out in the world for them all to see. "Please, Hans," Greta murmured.

"No, Greta. He comes back here after *five years*, strutting through the village like a damned *colonel*, throwing out coins in the Thorn this afternoon—"

"I would not have done so, Hans, if you had offered to pay," Jacob said.

"—and now he thinks to tell me how I should be running *my* household. Go on then, great man. Don't hold back on my account. I am only a poor country wretch, after all. A man of your experience knows far better than I!" He was on his feet. Greta willed him to sit down, but it was too late: Jacob shoved his bench back with a violent scrape.

"Someone has to have a care for Greta, if you will not!"

"How can you say that to me?" Hans banged his fist against the table so the cups rattled. "All I have done is care for her. I could have gone with you when you left. God knows I wanted to. To leave this place, to see the Empire—it is all I ever wanted! But I couldn't go, could I? Not when . . ."

He glanced miserably at Greta and away.

Another silence, even worse than the last. Greta stared at her brother, stricken. Had he truly wanted to leave Lindenfeld with Jacob? She had always known he was restless, unhappy. But she had never once thought that *she* was the cause.

"I'm going to bed." Hans swayed across the room, hollow, spent, and climbed the ladder to the loft.

Jacob helped Greta straighten the old pallet and gather blankets from the chest. "It wasn't just you," he whispered. "Your father made Hans promise to look after the mountain, too."

She nodded.

"He thinks it was all glory and riches, Greta, but you and I know . . ."

"Yes," she murmured. "I know."

When the pallet was neatly made and the candles extinguished Greta drew the curtain, undressed and slid into her own bed. She returned almost at once to the grim forest of her dreams. Hans, a man grown this time, was calling her name. She ran toward him and found him sprawled in sudden snow, his limbs torn from his body, his chest laid open, one blond curl lifting in the night breeze. A wolf howled. She spun in terror. Turned back and saw her mother, not Hans, lying there, her red hair tangled with blood. Lena blinked and sat up. She reached into her broken chest and withdrew something wet and shining.

"For the fairest," she whispered through dead lips.

In her hand was a perfect, crimson apple.

"Oh, Mother dear, let my bed be made . . ." Lena dream-sang. She bit into the apple and blood stained her teeth and tongue. Away in the woods a wolf howled.

And Greta woke, screaming.

"I heard you last night," Jacob said as he followed Greta down the mountain. He had bathed and shaved before dressing carefully in his new clothes. A pointless endeavor, as he had spent the best part of the afternoon with Greta, traipsing baskets of gingerbread to her market board in Lindenfeld. Now the day was closing fast and they were down to the last load. Further up the valley the first faint murmurings of the Walpurgis drums had begun. "Must have been quite the nightmare."

"I'm fine," Greta lied. How long had it been since she had slept well? There had always been dreams—of loss and loneliness, of a crone and an oven, and, worst of all, of her mother—but there was no denying they had worsened of late.

"Greta, we need to talk about what happened last night. About the book—"

"I won't burn it, Jacob. Don't ask me to."

"Yes, I can see that. I won't lie: your relationship with that *thing* scares me, Greta. The thought of you being discovered with it? Terrifying. But I can see now that you will not be parted from it. So, allow me to make another suggestion."

"Go on, then."

"I have money. Ill-gained money, undoubtedly, but money nonetheless." Jacob puffed and panted; he had taken the larger share. "I meant what I said last night about helping you and Hans. And it seems to me that if I did—if you used my money to pay Herr Hueber—you would have less cause to use that cursed book."

"And less chance of being burned in the Marktplatz, you mean."

"Well, as a matter of fact, yes." He shifted his baskets around a pair of pines crowding the path. "Hans would be free, you would be safe, and I . . . well, it would bring me peace, I think, to help you."

At his words, the heavy load in Greta's arms seemed to lighten. Perhaps Jacob was right. Perhaps he had found a way to ease not just her burden, but her brother's and his own, as well.

"We wouldn't have to tell Hans," Jacob added.

"No," she said, in agreement. "We wouldn't."

They grinned at each other.

"That was rather easy." Jacob readjusted his baskets and continued down the rough path. "I can only pray that my *other* proposition this night goes as smoothly."

"Did you see Ingrid today?"

"I did." He began to describe the encounter and was soon so engrossed that he missed the main path entirely and led Greta onto a little-used trail, thick with sweet violets. The second trail echoed the shape of the first but was hidden from view. As a child she had taken it often, delighting in the secret glimpses of Hans or her parents, oblivious to her presence, on the wider path below.

"I saw Christoph Mueller today, too," Jacob said. "At least, I think it was him. He is *slightly* larger than I remember. For a moment I thought it was Rob."

"He certainly favors his father." Greta adjusted her grip on the baskets. "Did he seem well to you?"

"He looked . . . nervous. I believe he wanted to speak with you and changed his mind when he saw me." Jacob maneuvered his baskets down the steepest part of the path and stopped to catch his breath. "What of you, Greta? Did you receive any visitors today?"

Greta, managing the difficult slope, was thinking of Christoph and his worry for his father. Had the soldiers Rob had argued with left the valley as he had demanded?

"Greta? Did anyone come to see you?"

"Hmm? No. Why would you ask me that?"

"Our Catholic friend seemed to enjoy conversing with you last night. I thought he might have found a reason to come back."

"That's very observant of you, Jacob." Greta moved smoothly past him, ignoring his grin.

"I meant it when I said he'd be a match for you. He's what, thirty? A good age. Strong. Easy to look at, too."

"Perhaps *you* should marry him."

Jacob laughed. "Wouldn't that get them talking, down in the village?"

"They would talk over far less."

The two paths split near the valley floor—the wider trail angling off toward the larger bridge, while the secret one continued upstream to the old bridge on Rob Mueller's land. Greta led Jacob across the new bridge and onto the village road. On either side, strips planted with the winter crop—rye, spelt, wheat—shivered in the breeze. Rich and green, they had not yet begun their slow fade to harvest gold.

Drums thrummed down the valley, prickling Greta's skin. Walpurgis was a night of light and shadow, and she could not dispel the notion that, while the villagers gathered behind their walls, the hills would soon be overrun by kobolds and other eldritch creatures.

A group of riders came up the road ahead, dangerously fast. Men-at-arms, their cloaks of Hornberg scarlet bright against the gloom, and a young woman in deep blue velvet, her petticoats trailing, her skirts split high to accommodate the saddle. A jaunty little hat spilling with veils and wind-tossed feathers perched on her black curls.

"Saints defend us," Jacob breathed as the riders veered from the road and thundered across the fields. "Who is that?"

"That," Greta said, "is the baroness. Elisabeth." She winced as the horses' hooves crushed through the soft bloom of winter wheat.

"Is she—is she looking at *us*?"

The men had turned their mounts back onto the road, but the baroness had drawn her horse in. She sat motionless in the saddle, affecting an unearthly stillness. Her eyes, though veiled, seemed to be fixed on Greta.

Greta's belly tightened. She felt a cold, creeping familiarity, as though this was not the first time she had met the baroness's gaze. Then, as suddenly as she had stopped, the lady wheeled her mount, long curls bouncing, and thundered after her guards. Greta watched her go, inexplicably relieved.

"She should know better than to ride through her own fields that way," Jacob said disapprovingly. "They've all but destroyed that wheat. I thought the aim was to rebuild."

"I thought the same." Greta looked once more at the trampled field, then hefted her baskets and hurried after Jacob. The sound of drums intensified as the sun sank behind the mountains.

# 7

## Walpurgis Night

*Years passed and Liliane became spoiled and cruel, even as her beauty grew. The viscount put aside his warring and hastened to fulfill her every whim and wish. He would have given his daughter the moon, if such a thing were possible. That she demanded it of him, and cried tears of rage when he could not deliver it, is indication enough of her true nature.*

The May Tree, an enormous spruce festooned with flowers, rose majestically over the Marktplatz. Beneath it a group of young men dressed as forest demons, kobolds and wild huntsmen heaved and sweated as they raised it into place, hauling at their poles and ropes, urged on by the good-natured cheers of the crowd. While Jacob watched their progress, a wurst in one hand and a measure of beer in the other, Greta joined the other sellers arranging their goods on the boards lining the square.

"Hello, Täubchen." Christoph approached, hat in hand. He had not dressed up like the other young men, but wore his best coat and a fresh shirt. "May I speak with you?"

"Can it not wait, Christie?" A gaggle of witches and wood-wives in grey and green, with moss for hair and faces made pallid with a dousing of flour milled behind him, eyeing the board eagerly.

"No." Christoph twisted his hat as though it had wronged him. "I can't be away long, you see. They're . . . they're watching me."

There was a tremendous cheer as the tip of the May Tree reached its zenith, its crown of ribbons breezing against the evening sky.

"Who is watching you, Christie?"

He tilted his head and Greta saw a band of soldiers across the cobbles. They were fearsome to behold, scuffed, greased and gritted, and armed with a fury of muskets, pistols, knives and swords. Her breath caught with instinctive fear. It had been months since a band of soldiers had passed through the valley. They had, she thought uneasily, looked very much like these men.

"They look as though they have come to do battle instead of dance," she said. The soldiers' frightening appearance was only heightened by the wolf pelts they wore rolled across their backs. The villagers were keeping a wary distance from the men, throwing disapproving glances at their muskets and blades.

Christoph hunched into his coat. "Maybe they have."

"I thought your father told them to leave."

"He did. But the council has offered them work here as watchmen. Because of those men near Hornberg, all cut to pieces. And there are French soldiers about, too. Making their way back to France, I suppose, now that the last of their garrisons are finally disbanding, but they've been causing trouble along the way. The council decided that having a few soldiers of our own wouldn't be a bad thing." He looked furtively in the mercenaries' direction. "And so, they remain."

A flourish of notes rose from the musicians, each dressed as a bockmann, or man-goat, on their dais beside the linden tree: the low drone of schäferpfeife and hümmelchen, the lighter sounds of shawm, zither and Bauernleier. Then they merged together, the drums joining them in a wild beat. Witches, wild folk, forest wights and elder queens spiraled into the first of the night's many dances. All was movement and laughter—all, that is, but the mercenaries, who remained silent and brutish, and Christoph, who seemed nothing like the carefree boy who had shared dried apples with Greta only days before.

She leaned across the board. "What do those men want with you, Christie?"

He opened his mouth to answer, then stopped, distracted by the clatter of iron-shod hooves on stone and the last of the day's light catching on polished breastplates and helms, blades and halberds.

A dozen mounted men-at-arms in Hornberg scarlet flowed into the Marktplatz, a wagon lumbering behind. The music, barely begun, wheezed to a graceless halt. The dancers stilled, all eyes upon the wagon as it creaked to a stop outside the Rathaus. Two guardsmen took up a wooden plank and laid it out, ramp-like, between the back of the wagon and the top of the council building's steep stone steps. Intrigued, Greta edged closer and saw a large round cage, as high as a tall man's waist, sitting in the back of the wagon. It was melded artfully together with strands of twisted iron. Inside stood a small man with a flowing white beard. He pushed on the sides of the cage with hands and feet and the gathered villagers gasped as it rolled smoothly out of the cart and down the ramp. Greta had seen children run field mice in balls of woven willow with much the same effect. Even so, the white-haired man in the outlandish iron ball was quite the strangest sight she had ever seen.

"Who *is* that?" someone muttered.

"Fizcko," came the reply. "The baroness's man."

"The baroness's pet, more like."

They both sniggered.

"The Lady of the Hornberg sends you tidings," Fizcko announced, in a voice both deeper and louder than Greta had expected. He spun the ball skillfully, taking in each and every face. As one, the villagers turned their heads, following his every movement.

*For certain, they would greet the sight of a dragon or a giant, with more grace.*

"The Lord of the Hornberg is dead. Let all who stand here know that the Lady Elisabeth is now your ruler and protector."

This was greeted by a silence so profound that the dribbling of the village fountain could be plainly heard. Whether this was due to sorrow at the old baron's passing, or shock at the white-bearded man and his strange ball, Greta could not guess.

"Furthermore," Fizcko continued, "there will be a change to this year's tithes. Bürgermeister?" He turned to where Herr Hueber stood on the Rathaus steps, the yellow feather in his hat bright above the swelling crowd.

"Indeed." Herr Hueber cleared his throat. "I have today had an audience with the baroness," he announced. "She has received word from Stuttgart. From the Duke of Württemberg himself. It seems the Queen of Sweden has demanded further compensation for her armies still residing in the Empire, and that Württemberg must do its part to provide it. To this end, let it be known that the summer taxes shall be raised from one-tenth of a man's earnings to one-fifth of them."

This news brooked a far worthier response. Resentful grumblings and cries of dismay rose from the crowd.

"But we've already *paid* the Swedes!" Klaus Wittman, the cooper, shouted. "Württemberg paid its share!"

"I heard the Swedes were gone—headed north months ago—"

"Haven't we done enough?" cried Hermann Messner, the smith, desperately. "We have only just begun to recover!"

There were shouts of angry agreement.

"The baroness understands what you have endured," the white-haired man in his cage said soothingly. "She is not indifferent to your plight."

"Then how can she think to ask this of us?" called Herr Tritten. "The amount is twice what we paid last year!"

"So it is, so it is," Fizcko agreed. "And I am verily pleased to see that you can count, my good man. I will expect no lapse in payment when we come to collect *your* tithe."

"But the baron promised—"

"The baron is *dead*!" Fizcko shrieked in sudden rage. A child near Greta wailed and burst into noisy tears. "But do not lose heart, good people. Your mistress is as generous as she is fair. If any here are unable to pay their taxes with coin or grain, they may offer themselves in service instead. They will pay their dues with their bodies, working my lady's fields or serving her in Schloss Hornberg. They will pay a Blood Tithe."

"I have never heard of such a thing," Hermann Messner said mutinously. He flexed his enormous shoulders, gazed about the square. "Has anyone?"

"I have not," someone said.

"Nor have I."

"This cannot be just. . . ."

The dissatisfaction grew louder, rippling through the people like wind over a field of summer grain.

Fizcko's final words fell like a scythe.

"The Hornberg's dungeons are mighty and deep. Any man, or woman, speaking against my lady will enjoy their delights. Think yourselves fortunate, good people. What lord would allow his people to pay with their own bodies? What lord would value his people more than coin or grain? Your baroness is a kind and generous woman. She will watch over you and your children. She will keep the Swedish army from ravaging these lands, as they have ravaged so much of Württemberg. She will watch over you all."

When Fizcko and his men had gone and the festivities resumed—though with a decidedly gloomier cast that even the lighting of the enormous Hexen fire could not brighten—Greta returned to her board. Christoph was still there. He seemed about to speak again, then caught sight of Jacob edging his way through the crowd.

"Excuse me, Täubchen," he blurted, lurching away.

"That boy *will* do his best to avoid me," Jacob said in mock bewilderment. He shrugged and slid in behind the board. "I'm glad we discussed my helping you with Hans's debt," he told her in a low voice. "Seems there's no choice in the matter, now."

"It would seem that way," she agreed. The baron was dead, the tithes doubled, and her brother still owed Herr Hueber money. It would take more than the best gingerbread in Württemberg to put things to rights, now.

Jacob was looking thoughtfully up at the Rathaus. Without the soldier's long, scraggly beard his face was surprisingly youthful.

"What's wrong?"

"I'm confused," he admitted. "The Swedish army began withdrawing last autumn. Most of the Swedes have already sailed home.

The men of the Empire who fought with them for coin, like me, were disbanded and paid months ago." He raised a shoulder. "Why else do you think I'm here?"

"Are you saying the Swedes *didn't* demand further payment?"

"Yes," he said matter-of-factly. "That's exactly what I'm saying."

The sun had set and behind him the Hexen fire was growing, tongues of flame-colored light mirrored in the Rathaus's windows.

"Then why would that man and Herr Hueber tell us so?" Greta asked. "The baroness has doubled the taxes, Jacob. They said it was for our protection."

"What's left of the Swedish army is five hundred miles away, Greta. I think you're safe enough."

"But why say it if it's not true?"

"Perhaps they lied," he said simply. "It would hardly be the first time a noble man—or woman—lied to their tenants."

"But why would the baroness lie to us?"

"Greed? Debt? Because she can?" The music kicked in again. Jacob cast the gingerbread Greta was arranging into neat rows a brief, disapproving glance before sliding his costume—a ragged dress and painted witch's mask topped with a startling nest of horse hair—out from under the board. "Or perhaps the lady is mistaken? She has lost her husband, after all. Maybe grief has addled her wits."

"Maybe," Greta said without conviction.

"You should speak to Herr Hueber about it tomorrow. I'll come with you, if you like." He yanked the costume over his head and adjusted the mask. "How do I look?"

"Awful."

"Excellent."

He threw her a salute and melted into the wash of customers approaching Greta's board. No time, then, for anything but smiling and serving, straightening the rows, unpacking more baskets. When the buying finally slowed, Greta stole a moment of rest on an upturned basket. The dancing had lulled, the musicians stepped down from their rough platform. A group of unruly young men were throwing wood onto the bonfire. Sparks fizzed across the sky.

"Pretty, isn't it?" A small woman Greta had never seen before stood before the board. "Men do love to light fires. They'll burn anything they can get their hands on, if you let them."

She winked, then leaned over the board, inspecting the remaining hearts and witches. Her uncovered hair was dark, her skin the soft, mellow brown of summer light on the forest floor. Beneath a cloak of grey wool, spiderweb fine, she wore a plain traveling dress. A knife hung from her belt beside several leather pouches and what looked to be a rather aged silver fox skin.

"I like your costume," Greta said.

"You are very kind." The woman's voice was rich and low, with an accent Greta could not place.

"Have you traveled far?"

"As far as a person can, I daresay." The woman bent over the baking, breathing deep. "Exquisite. Do you know, in Offenburg I heard tell of a young woman with fire in her hair—a baker whose gingerbread was the best in all of Württemberg. I think they must have been speaking of you."

"Some do say such things," Greta admitted, from the awkward space between pride and shame. She pointed to a gingerbread witch. "Please, try some."

The woman accepted the witch and took a bite. "Glorious."

She was older than Greta had first supposed. Closer to Rob Mueller's age than Greta's, though the memory of beauty shone through her high cheekbones and delicate chin.

"Have we met before?" There was something familiar about the older woman. Something vague and fleeting, as though Greta should know her. Remember her.

"Us?" The woman took a larger bite, swallowed. "No. I'd remember if we had. Indeed, who could forget such wondrous hair?" She smiled, and Greta was reminded sharply of the village's erstwhile healer. Frau Elma had been taller, her fair hair peppered with grey. But she had had the same gentle manner, the same kindness in her eyes.

"I'm Greta Rosenthal."

"It's good to meet you, Greta. I'm Mira." Mira's eyes were the color of tilled earth at sunset, rich and warm. She smiled and Greta could not help but smile back.

"I hope you won't think me overbold for asking," Mira said, "but I'm curious—where did you learn to bake like this? Did your mother teach you?"

"I wish she had," Greta said. "She died when I was seven."

"An aunt, then? Or a stepmother?"

Greta shuddered as though a pair of icy hands had settled on her shoulders. "No."

"Your father never took another wife?" Mira nibbled on the witch. "Goodness, but this is good."

"Oh no, he did. He married again the summer after my mother died." Greta fumbled for a way to describe her stepmother that would not sound uncharitable. Like so many others, Leisa had lost everything in the war; it was only chance that had brought her to Lindenfeld one summer day. How she had survived the forest, alone and on foot, no one ever knew. Peter, blinded by her beauty, never thought to ask. He married her on Midsummer's Day, as windflowers bloomed on Lena's grave.

"I take it you were not overly fond of your stepmother," Mira said.

"In truth, I hardly knew her."

Leisa was disinterested in her new stepchildren, enduring their presence with little grace when their father was by, and with ill-concealed contempt when he was in the woods or at the sawmill. She loathed her chores around the house, forcing Greta to fetch water and scrub the hearth, and once a week drag the heavy basket of washing to the falls. Were it not for the way her eyes followed Peter—hungrily—and the way she was with him when she thought the children were asleep, one would wonder why she had married him at all.

There was only one motherly task she seemed to enjoy: brushing and arranging Greta's long, red-brown hair.

It was clear that Peter's second wife would not mend the hole left in his heart by the loss of the first. His face became pale and thin, his body, once strong and capable, weak. The war raged on; there was little money and less food. And then one night Greta overheard her stepmother telling her new husband to take his children into the forest—and leave them there.

"And where is your stepmother, now?" Mira asked gently.

"She took sick and died a few months after she married my father. I was . . . not there when it happened. I believe it was sudden."

"You believe?"

"My father rarely spoke of her."

And she had never asked. It was with relief that Greta and Hans had discovered that their stepmother was dead: wrapped in their father's arms, kneeling in the dirt as they sobbed against him, a boy and girl returned.

"And your father?"

"He died when I was sixteen." A frail version of the man he had been, her mother's braid of hair vivid against his thin wrist. *Your mother made this for me, mein Täubchen. I'll never part with it, not while there's breath in my body.* He had never removed it, not even the day he wed Leisa.

Mira chewed the last of her gingerbread thoughtfully. "And what of your mother, Greta? What manner of woman was she?"

A shadow fell across the board. Brigitta Winter, dressed in an outlandish costume of rabbit and squirrel fur. Feathered wings stretched from her back and two small antlers sat atop her golden head.

"Let me guess," Mira said, squinting at Brigitta thoughtfully. "You're a wolpertinger. How strange and frightening you look!"

Brigitta grinned, revealing a pair of smooth wooden fangs. "Thanksh."

"I'd best move along," Mira said, with another smile at Brigitta. "This wolpertinger looks hungry."

"It was good to speak with you," Greta found herself saying. "I hope we'll meet again." The sense of having known Mira before, of comfort and familiarity, had strengthened. Her leaving filled Greta with unexpected disappointment.

"I'm certain we will," Mira said with another wink. As she moved away Greta saw that her feet were bare.

Greta helped Brigitta select gingerbread, then made space for her to sit on the board while she ate. The musicians were back, keeping time as Walpurgis ate its way through the night, growling and gamboling, a trail of wildness and firelight in its wake.

"Greta?" Brigitta asked, legs swinging.

"Hmm?"

"What did you mean the other day, in the forest? When you said the Devil was coming?"

The music drew to a resounding close, the drums falling silent. Greta looked around, fearful the girl had been overheard.

"And now for the crowning of the May Queen!" The lead musician's announcement floated across the square.

"It will be Ingrid," Brigitta said wearily. "Just you wait."

She was right, of course. They watched in silence as Ingrid, dressed as a forest wight with a pair of painted butterfly wings, was lifted onto the dais and crowned with a wreath of flowers. The heat and the crush of the festival had failed to fluster her: her hair shone like silver, and her cheeks seemed dusted with a fine, pink frost. Beside the musicians, with their strappings of faded leather and furred sackpfeifen, Ingrid was as fair and otherworldly as an elf maiden.

"I told you," Brigitta said bitterly.

"Perhaps it will be you up there one day."

"No. I'll never be May Queen. Not with my scars."

Later, Greta would wonder what compelled her to speak. Anger? Pity? The urge to give a gift, however small, to a lonely child?

"If I tell you a secret will you promise to keep it?"

Brigitta's eyes shone. "Oh, yes!"

Greta leaned her elbows on the board so she was eye-to-eye with the girl. "The other day, when we met in the forest? I was running from a bear."

Brigitta's voice was soft with awe. "What color was it?"

"Black."

"Did it chase you?"

Greta shook her head, remembering the bear's smooth tongue,

so like a dog's, and the warmth of its breath as it licked the honey from her fingers.

"Bears are dangerous," Brigitta said. "I should tell my father—"

"No," Greta said quickly. "He'll go to the council, and they'll send men to hunt it. The bear didn't hurt me. It would be braver—and kinder—to say nothing."

"I *do* like secrets," Brigitta admitted. She smiled, and some of Ingrid's beauty flickered beneath the fire's wreckage. "Very well, Greta. I'll say nothing." She pointed across the square. "Look. My sister is choosing a partner for the fire dance."

Every young man in the village had gathered at Ingrid's feet. Jacob had removed his mask and was gazing up at her, his face alight with hope—then confusion and dismay—as Ingrid pointed to someone else. Someone lounging near the fountain, dressed like a shadow wight, all in black. Someone more interested in his beer than the dancing.

"I choose Hans Rosenthal!"

Hans started at the sound of his name. He laughed, wafted a hand as though he would decline. Then his eyes met Jacob's. A hard little smile. He sauntered through the crowd to where Ingrid waited, her eyes too bright, her face too eager. The music rounded in and they were lost to sight amid the other dancers. When Hans next appeared, out of breath and grinning, it was to take a cup of beer Ingrid offered him. He drank deeply, then, to Greta's dismay, offered the cup to Ingrid. Ingrid, who sipped prettily, smiling up at Hans over the cup's rim.

"I told you," Brigitta said knowingly. "She waits for him in the Marktplatz. He never usually talks to her, though. I wonder what changed his mind?"

When the last of the gingerbread was sold and the board packed away Greta found Jacob by a pork seller, staring despondently into his empty cup. She sank down beside him, sighing deeply as she took the weight off her tired feet.

"They have danced all night together," Jacob said gloomily.

"Hans will soon tire of his anger and let Ingrid go," Greta said. "He knows how you feel."

Around them, the night swelled, rich with smoke and flame. She tried to imagine how the village would look from afar: a tiny bloom of fire beneath the mountains and the wide, smoky sky.

"Greta—*Ingrid* doesn't know how I feel." Jacob straightened his shoulders suddenly, brightening. "I should find her. Tell her."

*Curse him for a fool,* Greta thought. *And curse my brother, too.*

"Come, then," she said, forcing herself to her feet. "I'll help you."

She followed Jacob as he pushed through the dancing. Above, the May Tree loomed like some ancient talisman.

"I think she's near the fountain," Jacob said. "But we can't get through here."

"We'll have to go around."

Greta ducked into a narrow lane behind the Rose and Thorn, Jacob close behind, then slid to an abrupt halt.

"Odd's body, Greta!" Jacob stumbled into her, dropping his empty cup. "What are you . . ."

He trailed off. Seeing, as Greta did, the back of a man's dark coat in the greasy light from the tavern. Half hidden behind a stack of barrels and crates, the coat, and the shoulders beneath it, were nonetheless familiar.

Jacob's ragged gasp was so loud Greta thought her brother must surely hear it. But he did not. Hans was laughing at something Ingrid Winter was whispering, her sleek hair bathed in fire and flowers and moonlight, as she drew his face down to hers for another kiss.

"I do not think . . ." Greta struggled to keep up with Jacob's furious strides. "That is to say, I am certain that—"

"What are you certain of?" Jacob drew up abruptly and Greta almost collided with him. "Because *I'm* certain I just saw my oldest friend with the woman I had hoped to make my *wife*."

Greta fumbled for the right thing to say. Part of her wanted to lie—to soothe him, to tell him it was not Ingrid with Hans, but someone else; that their eyes had been deceived by shadows and the lateness of the hour. But there had been no mistaking Ingrid's silver-gold hair, or her smile. There had been no mistaking the way she had looked at Hans.

"I'm so sorry, Jacob."

"*You're* sorry?" He laughed bitterly. "I should have known. He was always selfish."

"That's not fair. You know what he went through—"

"You went through it, too! *And you are nothing like him!*"

"It was worse for him. . . ."

"How?"

*Because he was locked in the cage. Because it was* he *who held the bone.* Greta's mind flooded with memories: Hans's face when, three days after wandering lost in the woods, he had stumbled upon the crone's trap. No taller than Greta, the little house was made entirely of gingerbread, the windowpanes shaped of clear sugar. It was warm, too, as though it had just come from the oven.

"We shall have a glorious feast," Hans had said. "I will eat a piece of the roof, and you can eat the window. Will they not be sweet?"

He tore a piece from the gable, while Greta nibbled upon a fragment of sugary glass. Neither had noticed the old woman hobbling into the glade.

"Ah, you dear children! What has brought you here?" she had said kindly. "You are lost, I think, and hungry! Come, come. I shall take care of you."

And then, weeks later, Greta's frantic search for the key to Hans's cage when the crone had forgotten to chain her before leaving the house, heart thudding so loud she was sure the old woman would hear it and come shambling back, her eyes full of fire. When it was clear the key was not to be found Greta had tried to force the cage open until her small fingers were cut and bloody.

"It's no use, Greta," Hans had said. "Stop. You are hurting yourself."

Greta had shaken her head. She continued to work at the lock until the witch returned and gave her a beating for her troubles.

"Greta?" Jacob demanded. "How was it worse?"

She shook her head, unable to give voice to such thoughts. "We should go back to the house," she said. "You shouldn't be here, Jacob. Not like this."

"I'm not going anywhere." He swerved back to the square, a lone figure against the Walpurgis fire. "In fact, I believe I'll have another drink. And after that, another. I'll drink to love, and friendship, and to your dear brother, who at least had the good grace to make his feelings plain *before* any promises were made." The crowds swirled around him, stealing him from sight.

"Täubchen." Christoph was weaving his way up the alley. "I've been . . . looking for you."

Greta watched him come, frowning. He was moving strangely, his head oddly still while his body swayed beneath him.

"Christie? Have you been *drinking?*"

"No!" He teetered on the spot, wiped his mouth with the back of his hand. "Why would you . . . say that?"

Greta moved closer, then reeled back at the smell of beer on his breath.

"You *have* been drinking! Christie, you're far too young for that."

He gave her a mutinous look. "No, I'm not."

She grabbed his hand. "Come on. We'll get you something to eat. Your father will have your hide if he sees you like this."

"My hide." Christoph laughed sloppily. "My *hide!*"

Greta tried to pull him along with her, but only managed to make him trip and stagger clumsily.

"Just look at you! What will your father say? Come and sit down. . . ." She led him to the low wall encircling the churchyard, sagging as he leaned his considerable weight on her.

"I don't care what he says," Christoph slurred, slumping onto the wall. "It's all his fault, anyway."

Greta sank down beside him. "I hardly think it's your father's fault you drank too much."

Shrill laughter echoed down the street. Sparks flew into the sky above the rooftops.

Christoph hiccupped. "I need to speak with you, Täubchen."

"We can speak tomorrow, Christie, when you're feeling better."

"No," he said, with surprising clarity. "Tomorrow will be too late." He rose and pulled Greta through the creaking gate and into the churchyard. "Come with me."

It was quieter in the yard, the music dimmed by the bulk of the church. Smoke veiled the congregation of yew trees gathered among the graves. But for the faint light in the church windows, it was very dark.

"Christie," Greta said. "We should go back."

In reply Christoph grasped her face between his hands and pressed his lips clumsily to hers. She wrenched herself free, flinging a hand across her mouth.

"*Christie!* What do you think you are *doing?*"

"I know you are older than I," Christoph stammered. "I know you think me a boy. But you're wrong. I'm a man now."

*Yes,* she thought darkly. *Look how well you hold your beer.*

"I believe a man should be free to live the kind of life *he* chooses," he said. "But they say I must join them. That I must . . . *be* like them." He looked very young and lost.

"Do you mean the soldiers? The ones your father argued with?"

He nodded. "They say it is tradition. That none of them had a choice."

"But surely Rob—"

"There's nothing he can do."

"Then we will go to the men of the watch," Greta said firmly. "And the council. These men can't just traipse through Württemberg forcing young men to join them."

"Yes, they can. And we can't tell the watchmen, Täubchen. We can't tell *anyone.*"

"Why not?"

He shrugged helplessly. "We just can't."

Greta scuffed at the ground with her boot. "But . . . there must be *something* we can do!"

"There *is* one thing," Christoph said. "You can marry me."

The sounds of the festival—music and laughter—seemed to fade to perfect silence. Greta searched his face, desperate for a sign he was jesting.

"If we were married, Täubchen, they'd leave me be," Christoph said. "It's not their way to take on men with wives. We could ask Father Markus to do it now."

Father Markus had scowled through the night's proceedings with ill-concealed impatience before retreating to the sanctity of his small dwelling beside the church. She didn't want to think what the pastor would say if Christoph knocked on his door at this late hour and drunkenly demanded a wedding.

"Or we could leave," Christoph said eagerly. "Tonight. Take horses and go north on the Waldstrasse."

Greta stared at him in dismay. She did not see a man to risk all for or run away with. She saw a boy who had picked flowers with her at countless Mayings, who had cried to her when he scraped his knees. What kind of sell-swords were these, that they would press a frightened boy against his will? And why did the getting of a wife change things? Soldiers had kept wives for hundreds of years and no one had minded, so far as she could tell. Her own father had been one of them.

The church gate squeaked on its hinges.

"They're here," Christoph hissed, dragging her toward a stand of yews.

"Christie!" she hissed. "Let me *go*!"

"Christie? Are you there, lad?" It was, to Greta's everlasting relief, Rob Mueller's voice that floated across the churchyard. Torchlight flickered as he strode toward them, illuminating the thick sweep of his grey-blond hair. He held the torch in one hand and a pistol in the other as though he were perfectly used to prowling churchyards in the deeps of the night. Greta wondered briefly what his life had been like before he settled in Lindenfeld.

"There you are," Rob said, relieved.

"Christie has had altogether too much fun this Walpurgis," Greta said, pulling herself free of Christoph's clumsy grasp. He flailed, lurching like a colt on unsteady legs and toppled to the ground.

"He's drunk," Greta said bluntly. "And speaking nonsense, besides."

"Is he now?" Rob handed Greta the torch and bent to his son, checking him over. "I told you to stay close, lad," he said worriedly. "What were you thinking?"

*This* was not the reaction Greta had expected. Rob had never been one to lose himself in drink, or to condone such behavior in others. *It's a lost man who tries to find himself in his cups*, he was fond of saying. She had expected him to be angry. Not concerned.

Not afraid.

"Rob, who are the soldiers Christoph has been speaking of?"

He looked up at her, one hand still on his son, face half in shadow. "Just men I knew once."

"When you were a sell-sword?"

It was a hollow question, and they both knew it. Rob never spoke of his past.

"Please don't ask me, Täubchen," he said with a shake of his head. "I cannot speak of it."

"Cannot? Or *will* not?"

Drums, distant. Behind Rob, fire glow leered on the church wall.

"Come, Täubchen. Let me get you and Christie safely home, eh?"

"Christie is terrified, Uncle. He thinks these men want him to join them. As if you would allow them to just . . . to just *take* him!"

"You're right," Rob said, tucking his pistol into his belt. "I would never allow that." He scooped his son up from where he had slumped in the grass and slung one of his arms around his neck. "And Täubchen? That's all you need know."

# 8
## Lost Things

*Beauty, you see, can mask a thousand faults, and there was ever a seed of evil within Liliane. Selfishness and waywardness were its first manifestations. As she grew she became unruly, mischievous. And yet so fair was she no one could help but forgive her. She smiled sweetly, she lied prettily, and she wove deceptions and trickery into her father's failing ears.*

Jacob had not come home. Slants of golden sunlight, thick with flour and dust, pointed accusingly at his empty pallet.

*. . . mayhap he found a way to warm that icy girl of his,* the book said spitefully.

"I very much doubt that." Greta ran a hand over Jacob's still-smooth blankets. His shirts hung neatly on their respective hooks, his pack, bandolier and musket beneath them. Everything was as he had left it the day before when, filled with hope, he had readied himself for Walpurgis.

Walpurgis. Apprehension gnawed at Greta as she thought over the events of the night. The arrival of Fizcko and his news of the baron's death. The doubling of the taxes for the Swedish army's compensation, even though Jacob had assured her there was no Swedish army left to compensate. The baroness's strange new Blood Tithe, and Christoph's awkward, appalling proposal. In light of all that, Hans's betrayal of Jacob with Ingrid Winter had seemed rather insignificant. Now, seeing Jacob's belongings, his neatly made pallet . . .

Greta threw on her coif and checked that her knife was at her belt.

*. . . and where do you think you're going?*

"To find Jacob."

The May Day celebrations were well underway. She wended through streets festooned with blossoms and greenery, ducking as someone tried to press a wreath of flowers onto her head. There was no sign of Jacob. Herr Tritten refused to let her set foot inside the Rose and Thorn, and the inn was quiet, its doors barred, guests and owners alike gone out to join the Maying. Only one person had word of Jacob: Jens Gerber, the tanner.

"I saw him late last night." Jens was red-eyed and rough-headed, his clothes smelling of smoke and stale beer. He sipped at his drink and winced, and Greta wondered if he had slept at all the night before or simply rolled Walpurgis Night and May Day into a single, grueling campaign. "He was with a woman."

"A woman? Who?"

"Couldn't say."

"Was it Ingrid Winter?"

"Ingrid?" Jens belched softly and shuddered. "No. Didn't see her face but this woman was dressed fine. Too fine for Lindenfeld."

Greta paced the flower-strewn square, turning this piece of information over in her mind. It was not unusual for travelers to arrive in Lindenfeld for Walpurgis—she had met one herself, after all. But it was not like Jacob to seek companionship when he was troubled. No sooner had he seen Ingrid with Hans than he had begun to draw away from Greta, forsaking her company for the loneliness of a drunken crowd. When he was a boy he was wont to hide himself away, too, usually in the tree house he had built with Greta and Hans. . . .

Greta stopped.

*The tree house.*

She struck out for the forested slopes above the village, calling Jacob's name as she went. It was not long before she arrived at the feet of an enormous oak. High above, in the tree's generous, well-spaced boughs, perched a little wooden house. Years of weather had aged it; it had melted into the branches somewhat, misshapen walls sprouting tufts of leaves and moss.

"Jacob! Are you there?"

No reply.

"Jacob?" Greta peeled off her shoes and stockings, roughly knotted her skirts, and leaned against the tree, catching her breath. At some point on the walk from the village—she could not say exactly when—she had begun to feel unwell. Now that she was still, there was no denying the swirling in her belly.

"Shouldn't be here."

The voice was at her ear, so soft she hardly heard it. Frowning, Greta turned her head. Met a pair of huge, fey eyes in a tiny face framed by shaggy, mosslike hair. The owner of the eyes blinked solemnly, its skin a luminous green.

Greta stared. "What do you mean?" Her mouth was suddenly dry, her throat sore.

"She's here. You should go. Now." The little sylvan creature gazed fearfully about and scurried away across the tree, clinging to the bark with delicate claws.

Greta blinked as the bark began to blur, withering to black.

"Jacob?" she called unsteadily, rubbing her eyes. She looked up, saw the tree house standing stark against branches that were bare and gnarled, its roof drifted with snow. Beyond it, the sky was winter-grey. She stepped back in surprise, her bare feet crunching in the snow that coated the ground, the oak—the entire forest—in perfect, white silence.

Standing across the clearing was a woman in a long, dark cloak. Her face was hidden by her hood, but Greta knew that she was watching her. A cold rush of fear stole her breath. She rubbed her eyes, looked again. The woman was gone.

A squirrel skittered across the snow, then another, and another, until a thousand or more of the creatures seethed and chippered around her skirts.

"Greta! You found me!"

Sweet relief: Jacob leaned out of the tree house, beckoning. "Come up! It's warm and safe in here!"

Greta hauled herself into the tree. The going was hard; she was sick, cold, and confused. As she climbed trails of woody nightshade sprang from the snow below, weaving and choking along the branches, red berries bitter-bright. Bindweed, her father used to call it. Lena had always used a gentler name: bittersweet. It crawled over her arms and wrapped around her ankles. It took all she had to pull herself free and keep climbing.

"Almost there!" Jacob grinned from above.

She nodded blearily and pushed on, lungs bursting, heart thumping, throat burning. At last—*at last*—she was there. Jacob stretched out both hands and pulled her inside. She flopped into the woody shadows, breathing hard.

"Jacob?"

She rolled over, eyes adjusting to the gloom. The tree house was smaller than she remembered, the floor scattered with dried leaves and squirrel dung. It was cold and dank. Worst of all, it was empty.

"Jacob?" she whispered.

Far below, footsteps scrunched in the snow. Carefully, carefully, Greta leaned out of the tree house. Looked down. And there, sprawled in the snow with her hair spread around her like fire, was her mother. Lena's bodice was ripped and bloody, her chest a raw, gaping chasm. Her eyes were open, wide and sightless.

There was an apple in her hand.

"You found me."

A cold whisper, close to Greta's ear. She flinched. Turned.

Jacob was behind her. Jacob, ten years old again, eyes huge in his skinny face. He grinned in the gloom and held out an apple. Red, shining.

"It will be soon," he hissed. He bit into the fruit with a wet crunch and pointed at Greta's bodice. "Look."

Greta looked down at herself. Her bodice was ragged and torn, soaked with blood, and Jacob's little-boy hand was rummaging inside her broken chest. She looked up, stricken, and found not Jacob but her dead mother there in the dark.

"Soon," Lena whispered. Cupped in her hands, glistening and bloody, was Greta's still-beating heart.

No way to tell how long she had been cowering in the tree house. A few moments? The length of the afternoon? It was only when a voice carried up to her from below—a voice belonging to neither Jacob nor her mother—that Greta uncurled herself.

"Hello?" came the voice again. "Is someone up there?"

She crawled to the door. The forest outside was washed in springtime, silky with birdsong. No winter, no snow.

"Hello?"

Through the leaves she glimpsed a man's shoulder clad in mottled green. A breeze riffled up the valley and the branches swayed, revealing half a black-stubbled jaw and one blue—or green—eye.

"Fräulein Rosenthal?" Mathias called. "Is everything well?"

"I hardly know," she answered, a strangled croak. Part of her wanted him gone so she could recover in peace and make her way down the tree in her own time. But another, larger part of her feared that whatever had caused her to become ill and confused might return, along with the terrifying dream-winter. "Would you—could you wait for me to climb down?"

"Of course."

She flipped onto her belly and edged out of the tree house, legs flailing into open space. Her toes found a branch below and she swung down, panting, into the green heart of the oak. The sickness was gone, the soreness in her throat and the pounding in her head, but she was trembling all over. When a sparrow darted by she shrieked and clutched at the trunk in terror.

"I'm coming up," Mathias announced.

Greta was too shaken to refuse. A few moments later he emerged beside her, waist-deep in a river of leaves.

"Are you hurt?" He was close enough that she could see the surprising length of his lashes and the traces of red in the stubble on his cheeks. Close enough, too, to see that his eyes were green, like moss and light on water.

"I . . . No."

"I was hunting. I heard you scream."

"I don't understand what happened," she said helplessly. "I was fine, and then . . . I wasn't. My eyes blurred, and my throat tightened. I felt ill."

"You sounded terrified."

"Yes. I . . . *saw* things."

He shifted his grip on the branches. "What did you see?"

"It was winter, not spring. The ground was thick with snow and this tree was black. It was covered in bittersweet—"

"Nightshade?"

"Yes. The berries were so red. Like blood . . ." She shook her head, unable to describe the rest. "My brother ate nightshade berries when he was young. Mistook them for elderberries. My mother saved him, and afterward he told me what it felt like. His eyes, his throat, how sick he felt. He saw people who were not there. Said they were as real as you or I. Were it not May, I would wonder if I hadn't swallowed nightshade, too. I cannot explain it."

"There are some things that cannot be explained," Mathias said, frowning. "For now, we should get you down. If you slip through here . . ."

He stayed close as she descended, offering a hand or gesturing to a sturdy bough. Once, his hand closed around Greta's bare ankle, warm against her skin. She looked down; his gaze was on the tree, intent. As soon as he found purchase for her foot he gently placed it there and let go.

Mathias set foot on the ground first and lifted her down, waiting at a courteous distance while she unknotted her skirts and slipped on her stockings and shoes.

"I suppose you are wondering why I was up there at all," Greta said.

"Not really. My sister Katerina was forever climbing. I asked her once why she did it; she told me she was listening to the trees breathe."

"I think I might have liked your sister, had we met."

He glanced at her. "Yes. I think you might have." Greta, half listening to the reassuring chitter and rustle of a bird in a nearby spruce, remembered his face at the supper table when she had asked him of his family. *No home. No family.*

"So what *were* you doing in the tree?" he asked with a smile. "Were you listening to it breathe?"

It was remarkable, the way he folded away his feelings, as perceptible a motion as straightening his shoulders or getting to his feet. There was, Greta had to admit, something appealing about such practicality. From his clothing to the way that he moved, Mathias wasted nothing. He was infinitely capable. Endlessly calm. It occurred to her that if anyone was going to help her find Jacob, it would be him. And so she told him of Jacob's despair at Walpurgis, his absence that morning. When she was done Mathias's smile had vanished.

"You checked the tavern? The inn?"

She shook her head. "There was no one at the inn. And Herr Tritten never lets me anywhere near the Thorn."

"And Jacob was distressed when last you saw him?"

"Yes. I'm afraid my brother . . ." The bird chippered again and she stopped, distracted by the crimson tips of its wings; they looked for all the world as though they had been dipped in blood. "A waxwing. They say seeing one portends death. Do you think it's an omen?"

"I cannot speak of omens." Mathias shrugged on his bow. "But I think the sooner we find Jacob, the better."

The square had become a forest: freshly cut branches adorned the Rathaus and the fountain. Even the pillory was wreathed like a maid, its iron collar and chain swathed with leaves and flowers.

Greta waited for Mathias outside the Thorn. "They haven't seen him," he said, when he emerged. "We'll have a better chance if we stay still. Perhaps the fountain? We'll see the entire Marktplatz from there."

A space had been cleared beneath the May Tree for the dancing. Couples spun and ducked beneath each other's arms, or watched from the edges, clapping. The women were pink-cheeked and pretty, dressed in their best, their heads adorned with wreaths of flowers.

Mathias steered Greta to an empty bench near the linden tree, waited for her to sit, then wove deftly through the press of people to a row of tables laden with food and beer.

"Fräulein." Herr Hueber appeared, a new feather tucked into the band of his hat. "You're not dancing. Perhaps I can remedy that?"

Greta squinted up at him. The bürgermeister's confidence was truly remarkable. The last time they had met, he had flung curses at her as he pounded on her door. Now, he was smiling indulgently, as though his very presence was granting her most secret, fervent wish.

"I am happy as I am, thank you," she said coldly.

He sat himself beside her. "It must be difficult to enjoy the festivities when such worries weigh upon you. Tell me: Did you earn enough last night to pay your taxes *and* your brother's debt to me?"

"I might have," she said, "had the baroness not doubled the tithes." She searched the Marktplatz again, willing Jacob to appear, safe and well, purse in hand, ready to do as he had promised.

"A shame," Herr Hueber said happily. Greta was tempted to rip free her pocket strings and reveal the mysterious silver coins. Oh, what would it be to let them shimmer in the sun and watch his eyes widen, wavering between shock and greed? What would it be to end her obligation to him once and for all?

She would never know; the coins were not hers to give.

"And so here we are," Herr Hueber drawled. "May Day. Where *is* that brother of yours, do you suppose? If you won't favor me with a dance, I'd best find him and make good my debt. . . ."

"Please don't," Greta said, rising. *Oh Jacob, where are you?* "I will give you the money, I swear—I only need more time."

A smile flickered on his lips as he got to his feet. "And if I agree? What shall you give me in return?"

"I'll . . . I'll reconsider your offer of employment."

"And?"

"And . . . I'll dance with you."

He scratched his chin thoughtfully. "How *much* time?"

"A month."

The outer ring of dancers swept wide, arms raised. They skipped beneath the linden, almost hitting Herr Hueber. He laughed, raised his drink as they flowed away.

"Herr Hueber? Do we have an agreement?"

"Oh yes," he said, taking the opportunity, as he lowered his cup, to stroke Greta's wrist. "We do."

Greta risked a sideways glance. Dare she ask him? Jacob had been so sure . . .

"Herr Hueber, I wanted to ask you . . . this new war tax. For the Swedes."

"Hmmm?" He was content now, watching the dancers as they spiraled around the May Tree.

"Well, it's only . . . do you truly think the Swedes are a danger to us here in Württemberg? I heard they moved north months ago. . . ."

He turned to face her, no longer complacent. "Where did you hear that?"

"I cannot recall, now," she lied, hastily. The cold narrowing of his eyes, the speculative hunch to his shoulders, were a warning. "Perhaps I heard wrong."

"I daresay you did." He gazed at her a moment longer, as though deciding something. Then he smiled. "Sweet Margareta. Try not to dabble in matters you cannot understand, eh?" He tossed back what remained in his cup, set it on the bench, and took her hand. "Now. I'd like that dance you promised me."

Mathias returned with two cups of beer. "I'm sorry I took so long, Fräulein Rosenthal. I took the liberty of bringing you something to drink." He offered Greta a cup, allowing her to gracefully disentangle herself from Herr Hueber's grasp.

She smiled at him gratefully. "That's very kind."

"And who might *you* be?" Herr Hueber demanded, bristling. "What is your business in Lindenfeld?"

"I would say, with the greatest respect, that that is none of your concern."

At that precise moment the music wound down. Mathias's words—calm, firm—drifted out across the cobbles. One by one heads turned toward the little group beneath the linden tree.

"To whom do you connect yourself?" Despite his heeled boots Herr Hueber was forced to tilt his head back to meet Mathias's eye. "Or are you simply passing through, attaching yourself to young women and disrespecting your betters?"

"I always have the highest regard for those who deserve it. And I believe it was you, not I, who attached yourself to Fräulein Rosenthal just now."

The villagers, having caught the delicious scent of rising conflict, were gathering around, eager for their share.

"There is no place for vagabonds in this village." Herr Hueber gazed at Mathias as though he were an insect fit to be squashed. "Who speaks for you? If no man will, the watchmen shall remove you at once."

"I will speak for him."

As one, the onlookers turned. Rob Mueller's silvery-gold hair was tied back neatly, and he wore a fresh shirt beneath his simple coat and fitted breeches. His clothing might have belonged to any of the working men gathered in the square, so sharply did it contrast with Herr Hueber's pretentious garb, and yet everyone within sight of him quieted at once, stepping back to let him through. Waiting, as they always did, to hear what he had to say.

Herr Hueber frowned. "Rob? *You* know this man?"

"I do," Rob said easily. "He is both honorable and trustworthy. My word upon it."

"Well, then," Herr Hueber blustered. "Let his presence here be on *your* head." He threw a final, venomous glance at Mathias and elbowed his way through the crowd. The music wheezed into life once more and the dancers took their places.

Rob and Mathias grasped hands.

"It's been a long time," Rob said with a smile. "I am glad to see you are still alive. And that you are as good at making friends as ever."

Mathias grinned. "It is a gift of mine."

Greta looked between them in confusion.

"I did not think we would meet again," Rob said, releasing Mathias's hand. His tone was warm enough, but Greta noted the shrewdness of his gaze, the way it raked over Mathias from the ends of his long hair to the tips of his travel-worn boots. "What brings you here?"

"I would have thought you of all people would know the answer to that."

Rob blanched. "*Here?* But—*where?*"

"Hornberg. Two months, at least."

"Then she has come back," Rob whispered, almost to himself.

"She's been here before?"

Rob opened his mouth to answer, glanced Greta's way, and closed it again. "I see you've already met Greta," he said, over-bright.

"It was by chance," Mathias told him, a little warily.

A long, loaded look passed between the two men.

"But how do the two of *you* know each other?" Greta demanded.

"We met some years ago," Mathias said. "In Swabia."

"It's quite a story, Täubchen," Rob said. "Too long to tell, now. Suffice it to say we, too, met by accident."

"Doing what?"

"Hunting," they said, together.

Greta raised an eyebrow at Rob. "I have never known you to hunt."

"Oh, I don't. Though there was a time, if you can believe it, when I was rather good."

Music rose and fell around them, swelling as the dancing grew faster. Greta glimpsed Ingrid Winter smiling up at Hans.

"Might be time to sharpen those skills," Mathias said.

Rob did not reply. He was looking at Greta—or rather, past her. She turned. In the daylight Mira looked older than she had seemed in the glow of the Walpurgis fires; streaks of silver shone in her black hair. She was dressed as she had been the night before, her hair loose, the fox skin a smudge of silver wildness at her waist. Her feet were bare.

"Hello, Rob," she said.

"Mira." Rob nodded stiffly, sounding so unlike himself that Greta glanced up at him then quickly away, her cheeks flaming. She had never seen him look at a woman that way. "I wondered if I would see you. If you were still with Conran and the others. I hoped that it would not be so."

"Then I am sorry to disappoint you," Mira said. If she was as flustered by Rob's presence as he was by hers, she did not show it.

"You could never do that."

"You've spoken to Conran; you know what he wants. And so you know that isn't true."

Rob's face hardened. "You cannot allow Conran to think of taking Christie, Mira. He wasn't raised for it. *Trained* for it. He's lived most of his life here in this valley. He learned his letters beside the sons of farmers, and smiths. He knows my land and my mill almost as well as I do. And now Conran comes here, after all these years, and tells me that . . ." His voice cracked and Greta, her gaze resolutely on the cobblestones, knew that there were rivers of unspoken words lying between Rob and this woman. *Oceans* of words.

"I'll think I'll fetch us another drink," Mathias muttered, even though he, like Greta, had barely touched the first.

Greta nodded hastily. "I'll come with you."

She followed him into the crowded square. Behind them, Rob and Mira spoke on, oblivious.

"I've made a good life for myself here," Rob was saying. "A good life for my son. Don't you see?"

"Oh yes," Mira said resentfully. "I see."

"Look here," came another voice. "It's Mira and the miller, reunited. Oh happy day!"

Greta, glancing over her shoulder, saw Christoph's sell-swords, the wolf pelts at their backs lending them a wild, menacing air. She went to turn back, but Mathias caught her arm, pulling her around the fountain. The tall stone pillar at its center—crowned with a carved lion holding a shield bearing Hornberg arms—spilled water into the wide stone basin in four directions, obscuring them from sight.

"What's it been, lads? Fourteen years?" Angling herself just so, Greta saw that the owner of the voice was a Scot, like Rob. He stood ahead of the others, huge and harsh, a gleaming black fur across his shoulders.

"Fifteen," Rob said. The cadence of his homeland was never stronger than when he was angry, as he was now.

"Fifteen wonderful years," the dark man agreed with a smirk. "And now here we are, together again. Why, it warms my heart!"

"I cannot say the same," Rob said tersely. "In truth, Conran, I'd thought we'd said our goodbyes long ago."

Conran. The leader, no doubt, of this outlandish crew. Through plumes of falling water Greta counted seven men in all, lean and rangy, whip-tight, faces weathered as the stone lion above. Several wore plaids, gathered together and thrown roughly over their grimy jerkins, or hanging at their waists like a strange pair of petticoat breeches. The wolf pelts on their backs ranged from grey to brown, from rich cream to russet red.

"Temper, temper, Robert," Conran was saying. "We mean no harm. Do we, lads?"

"The hell you don't."

A chill crept down Greta's back. Rob Mueller could handle himself—not a soul in Lindenfeld could deny it—and it was plain that he knew these men well. Even so the possibility of violence was thick in the air. She glanced at the musket one sell-sword nursed, as loving as a mother with her child, at the easy way another rested one hand on the hilt of his sword. Beside her, Mathias was watching the proceedings carefully, half hidden, as she was, by water and stone.

Conran swaggered close to Rob. "You've made that boy of yours soft, here in this pretty valley. But don't worry. I'll toughen him up for you."

"Is that how you manage things now?" Rob demanded. "You would force him to join you out of fear?"

"It is not for you to question us," Conran snapped. "You gave up that right long ago."

"And see how well you have done for it!"

"Why, we *have* done rather well, now that you mention it," Conran said with a grin. "Between offering our professional services to the Swedes and then the French, as well as partaking in a little friendly looting here and there, we came out of the whole glorious, arse-shitting disaster with more than our fair share of brass."

"It was never supposed to be about money," Rob said. "You took a vow." He glared around at the other men. "You all took vows."

"We kept them too, for a while," Conran admitted. He shrugged carelessly. "But being honorable really is no way to make a living."

Rob clenched his fists. "And you expect my son to fight without honor or decency? Would you sell him to the highest bidder and take him to be butchered—"

"Who said anything about fighting? No, there'll be none of that." Conran looked around at his men, grinning. "Why, we could get hurt!"

His companions laughed with him, acrid, mirthless.

"Then what in God's name will you do?" Rob asked.

"The same as we did in the last war, I reckon: pilfer, pillage, maraud; enjoyable pursuits like that. We've had great success in switching sides, capturing officers, ransoming them—and then keeping their horses!" Conran leered. "But we need more men. That's where *your* lad comes in."

"No doubt you're disappointed, then."

"On the contrary! I feel full of the joy of living." Conran sauntered closer. "The lad's summer-bred, Rob. You were never meant to raise him. How did you even come to bring him here?"

"He's my son," Rob said through gritted teeth. "The where and how of it matters not."

"Oh, but it does," Conran said softly. The hairs on Greta's arms stood up. "You've interrupted the order of things, see, raising him yourself. Another of your poor choices, eh?"

Beside her, Mathias's hand moved toward his knife.

"That's enough," Mira said, stepping between the two men. "This is not the time or place for such talk." She looked small beside them, fey and fragile, and yet, strangely, they both heeded her. Conran drew back, signaling to his men with barely a tilt of his head. They began to move, Mira with them—*how is she connected to all of this?*—and Conran fell in behind them.

"You're forgetting you're old now, Rob," he said in parting. "Old and slow. You can't stand against me." He grinned a black grin. "You never could."

"You know those men," Greta said to Mathias when they were back on the bench beneath the linden. Rob and the sell-swords had gone their separate ways. "I saw you just now. You went for your knife."

Mathias had kept hold of his beer. He raised it to his lips, sipped. "I would have helped Rob, had he needed me to."

"You didn't want them to see you."

"No."

"Why?"

He sipped again. "Conran and his men are not unknown to me. Sell-swords who wear the pelts of wolves, with a reputation for being both fierce and unpredictable. I thought it best to avoid their notice, being, as I am, an outsider here."

"Rob knows you, though."

"He does." He hitched one knee on the bench, subtly shifting the shape of the conversation. "The two of you are related, then?"

"Not truly. He brought my father home after he was wounded at Nördlingen. Saved his life."

"Family, then."

Greta nodded. "Family." She thought of her father, and Rob, and Jacob, and all that they had lived through when they were soldiers. "I do not understand war. How can people be so cruel to each other? It is as though they forget who they are. Like . . . like animals."

"Most people are more like animals than they know," Mathias said. "See that pretty girl, there? She is eager for that man's attention. She reminds me of a turtledove, arranging its plumage just so, showing off its beauty."

"*That* is Ingrid Winter," Greta said with a sigh. "And the man she is trying to lure is my brother, Hans."

Mathias laughed. "Truly?"

"I wish it were not so. But yes." She watched her brother gloomily. Like Jacob, Hans had not come home after Walpurgis. He looked remarkably fresh for someone who had not slept in his own bed, had bruises covering the best part of his face, and was due to repay an enormous debt that very day. "Have you by chance lost a purse of coins?" she asked. "Silver ones?"

Mathias shook his head. "I haven't lost anything of late."

He listened patiently as she told him about the money in her shoe.

"Maybe the white wood woman, Perchta, left you a gift," he said with a smile.

"You're teasing me."

"You don't believe in Perchta? I assure you she is real. She and all her friends. Shrub women, moss folk, kobolds, wood spirits . . . I have met them all, in my time. Why, even the Elder Mother has graced me with her presence."

"Now I know you're teasing. The Elder Mother shows herself to no one. All the stories say so."

"You've not heard *my* stories."

Above them, the linden tree shivered in the spring breeze, its leaves flecking dappled light onto Mathias's eyes. Light and shadow.

"Tell me, then: How did you meet my uncle?"

"It was as he said. Years ago, in Swabia."

"And who was he speaking of just now? When he said 'she has come back'?"

The briefest of hesitations. "An acquaintance of ours."

"Is that why you've come to Lindenfeld?" she asked tentatively. "To see . . . *her*?"

"It is. Although I fear the reunion will not be a pleasant one." He glanced away. "This acquaintance stole from me, you see. And from my family. I have come to claim what is owed."

And then, as though there was nothing at all remarkable about this entirely remarkable speech, he got to his feet. "I'll search the pothouse again, shall I?"

Greta watched him cross the Marktplatz. Could not, if she were honest, look anywhere else. Mathias seemed brighter, and at the same time darker, than every other man there. She was not the only one to mark it; more than one young woman turned her flowered head to watch him pass. She forced herself to look elsewhere and saw Christoph on the other side of the square. He threw her a wounded look, then slunk further into the crowd.

Hans swaggered toward her, blocking her view.

"Found yourself a suitor, eh?" he said, winking over his drink. "Good for you."

"Have you seen Jacob today?" Greta demanded. "He didn't come back to the house last night."

"Didn't he? Well, perhaps he took a bed at the inn." Hans's gaze slipped away from hers.

"He saw you last night, Hans. With Ingrid. How could you *do* that to him?"

"He did? Christ." He slumped onto the bench beside her, sloshing beer onto her skirt. "It meant nothing, Greta, I swear. I was jealous and out of sorts, that's all. Things haven't been easy for me of late."

"And you think they have been easy for Jacob? For *me*?"

"I— No. No, I suppose not." He watched the dancing moodily.

"I've spoken with Herr Hueber, Hans. He's agreed to give you another month to pay him what you owe."

"Really?" He sat up, brightening. "That *is* good news! I've been avoiding the old fustilugs all day."

"Of course, there's still the matter of the new taxes to discuss. . . ."

"Yes, yes, we'll get to them, too, don't you worry."

"I *am* worried. And you should be, too."

"I do my best to avoid worrying whenever possible. Besides, a lot can happen in a month." He slid her a sideways glance. "Greta, I was speaking with Christoph this morning."

"Hmmm?" Across the square, Mathias was coming back. She

watched as one of the village girls caught hold of him, drawing him playfully toward the dance. He smiled apologetically and pulled himself free.

"He's grown into a fine young man, hasn't he?"

"If you say so." An image of Christoph on his knees on the river-bank the night before, retching violently between Rob and Greta while they kept him from toppling in, sprang into her mind. It had been a long walk home.

"He asked me—"

"Jacob is missing, Hans," she said tersely. "You should be thinking of him, not Christoph."

Hans clenched his jaw. "Very well," he said curtly, moving away. Around him, the villagers chattered and laughed. As though it hardly mattered that Jacob was not among them, or that Hans and Ingrid had together crushed his heart.

"Your brother?" Mathias asked, returning.

"Yes."

"He looks none too pleased."

"If he is unhappy, he has only himself to blame."

Ingrid's fair hair shone among the dancers, and Greta thought of the woman Jens Gerber had seen with Jacob. Who was she? Was it possible Jacob had left the village with her?

"I have asked it of myself again and again," Mathias said, interrupting her thoughts. "Why did you not tell the council about the bear you saw?"

Greta looked across the square to where Herr Auer, Lindenfeld's forest warden, hulked drunkenly in his furs, his hounds at his feet. The warden was charged with managing the birds and animals, the fields and the woods surrounding the village. This he did, but Greta had always thought he took more pleasure than was necessary in performing his duties, lingering over his kills. *Dallying with death*, was how Hans had once described it. There were whispers, too, that Herr Auer was wont to pilfer and poach the baron's game, selling the pelts to a merchant in Hornberg, or farther afield. In short, he hunted and sold the very animals it was his duty to protect.

"You see that man there?" She pointed. "That is Herr Auer. Warden of the Wald, and, by many accounts, Lindenfeld's finest poacher. I trust you can see what kind of man he is?"

Mathias watched as two of Herr Auer's dogs—huge, ill-tempered things—grappled and snarled over a bone, then cowered as the warden served them each a vicious kick. "I can."

"When men like that are about, nothing is safe."

"Even bears?"

"Especially bears."

He gave her a level look. "I thought you were afraid of that bear."

"I was. I *am*. But that is no reason for it to be killed, and its head mounted in the Rose and Thorn like some prize. What has it done to deserve such a fate? It is a living creature, the same as you or I." She glared across the square at the warden. "What right have men to take life where they see fit? What right have they to kill without need? I don't understand it. And I won't be a part of it."

Mathias was regarding her intently.

"Besides," she stammered, reddening, "the tales always say that bears are roaming animals. They seldom stay in one place for long."

"That is true," he conceded, looking out over the square. "That is true."

# 9

## The Devil's Color

*Rosabell, meanwhile, had drawn away from the intrigues of her father's court. She loved to ride, disappearing for hours in the forest. She lay by rivers and streams, listening to the water as it whispered. She scaled the oldest trees, breathing the wisdom in their branches. At night she watched the stars as they wheeled and danced, slow as time. Rosabell knew that the water and the trees and the sky were one. One, and everything.*

It felt wrong to leave the village without Jacob. All through the afternoon Greta was certain that he would appear at any moment, bashful and drink-sick, ashamed for having made her worry so. Thrice Mathias left alone to search the surrounding forest and roads, each time returning empty-handed and more troubled, Greta was certain, than he cared to admit. By the time the musicians were packing up and the villagers trickling homeward she was distraught. Were it not for Mathias's reasoning she might not have left Lindenfeld at all.

"Let me take you home, Greta. There is every chance Jacob is already waiting for you there. And if he is not," he said quickly, before she could protest, "I will keep searching."

"And if you find him . . ."

"I will bring him back to you at once."

It was the best she could hope for.

The fields were smoky in the fading light, the sky above the mountains palest violet, sprinkled with waking stars. Greta walked slowly, tense with worry. When the road curved to meet the river's edge, however, she slowed even further.

Christoph was waiting near the bridge.

"May I speak with you, Greta?" He narrowed his eyes at Mathias. "Alone?"

"Rob's son," Greta murmured. "He has been troubled of late. I had best speak with him."

"Of course."

"You seemed to enjoy the Maying," Christoph remarked as Greta approached. He flicked his chin at Mathias, now removed to a discreet distance. "Who is *he?*"

"*He* is Herr Schmidt. A friend of your father's."

Christoph glared. "I've never seen him before."

"That doesn't mean he's not your father's friend, Christie."

"Don't call me that," he snapped. "It's a child's name. If we are to be wed, you must call me Christoph. It is only proper."

Greta winced. "Please don't start this again."

"I thought you would be happy. My offer is likely to be the only one you'll get, after all."

Until now, Greta had tried for pity and patience. But at the insult, anger blossomed. "Well, that *is* a fine thing to say!"

"You said it yourself! You, and the Winter girl. I have money, Greta. I don't *care* about the dowry. Or any of it. Don't you see?"

"Christie—"

"*Christoph.*"

"—whatever has happened, whatever those men have asked of you, I'm sorry for it. But you must give up this idea of marriage. It is a fancy, nothing more."

He clenched his fists. "You are wrong. We will leave Lindenfeld together, and none of this will matter. My father and those men won't matter." He eyed Mathias balefully. "*He* won't matter."

Greta turned on her heel and headed back to Mathias. "I will not hear any more of this foolishness, Christie."

He stomped after her. "You should be grateful, Greta. Grateful! That little girl—she was right. The villagers don't trust you. I didn't tell you, the other day by the river. But it's true. What you did to that old woman in the woods . . . and then Herr Drescher's spelt.

The stone and the storm. They remember it all." His voice was harsh on the still evening air. "They'll turn on you. It's only a matter of time. Better that you leave now, with me. It's the only chance you'll get. Why, even a *child* knows no man will ever ask for you!"

Greta stopped. Wondered, through the cold horror, if his words had carried far enough for Mathias to hear them. The thought that they had was enough to make her turn back.

"It is not for you to say what a man might do," she told Christoph, low and trembling. "You cannot know, for you are a boy, yet."

It was there on Mathias's face: he had heard every word.

"You do not have to walk further with me," Greta said flatly, hurrying past him and onto the bridge. Why did she feel like crying? Christoph's hurtful words were nothing new; she had known since childhood that whatever had happened in those long-ago woods had marked her for life. Why did it matter now? "We are not far from my brother's land."

"I promised I'd see you home," Mathias said, following.

He drew ahead of her as they climbed, stopping now and then to hold aside a branch for her, or hand her up a steep turn in the trail. Hoping to avoid further conversation, Greta let him.

"What did the boy mean when he spoke of the spelt?" he asked during such a moment.

Greta looked at him. "You don't have to do this," she said sincerely. "It is enough that you're helping with Jacob. I do not expect you to subject yourself to my troubles, as well."

He looked back at her, impassive. Waiting.

"Very well." She sighed. "When I was ten years old, I walked by a field of spelt. It felt . . . sad." She remembered that spelt, still; bowed and weary, as though the act of staring at the sky was an ordeal past endurance. "I knew it was going to fail. I told Herr Drescher, who worked that field, that it was unhappy, and that if he did not have a care with it, it would die. He laughed at me and told me not to fret—his fields were in good order. A week later, that spelt was dead. Herr Drescher stopped smiling at me when I passed his land after that."

"What of the stone? And the storm?"

"When I was fourteen I was helping in the fields. Without thinking I picked up a stone and threw it over my shoulder. My *left* shoulder. Soon after, a great storm came up the valley. They say a witch can summon a storm with a stone like that." She shrugged. "I was just trying to clear the field."

"And the old woman?"

Greta hesitated. Glimpsed, through the trees, the lights of Lindenfeld flickering below. The village was closing in upon itself for the night: locking its gates, lighting its lamps, tending its fires. Families were gathering close around their supper tables, tired after the day's festivities.

"Something happened to Hans and me when we were children."

And despite her careful misremembering, the fragile web of time and distraction she had crafted for herself, she was there again, in the forest.

The kind old woman who had baked the wondrous little gingerbread house lived nearby, the children had soon learned. When she led them to her home, they found it to be filled with bags of flour and pots of honey; dried apples and other sweet and tempting treasures. There was a great stone oven, too, flame flickering bright in its enormous belly.

The woman made the hungry children pancakes, and when they had eaten their fill she bade them lie down on two little beds. Greta fell at once into a restless sleep in which she dreamed of all manner of fearful things: the wide and empty forest, the deep, deep dark of the night. She woke to the sound of her brother screaming. The old woman had seized Hans and thrown him into a cage. She came next for Greta, chaining her by the ankle so that she could not escape when the old witch—for witch she certainly was—forced her to help with the chores.

"Lucky, lucky girl!" The witch's eyes were red and leaking, her hands curled like claws. Stale breath hissed between her rotting teeth. "You shall help me bake for your brother. Yes, yes! Together we will make him plump and juicy-sweet." And she cackled gleefully.

Above all else, the witch had wanted to fatten Hans up. "Too thin, too thin," she muttered over and over again. Each morning she asked him to stretch out his finger, so that she could feel if he was getting fat. Greta had found an old bone and given it to Hans, and he held that out instead. The witch, with her bleary, wasted eyes, was fooled by the ruse.

"Each day she insisted that Hans be fed well," Greta told Mathias. "That's how I learned to bake." She studied his face, expecting disgust or, even worse, disbelief. She saw none.

"Go on," was all he said.

The Ave Maria bell sounded faintly from the monastery on the other side of the valley. Greta pulled her shawl around her shoulders, warding off the rising chill.

"Three weeks after our arrival," she said, "I baked a tiny gingerbread house."

"Not bad," the witch had remarked grudgingly. "There may be some hope for you, yet."

That same day, Greta found the mouse. It had rounded ears and long whiskers, which it cleaned with dainty pink paws. At night, while the old woman slept, Greta whispered to the tiny creature, feeding it crumbs of gingerbread. It spoke back to her sometimes, small sounds that made the long hours of the night seem shorter and helped Greta forget, for a few moments at least, that she was chained to her bed, and that she and Hans were prisoners, far from home.

When four weeks had passed, the witch tested Hans's finger. By then the children understood that she meant to eat him. Hans, as he usually did, held out the bone, his small hand trembling so badly Greta feared he would drop it and doom himself.

"You are as thin as when you first came to me!" the witch

screeched. "How can it be so? Hasn't your sister been feeding you? Have you not enjoyed her beautiful baking?"

She stomped around the workbench, muttering. "It will not do. It will not." Her reddish eyes bored into Greta. "We must bake more, that's all. Fetch some wood."

Greta obeyed. When the oven was good and hot, she bent to close the heavy door. The mouse, sleeping in her apron pocket, slipped out.

"Agh!" the witch shrieked. "Vermin!" And she plucked the mouse up and tossed it into the flames.

"No!" Greta screamed. A terrible loss welled up within her, quickly followed by fury. Outside, a wind blew, and the fire in the oven leapt and sparked. Greta's rage, boundless and bountiful, matched it. She ran toward the witch, her hands outstretched, and—

"And what?" Mathias breathed.

"I cannot remember," Greta said. "I have never been able to remember. The next thing I knew, I was in the forest with Hans. We ran and ran, until we were home again."

"But what of your brother? Surely he knows what happened?"

Greta nodded, swallowed. "Hans said I . . . He said I pushed her."

"I see."

"My father warned us to say nothing of what I had done. He knew what it would mean for me. But somehow the story got free."

"And the people"—Mathias tilted his head toward Lindenfeld—"believed it."

"Yes. They believe it still."

She waited for him to turn away from her in disgust. He didn't.

"But if you *did* push her—and I am not certain that you did," he said thoughtfully, "would not the act deserve praise in lieu of contempt? Lindenfeld should have been grateful to you for ridding the forest of such evil."

"They did thank me, at first. But then . . ."

He sighed. "You walked by a crop that died and threw a stone over your shoulder while you were clearing a field."

"Yes. They burned a woman for witchery, too, the year after my father died. Frau Elma. She was my friend."

"I'm sorry. It is barbaric, what they do to so-called witches."

The light shifted around them, a reminder of the passing of day. Greta watched Mathias consider her, his gaze drifting over her hair, the auburn wings of it beneath the edges of her coif. *Witches always have red hair. It's the Devil's color.*

"And so, because of a storm and a stone and a field, you are judged."

Greta nodded.

"There is a fault in that reckoning." He gave her a regretful smile and continued along the path.

He was right. Greta knew it. But even so the villagers had never forgiven her for what they believed she had done.

*They remember it all. They'll turn on you. It's only a matter of time.*

With a stab of shame she realized that Christoph's final words at the bridge—words she had taken as nothing more than the insults of a frustrated and frightened boy—were true: she had never belonged in Lindenfeld. The villagers were kind enough to her. They bought her gingerbread and passed a word or two with her at market or after church. But aside from Herr Hueber, the men never asked her for a dance at May Day, or the harvest feast. And the women never invited her to join their spinnstuben on winter evenings, when they gathered to gossip and knit. The past hung about Greta like a ragged dress, stained with smoke and witchcraft, threaded with bones and shadows. With every step she took it itched against her skin, heavy with ash and scandal, dank with mud and blood. It could be neither unlaced nor unmade; it would be with her always.

"We should keep moving," Mathias called. Framed against the dusky trees above, he looked like a warrior in one of the old tales.

Greta hurried after him. "You don't seem troubled by any of this."

"That is because I am not."

"Are you saying it doesn't concern you? What Christoph—what they say?"

He stopped midstride and turned back, so that Greta all but collided with him. "Could you change it, if it did?"

"Of course not."

"Then what does it matter?"

Night was coming, with its secrets. Below, the village was secure behind its wall. She thought again of Frau Elma; Lindenfeld had not been a place of safety for her. And what people had said about her had mattered. In the end, it had mattered very much.

"It is not many men who would speak of witchcraft as you do," she said.

"How do I speak of it?"

"With ease. As though you were discussing the summer planting. Or hunting, or praying."

He shrugged. "I have seen too much in my time to do otherwise." His smile caused Greta's belly to do an odd little flip-flop. "Know this, though: no amount of talk can change who a person is, in their heart. Remember that."

They were not far from the house. Greta could all but see it through the trees. She drew away from Mathias and made her way up the last turn of the path, eager, of a sudden, to be home.

"I'll come back when I've found Jacob," he called after her.

Greta raised a hand in acknowledgment and hurried on. She was careful not to look back.

"You are home late."

Greta, hanging her shawl on its hook near the door, snapped around. Hans was lounging in the old chair that had been her father's favorite, one boot propped on the oven.

"Stars above, but you frightened me!" She found a candle, lit it. "Why are you sitting in the dark?"

"I wanted to speak with you about Christoph Mueller." Her brother's face was solemn in the candle's glow.

"Oh?" Greta did not want to speak of Christoph. She poked about in the wood basket, feigning interest. "Are you hungry? I could make us some supper. . . ."

"He told me he asked you to marry him," Hans said flatly. "And that you turned him down."

"He didn't mean it. There's been . . . some trouble between him and his father." She would go to Rob first thing tomorrow and tell him of Christoph's behavior. Enough, after all, was enough.

"He seemed serious to me."

The coals beneath the oven were still glowering. Greta stirred them until they woke, then laid slivers of wood across them, blowing gently. Anything, to avoid the entirely new, and frighteningly speculative, look in her brother's eye.

"I mean it, Greta; Christie's offer was sincere. And though I do not like to say so, it seems to me it's the best one you'll get."

"Why do people keep saying that?" Greta slammed the oven's door. "Am I really that hideous? Could no one possibly love me?"

Deep in the oven's belly, the fire sparked and hissed in sympathy.

"That is not what I meant and you know it." Hans unhitched himself from his seat and came to her side. "Surely you do not wish to remain unmarried? By all accounts it is a lonely life to choose."

"You speak as though I had a choice. Tell me, what choice did I *ever* have? There was never any money for me. I reconciled myself years ago to a life without a husband, without children. I have asked for nothing, though Heaven knows I am reminded often enough of what I do not have!"

"But that is what I am *saying*." Hans took both her hands in his. "If you married Christie, you wouldn't be alone anymore. And the Swedish tax, my debt with Herr Hueber . . . None of it would matter. All our troubles would be over."

. . . *he means all* his *troubles would be over,* the book said dryly.

Greta ripped her hands away. "I *told* you, Hans. I spoke to Herr Hueber today. He has given us another month!"

"Odd's bodkins, Greta, are you thick-witted?" Hans's voice rose.

"It will take more than a month to make that kind of money, even with baking like yours. Besides, do you really think Herr Hueber is the only man in the valley I owe coin to?"

*. . . the plot thickens.*

Greta went cold. "What do you mean?"

His gaze slid away from hers. "Perhaps I have a debt or two, here and there. It hardly matters. Christoph is willing to pay a very pretty bride-price for you—"

"Money he stole from his father, no doubt. Are you listening to yourself, Hans? You would steal Rob Mueller's money, and agree to his son's marriage without his knowledge?"

"Rob would forgive us all, in time—"

"But you would be *selling* me, Hans! Your own sister!"

Hans looked down, unwilling to meet her glare.

Greta felt as though the floor between them had cracked and fallen away, widening into a chasm neither one of them could cross.

"I am doing this for *you*," Hans said at last. "It's a good match. Can't you see? I only want you to be happy."

"Of course. That's you, isn't it? Always putting others first. Like Jacob. He wanted to help us. But you had to be jealous and selfish—"

He raised a hand. "Don't, Greta."

"You broke his heart!"

"That's enough!"

"You broke his heart, as you are breaking mine." Her voice cracked as she fought back tears. Unbidden, an image of Mathias, his moss-colored eyes, flickered in her mind.

"Please, Greta." Hans took hold of her shoulders. "Please do this for me. I can't stand it any longer. I must get away. I should have gone years ago, with Jacob. I stayed because of you. And what good has it brought us? This marriage, this money—it would mean a new start for both of us." He swallowed. "I'm begging you."

The tears had come, flowing down her cheeks. "You cannot ask this of me."

"I do not ask," Hans said in a different tone. "The deal is already struck. You'll leave tonight. Christoph will be waiting at the river with horses." He sighed, and brushed Greta's tears away with his thumb. "You will thank me for this one day, sister. He'll take better care of you than I ever could. Now, you'd best pack your things."

# 10
## Bitter and Binding

*It was only when her young body ripened and curved that Liliane understood the true power of her beauty. Narrow-chested noblewomen looked at her with envy, and the men of the court, old and young alike, followed her with their eyes.*

*Liliane indulged them. She cared little for the feelings of others. She was like the moon she had so longed for as a child—beautiful, cold and distant—and as dark as the sky surrounding it.*

Strange, how in a few moments everything can change.

The Greta who tearfully scrambled together her belongings— comb and clothing, baking molds and ribbons—and thrust them into a pack was not the Greta who drew tight the strings. *She* was dry-eyed and cool as stone. *She* followed her brother out into the night without a word of protest.

Hans had never liked the forest. He moved quickly, lantern held high, eyes carefully forward as though he were afraid of what might lurk at the edge of the path. It was easy enough for the second, more purposeful Greta to hang back and let him pull ahead of her. Easy, too, to let her eyes adjust to the dark, and to slip silently onto the narrow trail where the wild violets grew, not stopping until she reached the little footbridge that led to Rob's land.

She crouched by the riverbank, catching her breath. High above, Hans was calling her name, faint and furious, his lantern swinging through the fir trees like a will-o'-the-wisp. Hard not to smile a little, in triumph. Downstream, two horse-shaped shadows waited near the main bridge. There was no sign of Christoph.

A wolf howled, very close, and the horses nickered in fear. The hair on Greta's arms prickled. She straightened and ran for the footbridge: for Rob's land, and safety. But hands grabbed her, half lifting her off her feet.

"Be still, Täubchen."

It was Christoph.

"Let me go!" she hissed, struggling. "How could you—"

"There's no time for that. We have to go."

He jogged toward the horses, pulling Greta with him, then juddered to a halt. Three wolves, their fur rimed in moonlight, blocked the path. A fourth, with fur so black it was barely visible, stood on the bank above. Its lips were drawn back in a snarl.

"Run," Christoph breathed.

To run is to die. Greta knew it. But there was no question of stilling or dropping to the ground this time. The bear and the wolves were different creatures, entirely. She turned and ran, her feet slipping on the slick riverbank, Christoph close behind. More wolves appeared, swift shapes at the edges of her sight. They cut between Greta and Christoph, separating them. She ran on alone, moving deeper into the old forest that skirted the mountain. A tiny fey creature moved with her, its wings a frantic whirring at her ear.

"Run," it said. In the moonlight the creature's skin was lucent, its lips soft as rosebuds. "They come. . . ."

Greta stumbled as the wolves snapped at her ankles and tore at her skirts. Gasping, breath hot in her burning chest, she lost her footing and fell. The wolves closed in.

This, then, was death. Greta dropped to the ground at last, burrowing around herself like a small, terrified creature taking refuge in the earth. She shut her eyes, waiting, ears thick with looming snarls.

There came a different growl, then—deeper, hoarser—and a huge shape cleaved itself from the night. The black bear ignored Greta, haunching slowly past her until it stood between her and the wolves. It growled again, a monstrous sound.

And the wolves answered. They rushed in, fanning out around the bear, darting and snapping. Greta scrabbled backward in the pine needles. She counted five wolves in all. Five wolves against one. They tore at the bear from one direction, then the other, scratching and panting, snarling and biting. They were fast but the bear was faster. It struck out with unbelievable speed, standing on its hind legs and pivoting hither and thither, great paws slicing the air. Thrice it found its mark and a wolf went down, scrambling and whining. A fourth fell under the bear's jaws, where it was shaken viciously then tossed across the clearing. It hit a tree with a sickening crack and slid to the ground. Only the black wolf was left unscathed. Outmatched, it bared its teeth and retreated, the others limping after.

All was still but for the pounding of Greta's heart and the roughness of the bear's breath, in and out again, its sides heaving with effort. It swept its head around and blinked at her, then rocked slowly back into the woods. In moments there was no sign that it, or the wolves, had been there at all.

"What in God's name are you doing here, Täubchen?" Rob swung wide his door, allowing Greta to stumble inside. He peered out into the moonlit yard, then closed the door firmly, locking it.

"I h-had to come." She was shivering uncontrollably, the molds in her pack clanking. She slipped the pack off, dropped it on the floor. "Hans did something a-awful."

"You're soaking wet!"

"I forded the river. C-couldn't risk going back to the bridge. The wolves—"

"Wolves?" He gripped her arm. "Where?"

"By the bridge. They chased us. Then I lost Christie, and—"

"*Christie?* That can't be. He's upstairs." Rob touched a key hanging from his belt beside a pistol and a dirk. Behind him, Greta glimpsed a musket lying casually across the big, worn table.

"No. He's not." She eyed the weapons warily. "What is happening here?"

"Tell me everything you saw tonight. Quickly, now. Much depends upon it."

Greta told him, then watched wide-eyed as he strode across the room and took up the musket. "You're . . . you're not going to shoot Hans?" she stammered.

"It would be less than he deserves," Rob grunted, ripping down a lantern from a hook by the door. "But, no. Come, Täubchen. Show me where you saw my son."

And so Greta found herself stumbling once more into the night, shivering with cold and dread, her sodden skirts clinging to her legs.

"Christie!" Rob hissed, when they were at the river. He raised the lantern. But for the river rushing beneath the bridge, all was still. "Christie! Are you there?"

His voice was low and urgent, as though he feared someone other than Christoph might hear. Greta could feel his distress. It had begun at the house, intensifying as he crossed the yard and saw Christoph's window flung open to the sky, the shutters wide and accusing.

"Was it here, Täubchen? Did you see him here?"

"It was on the other side, but yes, it was here." The horses were gone—frightened, no doubt, by the wolves. A faint glimmer of light high above on the mountain: Hans, returning to the house.

"Christie!" Fear outweighed caution, and Rob's voice echoed along the riverbank. "*Christie!*"

A faint cry from the direction of the old mill. Rob followed the sound, Greta behind him, until they came to a large, firelit clearing. The mercenaries were there, standing in a tight circle with Mira at its center, the animal furs on their backs more predatory than ever.

Mira held a wolf skin, soft as new snow. Conran loomed at her shoulder. Before them, on his knees, was Christoph. His face was bleeding and he was breathing hard, as though he had fought for his freedom before losing it. Tears and dirt smudged his cheeks.

"What in Hell's name is happening here?" Rob roared.

Conran raised a casual brow. "I should think that was fairly obvious."

"You mean to force him, then? Against his will?"

Conran shrugged. "Did any of us really have a choice?"

"You were rough with him."

"Aye, and he with us," put in a big red-haired sell-sword. He touched his swollen lip. "Fights like his father, this one, and no mistake." He looked at Christoph regretfully. "A shame."

"What is?" Rob demanded.

"All of it."

"Aye, well," Conran snarled. "It'll be over soon enough." He jerked his chin at Mira. "You know what to do."

Mira hesitated, her gaze flickering toward the edge of the clearing. One of the youngest mercenaries was there, propped against a tree. He was drawn with pain, clutching at his side.

"Who is that?" Rob, too, had seen the wounded man.

"That there's Tavey," the big redheaded mercenary said. "The youngest."

"He's wounded."

"I fear his ribs are shattered," Mira agreed tonelessly. "I wanted to take him back to camp. Time matters, in such things. You know that, Rob. But Conran thought it best we finish the ceremony first."

Silence. Every man there, watching.

Firelight glinted in Conran's eyes. "Are you criticizing me, Mira?"

"Tavey needs help," she said. "It is my duty to care for him—"

"It's your duty to do as I damn well say." He seized the wolf skin and thrust it at her, so hard she almost stumbled. "You want to help Tavey? Change the fucking boy."

Rob's back was to Greta. Even so the anger rolling from him was palpable. Mira, for her part, looked as though she would like nothing more than to throw the grey pelt onto the fire. But whatever power Conran had over her, over them all, held fast. Mira merely took a small pot from within the folds of her cloak, spreading its contents, a thick salve, over the fur. Around her, the men and

Conran each unrolled his own pelt—black and iron-grey, old cream and ash, autumn brown and copper—and did the same. The salve gleamed silver on the furs. The scent of it—bittersweet earth and flowers—hung heavy on the air.

A thread of understanding tugged at Greta. Understanding, and something more, like snatches from a half-forgotten dream. The river's murmur and the faint creak of the old sluice gate were ordinary enough sounds. But the night, alive with fire and the gleam of the rising moon, was ripe with otherness.

"What is this?" she whispered.

Rob barely looked at her. "Go, Täubchen. Back to the mill. Now."

"Perhaps you should take her back, Rob," Conran leered. "The woods can be dangerous at night. We'll see to your brave son, have no fear."

Rob responded by raising his musket and pointing it directly at him. In the blink of an eye Conran hauled Christoph to his feet, shielding his own body with the boy's.

"Put it down, Rob," he said. "You're cannier than that."

The musket was steady in Rob's hands.

"You're as like to kill him as me," Conran said reasonably.

Christoph whimpered.

With agonizing slowness, Rob lowered the gun.

"There, now. Isn't that better?" Conran drew his knife and scored Christoph's palm neatly. Blood glimmered.

"I want no part of this," Christoph said, hoarse with fear and pain.

"It is the Way," Conran told him.

"It is the Way," the men echoed. They drew blades across their open palms and wiped the wounds over their own wolf skins. Blood and moonlight mingled.

"Go, Greta," Rob whispered. "Please."

She wanted to obey him: the fire, the salve, the menacing men with their bloody pelts all seemed part of some unholy ritual, frightening beyond measure. And yet she found she could not look away.

Conran was glowering at Mira. "Hurry up, then!"

"It is the Blood," she whispered.

"Louder!"

Mira took a shuddering breath. "It is the Blood!"

"You'll not do this, Conran!" Rob's voice rang out across the clearing, solid with authority. "Stop now, all of you!"

The men hesitated, gazes twitching from Rob to Conran and back again.

"Finish the words," Conran snarled.

The sell-swords shifted uncertainly. Cursing, Conran ripped the pelt from Mira and held Christoph's wounded hand over it. Drops of blood, set to fall.

*"Finish the fucking words!"*

"Don't let them do this, Da!" Christoph implored his father. *"Please."*

"It is the Blood," the men intoned.

"The Devil it is," Rob said. And before Greta knew what he was about he had thrown his musket aside and seized his dirk. Blood welled as he sliced his palm.

"I'm sorry, Täubchen," he muttered.

Then he was running, throwing himself between Conran and his son, snatching the wolf skin and pressing it against his own wounded hand, blood and fur together.

A curious prickling sensation ran over Greta's skin. The glade whispered, willow-dark. The fire flickered.

Rob swept the pelt over his shoulders. It trailed to the backs of his knees, tail brushing the grass. He crouched low and the fur rippled and clung to his back as though it were alive. His shoulders narrowed, his hips became haunches, his arms, forelegs. Fur melded smoothly with leather and linen. There was a brief creaking of muscle; a shudder, a snap . . . and Rob Mueller was gone. Standing in his place was a huge, pale grey wolf.

Greta glimpsed Christoph's face, bloodless with shock, before the other men donned their wolf skins, too, relentless as a ring of standing stones falling one against the other. In moments, eight more wolves appeared. Conran changed last, and Greta recognized the black wolf who had pursued her near the bridge. She would have run, then, if her limbs had not been iced into place. If Mira had not raised a calming hand and shaken her head. *Be still.*

But the wolves were not intent on pursuing Greta, now. They whined and circled uneasily. All of them, that is, but Conran, whose yellow eyes were fixed with unwavering malice on the wolf who had been Rob.

"You'll not fight—" Mira shouted, even as the black wolf leapt at the grey. A writhing mess of wolf tore through the clearing, jaws snapping and tearing, claws ripping the earth. They rose on two legs, forelegs gripping, mouths open, each rending the other's neck. They faltered and dodged, lunged and jarred and skidded, until both wolves were so torn and bloodied that Greta, who had seen dogs fight countless times in the village or in the busy streets of Hornberg, and who had thought herself used to such things, was sickened.

"Enough!" Mira cried.

The other wolves milled around her. One of them—large and reddish—whined.

"Yes, Roebuck, yes. I will try." She closed her eyes. Power rose, surging through the clearing, so strong it near knocked Greta off her feet. The wolves surrounding Mira staggered. Their skins came free and they stood upright, men once more. Beyond them, the battle between the black wolf and the grey raged on.

"Why didn't they turn back?" It was the big ginger sell-sword. "Mira?"

"I don't know," Mira said, helpless. "I don't . . ."

The crack of a musket filled the air, and the-wolf-who-was-Conran yelped and staggered. Greta whirled to see Christoph holding his father's smoking musket.

There was a terrible silence. Then the black wolf shook himself and, despite the ball lodged in his flesh, plowed toward the boy. Rob, in his turn, rushed to defend his son. The fight began all over again.

"You have to stop them, Mira." The ginger-bearded soldier cringed as Conran's teeth razed Rob's pale shoulder. "Mira? He'll kill him!"

"Two leaders," Mira murmured. "Two . . ."

Conran bore Rob to the ground and sank his teeth into his throat, shaking viciously. Rob struggled to rise, could not, and gave a panicked, throaty yelp.

"Mira!" the sell-sword bellowed. "*Change them back!*"

"Two, then," Mira murmured. "Two for two." She gripped Greta's hands. A surge of power thrummed from her fingers and Greta drew back, startled.

"Don't be afraid," Mira gasped. "For the love you bear Rob, hold on to me."

With a brief, fearful glance at Rob, Greta obeyed. Power—there was no other name for it—gathered at her feet, surging upward. It hit the fighting wolves, drenching them in light, hurling them into the air. They landed with a mighty splash in the river. And surfaced, gasping and thrashing, men once more.

The sell-swords gathered on the bank as Rob and Conran limped from the water, clutching their sodden skins. Rob flopped on the grass, gasping like a fish, but Conran fumbled for his knife.

"That's enough," Mira called sharply, "for one night!"

Conran hesitated, then collapsed beside Rob. "You're stronger than I remember," he panted.

"Fifteen years . . . hauling grain . . . will do that."

All this Greta saw from a great distance. She was awash with light, as if every sylvan creature in the forest was winging around her, buffeting her with the force of its flight. As if the very stars had wheeled and realigned. Every leaf on every tree, every drop of water in the river, screamed her name. The force of the earth beat through her like a drum. She sank to her knees gasping the stars swirling above, then smearing the sky with silver as they fell.

"What's wrong with me?" she asked numbly, realizing it was she, and not the stars, who had fallen, and that, most curiously, her soul and her body were now separate. She was floating, looking down upon herself on the moon-soaked grass, her face ashen, her hair a tangle of flame.

"It is the greenstrength." Mira was kneeling at Greta's side. She was luminous, traced with starlight, her voice hollow and distant. "Cauley, Clays, help me lift her . . . gently, now."

Greta floated over oceans of stars, realms of light. All the trees in all the forests bent to her grace. The rivers flowed through her veins and the mountains thrummed in her bones. Then light enfolded her and she saw no more.

# 11

## Green, Wild, Moss, Storm

*Rosabell could be found most often in the meadows, the forest, or the castle gardens, gathering flowers, roots and herbs. She chopped them, stripped them and crushed them, made oils and salves and poultices to help the sick and wounded.*
*There was power in such doings.*

"You shouldn't have done it, Mira. You shouldn't have used her like that."

Greta stirred at the sound of Rob's voice. She was warm and snug, half sunk in the deepest, sweetest sleep she had ever known. It took all her strength to crack one eye open. Moonlight seeped through a shuttered window, mingling with the familiar sound of running water and, fainter still, the murmuring of willows. She was at the mill, in Rob's own room.

She heard the soft swish of Mira's skirts and closed her eyes again. "Oh? I should have let Conran chew through your throat, then, should I?" A shifting of weight on the edge of the bed, a cool hand on Greta's brow. "It must have come from her mother. Tell me, what was she like?"

Greta felt Rob bristle. "What do you mean by that, then?"

"You know *exactly* what I mean."

"Lena Rosenthal was a good woman," Rob growled. "She lived and died here in this valley. Her husband Peter, too. That's all you need know."

"Peter Rosenthal... Of course. The soldier you saved after Nördlingen. She's *his* daughter." Another touch on Greta's brow, smoothing away her hair. "Perhaps that's why you saved him, eh? Perhaps you sensed it, even then."

"You'll not meddle with Greta! Do you hear? I won't have it. Keep away from her."

"No amount of meddling can change what a person is, or will be, Rob. Blood is blood."

"That's right," he said. "It's red and wet. Cut yourself, you'll bleed. Lose too much, you'll die."

"There's more to it than that and you know it." Mira got to her feet with a sigh. "You cannot keep a witch from her nature. Sooner or later it will bite back. It did just that tonight—it also happened to save your life."

"And what of Greta's life?"

"She will recover. Which is more than I can say for you, if you don't let me see to those wounds."

The night's events drifted back to Greta. Hans's betrayal and her flight to the river. The wolves. The bear. Rob turning into a great, pale wolf. The battle with Conran and her own part in ending it. The wheeling of the stars and an unbearable power rising from deep within the earth, drowning her.

She slipped toward that wondrous sleep again. *Tired. So tired.*

"Are you *certain*, Mira?" Rob was saying. "After all, you hardly know her. . . ."

"I suspected it from the first. But I wasn't sure until tonight." Mira chuckled. "Did you know she's been bewitching the villagers with her baking?"

Greta, sinking luxuriously, forced herself back to wakefulness.

"All these years I've searched for someone like her. And now here she is. With you! There is a beauty to it, is there not?"

"I suppose so," Rob said dolefully.

"I'll tell her everything when she wakes." Mira's skirts whispered as she moved about the room, restless with knowledge and plans. "Her mother died when she was young, she told me. A shame; by right, Lena should have passed her knowledge to her daughter years ago. There's so much to teach her!"

"*Teach* her?"

"Of course! The poor thing hardly knows herself. She's like a bird that's been kept in a cage all its days, never knowing what it is to fly."

"Caged birds are safer than wild ones, in my opinion," Rob said gruffly.

"Caged birds are miserable," Mira told him. "I make a point of releasing every one I come across."

"And after you've 'released' Greta?"

"Well, it will be up to her, of course—"

"Of course," he agreed bitterly.

"—but I'd like to think she'd want to join us. You know as well as I do that she'd be safer out there with us than here in this village. And I'm not as young as I used to be, Rob. The pack will need another witch when the time comes."

*Witch.* A shiver of horror ran down Greta's back. The last person to utter that word alongside her own name in Rob's presence was Herr Tritten, at Frau Elma's trial. Rob had responded by quietly vowing to kill him. She braced herself for the onslaught that would, at any moment, burst from his lips.

It never came.

"But surely there are other witches, Mira?" he asked, hardly missing a beat. "Someone else to take your place?"

"There are no others. Not after the trials. So many died, Rob. In France and Scotland. In England, my home. And here in the Empire, too. Mutilated or burned. Drowned or strangled. Surely you remember what they did in Würzburg? In Bamberg? No woman with a trace of green in her blood was safe. Until two days ago I believed I was one of the last."

"Even so. Greta is . . ."

"Greta is *green*, Rob," Mira said firmly. "Green as a moss maid, and strong, too. I can feel the power rolling off her like heat from a fire. You've done well to protect her all these years. But now it's time for you to let her go."

Rob was quiet for so long that Greta risked another peek. His face was drawn in the candlelight. He looked old, suddenly. Old and sad.

"Mira," he said at last. "I must ask you to leave her be."

"I can't do that. Greta's path has been hidden from her. It is my duty to help her find it."

"Aye," he snapped. "A path of loneliness. Of constant danger, and hardship."

There was a strained silence.

"I know what it was like for you," Rob went on, softer. "The dangers you faced. The sacrifices you made."

"I made them gladly, Rob."

"Even so. You gave up everything you knew. Your home. Your family. The chance to take a husband and have children of your own. You followed first my whim, then Conran's, chained to your duty, half starved and adrift, peddling war. Tell me, why should I want that for Greta? To be trotted around the countryside at the mercy of that reckless bastard, knee-deep in blood and rot? No. Greta has suffered enough. I cannot let her struggle through life, never to love, never to marry, never to bear children—"

"There are some who would say that marriage is its own kind of drudgery," Mira cut in. "A wife, too, is chained to her duty, tied to her hearth and table. She lives at the whim of a man who may beat her when he pleases and no one will say otherwise. She'll bind herself to him with child after child, weighed down by her own treacherous body, never to be free, never to see what lies beyond the next valley—"

"And what of the battlegrounds?" Rob hissed. "The wounds and the sickness? The stink of rotting flesh? Men half crazed with fear, or so relieved they survived the day they'll force the first woman they see. . . . Have you forgotten the villages? Whole villages burning or emptied by plague, bodies left in the streets with none to bury them. Children bloated with hunger and disease. Fields ripe with dead horses. Have you forgotten—"

"It is *you* who has forgotten," Mira said. "You have forgotten that there is wonder and beauty, too. To run with wolves over winter snows. To walk the woods in bare feet, with the sun on your face and not another soul for miles." Her voice strengthened. "You think I have thrown away my life. But I tell you, it is something indeed to be free."

Greta's breath caught in her chest. Her skin tingled all over, sunlight sparkling on snow.

"I'm not denying that," Rob said. "But I promised Greta's father I would take care of her. He almost lost his children, once. It haunted him until the day he died."

"You've kept that promise, Rob. Greta and her brother are children no more."

"There is more to it than that."

"Tell me, then."

"It is a sad tale," he warned.

"I know about her mother. Lena."

*Blood on the snow, red as her hair.*

"Her father married again, she said."

"That's true."

"The second wife was cruel, she said."

"That, too, is true." He sighed, and Greta imagined him glancing her way, checking that she still slept.

"I was not here when Lena died," he said. "Or when Peter took another wife. I could not help their children. . . ."

"How bad can one stepmother be?"

"I have never forgiven myself for what happened," Rob muttered. *"Never."*

"What happened, Rob?" Mira asked. The amusement was gone from her voice now. "Why do you blame yourself?"

Greta waited for his answer, every muscle taut with expectation. Then Conran's voice bounced up the narrow stairs, shadowing whatever truth Rob had been about to bring to light.

"Come now, miller!" he called irritably. "She's well enough, isn't she? No one bit her."

"He has no idea it was Greta who helped me put down the

magic," Mira whispered. "He thinks her nerves are simply frayed after he and the men hunted her in the woods."

"As well they might be," Rob said bitterly.

"We're all waiting patiently for you!"

"You must run out with them," Mira said. "Seal the bond."

Rob sighed as he pushed himself to his feet. "I wanted to be here when she woke. But I suppose I must go."

"I suppose you must."

Rob picked up Greta's hand. "I remember when she was small, all wild hair and big gray eyes. What will you tell her, Mira?"

"The truth."

"You don't have to. You could tell her . . . that she dreamed. That it was all a horrible nightmare."

"She's not a child, Rob; I'll not coddle her or lie—"

"I never lied!"

"You never told the truth, either. She deserves to know. To make her *own* choice." Greta heard the scuff of bare feet as Mira came to Rob's side. "Let me teach her, Rob. Let me show her how to protect herself."

"*I* can protect her."

"How will you do that when you are miles and miles away?"

Silence.

"I will speak with Greta when she wakes," Mira said. "I will tell her everything, and I will let *her* decide."

"And what if I say no?"

"You have been too long away, Rob," Mira told him, releasing Greta's hand from his hold. "You forget there are greater powers in this world than your will."

"That's it, then?" Rob's fury was plain, despite his stifled whisper. "You'll go your own way, regardless of my feelings?"

"At this moment your feelings are not my concern."

"Then I shall remove them from your presence!"

Footsteps.

"Wait, Rob. Your wounds . . ."

"I survived fifteen years without you," Rob flung at her before he left the room. "I think I'll manage."

"You can stop pretending to sleep, now," Mira said dryly, when the sound of the departing men below had faded into night-quiet.

Greta opened her eyes. "Is it true?" She tried to sit up and flopped weakly back against the bolster. "What you . . . what you said about me?"

Outside, the willows stilled, listening.

"Oh, yes," Mira said. "As much as it may displease Rob, you have the green." She drew a chair close to the bed and sat down.

"The green?"

"Greenstrength. The ability to use greenmagic. It's strong in you."

"And that means . . ."

"You're a greenwitch. A wild-wife, a moss maid, a storm hag. We have many names."

Greta stared at her. She felt adrift, confused—a woman pulled apart, then stitched roughly back together again.

"I thought w—" She trailed off, unable, unwilling. "I thought women like that were evil. Malicious and cruel."

"More's the pity. The situation would be different had your mother lived."

"You're wrong about her. She wasn't . . . what you think."

"Of course she was," Mira said reasonably. "Greenstrength always comes from the mother."

"That doesn't mean she was a . . . witch." Greta forced herself to say the word.

"But did she know things, your mother? About the trees? About the weather?"

"Perhaps. I cannot rightly say."

"And did she heal others? Did she know a little rhyme or two, a secret song, to cure an ill or ease a hurt?"

*Leaf that's green, earth and air . . .*

"Perhaps," Greta whispered. "Perhaps she knew a little."

Mira's skin was burnished in the candlelight. "It is possible she did not know her own power. Many women born with the touch never do. They grow things, and heal the sick, and walk the wood. But they do not shine." Mira leaned close. "Now, you, on the other hand. I knew you had it the moment I saw you. But I did not know how strong you were until tonight."

"I don't feel strong, Mira. I feel as though I've been run over by a cart."

The hint of a smile. "It's a different kind of strength. It was *you* who stopped the fight tonight. *You* who saved Rob's life. Don't look so shocked; Conran would have killed your uncle if we'd not intervened."

"But . . . why?"

"There can only be one leader. The First, we call him. Your uncle was First before Conran. His return went against the natural order of things. As you saw, Conran did not take kindly to it."

Greta shuddered at the memory of the fight. The sound of it, the violence.

"Why did Rob . . . return?"

"For his son, of course. The boy does not wish to claim his birthright. Didn't he try to buy you like a wheel of cheese to escape it?"

"My brother called it a bride-price."

Mira wafted a hand. "Cheese, bride. I've found they mean much the same thing in such transactions."

Something stirred, deep beneath the fatigue and turmoil. Something that sparked and burned.

"But why would marrying me have made a difference?"

"Because once a wolf is wed he must give up his pelt; his place is with his wife. Ordinarily he'll marry *after* he has served for many years and go with his brothers' blessing. When his sons are of age, *they* will take his place. It works beautifully, for the most part."

"But *why*?" Greta asked. "Why would a man choose to change his shape? And why must you be with them?"

Mira laughed. "You think them wild and uncouth. Dangerous. And you would be right. But they were not always that way. For many, many years they were honorable. Good. When Ashildr created the First Wolf and his men, she did so because she wanted to protect the land and every creature who walked upon it."

"Ashildr?"

"The first of our kind. She lived long ago, in Gothia. It was Ashildr who learned to wield the green. To spell a pelt and turn a man into a wolf. A witch has power enough of her own, but oftentimes she needs more. She needs iron; warriors to help her protect what is green and good in this world: the small things, the wounded and the weak, the young and innocent. All things evil, be they man or fey, were the enemy of Ashildr and her pack." Mira sighed. "But that was six hundred years ago, before the High King banished the old ways. Ashildr and her warriors traveled to Scotia—Scotland—after that, and their ancestors remained there. Until the Scots king ordered the great wolf hunts, at least. It became too dangerous after that, and they left for the Empire."

"They became sell-swords." Greta was unable to keep the derision from her voice. It was well known that mercenaries had wrought the greatest damage upon Württemberg during the war.

"They did. But not for the reasons you think. Remember, they already knew how to fight; it was all they had known since the earliest days. And they were needed. Evil men and fey creatures alike will always prey upon the weak, but in a land at war they thrive. What better place to find them?"

It made sense in a grim, dangerous sort of way.

"But those days are gone, now," Mira said. "The pack is weak. Wild and unwieldy."

"Why?"

"We lost Rob." Mira's face was troubled. "The men would never have attacked you as they did tonight if Rob were their leader. That they did so proves how far they have fallen."

"And what of you? How did you come to be with them?"

"The pack must always have a witch. They found me when I was just a girl—a housemaid in a village near the New Forest. I went with them willingly. The Empire is not the only land where witches are at risk; England, too, had its share of hunts. I was already being treated with suspicion. Besides, I wanted to see the world." She smiled. "You heard what Rob said just now. It was not always easy for me. But the years I spent with him were the best of my life."

"Did you and Rob ever . . . ?"

"No. The greenwitch is mother to the pack. Sister, advisor, healer. Never wife. Never lover."

"That seems cruel."

"Every wolf must be equal in the witch's eyes."

A chorus of howls seeped through the night.

Greta froze. "Is that . . ."

"Yes."

"What are they doing?"

"Running with the moon. Sealing the bond."

"The bond?"

"The blood bond. Rob has come back to them after many years. He must find his place again."

Another howl.

"He didn't want you to tell me," Greta said. "About . . . what I am."

Mira leaned across the bed, took Greta's hand. "You have the potential to do wondrous things, Greta. Rob knows this. But he also knows, as I do, that such gifts can be dangerous. I don't have to tell you what happens to women who are accused of witchery."

The Marktplatz. Flame and smoke, a seething crowd.

"No," Greta whispered.

"Rob wishes to protect you. I understand that, I do. But to not teach you now would be a grave injustice to us both, as well as to all the greenwomen who have walked before us and will come after. So." Mira leaned closer, and Greta caught the scent of yarrow and earth. "I can teach you how to wield greenmagic and bend it to your will. How to harness the power of the mountains, the rivers, the trees. How to protect yourself and others. How to cloak the land in rain or mist. How to remain unseen. If you wish, I can show you *everything.*"

Moonlight shone on Mira's silver-dark hair. On her heart-shaped face and the fox skin hanging at her waist.

Greta thought of the witch, long ago, entrapping two helpless children and no one to stop her. Herr Hueber's desire, his threats, the weight of them pressing down, smothering her. Frau Elma, burning. Hans and Christoph, conspiring. How would it feel to be powerful enough to protect herself? How would it feel to never again be at someone else's mercy?

"Yes," she said. A single word springing from somewhere deep inside her, somewhere beyond reason and fear. She gripped Mira's hand with sudden strength. "Yes."

When the first breath of dawn silvered the eastern hills Greta followed Mira to where the river dozed beneath the willows. She had slept through the remainder of the night, deep and dreamless. The morning seemed fresh and new, the air so clear and cool it tingled in her nose and on her skin.

"This is a good place for us," Mira said. "Spellwork is always easiest in the sacred places."

"Sacred places?"

"Old forests. Forgotten springs. Mountaintops. But this will serve, too."

They entered the cool secrecy of the willow grove. As a child Greta had spent hours roaming its leafy halls and chambers, enjoying the quiet, the knowledge that she would not meet another person for hours and hours.

"There are two kinds of magic," Mira murmured, seating herself on an old, moss-covered boundary stone. "Greenmagic, which heals and protects, and tattermagic, which does the opposite. My kind, and yours, is greenmagic." She trailed her fingers through the willow leaves.

"Greenwitches honor the earth. They feel the breath of the seasons,

the changing moon. They carry their craft with them. Fire and air."
Mira gestured to the tinderbox and knife hanging at Greta's waist.
"Water and earth." She pointed to the river, and Greta's bare feet. "It's
no wonder you spelled the village with your baking."

Greta frowned. Surely the book, too, had played a part?

"And as they honor the earth, so do they borrow their strength—
their *magic*—from it," Mira was saying. "Hear me, though: we must
go gently, always. If you borrow a tree's strength you will weaken it.
Autumn will come to its branches, even in high summer. In winter
you may kill it. You must learn to listen. Be mindful of every living
thing, and never take too much."

"Forgive me, Mira, but should I not be writing this down?"

A meeting of those once-black brows. "No. Greenmagic is felt
in the heart, and remembered in the soul. It is a living thing. Not
scratches on the dried skin of some poor dead creature."

The derision in Mira's voice turned Greta cold. "A greenwitch
would never keep her spells in a book, then?"

"No. Only tatterwitches do that."

She had known, of course. Only a fool would believe that the
book's magic was the same as Mira's. She wondered if she should
tell Mira of its part in her past, how it had helped her, again and
again. The disdain lingering on Mira's face, coupled with the ever-
present instinct to protect the book, stopped her.

"What *is* tattermagic?" she asked instead.

"Tattermagic rends and destroys," Mira replied. "It is a bitter,
ill-gained sort of magic, wrought of pain, fear, and sadness. A
tatterwitch—or tattermage—is the opposite of a greenwitch in
every way. *We* heal and protect. A tatterwitch seeks to destroy, remaking what is broken for her own selfish purposes."

It couldn't be true. The book had saved Greta. *Cared* for her. Its
gingerbread had kept her, and Hans, fed and safe for years. Surely
there was nothing selfish in that?

Mira noted Greta's consternation. "I'm rushing this, aren't I?
Forgive me. It's just . . . I had all but given up on ever finding another greenwitch. It's been some time since I thought on how I

might teach one, should the opportunity ever arise." She stood very still, thinking, and Greta wondered at how *different* the greenwitch was. Mira wore her magic like a cloak; it pooled at her feet and shimmered in her hair.

"There!" she said suddenly, pointing. "The spider there, in the tree. Do you see?" A delicate grey spider had strung a web between two willows, the strands golden in the rising sun, hung with liquid jewels. "She sits at the center of her web, connected to all things: the trees, the air, the sky. She feels everything, because everything is connected." Mira gestured at the sky, the willows, the earth at her feet. "We, too, sit in the center of a great web. We, too, are joined to all things. Can you feel it?" Mira raised her hand, plucking one graceful finger. The air trembled as a web will when it is disturbed. Greta *saw* it then: golden with dew, stretching from the heights of the mountains to the secret places of the earth.

"You try," Mira said.

Greta sank to her knees. She grasped the web as Mira had done, flicking her fingers over the strands. She could pull on them, if she wanted to. Instinct told her so. The mountains, the trees, the very earth, would lend her their strength. How had she not felt it before? Gently, gently, she took up the strands. There was a slight resistance, like the intake of breath before song. And then it came. Slow and small at first, then faster and faster, a storm rushing from the trees, pouring from the river, flowing from her fingertips. The river ceased its rambling; high above, the falls forgot to fall. Every pebble, leaf and feather stilled, waiting for the witch's bidding.

"Stars above," Greta muttered. A glance at Mira. "Can you . . . can you feel that?"

Mira grinned. "Oh yes."

The clang of distant church bells broke over the valley. Distracted, Greta released her hold. At once things returned to their former occupations. The river ran and, high above, water foamed over the falls. Birds skittered through the undergrowth. The willows shivered happily in the warming sun.

"It's Sunday," Greta said, listening to the bells.

"Is it? I'd not noticed."

"Stars above!" Greta cried in horror, lurching to her feet. "Jacob!"

"Who?"

"My friend." She strode across the glade, managing, in her haste and guilt and shame, to entangle herself in the willows. How could she have forgotten? She wondered if Mathias had found him. If they had arrived back at the house, only to find Hans incensed, his plans ruined, and Greta gone. "He'll be at the church. He *has* to be."

"Devout, is he?"

"Do you mind if I go, Mira?" Greta pushed free of the long, thin branches. They trailed down her back, a willow cloak. "I really do need to speak with him."

The bells throbbed up the valley, grating against the morning. Even now the villagers would be milling in the churchyard, dressed in their best. Desperate as she was to know that Jacob was safe, Greta knew a moment of reluctance. The morning seemed fresh and new, sparking with light and magic; as though she had woken from some dim dream and stepped into the light again. At the thought of the long, dull service, packed close in the musty confines of the church, her heart sank. "Besides," she said. "People will notice if I am not there. They'll talk."

"Mind?" Mira said. "Of course not. I'm no fool, and neither are you. Go. Find your friend. Appease the good folk of Lindenfeld." She turned her face up to the sun, basking in its warmth. "We'll continue your proper instruction later."

# 12

## The Devil in the Woods

*The scent of the wind and the whisper of the forest were Rosabell's tutors. She watched a spider weave its web, the strands shimmering with dew and sunlight. The web was strong, connecting everything—water, branch and earth. Rosabell began to understand that she too was part of a vast and mighty web. And that, like the spider, she could draw upon its power.*

The bells ceased their ringing as Greta passed through the village gates. She hurried toward the church, braced for Father Marcus's disapproving glance, and slid to a halt. Instead of sitting quiet and neat in their accustomed pews, the congregation was spilling from the church's open doors and rushing toward the Marktplatz, as unwieldy as the river Schnee when the snow has melted.

"What has happened?" Greta fell into step with Jens Gerber.

"They're saying another man has been found dead," Jens said. "The watchmen are bringing him in now."

"Who is it?"

"They didn't say."

A cool breeze blew across the square, picking at the crushed flowers and dirty ribbons strewn across the cobbles. Hans and Christoph were already outside the Rathaus. Christoph blushed when he saw Greta and looked quickly away, but Hans jostled through the gathering crowd.

"Thank God," he said. "I was so worried last night, Greta. I heard wolves. Wolves, in Lindenfeld! I could not sleep for fear that something had happened to you."

"Something *did* happen to me," Greta said pointedly.

Hans winced. "I've treated you wretchedly, I know. I've just returned Christie's money—"

"Rob's money, you mean."

"—and I'll find another way to pay Hueber. Say you'll forgive me?"

A hush came over the crowd as a cart jolted into the Marktplatz, Dieter Abendroth, the first watchman, at the reins. His men followed on foot, pikes glinting above their black robes. Dieter drew to a stop before the Rathaus steps.

Greta glimpsed something in the back of the cart—something large, wrapped in a bloody blanket—before the people around her pressed forward eagerly. She was jostled and pushed, separated from Hans. Women balanced on tiptoe, desperate to see. Youths clung to the linden tree's branches. A boy clambered onto the pillory, only to be snatched roughly back by his mother.

"Who is it?" someone cried.

"Is it my boy? Is it my Günther? He did not come home last night—"

"I'm here, Mother." This from Günther, apparently, on the other side of the square. There were smatterings of nervous laughter.

Someone took hold of Greta's hand.

"I need you to come with me." Mathias, his voice low and urgent at her ear. She looked up at him.

And she knew.

*Jacob is dead.*

The men of the council were climbing the Rathaus steps, Herr Hueber among them. They looked on as Father Markus climbed into the cart, drew back the bloodied wrappings.

*That is Jacob, dead in that cart. Jacob, dead . . .*

"Come away," Mathias said. "You should not be here now."

*You should not be here, Jacob. Not like this.* Fire and flowers and moonlight. And Jacob, walking away from her for the last time.

"What happened?" Greta managed.

"I found him last night. Took the watch to him at first light. I went back to the house to tell you, but you weren't there. . . ."

"Well, Abendroth? Father Markus?" Herr Hueber's voice carried easily over the square, cutting through the roaring in Greta's ears. "Who is this man and what has killed him?"

"It is Jacob Peters," Father Markus said. A murmur ran through the crowd. "As to what has killed him, I cannot be certain. Such wounds . . ." He tore his gaze away from the contents of the cart, swallowed.

"Was it the Bavarians?" someone called. "They've made camp near Wolfach. My cousin in Hornberg told me not three days ago."

"Yes—the Bavarians—"

"Something must be done!" Anna-Barbara Wittman cried, her plump face beaded with sweat. "They cannot terrorize us, thieving and murdering as they will. The war is over!"

A tide of angry, frightened voices rose, then fell as Herr Hueber raised a placating hand.

"Something *will* be done," he said. "Isn't that right, Captain?"

He spoke to someone at the back of the crowd. As one, the people turned.

"Aye," Conran said easily, from where he lounged with his men around the fountain. "Those Bavarian rogues will cause no more trouble. My word upon it."

The sell-swords looked, if it was possible, even wilder and more fearsome than before. They fairly bristled with weapons, and all wore baldrics and vambraces of worn leather. Rob, Greta saw with some relief, was not with them, nor was the young soldier who had been wounded the night before. Mira had told Greta that she had done all she could for his damaged ribs; even so he would need time and rest to recover.

"When will you go?" Herr Hueber called to Conran.

"As soon as you wish," Conran replied. "My men are ready. We don't much mind the how or when of things, so long as there's a little brass waiting for us at the end."

"You shall have it," Herr Hueber promised. "We would be grateful if you would go at once, and rid us of these marauding devils all the sooner."

"All right then, boys," Conran said, sliding off the fountain's edge. "You heard the man. Off we go."

The villagers watched in silence as Conran—with a final, rather mocking salute to the council—led his men out of the village.

Dieter Abendroth, it seemed, was not so squeamish as the pastor. Out of resentment for the council's appointment of mercenaries to do what was by right the watchmen's duty, or mere curiosity, the first watchman was examining Jacob's body.

"Part of me wonders," he said thoughtfully, "if this was not the work of wolves."

*Wolves.* There was a stirring of fear among the people. Greta's heart stuttered and thumped. She looked down. Her hand was still holding Mathias's.

"Who found him?" Herr Hueber demanded. The feather in his hat dipped as he searched the square.

"Him," someone said, pointing at Mathias. Heads swiveled, revealing a sea of curious faces. At once, Mathias's grip on Greta's hand loosened, allowing her to step away. She only wound her fingers more tightly between his, holding fast.

"How came you to find Herr Peters?" Herr Hueber demanded.

"Fräulein Rosenthal was concerned," Mathias said. "And so I went looking."

"You tracked him?"

"I did."

"What, in your opinion, killed this man?"

"I hardly think my opinion matters."

Herr Hueber's eyes narrowed. "Wolves, would you say?"

"Maybe."

"Where is Herr Auer?" Herr Hueber snapped. "Where is the forest warden?"

Herr Auer, heavy in furs despite the warmth of the morning, shouldered his way up to the steps.

"What manner of creature could do this?" Herr Hueber demanded, as Herr Auer drew aside the coverings. He was less dis-

creet than Father Markus and Dieter Abendroth, and gasps of
horror rose from the nearest villagers. Someone retched. Mathias
tried to turn Greta away from the cart, but too late: she had seen.
An image of her father flooded her mind. Broken with grief,
boots crusted with snow, clutching a musket in helpless rage. *I
couldn't find their tracks,* he sobbed. *I couldn't kill them. It was like they
were never there.*

"Well?" Herr Hueber asked.

"Could be wolves," the warden growled.

The Marktplatz seethed.

"I saw wolves not two nights ago!" a woman shrieked. She
slapped her husband's arm. "I told you I saw them! I *told* you!"

"I have heard howling, too," called another.

"I was in Grünwald last week," someone else cried. "A man was
killed there—by wolves, they said!"

"What's that, then? Three men dead?"

"Three that we *know* of! Who's to say how many more might be
dead across these mountains? And women and children, too!"

Voices rose and rose again, shrill with fear and loathing. Greta
looked about. Conran and his men were nowhere in sight. *The pack
is weak. Wild, and unwieldy,* Mira had said. She thought of the
black wolf and his unaccountable malice. Her terror as he and his
companions chased her through the woods. *Running with the moon.
Sealing the bond.* How was such a bond sealed?

No, she told herself, stemming the panic that seemed to be flowing from the villagers into her own heart and mind. *No.* Mira had
admitted that the mercenaries were dangerous. But they were sworn
to protect innocent people, not kill them. And however dangerous
Conran might be, she would never believe that Rob would allow
him to hurt Jacob.

"What about a bear?" A high, sweet voice broke through the
uproar. The crowd parted, revealing Brigitta Winter.

Herr Hueber frowned. "What's this, child? A bear, you say?
There are no bears here. Not for two hundred years or more!"

"Greta Rosenthal saw a bear," Brigitta said. "Not four days past."

"Is it true, fräulein?" Herr Hueber demanded. "Did you see a bear?"

They were all of them watching her: Mathias, Herr Hueber, Father Markus. The men of the watch, Herr Auer . . . and every man, woman and child of Lindenfeld.

"I-I could not be sure." The bear had fought off the wolves. It had *saved* her. To speak of it now would mean its certain death. "What I mean to say is—I did not see the beast closely."

"And yet you admit you saw a beast. Why did you not report what you saw to the council?"

"It did me no harm. I . . . pitied it."

There were mutterings and misgivings at that.

"The Devil oft comes in the guise of wild beasts, my child," Father Markus said. "And the bear, who wears his colors, is his favorite. I have heard of bears who have ensnared young women such as yourself, taking them to caves deep beneath the earth. There they lie with them, performing all manner of gross and unholy atrocities. The Devil is a beast. You must guard your soul against his wickedness."

Greta bowed her head meekly as the crowd's judgment washed over her. Inwardly, she seethed. *Superstitious fools.*

"Surely Fräulein Rosenthal meant no harm." Herr Hueber's gaze was full of meaning. "Doubtless she cannot stand to let any creature, man or beast, suffer."

A sudden, wonderful thought.

"But I *did* tell you of the bear, Herr Hueber," Greta said. "I have just remembered. Cannot you? It was that evening last week, when you came to my house and . . ."

"But of course!" Herr Hueber exclaimed, with a titter. "With so many important matters to think upon, I had quite forgotten! In any case," he declared, raising his palms against the misgivings that had swung from Greta to himself, "whether we are facing a bear or a wolf hardly matters. A beast is still a beast, whatever the form, and I propose we rid the forest of this threat before more harm can be done. Who's with me?"

A great cheer went up. Herr Hueber glared at Greta. Behind him, the other councilmen nodded in agreement.

"Very well," Herr Hueber said. "Herr Auer, choose your men. Take what you will from our stores. I want the creature's skin nailed to the village gates before the week is out!"

The people clapped and cheered. Several men, feverish at the prospect of a hunt, pressed forward to join Herr Auer.

"You, there." Herr Hueber turned to Mathias, mouth twisting with dislike. "You possess some skill in tracking, do you not? You will join them."

Mathias frowned. Greta watched him, waiting for him to refuse. But then, to her horror, he nodded. She shoved away from him, sickened.

He caught her beneath the linden tree.

"Greta . . ."

"How could you agree to go with them?"

"My welcome in this village stands on Rob's good word and not much else. I don't have a choice."

Greta went to answer, then stopped as a little boy and his mother passed by.

"I would like to see a bear," the child was saying.

"You *have* seen a bear," his mother replied. "At the Marktplatz in Freiburg, remember?"

"That was an old, sad bear on a chain. I want to see a *real* bear with big teeth."

"Saints preserve us!" the woman said as she led her son away. "Let us hope you never do!"

"The bear is no threat, Mathias," Greta said when the woman and her child were gone.

"You cannot be certain of that."

"I can. I have looked into its eyes. It stood before me as you stand before me now."

Men armed with muskets, spears, and hunting swords gathered outside the Rose and Thorn. Others brought packs of supplies from the storehouse. A few clutched crossbows, while Herr Auer wielded a fierce-looking boar spear. Axel Lutz and Jan Karsten, brothers-in-law and members of the night watch, both carried long pikes. *They think themselves heroes in one of the old tales,* Greta thought bitterly, *proving their worth.* Would they wear the bear's skin into battle when they were done, so that they too might fight with the beast's godless rage?

Mathias propped his bow against his boot and bent it into a half-moon, fitting the string neatly to the nock. "Such a creature cannot be trusted. It could tear you apart."

Greta paled. "How can you say that to me? Here? Now?"

He glanced across the square to where Father Markus was covering what remained of Jacob. "I say it because it is true."

"No. The bear was *not* responsible for this."

The hunters cheered, tankards of beer raised. Kissing their wives and children goodbye, promising a swift return.

Mathias touched his sword, his knife, his waterskin. "That may be. But whatever *is* responsible is still close by. Promise me you will keep away from the woods while I am gone."

As though she were too stupid, too weak, to survive alone. "You think I don't know what's out there," she said. "But I have been there. I have seen it. I am not afraid of the forest."

His eyes were like the falls in winter. "You should be."

There would be no sweet farewell for them. No promises of swift return.

"You are the one who should be careful," Greta said frostily. "That bear is the largest creature I have ever seen."

"Do not fear for me," Mathias muttered, shouldering his bow. "I can take care of myself."

He strode to join the hunt, taking the best part of Greta's anger with him. She sagged onto the bench beneath the linden tree.

"I'm sorry I told them about the bear," came a small voice. Brigitta Winter, her blue eyes huge in her face. "And about your friend. He seemed kind."

"He was." Greta's voice splintered. Brigitta put her arms around her, and she leaned in, comforted by a child who knew more of pain than anyone her age had a right to.

When Greta returned to the house that afternoon, Hans was on his knees beside Jacob's pack. It was laid open, the contents spilling across the earthen floor.

"It's not what you think," he said at once, leaping to his feet.

Greta stared at him. She was numb. Bone-weary and aching with sorrow. But at the sight of Jacob's things, crushed and discarded, anger flickered within her, ember-bright.

"Do you know where I've been today, Hans?"

He would not meet her eye. "No."

"I've been at the church. Helping Father Markus wash Jacob's body. He's ready now. All he needs is fresh clothes." She pointed to the pack. "I came back to fetch them."

Hans swallowed. "Greta . . ."

"Tell me you're not doing what I think you're doing."

"Greta, please. If you'll let me explain—"

The little flame wavered, grew. "Tell me you're not stealing from him."

"It's not stealing!" he blurted. "He told us he wanted to help us. He said if we needed anything we had only to ask!"

"*But you didn't ask!*" Greta cried. "*You never do!*" It didn't matter to her that Jacob had *wanted* to help, that he would have gladly parted with the coin. Hans's selfishness at Walpurgis had changed everything.

A muscle in his jaw quirked. He looked down at something clenched in his fist.

"Jacob would want me to have this."

It was a soldier's purse. The leather was worn, darkened with years of grease and dirt. Greta's heart clenched at the thought of Jacob carrying it with him through long marches and cold rains, through battles and fear and hopelessness. He had given his soul for it. And now, in the work of a moment, Hans was snatching it away.

"He wouldn't," she said. "Not after what you did. You cannot take it, Hans."

The house gave a soft, unsettled creak.

Her brother's eyes narrowed. His face was healing now, the bruises fading to a sickly yellow. "It is not for you to tell me what to do, Greta. Besides, this is for you, too. Surely you don't want to work for Herr Hueber?"

"I would rather that than have you steal from my friend!" Tears, hot and painful. She wiped them away.

"He was my friend, too." Hans looked at Jacob's pack, his scattered belongings, and sighed. "You're grieving, Greta. When you are yourself again and seeing clearly, you'll realize that Jacob would have *wanted* me to have the money. After all, it is no good to him, now, is it?" He squeezed her shoulder. She flinched away.

"Jacob was right about you," she said. "He always knew you were selfish. That you were no good."

The blood drained from Hans's face. "You don't mean that."

"I do. Jacob knew it. And the witch knew it, too. Why else do you think she locked *you* up?"

She turned abruptly from him, ignoring his anguished expression, and scooped Jacob's clothing into her arms. She walked as fast as she was able on her way back to the church. Hoping it might help her anger, still fire-bright, fade.

"You're still alive, then," said a bored voice.

Greta, in the midst of readying the house for the night—lighting candles, waking the oven—froze. The room was chill, dusk stroking its edges with long, cold fingers. She held a candle high, peering into the gloom. There was no one there.

"When you didn't come home last night I began to worry," the voice continued. It belonged to a woman, low and rasping. "Must say I'm impressed, dearie. Didn't take you for the type."

"Who is that?" Greta fumbled for the knife, drew it from its sheath. "Who's there?"

"Poor child. It's me. *Here.*"

The voice was coming from the book's garner. Greta put down the knife and lifted the lid.

"Good evening," the book said politely.

"Good evening," Greta replied, without thinking. Then, "You're talking! I can hear you!"

"Couldn't you always?"

"No. I mean, yes . . . but no. It is as if you are a real person now, here with me."

"Rude," the book muttered. "I've always been a real person."

"Of course you have," Greta said apologetically. "I only meant . . ."

"Fiddle-faddle." The book harrumphed, and its pages lifted a little. "Besides, it's not I but *you* who has changed. Something happen, did it?"

Greta nodded slowly, remembering the strange magic Mira had summoned amid the circle of wolves. The world glittering with dew and sunlight. *You're a wild-wife, a moss maid, a storm hag.*

"Thought as much."

"I met someone. A witch." Easier and easier to say the word. "Her name is Mira."

"And who is this Mira to you?"

"A friend."

"Pah! And what am I, then? A sack of beans?"

Greta lifted the book from the garner and set it on the bench. "She says I have the green."

"Weed magic?" The book's pages rustled ominously. "That explains the smell."

"What smell?"

"You stink of marsh mildew, dearie. It's as if you strolled through a swamp."

Greta sniffed cautiously at her sleeve. To her relief she found that it smelled as it did any other day.

"So this hedge witch is a better teacher than me now, is she?"

"Of course not."

"And yet you are willing to learn from her. *Listen* to her."

"I listen to you, too."

"Do you, though? How many times have I tried to show you more than just that sick-sweet gingerbread? A hundred? A thousand? Why, I could teach you such things—magic with sizzle and bite!"

*Tattermagic rends and destroys. It is a bitter, ill-gained sort of magic wrought of pain, fear, and sadness.*

"Yes, but . . ." How to say it? "Is your kind of magic . . . harmful?"

"What do you mean, harmful?"

"Sizzling and biting are hardly pleasant sensations."

"So says you."

*It's witchcraft, Greta. No good can come from using it.* Jacob's words, right here in this very room. Had he been right all along? The thought, together with the sight of his belongings, still strewn across the floor, woke a searing pain in Greta's heart. She knelt to tidy them away, trying not to think of how he had looked when she had left him in the church, his fine new shirt as white as his bloodless skin.

"Poor child," the book said, not without sympathy. "I know you're hurting. But he *was* wrong about me, you know."

"It wasn't just him. Mira said that your kind of magic is destructive. Cruel."

"And what is *my kind of magic*?"

"Tattermagic."

"The shrub sorceress is wrong. Tattermagic remakes what has been damaged or lost. It begets something new from emptiness."

"Even so," Greta said. "I think it might be best if we stopped working together, for a time."

"I see." There was a nettlesome silence. "And what will you do when you have put me aside? You'll soon find there's little money to be made from talking to trees and playing in the mud. Unless you plan to sell herbs and heal the sick? We all know how *that* turns out. Nothing screams 'witch' like a crone with green hands."

Rain *tap tapped* on the roof. Gentle at first, then rising to a steady patter.

"Well?" the book urged, ruffling its pages. They began to turn, faster and then faster, blurring under the invisible fingers of some mad and mighty wind. "How will you earn your living? Will you find work in the village? *As what? A servant? And live in a cramped room with one Sunday a month to yourself? No hearth to tend, no woods to walk when you please? You could sew, but not well enough. . . .*"

Greta listened, appalled, as the book regurgitated, with remarkable likeness, the very conversation she had had with Jacob the night he had threatened to burn it.

"*You could chop wood, or raise pigs, or serve ale in the Rose and Thorn—*"

"Stop that!" Greta cried. "Stop it at once, or I really will throw you into the fire!"

Ancient pages settled into stillness. "I'm sorry. It's just—the thought of you turning from me and learning spellwork with another . . . I really am a very jealous book, you know."

Greta hesitated, caught somewhere between pity and disgust. Guilt and irritation. "Very well," she said at last. "I won't burn you today." Perhaps she would speak to Mira of the book when next they met. If there really was evil in its pages, she would know it. "But you must promise to behave."

"Agreed!"

"And you *will* keep yourself hidden. But not in the garner. . . ." She peered around the room. "You can stay under the hearthstones."

"The *what*—?"

Greta was already on her knees, prizing the loose stone from its resting place. "There's plenty of room down there. No one would ever find you."

The book grumbled something that included the words "ungrateful," "filthy" and "wench."

"It's this or the fire," Greta told it. "Make your choice."

The book gave a long-suffering groan. "Very well. And now that that's settled you might want to have a wash. You really *do* smell like a swamp."

# 13
## Windflowers

*Though different, the sisters loved each other dearly. They shared a chamber and slept curled together. They helped each other dress and brushed each other's hair, one red and tangled, the other dark and shining. They vowed never to part, even when they married, for they were stronger together. Two halves of one whole.*

The telling of a tale is always the richer if one can say one was there, and so it was only natural that on the day of Jacob's funeral the churchyard overflowed with mourners. They gathered around the grave as Father Markus began the familiar words, heads bent against the rain, gathering details like fresh herbs to be shared later. High above, the mountains looked on, steeped in cloud.

Greta felt Hans's eyes on her across the open grave and kept her head firmly bowed. Two days had passed since Jacob had been brought in from the woods, and she had discovered her brother stealing from him. She had not uttered a word to Hans since.

Jacob's coffin was already in its place at the bottom of the grave, rain pattering dully on its top. Greta would rather have not looked at it, would rather have not listened to the rain as it soaked into the fresh timbers, but she was caught, her gaze pinned in place by her unwillingness to meet her brother's eye. She went inward, her mind roving over the sodden churchyard, the gathered mourners, the headstones standing vigil between them. Jacob's father lay nearby, as well as the graves of her own parents. Impossible not to think of her mother's burial. All winter Lena had lain in the village storehouse, waiting for the thaw. Each time Greta and Hans had passed it on their way to Father Markus's school, Hans would all but run by, dragging his sister with him. Greta would always look back, imagining her mother within. A queen in a fireside tale, cold and beautiful, her skin washed clean, her wounds hidden beneath her best dress, auburn hair spread around her.

Peter, too, had been drawn to the storehouse. Many were the nights he staggered from the Thorn to slump in the snow before its locked door. Rob had not been in Lindenfeld, then—he had disappeared not long after he and Peter had arrived, though Greta had never known where he had gone, nor why—and so it was Father Markus who helped Peter home, leading him patiently up the mountain and settling him in his empty bed.

When spring came Lena was laid to her rest at last. Greta heard the village women whisper prayers of thankfulness: more than one had glimpsed a pale figure roaming in the dusk.

"Best for everyone that Lena Rosenthal take her rest," they said sagely, scattering salt upon the grave. Greta, misunderstanding, cried tears of anger as well as loss. Who were they to say it was better her mother was dead?

That night she had dreamed that her mother walked in the woods, a silent figure in white, her skin white as falling snow. Greta could not understand why Lena would not come inside and warm herself, and hold her as she used to. She called to her and threw out her arms to the bitter night. Her screams woke Hans, who locked the shutters and held Greta in his thin arms till she sobbed herself back to sleep.

Her brother came to her as Jacob's service ended and the mourners began to drift away. He was soaking and bedraggled, his shirt crushed, the holes in his coat sleeves worse than ever.

"Greta . . ." Arms open, as though he would comfort her once more. She drew away from him, shivering in her wet cloak, and trudged to the far edge of the yard where the yew trees were quietly weeping.

LENA ROSENTHAL and PETER ROSENTHAL, the wooden markers said, and the years plainly beneath. Lena's marker was surrounded by windflowers, the small, white blooms trembling in the rain.

Greta knelt in the wet grass. Frowned. Leaned forward, peering at her mother's name. Something had been scratched into the wood beneath it. A single word. *Hexe.*

*Witch.*

"About time the truth was there for all to see, instead of hidden away beneath moss and dirt," came a voice. She turned. Herr Tritten, the innkeeper, and his wife, Barbara, were watching her.

"We always knew what your mother was," Herr Tritten said, his lip curling. "What *you* are. It is no coincidence that wolves have returned to our forests after so long. That a bear is even now stalking our village. You, and no one else, saw it. You tried to hide its presence from the rest of us."

"You summoned it, didn't you?" Frau Tritten hissed. "You brought it here. Poor Herr Peters, those other men in the woods—they died because of you!"

Greta looked back at her mother's grave. The flowers there had lost their beauty of a sudden. Windflowers, they were called. But also ghost flowers. And witch's flowers.

"Did the bear speak to you?" Herr Tritten hissed. "Did the Devil's own voice issue from his jaws? Did he promise you money or power if you would do his bidding? You were with poor Jacob Peters the night he died. Did the Devil-Bear ask you to bring that poor man to him, so that he might sate his hunger by feasting on his flesh?"

"Perhaps you danced for the beast," Frau Tritten said, her face twisting with an ugly eagerness. "Perhaps you unlaced your clothes and let him lie with you as Father Markus said—"

"How dare you?" Greta caught up her soaking skirts and got to her feet. "How dare you say such things to me? I never saw the Devil. I never spoke to him. Indeed, I never saw evil in any living creature—except people like *you!*"

They staggered back from her as though she would leap at them, their fingers crooked.

"There is witchery at work here," Frau Tritten snarled. "I was in Bamberg. I saw the trials. And I see you for what you are."

"I see you, too," Greta said. Her voice shook. "Whatever evil you witnessed in Bamberg has blinded you. Now, you see nothing else. It is you, not I, who hears the Devil!"

Anger coursed through her, rich and bright. She wondered what it would be to flex her fingers and bring some biting, sizzling spell upon the Trittens. A spell that would leave *them*, not her, small, helpless and alone. Leave them, not her, afraid.

*Oh, what would that be?*

There was a commotion in the Marktplatz: Lindenfeld's brave hunters had returned. Greta hurried to the square, where the slow procession of mourners was mingling excitedly with Herr Auer's rather weary-looking men. *Did they kill the bear?* A single glance at their dejected faces and muddy boots, at their coats plastered wetly to their drooping shoulders, told her that they had returned empty-handed.

Relief at that, there and then gone again as she searched despite herself for someone else. Someone taller than the rest of the men, someone darker and brighter at once. Greta searched each and every face, again and then again, until she was absolutely certain: the hunters had returned, and Mathias was not with them.

"The Tyroler?" Jan Karsten's hat was pulled down low against the rain. Beside him, his brother-in-law Axel Lutz shivered as he gazed longingly at the Rose and Thorn. Both men were part of the night watch, and well used to long nights and broken sleep, but it was clear to Greta that their time in the forest had been anything but easy. "We lost him the day after we left the village. He said he would head west and sweep around northward. Meet us where the Storenbach and Offenbach join."

Axel nodded. "That's right. He never did meet us, though."

"No. We haven't seen him since."

Greta's mind flew to the darkest of possibilities: Mathias, lying in the forest alone and wounded. Mathias, surrounded by wolves. Mathias, dying . . .

No. Surely, *surely* not. He was nothing if not capable. He had said as much himself.

"And did you wait for him at the river?"

The men exchanged a look. "We would have," Jan said uneasily. "That is, we wanted to . . ."

"Some of us thought it best to push on without him," Axel said.

"Why?" Greta demanded.

Jan shrugged. "There was unrest among the men."

"Unrest?"

"Well, at first there was that business with Herr Auer's hounds," Axel said.

"What business?"

"Something killed them. Killed them good, too, not a day after we'd left the village. And then . . . a few of the men claimed they'd seen things."

Jan threw Axel a warning look.

"What kinds of things?" Greta pressed.

"Viktor said he'd woken one night to find his mother bending over him," Axel said. "Thing is, his mother died last winter. And Hans Mott felt ill, as though he'd eaten something that had gone bad. He was sure he was being followed when he went into the woods to, well . . ." He looked away, awkward. "You know."

Greta waved her hand impatiently. "Go on."

"Johann Hoch was the one who really set the men to clucking," Axel said. "He said a voice woke him, and when he followed it into the trees, someone whispered his name. And then he saw . . ."

The clouds parted and the rain stopped. Sunlight bathed the square in silver and gold. A chill went down Greta's spine all the same.

"What?" she said. "What did he see?"

Axel looked at her a moment as though weighing her trustworthiness. Then he leaned in close, so that Greta smelled sweat and damp wool. "He could not be sure, on account of the dark," he whispered. "But he swears it was a woman."

"A *beautiful* woman," Jan added. "He said she was beckoning to him—drawing him into the forest. He would have gone, too, if

Herr Auer had not followed and fired his musket into the trees above the woman's head. No one saw her again, after that."

"I worried a bit for the big Tyroler, though," Axel added, after a moment's thought. "Catholic or no, I do not like to think of him out there in the woods alone. I'm sorry we did not wait for him, now."

"He was well able to handle himself," Jan said gruffly.

"Maybe so," Axel mused. "Thing is, I can't help but think there was something, or someone, out in the woods with us. And whoever it was, they did not wish us well."

Jan guffawed. "Look out, Axel. There are turds falling out of your mouth again!"

"I mean it," Axel said to Greta. "And if I was completely honest I'd say that there was something *else* out there in the forest, too. Something that watched us the same as the other, but in a good way. A *protective* way. How else do you explain us all getting back here safely?" He glanced at his brother-in-law, at the other men trailing into the Thorn, eager for warmth, beer and food. "No, there was something watching over us. I'm certain of it."

A cart rolled into the Marktplatz, surrounded by mounted guards wearing Hornberg scarlet, their mounts splashing up dirty rain.

"It's true, then," Axel said somberly. "The Blood Tithes are beginning."

The poorest folk, the ones who knew they could not hope to make their tithes with coin, stock or grain, were going first. Mothers kissed their babies and climbed into the cart. Husbands reassured their worried wives. Greta's heart turned over as the children cried. There were young men and women going, too. They would be sorely missed by those families still sowing their spring crops.

"It will be the same in Wolfach and Grünwald, and in Hornberg, too," Axel said. "We all of us must pay our dues."

"I dislike this," Jan muttered. "In truth there's part of me thinks we'd be better off in that cursed forest."

Dark days, and even darker nights. Two, then three, then four. Greta went through the motions of her life with a tense new emptiness. Her thoughts were often with Mathias. Was he safe and well? Or was he dead, murdered like Jacob and the other poor souls in the forest? She asked about him each time she went to the village, but the answer was always the same: no one had seen the Tyroler since the hunt.

Hans, too, was troubled. At night Greta heard him thrash and mumble in his bed in the loft and knew his nightmares had returned. She was still angry enough with her brother to find some comfort in that, despite the fact that she too was plagued by ill-natured dreams.

Sometimes she was lost in the forest. Church bells rang discordantly and she ran toward them, only to grow more and more disoriented. Other times a trail of white pebbles led to a rising moon, full and silver. It glowed upon Jacob, or her mother, staring up from a bed of bloodied snow. One harrowing night she dreamed a little-boy Hans crouched over Jacob's broken body.

"We shall have a glorious feast," he told her. "I will eat a piece of his liver and you can eat his heart. Will they not be sweet?"

She had woken on the edge of a scream, caught between dream and wakefulness. Shadows crept along the walls, reaching for her with clawed hands, and Greta, who knew a little of wickedness, and of things that cannot be explained in the light of day, could no longer deny that something had changed. There had always been dreams. Their presence was a constant, if not unsettling, part of her life. But never like this. Never had she woken night after night, sweating and shaking, sick with the certainty that someone had been watching her sleep. The presence of the book, which used to soothe her, did little to help.

When the Sunday church bells began to peal across the valley Greta made her way obediently down the mountain. When she came to the point where the road forked between the village and the mill, however, she faltered. Herr Tritten and his wife would be at church. Herr Hueber and Hans, too. The thought of sitting pew by pew with them in the very place where Jacob's poor, broken body had lain while Father Markus prattled about the Devil suddenly seemed too much. Too much to ask, and far too much to give.

Rob had not left the village with the rest of Conran's men. His embrace—flour, soap and linseed oil—was as comforting as Greta remembered. She held on to him for a long time, until Mira took her turn, enveloping her in yarrow and sweet violet.

"I'm so sorry about your friend," she murmured. "I wanted to visit you after it happened. But Rob thought it best to wait."

Greta drew back from her. "Why?"

"Because a part of me worried you'd blame *us* for Jacob's death." Rob pulled a bench out from beneath the table for Greta and Mira, then sat down himself. "After all, we were out in the woods when Jacob—when he . . ."

Greta shivered, remembering the black wolf's vicious snarl, the pack pressing in close, their breath hot, their teeth bared. She did her best to smile reassuringly. "No. I never thought that. Besides, Father Markus believes that Jacob was killed on Walpurgis Night, not May Day." She clasped her hands before her on the table. "Who killed him? Do you know? If it wasn't the pack and it wasn't the bear—"

Rob frowned. "How can you be sure it wasn't the bear?"

"I can't," Greta said. "It's just . . . a feeling I have, I suppose."

His brows drew so deeply together they almost touched. "A *feeling?*"

"Let her speak," Mira said, touching his arm. "Go on, Greta. If not the wolves or the bear, then . . . ?"

"It must have been those soldiers passing through," Greta said. "The Bavarians."

"Wrong!" Conran entered the kitchen, stooping sideways so his weapons cleared the doorframe.

"You're back," Rob said in surprise.

Conran smirked. "Disappointed?"

Through the open door behind him Greta glimpsed the rest of his men. Though standing upright on two feet—not padding about on four—a sense of the woods and the wild clung to them still. They looked too large, too unruly, for the neat mill yard.

"Why not the Bavarians?" she asked.

"Because, Carrots, the Bavarians are dead." Conran helped himself to bread and dipped it into a pot simmering on the oven's top. "And no, *we* didn't kill them, if that was your next question. They were dead when we found them."

Rob cleared his throat. "I hardly think this is an appropriate conversation for Sunday morning."

Conran shoved the bread in his mouth, chewed. "Seems a good enough time to me."

"And me," Greta said quickly. "Go on, Conran."

"By all means. We found the Bavarians not a day after we left the village meeting." He grabbed another slice of bread, dipped again. "I'm not sure if you've seen many dead men, Rosebud, but believe me, *we* have. And these men? They were very, *very* dead."

"I've seen bodies pulled out of year-old graves that looked better," one of the sell-swords added from where he leaned in the doorway. Conran tossed him the bread. He caught it neatly.

"So," Greta said, doing her best not to imagine exactly how or why the mercenary had come to make such an observation, "you're saying that the Bavarian soldiers were dead *before* Jacob was killed?"

"Precisely, Sunset." Conran threw Greta a wicked grin. "Although, I didn't tell your council that. Far better to let them think it was *us* who finished the job. And, of course, pay us for our trouble."

"Then who killed Jacob?" Greta said. "And the other men?"

"That," Rob said, getting to his feet, "is not something you need concern yourself with. Whatever is out there, we'll find it. Won't we, Conran?"

"What?" Conran had lifted the entire pot off the oven and was heartily attacking its contents with the last of the bread. "Oh. Yes. Of course."

"The council has tasked the pack with keeping the village safe. And even if they hadn't, it's our duty to protect it. There's no need to be afraid. We'll be here, watching over all. I promise." He tilted his head at Mira. "Now. Don't you two have work to do?"

"Work?" Greta echoed, confused.

"Work?" Conran looked up, bread poised halfway between mouth and pot, one bristly black brow arched. "Missed something, have I?"

"Greta has the green," Rob told him.

"That so?" His mouth hitched in brief approval before he bit into the bread. "Huh."

"Does that mean you'll take no issue with Mira teaching her?"

"Me? Take issue?" Conran chewed noisily. "You wound me, Rob."

Greta was watching Rob closely. "I thought you did not want Mira to show me greenmagic," she said. He had made his thoughts on the matter clear the night he rejoined the pack, and it was plain to her now that his change of heart was nothing more than a clumsy ruse. He was keeping something from her. It was written in his tensed shoulders and the forced smile stretching his face.

"I had my reservations, of course," Rob said. "But it can't hurt to learn how to defend yourself, eh? Besides, if Mira's made up her mind to teach you there's nothing I can do to stop her." He grinned that false grin of his and patted Greta's hand. "Now. I'd best check on Christie. God only knows what he's doing to my mill."

"*His* mill," Conran corrected. "Don't forget we're only here as long as the council's coin keeps flowing. When it dries up, we go."

"Of course," Rob said. He turned to leave, but not before Greta saw the anguish he had been trying so hard to hide. "How could I forget?"

"Even the strongest witch needs guidance," Mira told Greta when they were standing in the willow grove once more. "To summon a storm or turn a seed into a tree—or a man into a wolf—requires practice and patience. The storm comes because a thread in the web is plucked, because air and water mingle. All magic is a blending, a giving and a taking."

"Even tattermagic?"

"No," Mira said firmly. "Tattermagic gives nothing. It only

takes." She tilted her head. "This is not the first time you've asked me of such things. Is there a reason?"

"No," Greta said hastily. "It's just . . . the old woman who stole Hans and me when we were children? *She* had a book filled with recipes and spells. I suppose that means she practiced tattermagic?"

"I suppose she did," Mira said, her mouth curling with distaste. "Although the stealing-children part also reveals something of her nature."

*And what if a greenwitch were to use that book?* Greta longed to ask. *Would that make her a tatterwitch, too? Would that make her . . . evil?* The look of disgust on Mira's lovely face stopped her. She could not bear it should Mira turn from her. If she too saw shadows at Greta's heels and the Devil in her hair.

"Greta?" Mira was watching her. "Is something wrong?"

"No." Greta forced a smile. "Well, actually, yes. I was wondering why Rob changed his mind. About us, I mean." It wasn't a complete lie; her uncle's behavior back at the house *was* concerning.

"Rob and I," Mira said, "have had time to speak plainly to one another over the last few days. Accordingly, we have come to an arrangement." She raised a hand, warding off further questions. "I swore that's all I would say on the matter. If you want to know your uncle's mind you'll have to ask him yourself. Now." She rummaged in her pocket and withdrew something small and fine. "See this seed?" She pushed it into the earth and stepped back, hands on hips. "Make it grow."

Greta nodded. Pushing aside all thought of Rob's, and her own, dishonesty—after all, there would be plenty of opportunities to tell Mira about the book—she threw her mind into finding the strands of the web. They were all around her, earth-deep and sky-high, and she drew upon them gently, easing their power toward the seed. The earth shuddered and woke beneath her bare feet. Magic surged. She felt it hit the seed, felt the seed tremble.

"Gently," Mira murmured. "Gently, now."

Greta closed her eyes, palm outstretched above the seed. The magic softened at her will and she felt the first faint stirrings of life:

water and root, a fine green tendril. She opened her eyes as the first shoots broke the surface and climbed steadily toward her hand. The stem thickened and offshoots sprouted, so that as the little plant grew in height it stretched outward too, uncurling itself, swirling, moving rapidly through the stages of its growth. The stem became the slender trunk of a young apple tree. Lacy branches stretched toward the sky, frothing with leaves and creamy blossoms.

"Good," Mira said approvingly. "Very good indeed. And now, something a little more difficult." She reached into the folds of her cloak and drew forth a beautiful coppery pelt with delicate points of black and white.

A fox.

Greta's eyes widened. "Surely you're not suggesting—?"

"Oh, but I am."

"I couldn't—I wouldn't know where to begin—"

"That's why I'm here." Mira pressed the pelt into Greta's hands. It was coarser than she expected. Shards of the little creature's life force, its wildness, remained.

"There must be other things I should learn first?"

"Rob asked me to show you how to protect yourself," Mira said. "There is no better way." She took out the little pot of green salve Greta had seen at the ceremony on May Day and opened the lid.

"Sweet flag and cinquefoil, lunaria and ivy. Vervain, henbane and wolfsbane. The last two are poisonous. You must take care when gathering them, though they'll do no harm now." She nodded encouragingly, and Greta scooped a glob of the salve onto her finger—her skin tingled at the wolfsbane's touch—and wiped it onto the pelt. It left a mark on the fur, silvery as a snail's path, before fading.

"And now?"

Mira unhitched the silver fox skin from her belt, painted a trail of her own. "Now, you step back and let the green do what it must." She drew the pelt over her head, falling smoothly onto all fours—a lithe, frost-colored fox with beautiful black ears. Greta drew back in surprise. The fox clawed at her own black belly and the fur came away. Mira rose, a woman once more.

"Now you."

"Very well," Greta said doubtfully. She settled the fox skin over her shoulders. It quickened of its own accord, flowing down her back, warming her skin through her clothes. The world seemed larger, brighter, louder. The willows loomed above. Greta looked down at her feet and found two dainty black paws in their place. She twirled and glimpsed the length of her own body, a deeper red than the fox skin had been, as though her own coloring had seeped into the magic. The tip of her tail was white in the sun. She skipped, delighted.

Mira, back into her own fox body, looked on, her muzzle split in a wide, vulpine grin.

*Come,* she said in Greta's mind, loping down the riverbank and into the willows.

The-fox-who-was-Greta followed.

# 14
## Of Spices and Stars

*Suitors began to appear at the castle gates. Counts and dukes, even a prince or two. From lands both near and far, they proclaimed there was no one in the world fairer than Liliane or sweeter than Rosabell.*

When Greta arrived home that evening it was to find a man sitting on her front step. She hurried forward, heart leaping in joyous certainty—it was Mathias, it had to be—then slowed as she recognized her brother.

"You still leave bread and moss out for the fairies," Hans said, absently touching the empty dish. When she made no answer he squinted up at her. "You were not at church this morning."

Greta said nothing. She had spent the day roaming the forest with Mira, practicing with the fox pelt, observing how a leaf unfurled or a flower slowly bloomed, while Mira's soft voice spiraled into her mind, filling it with knowledge and memory. She tensed, ready for the inevitable reprimand, but her brother continued speaking in the same mild, slightly distant, tone.

"You missed the banns," he said. "My name was there. With Ingrid's. We're to be married, Greta."

For a moment words betrayed her. Her mouth opened and closed, but not a single sound came out. "Married? But . . . *how*?"

"In the usual way, I expect. We'll go to the church and Father Markus will open with a prayer or two—"

"That's not what I meant."

Hans exhaled wearily. "Ingrid's sister Brigitta saw us together at Walpurgis."

"Saw you . . . ?"

He cleared his throat. "In the hay behind the smithy."

Greta slumped on the step beside him. "Oh, Hans."

"Brigitta told her mother. And she, of course, told Herr Winter. He asked Ingrid—beat her, in truth—and she confessed it. He went straight to the council and complained that I had stolen Ingrid's virtue. I am to marry her in three weeks' time." He spoke as though he were a man condemned, facing the gallows instead of a bride.

Greta groped for the right words. "I'll admit it is a . . . surprise. But I'm certain that once you are settled together you will be happy."

Settled together *here*, she realized, dismayed. She tried, and failed, to imagine sharing her home with Ingrid Winter.

Hans shook his head. "You don't understand. Every time I look at Ingrid I see Jacob. I only took her to spite him." He seized a pebble lying near the door and hurled it at the trees. "This marriage is my penance. Didn't I steal Ingrid? Didn't I try to force you to marry Christoph? I even took Jacob's money. You were right, Greta. I am selfish and foolish, and cruel."

He looked so lost and bewildered that Greta pushed her own misgivings aside.

"That's not true, Hans."

"No, it is. Everything I did, I did for money. And now I am to marry into one of the richest families in Lindenfeld." He gave a shaky laugh. "You'd think I'd be happy, wouldn't you?"

"Hans . . ."

"We're to sign the betrothal papers the day after tomorrow at the Rathaus. There'll be a gathering afterward. Could you—will you— bring gingerbread?" He gestured to a pile of sacks and packets nestled in the shadows beside him: flour, and other familiar ingredients. "There'll be wine and perhaps a little food. It's all the celebration there will be, I'm afraid. Herr Winter won't permit a wedding feast, on account of the . . . circumstances."

Greta laid a soothing hand on his shoulder. "Of course I will. And I'm sure that everything will be fine."

"Will it though?" the book muttered later. "With a wife like Ingrid Winter? I would as soon marry a salamander. It would make, in my opinion, a much warmer companion."

The next morning Greta rose early and busied herself with baking for the betrothal. She had slept well for the first time in what seemed like months after falling asleep to the sound of wolves howling on the mountain. *There's no need to be afraid. We'll be here, watching over all.* The old fear of them had gone, to be replaced by something completely different: gratitude.

"What are you planning to wear?" the book asked as Greta poured flour into a large bowl.

"Wear?"

"To the gathering."

"I hadn't thought about it."

"I thought as much."

Greta finished pouring and swiped a piece of loose hair away from her face, leaving a trail of flour dust behind. She brushed it away. "What are you suggesting?"

"Nothing at all. Just thought it might be nice to make an effort, that's all. It wouldn't take much to freshen up your cream-colored bodice and the darker of your skirts."

"And what would you suggest I use?"

"For the bodice, elder bark and ivy. Blackberry leaves would do for the skirt."

"You have it all planned, don't you?"

"If there's one thing I have in abundance, it's time to think."

Greta added ginger, cloves, nutmeg and cardamom to the flour, measuring each of the precious spices carefully.

"Why not add a few drops of your blood?" the book suggested.

Greta, spooning cinnamon into the bowl, paused. "What would it do?"

"Why, whatever you desired! But why not start by adding some spice to this gathering? Wine, and perhaps a little food, Hans said. Sounds like a failure to me. We could change that. Really make them celebrate!"

"And why would we want to do that?"

"To ensure the marriage is a success, of course! With a few additions to the recipe—a touch of joy, say, or a drop of flirtation—we could really change things for your brother. We could make him happy at last."

Greta considered that. "And we could do that? With a few drops of my blood?"

"Of course! I told you, dearie—sizzle and bite!"

It was tempting. A few drops to ensure Hans's happiness and his future. And though she would not admit it to anyone, least of all the book, Greta *had* been wondering what it might be like to really try her hand at tattermagic. She had felt different since wielding the fox skin—even now she could feel the magic weaving its way from the book's pages to the bowl—and she liked it. Tattermagic remade what was lost or damaged, the book had said. It cast something new from emptiness. Now, as Greta baked, her loneliness and fear—a pair of constant shadows at her side since childhood—lessened. She felt stronger. Safer.

Powerful.

"I'm listening," she said, drizzling honey.

The book cackled happily. "I suggest one drop for your brother and Ingrid's happiness . . . and a few more besides. Why not cast a little charm that will allow *everyone* to feel as happy and loving as your brother and his salamander-to-be?"

"I think not," Greta said, kneading the ingredients between her fingers. "Herr Winter is a councilman, remember. That means the whole council will be there, including Herr Hueber." The last thing she needed was the bürgermeister's happy and loving attentions all evening.

"Herr Hueber? Another drop of blood and we can remedy that, too."

Greta blinked. "You can do that?"

"No, dearie. *You* can. All you need do is cut yourself, just a little, and let your blood fall into the dough. Such a simple thing, really. But worth it, is it not, to ensure your brother and Ingrid's happiness forevermore?"

*A little blood, a little pain . . .*

"I *do* want Hans to be happy."

"It's only natural, dearie."

Kneading, kneading.

"And I *would* like to be free of Herr Hueber. . . ."

"Who wouldn't?"

The ingredients were melding together now, forming a thick, golden dough. If Greta was honest with herself, she would have to admit that she wasn't entirely sure her brother deserved to be happy forevermore. But if . . .

"Let us add another drop—for *me*," she said. "After all, why shouldn't *I* enjoy the party, too?"

"Why, indeed? Poor child, you've had so little joy!"

"I deserve it!" She had endured enough, surely, to warrant some happiness of her own? A drop of her blood was all it would take. So little, for so much.

"Very well, then." Greta slapped the dough onto the workbench and pushed the heavy tail of her hair over her shoulder. She was out of breath, rosy-cheeked with magic. "Show me what to do."

When the gingerbread hearts were cooling Greta went out to gather blackberry leaves to make a dye. She had just finished cutting a neat bundle when a rustling step sounded in the undergrowth nearby. Her heart skittered in fear, then settled as she saw Christoph.

"I came to apologize, Täubchen," he said with a shrug. "For . . . everything."

They had not spoken since May Day; since a pack of wolves had undone his careful plotting with Hans. Since that same pack of wolves had turned into men before his very eyes, and he had faced them in a circle of fire with a witch, a pelt, and a knife at its center. Since he had shot Conran, and seen his own father turn into a snarling beast.

"How are you, Christie?" He was pasty and drawn, his eyes ringed with shadows. At the sight of him the elation Greta had felt while baking, the tingling in her hand where her blood had been spilled, diminished.

"In truth? Not well at all." He fell into step with her as she returned to the house. "I've barely spoken to my father since he . . . since he . . ." He shook his head helplessly. "Those men have set up camp with us, now. Eating in our kitchen, bedding down in our rooms or out in the yard. They drink and throw dice and play their music all through the night. When they're not out 'protecting' the village, that is." He sighed. "Their captain is the worst. Conran. I've seen him change his shape and run alone in the night. He . . . he frequents houses of . . . well. You know. I have heard the way he speaks of women. He is the vilest sort of man."

They had reached the house. Greta fiddled with the linen binding her newly cut hand; it was throbbing, though from the cut itself or the magic the book had drawn from it, she could not be sure.

"Conran says other things, too," Christoph said. He looked up into the gnarled branches of the old apple tree, absently tweaked a leaf. "He calls me 'summerborn,' or 'fireborn.' I asked my father what it meant. Do you know what he said?" He looked at Greta, his eyes huge and troubled. "He said that 'summerborn' is the name for a packmate's child who was conceived at midsummer. He said that it is the pack's custom to visit certain villages, in the Empire and in Scotland, too, during the midsummer celebrations. The people of these villages are aware of my father and his friends' . . . *condition*. They're aware, but also, they're accepting. They . . ." He swallowed, a furious blush creeping up his neck. "They allow their women to lie with the men at midsummer, if they should wish to. And then, if there is a child, the village cares for it and the mother. To ensure the line survives, my father said, if one of the men happened to be killed during battle."

Greta stared at him. "Are you saying . . ."

"I always believed—was always *told*—that my mother married my father when he was soldiering in the Empire. That she traveled with him and the army as many wives did. After I was born my father feared for us. My mother was trailing along after a huge army, trying to care for me, struggling to find enough food. It became even harder when things began to go badly for the Swedes. And so he left us in Bavaria before going north with the army to Nördlingen. I was told that after the battle, and after he brought your father home, he went back to find us. But when he got there he found that my mother had died. That's when he brought me back to Lindenfeld with him."

Greta nodded. She had always believed the same.

"But it was all a lie," Christoph said bitterly. "My father never married my mother. He barely knew her. She was just a woman he met one midsummer in some tiny, pagan village. And when the sun rose and the fires died and he was done dishonoring her he left with Conran and the others. As though there were nothing wrong with taking a woman, with starting a baby in her belly and then just . . . *abandoning* her."

A sick twist in Greta's own belly. Her father had lied to her, and to Hans, before he had left them in the forest. Before he too had abandoned them.

"Are . . . are you sure, Christie?"

Rob was the most honest, and most honorable, man Greta knew. To think that he had lied to his only son—and to her, to everyone—for years was unthinkable. "Did your father tell you all of this?"

"He did." Christoph bowed his head, wiping at his eyes with one stained sleeve. "It's funny, isn't it? You think you know someone."

"But—what happened to your mother, Christie? Your *real* mother."

"That part was true. He *did* return to my mother's village. But when he got there he found that it had been burned. All but a few were dead or had fled. My mother had died the winter before. The villagers were true to their promise to the pack, and looked after me, even though they were starving. My father could not leave me there to die, he said. So he brought me here and fed me lies."

He sounded so young and so lonely that Greta put her arms around his waist and her head on his shoulder. He held her tightly for a moment and she could not help but think of his poor mother, and her own.

Christoph sniffled and wiped his eyes again. "Are you dyeing today, Täubchen?" he asked, gesturing to the blackberry cuttings in Greta's hand. "You'll need plenty of water. I could help you fetch it?"

Despite the pack's watchful presence Greta had become nervous of going into the woods alone. Twice she had become sick there, once while collecting honey and again when she had searched for Jacob. There was no forgetting the blood and the snow and the horror. The icy chill of the tree house and the fear that had seized her in the darkness: her mother's death-white hands, holding Greta's heart.

There was no forgetting that Jacob had died beneath the ever-dark trees. That the hunters from Lindenfeld had seen, and heard, strange things there.

And there was no forgetting Mathias. He had disappeared completely, as though the forest had swallowed him whole. His last words to her had been of its dangers, and though a small, rebellious part of her wanted to disregard his warning, she had nevertheless found herself avoiding it whenever she could.

"That would be lovely," she told Christoph.

And so they walked to the falls together, the empty water buckets clanking comfortingly at Christoph's side.

"They're speaking of your brother and Ingrid in the village," Christoph said. His anguish seemed to ease the higher they climbed. "They talk of little else, besides the Blood Tithes and the beast in the wood."

Greta said nothing. It loved a good scandal, did Lindenfeld; gossip there was like a fresh-baked loaf: to be broken apart and savored.

"They're saying Ingrid is refusing to live outside the village walls."

"Is she? Perhaps she should have thought of that before she set her sights on my brother."

Christoph laughed. "She has asked her father for a small house in the village after the wedding. But he is still too angry. If his daughter wants to marry a day laborer, he said, then she can live like one."

"That must be difficult for her," Greta said. She thought of the day laborers and poorer folk she had seen climbing into the tithing cart bound for Schloss Hornberg. "What about the Blood Tithes, Christie? What are they saying about that?"

"Everyone's worried," Christoph said. "They're saying that with so many laborers going to the Hornberg, or thinking of going, there won't be enough men to plant the rest of the spring crop. We could soon be struggling again."

They climbed higher, until the air cooled, and the sullen rumble of the falls filled Greta's ears. Christoph went ahead to fill the buckets while she picked ivy and left an offering of bread beneath an elder tree.

"Mother, give me of thy wood and I will give thee of mine when I become a tree," she whispered, bowing her head. How often had her parents warned her to say those ancient words? Peter had never taken wood from elder trees, and Lena was always careful to ask permission when gathering elderberries and flowers. "She'll pinch you black and blue, should you upset her," she would say. "You must treat the Elder Mother with respect."

When she was certain it was safe Greta cut away strips of elder bark with her knife, smoothing the tree's trunk with her fingertips in thanks. She could have sworn she glimpsed the silvery softness of tiny wings and heard a faint chuckle, high and sweet.

*Now I know you're teasing. The Elder Mother shows herself to no one. All the stories say so.*

*You've not heard* my *stories.*

She tucked the bark into her pocket and climbed the path to the falls. Thoughts turning, as she knew they would, to Mathias.

Perhaps he was safe and well somewhere and had simply chosen not to return to Lindenfeld? She could hardly blame him. He owed the village nothing and Greta herself had certainly given him little enough cause to think she would be glad to see him again. There was no denying she had been shrewish with him when he left with the hunt. But had he not deserved it? *He had no choice but to go with Herr Auer,* an irritating inner voice reminded her.

Birdsong drifted through the trees and the distant, rhythmic *clop* of an ax into timber thudded up from the south. Calming sounds, ordinarily, but today they brought no contentment. How could they? Mathias could be wounded and alone in the woods somewhere. Starving. Or, worse still, wrapped in a bloody blanket in the back of the watchmen's cart. *Or perhaps he is in Hornberg,* the little voice whispered. With *her.*

*Ah.* That *was* a possibility. After all, it was the woman in Hornberg, and not Greta, who had brought him to the valley. *I have come to claim what is owed.* A simple enough explanation. But what if the woman had stolen not just money from Mathias, but his heart? And what if he did not truly want it back?

*So?* Greta demanded of herself, walking faster. *Mathias's heart is nothing to you. Why should you care whom he gives it to?*

"There you are," Christoph said, as she neared the first of the pools. He raised his voice, competing with the sound of falling water. A fine mist beaded his hair. "Look here. Do you see that?" He pointed at a print in the mud. It was broad and round, five large toes topped by five deep gouges. "Might be this belongs to your bear."

"Perhaps." Greta touched the print. Her savior was still near, then. She had assumed it was far away. South in the Alpen, perhaps, or east in the Swabian Mountains.

"We should follow these tracks and find out."

All at once Mathias was back in her thoughts. *Such a creature cannot be trusted. It could tear you apart. . . .*

"I don't think so, Christie. . . ."

"Oh, come, Täubchen. We could use an adventure!"

He set off eagerly up the slope. After a moment's hesitation, Greta followed. Surely if Herr Auer and the hunters had been unable to track the beast, she and Christoph would have no more success?

Christoph, however, proved to be a worthy tracker. He led Greta upward, past the pool where Mathias had handed her stays back to her—her heart panged mutinously—and higher still, to the top of the cascades. The roar of water, the mist of the falls as they poured themselves down the mountainside, was everywhere.

"The tracks stop here." Christoph's gaze swept across the narrow river. "Look! A cave!"

A fissure yawned in the stony slope, concealed by a half-fallen tree and knots of ferns. Were it not for Christoph's keen eyes Greta would not have noticed it.

"The tracks lead to the river's edge," Christoph said. "And there, in the water, see? Stepping stones."

Greta was very aware of what could lie, unseen, in the cave's depths. "Please tell me we're not going in there, Christie."

"Of course we're not. But look—there are tracks everywhere! Here, and here . . ." He crouched in the wet fernery, pushing fronds aside to reveal the damp, dark earth. "There are boot prints, too."

"Herr Auer must have passed this way." She had heard the forester still coveted the bear, for its hide as much as vengeance for his slain dogs.

Christoph had already lost interest in the print. "Look. There are clumps of fur on this tree. I think your bear must use it to scratch himself."

"He is not *my* bear."

"You tried to keep him a secret," Christoph reminded her.

"Only because I did not want its head mounted on a wall."

Greta freed a tuft of black fur from the tree. It was long and coarse. Higher up, more fur clung to the bark. She imagined the bear towering on its back legs, scratching itself in bliss.

"Herr Auer would pay a pfennig or two to know where this cave lies," Christoph mused.

Greta rounded on him. "He will never know. As you value our friendship, Christie, you will say nothing of this. To *anyone*."

"Of course," he stammered, raising his palms. "Of course. I would never tell."

Of all the wild places dear to her Greta loved the Sturmfels best. It was a place to be still at day's end. To lean upon a mossy half wall, wrap yourself in your warmest shawl and watch the sun cast itself into the west.

The mountaintop ruin had been a grand schloss, once. Now, lindens flourished where the hall had once stood and mountain roses blushed within broken chambers. Half a stairway stretched to the empty sky, crumbling into magnificent nothingness. If you looked south, you could see Lindenfeld far below. To the north the forest flowed toward Baden. Eastward, the white towers of the Hornberg nestled between the mountains.

"I see you did not manage to keep your promise to me and stay out of the woods."

Greta leapt to her feet. Mathias leaned against the ruins behind her, arms folded within his cloak. Entirely relaxed, as though they had planned to watch the sunset together all along.

"I made no such promise." She willed her heart to slow as she pulled her shawl more tightly around herself. "You did not return with the hunt."

"They were slowing me."

"It's been more than a week."

He picked his way toward her, through ancient lindens and banks of broken stone. "You didn't think I would come back?"

She lifted a shoulder.

"I do not like the way we parted. You had had a shock and I was hard with you. I would ask for your forgiveness, Greta."

"I should ask for the same. You were not the only one who spoke harshly that day."

Late sunlight burnished his skin, lending the stubble on his cheeks a coppery sheen. "We agree to forgive each other, then?"

"It would seem so."

She caught the edge of his smile before he settled himself beside her. Looked westward, where the mountains tumbled in pink-gold cloud. "And how are you?"

"I am well enough."

"I wanted to tell you how sorry I am about Jacob."

Greta's throat was suddenly tight. She forced herself to look away from Mathias's eyes and the sorrow she saw there. "He came back to Lindenfeld to begin a new life," she said. "He wanted to marry. Start a family and live in peace. Everything he did during the war, everything he endured . . . it was all for nothing. He spent all those years thinking of what might be, the happiness he might have had, and then, just when it was within his reach, it was ripped away from him. It seems unbearably cruel."

Mathias looked out over the darkening forest. "Life often is."

"And what of you?" Greta asked. "Where have you been all this time?"

"I parted with the hunt the day after we left the village," he said. "When it was clear I'd have a better chance of discovering whatever killed Jacob on my own."

"And did you?"

"I came very close."

"What *is* it?" Greta asked. "I know it was not the wolves. Rob would never—"

He turned to her sharply. "You know about Rob and the others?"

"Yes."

"And you're . . . not afraid of them?"

"Afraid? Of Rob? No." She looked down at her hands. The cut she had made was still pulsing. Not painful, but not comfortable, either. "But if I was honest I would say that I *am* rather angry at him. For all these years he made me—he made *all* of us—believe he was something other than what he is. He lied to me. Even worse, he lied to his son. I was with Christoph today. That poor boy is distraught. Not only has he discovered his father is a . . . a *wolf,* but has also found that his whole life, his whole world, is based upon a lie. Christoph's mother—" She stopped herself, unwilling to describe how Rob had lain with a woman not his wife, then abandoned her and their child.

"I fear you are judging Rob too harshly," Mathias said gently. "No doubt he had reason enough to keep the truth to himself. It is not as though having such . . . abilities comes without its own dangers."

"You think he had cause to lie?"

"Undoubtedly."

"And what of honor?"

"What about it?"

"Would an honorable man lie?"

"Any man—or woman—will lie, when forced," he said reasonably.

*I'll be back soon,* her father had said. *Wait here, with Hans.* The first lie of her young life. She woke sometimes, shaking with the horror of it. He had promised he would return for them.

He had lied.

"Yes," she pressed. "But do you think what Rob did was honorable?"

A shrug. "I think Rob did what he had to."

"I cannot believe you're defending him!"

Mathias did not flinch. "He helped me once, when I most needed it," he said. "I'll not forget it."

Greta crossed her arms, irritated. Above the mountains the first stars glimmered.

"Tell me, then," Mathias said. "What makes an honorable man?"

"He helps others when they are in need, without thinking to gain anything for himself, yes. But he is also good to women. He keeps promises. He tells the truth. I always thought Rob was like that." She stilled. "I thought—I thought he was like *you.*"

"Greta—"

"No, Mathias. No. Do not defend him. Truly, I do not know if I shall ever be able to look at him the same way again."

There was a silence, broken only by the pensive shifting of the lindens.

"Rob Mueller is a better man than I could ever hope to be," Mathias said quietly. "I'm sure he did what he thought was best."

"Perhaps."

The sun was all but gone behind the mountains now. To the

east, the windows in the distant Hornberg glinted with light. Greta shivered in the evening breeze.

"Are you cold?" Mathias asked. "I could start a fire? Make supper . . . ?"

"Supper? *Here?*"

"Why not? It's a lovely evening." He gestured at the moon, rising against a smattering of early stars. Lovely, indeed. And completely impossible. She could *not* stay out here with him. Greta turned to tell him so, but Mathias had gone. She waited, uncertainty and confusion and happiness warring within her, until he returned with an armload of kindling and dry branches, as well as his bedroll, his bow and a pair of rabbits, freshly skinned. She watched him set everything neatly down, then lay out his cloak for her to sit upon.

"Or, I could take you home, if you'd prefer it," he said, when she hesitated.

It would be lonely at the house, the air stuffy with the dyed, still-damp clothing she had laid across the oven to dry. Besides, it was only supper—surely it could do no harm? There was no one here to see them, after all. A curious feeling, somewhere between dread and excitement, fluttered in Greta's chest.

"No," she said, settling herself on the cloak. "Let's stay."

A fire was soon burning. She watched Mathias fashion a rough frame and lay it over the flames. His shirt was ripped, the edges daubed with blood.

"How strange," she said. "You've cut yourself again—and in exactly the same place you did that day at the falls."

"What? Oh." He looked down at himself and laced his tunic. "I hadn't noticed."

Night fell, a velvet cloak embroidered with stars. Mathias skewered the rabbits on a length of green wood and laid them on the frame. He had rubbed them with garlic root, and the scent of their roasting soon filled the air. When they were cooked through he broke them apart, laying the pieces in a much-beaten bowl and offering it to Greta.

"My father was like you," she said, taking some. "He could make a feast from nothing when we went out cutting. At least he *could* before my mother died." *Wait here, with Hans.* "He changed after that."

Peter had never truly recovered from her mother's death. He struggled to cut as he used to, and the pitiful amount he managed had curled his back like an old man's. He was heartsore. Weary.

"My father was the same when he lost my mother."

"How old were you when she died?"

He finished another piece of rabbit. "Fifteen."

"I was seven."

"I'm sorry to hear that," Mathias said. "You had so little time with her. Was she like you?"

"To look at? I think so. My hair is the color hers was, at least."

He poured the contents of his waterskin into a scuffed pot and rested it in the fire, tossing in a handful of pine needles. "I spent my whole life in the woods as a boy. I think I ate more meals out of doors than inside them."

"And where was that?"

"When we've eaten, I'll show you."

He was true to his word. When Greta had finished her share of the rabbit he led her through the moonlit ruins to the old stairway. They were soon higher than the ruins, higher, even, than the tops of the trees. Far below, Lindenfeld twinkled.

"There." Mathias pointed. In the far distance, Greta discerned a range of mighty mountains, the moon glowing white on summer snow.

"The Alpen," she said. Always, the view had called to her. "What are they like?"

"In winter the snows there are deep, but in summer the forest sings. My father's house sits high above a lake as blue as a jewel."

The wind was stronger at the top of the ruin. Mathias stood close, shielding her from its bite.

"There are places—high places—where the spirit of the world can be felt," he said. "Some say there is a grove so high, so pure, that the very air is magical. There is a spring there from which the Water of Life flows."

Greta was enchanted. "What is the Water of Life?"

"They say it can heal any ailment and break any curse. Some even say it will make the man, or woman, who drinks it live forever."

"I cannot imagine living so long."

"It would be more curse than blessing, by my reckoning."

"Is it real?" she asked. "This spring? Has anyone ever found it?"

"Many have tried."

"Have you?"

"Once. When I young and foolish." He turned away then and Greta followed him back down the steps. It was dark, despite the moon, and when he offered her his hand, she took it. She did not let go when they reached the ground, and weaved their way back through the lindens, the trees' honey-sweetness mingling with the mountain roses. Neither did he.

"Tell me more of your home," she said, when they were settled once more beside the fire.

"In midsummer the people light pyres upon the mountaintops." Mathias poured pine tea into two wooden cups and handed her one. "The men strap loads of wood to their backs and climb to the highest peaks. Sometimes it takes half a day to reach the top." He sat beside her on the cloak. "As the sun sets the pyres are lit and the mountains glow with the light of a hundred fires, burning like stars."

Greta tried to imagine anything so beautiful.

"They welcome the sun, you see," Mathias said. "The fires. People say that they chase away the darkness, and with it, dark things—devils and witches. But I always felt that it was like a meeting of earth and Heaven. That the two realms were close—closer than they had any right to be—and that my mother would come back to watch them. I used to imagine I could feel her sitting beside me."

Greta watched him in the firelight. "Who are you?" she asked. "Where have you come from?"

"I just told you," Mathias said with a smile.

"My brother is to marry Ingrid Winter," she said on a whim.

"The pretty bird caught him, then?"

"Yes. I suppose she did." The fire crackled, popped. "There'll be a gathering tomorrow to celebrate. Will you . . . will you come?"

He hesitated, and for an awful moment she thought he would refuse.

Then, "Will I have to dance?"

She laughed. "Goodness, no!"

"And will there be gingerbread?"

"Of course!"

They grinned at each other.

"Then I would be honored," Mathias said.

They sat together for a long time after that, watching the fire flicker and bloom, imagining the mountains aflame against the night sky.

# 15

## Gingerbread Hearts

*The suitors brought the sisters gifts of silks and gemstones, pearls from the southern seas, spices from the east. Chests of gold and silver, gowns of damask and velvet, veils and crowns and rings. Finest of all a mirror, its edges traced in whorls of beaten gold, its face polished as a silver lake. Liliane spent hours gazing at her reflection, reveling in the knowledge that she was fairest.*

Greta." Hans's grip on Greta's elbow as he steered her into the courtyard behind Jochem Winter's fine half-timbered house was painfully tight. "Tell me. What did you do to it?"

"Do to what?"

"The gingerbread, of course!"

The sounds of the betrothal gathering were growing steadily louder on the night air. The guests, no longer content to remain indoors, were spilling into the street.

"The hearts? Well, I iced a little 'H' and 'I' on them . . ." She scrunched her nose. "Too much?"

"I'm not talking about the cursed letters." He dragged her with him, forcing her to look down the long, cobbled hall that ran the length of the Winter house, from the courtyard with its stables and storerooms to the street beyond. "Look!"

There was no doubt the mood of the gathering was changing rapidly. When first she and Mathias had arrived, it was to find a small collection of Lindenfeld's councilmen and their wives stuffed into the Winters' home, sipping wine and picking at platters of wurst and soft, buttered bread. They had been quiet and reserved as Hans and Ingrid exchanged the traditional betrothal gifts while Herr Winter looked on, glowering. Now, most of the guests were outside, laughing and jesting as Herr Winter's bewildered servants obediently dragged a table, several benches, chairs and even candles onto the cobbles. The wine came too, and a cask of beer, rolled merrily up the long hall from Herr Winter's large storehouse. Its appearance was greeted with a resounding cheer.

"What are they doing?" Hans's voice rose in panic.

"Perhaps they want some fresh air?"

He pulled her back into the shadows. "*What did you do?*"

Greta yanked her arm free of his grip. "You think this is *my* fault?"

"It has to be. Everything was fine until the gingerbread came out."

Greta peeked down the long passageway again. Frau Winter and Ingrid had gathered up the platters of wurst and bread and were moving them outside. Hard not to laugh, really. Especially when Herr Winter kissed first his wife and then his daughter. "More, bring more!" he shouted, joyously. "Aren't we here to celebrate?"

"Well," she said, biting her lip. "Perhaps I *did* add a little something when I baked. . . ."

"*What?*" Hans spluttered. "No, Greta. *No.* That is *not* what I want to hear from you!"

"It won't do any harm," she assured him. "It's just a tiny spell. Quite subtle."

More people were crossing the square bearing food and beer, lanterns and flowers. Herr Winter welcomed them all, a half-eaten gingerbread heart waving happily in one hand.

"Come join us, friends! Come celebrate my daughter's betrothal!"

"Really, Greta? *Subtle?*"

"Well, it's better than the alternative," Greta said with a shrug. "Herr Winter was so angry before, and you were so upset. Can you blame me for wanting everyone to be happy?"

More tables, more wine, more food. People flooded in from all directions, as high-blooded and merry as they had been first thing on May Day morning.

"Sweet Jesus," said Hans as a drum stuttered into life, accompanied by a schäferpfeife and zither. "We're to have music, too?"

"Why not? Relax, Hans. Enjoy yourself." Greta gestured proudly at the gathering, unfolding like a glorious flower. "Everyone else is."

Oh, but it was satisfying. Perfectly, deliciously satisfying. The newly made cuts in her palms throbbed sweetly in time with the beating drum. As though the entire evening, its rhythm and magic, belonged to her.

"You shouldn't have done it," Hans muttered. "What if someone suspects? What if they blame you? It wouldn't take much; I've heard three different people speak of witchcraft this week."

"You give them too much credit," Greta said lightly. "They will have a marvelous night and celebrate your betrothal in the best of spirits, and tomorrow they'll wake and remember all the fun they had. By the looks of things, you and I are the only ones who *haven't* eaten a heart or two. Which means we're the only ones who will know."

Hans glanced at her. "You didn't eat any?"

"No."

She had wanted to. The hearts had smelled deliciously enticing as they came from the oven. But the book had been adamant: Greta herself must not partake.

"Well, that's something, I suppose," Hans grumbled. "Thank God I don't eat the blighted stuff, that's all I can say."

"Where is my new son-in-law?" Herr Winter was gazing about, his arm around Ingrid's shoulders. "The bride is waiting for a dance!"

"You had best go to Ingrid," Greta told her brother. "Try to enjoy yourself, won't you?"

"Very well. I'll play my part in this farce," Hans muttered, "on one condition. You remove the rest of the gingerbread *right now*."

"Oh, Hans, you can't be serious!"

"I am. I don't want anyone else eating it, Greta. You've had your fun—"

*Have I, though?*

"—and now it's time to be sensible. How much is there?"

"Well, there's the tray I took to the house," Greta told him resentfully. "The rest is in the storehouse." She had stacked the baskets neatly alongside Herr Winter's grain and vegetables, ready to replenish the platters as required.

"Well, gather what you can from the house, and then empty the storehouse before Frau Winter or one of the servants finds it. How much is there?"

"Not so very much." *Four packed baskets, but who's counting?*

"That's good, then. The worst is over." He patted her shoulder, certain in the knowledge that his word—like that of any brother, any husband or father—would be obeyed. Greta watched as he headed for Herr Winter and Ingrid and was enfolded in a warm haze of beer and good wishes.

"Have fun, Hans," she whispered. She had no intention of removing the gingerbread, though it would not hurt to *look* as though she did, and so she left the courtyard and skulked down the hall toward the food.

Hard not to be impressed, really. Flowers crowded the table as thickly as a spring meadow. Besides Frau Winter's wurst and bread there was a salad of gooseflower leaves, cabbage, wild carrot and hedge garlic, spätzle, a platter of sliced venison and a gleaming smoked ham. Maultaschen burst with spinach and pork, and fried onions glittered in butter. And at the center of it all, surrounded by fried elderflowers and sugar cakes, was a tray of gingerbread hearts.

Greta grinned. Someone had already brought it from the house. She made a show of reaching for the tray in case Hans was watching, then stopped as Mathias came to her side.

"For a quiet betrothal, they've put on quite the feast," he said, perusing the table and popping a slice of venison in his mouth. It was clear that he had gone to some effort for the gathering. His dark hair was tied neatly back, and he wore a crisp new shirt and a buffcoat of smooth, undyed deerskin over his breeches. He looked different. Tamer.

Several more guests drifted to the table, grasping for the hearts. Greta stepped back to give them space. Out on the lantern-lit cobbles,

Hans was leading Ingrid into a dance to deafening cheers. He gave a strained smile, an awkward little bow.

"I thought you said I wouldn't have to dance," Mathias said, watching them.

"You won't," Greta promised.

More people came for the hearts, reaching across each other greedily, knocking platters and nudging plates. The table was soon surrounded by people nibbling and crunching, flirting and giggling.

"*Quite* the feast," Mathias muttered.

"It is, at that," agreed Rob Mueller, surprising them both. "You're looking well tonight, Täubchen," he said, after giving a decidedly cool nod to Mathias. "The very picture of your mother."

"Thank you." Greta's throat was suddenly tight.

After simmering in a bath of ivy leaves and elder bark, her bodice was the lavender of a winter sunset. The blackberry leaves, too, had done their work; her skirt was now a rich, satisfying brown. She had arranged her hair carefully, tucking it under a coif the same soft hue as her bodice. Pinning it in place, she had felt the loss of her mother's ribbon all over again; it would have matched perfectly.

"Can I speak with you a moment, Täubchen?" Perceiving Greta's reluctant glance at Mathias, Rob cleared his throat. "It won't take long."

Did Greta imagine the tense look that passed between the two men? Gone was the warmth and gladness of their reunion on May Day. Frowning, she followed Rob a little way down the street.

"Täubchen, I wanted to discuss—"

"I saw Christie yesterday," Greta cut in. "He told me of his mother, of the . . . *circumstances* of his birth."

"Christ." Rob winced. "He told you?"

Greta raised her brows. "It was indeed a revelation."

"Truly, it is not as sordid as it sounds," he said. "The men take a vow, you see. They . . . er . . . they *save* themselves until such time as they give up their place with the pack and start their own families." Rob's blush was bright and furious despite the dimness of the street. "But soldiering is a dangerous business. And so, at midsummer, in certain villages, the men are permitted to break their vows.

The women must be willing, of course. And if a child should come from the union, they are raised in the village until they are old enough to join the pack. Christoph was such a child."

"So it's true, then. You *did* abandon him."

"I didn't know he existed."

"And his mother?"

"I could not know that the village would be destroyed. It was not until later, when I returned to Bavaria, that I discovered her fate. That's when I brought Christie home."

"And lied to us!" Greta said hotly. "To all of us! Christie, my father, me—"

"Your father knew," Rob said. "He knew everything, from the first. How else do you think I saved him at Nördlingen?"

Behind Rob, more couples had joined Hans and Ingrid's dance, swirling over the softly lit cobbles.

"What do you mean?"

"It was during the retreat. We were crossing the river, making for the Arnsberg Forest. Peter was half dead in the water, about to be butchered by Imperial cuirassiers. I knew him by the braid of red hair at his wrist. . . ." He sighed. "We had met in camp. I had heard him speak of you and Hans. Of your mother. *I carry a lock of her hair with me,* he said. *It is what I take with me, into the dark.* Well, that stayed with me. I wondered how it would be to have a wife of my own. Something to take with *me* into the dark. So when I saw him there, wounded, drowning in blood . . . You have to understand, the Imperials were closing in. There was no time to think. We had lost a man, Malachy, and I threw his pelt over your father. Conran argued with me—even then he questioned my leadership—but I held firm. There was a chance, however small, that Peter was shape-strong. As it turns out, he was."

Greta raised a hand. "Are you saying that you saved my father—brought him home to us—by turning him into a *wolf*?"

"I am. Wolves are hardier than men; with a pelt on his back Peter was able to run, despite his fearful wounds. Every man from his company died that day, in the battle or on the banks of the river during the retreat. But he survived."

As a child Greta had heard Peter's return to Lindenfeld described as nothing short of miraculous; his wounds were severe, the distance great. The entire village had prayed its thanks in the church. She tried to imagine their reaction had they known it was not God's hand but a wolf's pelt that had brought Peter Rosenthal home.

"He never told us," she said softly. "He never said."

"No. Sometimes I wondered if he remembered it at all. He was so badly hurt, and Mira gave him dream herbs. . . ."

"You never thought to ask him?"

"I thought it best he forget. A soldier returning from the war because he was rescued by a pack of shape-changers? He would have been thrown out of the village at best and accused of witchery at worst."

*Hard to argue with that.* "I just wish you had told me the truth."

"I wanted to, Täubchen. But I thought it best—safer—if you didn't know."

"And what of my father? Did the wolf magic—*damage* him?"

Lena had used all her skills to tend Peter when he returned to Lindenfeld. Under her devoted care he had healed quickly. But then, when she died . . . Peter had sickened rapidly that winter, worsening and weakening, never fully regaining his strength. Why had a strong, healthful man been brought low so suddenly? The wolf magic had saved Peter's life; but at what cost to his body—and his soul?

"Damage him?" Rob said. "Why, no. He recovered well. Why?"

"He grew so sick after my mother died. . . ."

Through the dancers, Greta caught Hans's furious frown, his swift nod toward the storehouse. "I have to go," she said.

"Back to Mathias?"

The bitterness in his voice froze her in place. "I thought you liked him."

"I do. But that doesn't mean he's right for you."

The man in question was visible at the edge of the dancing. The change in his appearance had not gone unnoticed by the other guests. Even now, he was disentangling himself from the grip of not one but three of the village's more self-possessed unmarried women as they vied to make him their partner.

"It would take a greater fool than I not to see that you're drawn to him," Rob said, not ungently. "But Mathias isn't the kind to settle in a place like Lindenfeld." He weighed his words carefully. "He is not like other men."

*No, he is not, thank the stars.* "I hardly think *you* can judge him on that score."

She ignored Rob's protest and returned to the Winter house, hurrying through the long hall. In the courtyard soft light from the windows above illuminated the storehouse and the stables.

Brigitta Winter was sitting on the back step, munching on a sugar cake.

"You should dance with the Tyroler," she announced. "It won't be right, if you do not."

"Why?" Mathias asked, coming up behind Greta.

"Because you're the talk of the party, that's why!" Brigitta leaned in conspiratorially. "They're all wondering how long it will be before the *other* Rosenthal is betrothed. Or if you will do something strange and ruin your chances."

"Oh," Greta said faintly.

Mathias crouched down to Brigitta's height. "I do not much like dancing," he told her. "But I should hate to disappoint you."

Brigitta clapped her hands. "Oh, good!"

And so Greta was led, protesting, into the midst of the dancing. It had intensified somewhat since the ordered prettiness of Hans's first dance with Ingrid. The music was wilder now, and fast. It seemed the entire village had joined in, an unruly mass of bodies pressed too close or whirling too fast. Greta was ripped away from Mathias and held tightly by first one man, then another. "Let me have Greta," someone else grunted, and she was spun away again, hardly knowing where to look, where to put her hands. There was a crush of men around her, pressing, reaching. "Such pretty red hair," someone muttered, close. "I never noticed, before."

*Why not cast a little charm that will allow* everyone *to feel as happy and loving as your brother and his salamander-to-be?*

She reeled back, only to find more men crowding in around her. She was horribly aware of their eyes eating into her, bright with wanting.

And then, less horribly, Mathias's cool hand was closing firmly around hers. A new song started, slower and sweeter, and the men surrounding Greta backed away. There was no shortage of breathless, rosy-cheeked women waiting for partners and they soon paired off, moving into two large rings. Mathias fell smoothly in with them. Two steps, three steps, four. When the other dancers changed direction he moved, too, turning Greta neatly.

"You know the steps," she accused.

"I said I did not *want* to dance," he murmured. "Not that I could not."

Greta was very conscious of how close they were, of the way his hands lingered on her waist each time they stepped apart and drew her firmly back to him when they came together again. One song became two, two became three, and she understood why people made such a fuss of dancing, after all.

"Why didn't you throw away the rest of the gingerbread?" Hans pulled Greta aside during a break in the dancing, sloshing beer onto the cobbles and narrowly missing her skirt. "I've just seen Frau Winter bring more out from the storehouse." He searched her face fearfully. "You didn't eat any, did you?"

"No," she said, lifting her skirt away from the spill. "Why?"

"I saw you dancing with the Tyroler. I thought perhaps . . ."

"No." She blushed. "*No.*"

The gathering swelled and pulsed around them: a young couple kissed passionately in a doorway, hardly caring who saw. Father Markus sat at a table littered with scraps and empty jugs, stuffing handfuls of wurst into his mouth. Atop another table Anna-Barbara Wittman danced madly, skirts high, plump legs bared to the knee.

"Sweet Jesus." Hans tossed back the contents of his cup in a single gulp.

Greta cringed. "Perhaps you should . . ."

"I can't get through this night sober, Greta. Do not ask it of me." He wiped his mouth on his sleeve. "Although, perhaps I should thank you, after all. Herr Winter has just informed me that he's secured a house for Ingrid and me here in the village. It would seem that we're forgiven."

"Well! That *is* good news!" Greta was unable to hide her grin.

"I know what you're thinking," Hans said. "And I won't force you to come and live with us. If you want to stay on the mountain after the wedding, I won't stop you."

"Oh, Hans!" She hugged him. "How can I ever thank you?"

"By destroying what's left of that godforsaken gingerbread. If Herr Winter eats any more, I fear he will throw my new mother-in-law on the table in front of everyone and—"

"Yes, yes." Greta hurried into the hall. "I'll do it now." There was no denying that the gingerbread had done its work perfectly. Enough, after all, was enough.

She was halfway down the dim passageway when Herr Hueber tottered out of the shadows.

"You and the Tyroler seem to be getting along, fräulein. I see now why you balked at my offer."

Soft footsteps behind her.

"Is everything well, Greta?" Mathias asked.

"*Greta,* is it? My, my, things *are* moving along." Herr Hueber took a swig from his cup. "I was just bidding Margareta a good evening. She looks well tonight, doesn't she? Such a shame. About the dowry, I mean."

"Herr Hueber—"

"Hush, fräulein." Herr Hueber flapped a hand in Greta's direction. "Best that your gallant suitor knows what he's getting—even if he *is* Papist scum." He cleared his throat pompously. "You see, woodsman, the Rosenthals have always had but little with which to feather their nests. Peter worked hard—but I never knew a rich woodcutter, did you?—while dear Hans does the opposite. Never worked a full day in his life and gambles what he *does* earn at the earliest convenience. His lucky match with a Winter will no doubt help, but even so . . . I'd bet my last pfennig that there is no dowry for his pretty sister. I take it you know the family history? Lena died tragically—killed by wolves, of all things. Peter was never the same, after. Went mad with grief, if you ask me—how else could a man abandon his children in the forest? Simply leave them there to die? What were you, Margareta? Six? Seven?" He sipped his wine thoughtfully. "Hard to imagine, really. And then, of course, there was that business in the woods. What sort of child is capable of burning an old woman to a crisp in her own oven?" He gazed at Greta, considering. "Such wickedness always lingers. If it's a wife you're after, woodsman, I'd suggest you look elsewhere. Unless, of course, it's sport you seek. If that is the case, I doubt you'll be disappointed. You know what they say about red hair. . . ."

Greta could stand no more. Time and time again the bürgermeister had taunted and disrespected her. He had touched her, threatened her and bullied her, and each time she had stood by and let him do it. Perhaps it was the spell she had worked with her blood. Perhaps it was Mathias, standing witness to every one of Herr Hueber's disgusting words. It hardly mattered. Anger rose in her, flowed through her, iron-strong.

"If being poor and wicked are one and the same," she said, "then it is no wonder you hold yourself in such high esteem, Herr Hueber. Tell me, how much did the baroness pay you to collect this false war tax of hers? When can we expect her imaginary Swedish army to arrive?"

Herr Hueber gaped at her.

"My father and brother have made mistakes, it is true," Greta said. "But the only wickedness lingering here is *you*."

She dug fingernails hard into the bound cut in her palm, wincing at the sudden pain. It coiled in her hand, hot and violent, and she

pushed it toward the bürgermeister, forcing her hurt and her
anger—a beautiful, bitter-dark brightness—into his mouth and
down his throat, past his stinking teeth. He had eaten the magicked
gingerbread that night, but instead of making him joyful and loving
it had festered, rotted. She teased it further, curdling and squeezing
until Herr Hueber's guts quivered and shuddered.

He blinked. Gulped. Blinked and gulped again. A sweat broke
out on his skin and he tottered, steadied himself clumsily against
the wall. He glanced at Greta, fearful, panicked, and heaved himself
away. She followed. The cut was bleeding, blooming wetly on the
linen binding, but she was past caring. All that mattered was her hatred for Herr Hueber, his wonderful, glorious suffering. He groaned,
staggered out onto the street. She saw, through his eyes, that the
table, which only moments before had been laden with food that was
deliciously fresh and inviting, was now furred with mold and writhing with maggots, thick and flour-pale. He cried out and backed
away, bumping into Herr Winter, who bumped into Hans, who
bumped into Frau Tritten and her husband, who all turned in time
to see the bürgermeister groan and fall to his knees, heaving a belly-
ful of maggoty gingerbread onto the cobbles. He heaved and then
he heaved some more, and only when he had flopped, exhausted
and empty, facedown in his own vomit, did Greta relinquish her
grip upon him. Her fingers uncurled, white and bloodless, the linen
soaked with blood. She stared down at it, her horror at what she had
done deepening as more people stopped to stare at Herr Hueber.

"Come now, Bürgermeister!" someone called merrily. "You'll
need to do better than that if you wish to keep up!"

Laughter all round at that, and a few generous souls bent drunkenly down to scoop Herr Hueber up. The music and dancing started
again, and the gathering found its stride once more. Not so Greta.
Heart thumping with disgust and fear she turned, pushing wordlessly past Mathias, and fled down the shadowed hall. She crossed
the courtyard in a few strides and threw open the door to the storehouse, slamming it shut behind her.

She leaned against it, panting and trembling in the soft, cool dark, the music fading to a low, woody murmur. The little room, with its long shelves and grain holds, was lit by the glow of a single candle set high on one wall. She turned, pressed her brow against the smooth, old wood as though it could offer her protection or forgiveness.

*Herr Hueber deserved it,* she tried to tell herself. *His privilege, his power, have allowed him to get away with such behavior for far too long.*

*You shamed him,* another part of her replied sadly. *He was frightened, confused. . . .*

*Yes, yes, he was all of that. And more, besides: rude, cruel, selfish, arrogant . . . Did you hear what he said about you? About your father?*

*Even so. Does anyone, even Herr Hueber, deserve such treatment?*

*Yes.* And with a suddenness that was sickening Greta realized she had *enjoyed* hurting him. She had enjoyed it very much.

"Oh my God," she whispered.

One song had ended and another begun when Mathias found her. Moonlight slipped into the storehouse with him, skimming the baskets of grains and vegetables lining the walls, the long bench lined with trays of gingerbread and Greta's baskets. A wave of music and laughter rolled in, then out again, as he closed the door.

Silence.

Greta spun away, brushing at her cheeks. She busied herself by packing the hearts back into their baskets. Anything, to avoid looking at him.

She continued working as Mathias moved through the dark. Continued as his warm breath touched the back of her neck. Continued as he reached around her, took a heart from the tray and laid it carefully in the basket beside the others.

Greta's hands slowed. It was a startling thing, the bloom of emotion that came with the curve of his smile or the touch of his hand. She had felt it from the first, that day at the falls. He had seemed to be made of the forest, then: leaf and moss and stone carved into the shape of a man.

*Enough,* she told herself fiercely. *Do you truly think the forest cobbled together a person for you? Formed him of mud and breathed life into*

*him for you? He is a man like any other. He will want a good name and*
*a dowry as much as the rest. And despite what he says, he will remember*
*what you did to Herr Hueber. How could he forget?*

"Most people," Mathias said, "like to talk. But I have found the
people here have a rare talent for it. On May Day, when I searched
for Jacob, the taverner warned me of you. He told me I lingered
with a woman who was ill luck, with hair as red as sin. Who was, if
he was completely honest, more than likely a witch."

Mathias took another heart, and another, his hands moving from
tray to basket and back again, his arms echoing the shape of her
own. There was no ignoring the way his hands lingered near hers at
each pass of the basket's edge; the way they brushed against her skin.
The way his thumbs traced the inside of her wrists.

"This I heard. And just now, I saw you do something to that man
that was surely witchcraft. And yet when I look at you, I see only
your eyes, grey as a storm, and your hair like autumn. I do not see
evil in its color. In truth, I have not seen anything more beautiful
in my life."

She stilled. Caught—torn—between joy and shame.

"Herr Hueber was right," she said. "About my father. About . . .
what I did."

"That's not true." He was so close Greta could feel the steady rise
and fall of his chest against her back.

"It's my fault," she said. "My fault my mother was killed. Hans and
I were playing in the snow that day. It grew late and Hans wanted
to go back to the house. I refused. I loved being out in the woods."
She had torn open the wound; the words bled forth, running one
into the other. ". . . By the time we got back it was dark. My parents
had gone out to search for us. They separated to cover more ground.
My father came back. But my mother . . . In the morning there was
a search. And . . ."

And.

"My father never said so, but I know he blamed me. If not for
me, Hans and I would have returned when we were supposed to,
and my mother would never have been out that night. That's why he

left us in the forest after he married Leisa . . . he could not love us anymore. He could not forgive us. How could he?"

Mathias stroked her hair. "Whatever troubles your father had, whatever he did, I know he loved you."

"How . . . how do you know?"

"How could he not?"

She bit down tears. Why was he making this so hard? She knew the ways of the world. You could have marriage without love—just look at her brother. But without money . . . ? "Herr Hueber spoke the truth, Mathias. I have no dowry."

"I don't care."

"I have nothing to give you. . . ."

"I don't care."

"I *did* hurt Herr Hueber tonight. And I bewitched the gingerbread. I bewitched *everyone*."

His hands, less gentle than his voice, turned her around. "I don't *care*." He grasped her face, raising it to his. And then—one swift movement, one dip of that dark head—he kissed her.

Time slowed its beating wings. Mathias's words, his lips, sparked against Greta's soul, burning away a lifetime's worth of doubt. She wrapped her arms about him, pulled him close. Gave him kisses, only to steal them greedily back again. He gave and stole them, too, his fingers moving over her hair, drawing away her coif, loosening her hair pins until his fingers were wound in the long, loose lengths. He pressed his lips to her neck, her collarbone. Kissed her again. She felt, shockingly, the touch of his tongue. Her breath quickened and something flickered, fire-bright, within her.

*I don't care.*

He felt it, too. It was there in the way he drew her to him, the way he lifted her, easily, onto the bench. Gingerbread crashed to the floor, scattering across the grainy boards. Greta hardly noticed. The top of Mathias's buffcoat was loose, the collar beneath it untied, revealing a narrow swath of skin, golden in the candlelight. She wanted very much to see more of it.

She pushed the coat open, clumsily unfastened the shirt: she had never undressed a man before. It was easier than expected; her hands soon smoothed over his bare shoulders, the hard slope of his chest. Mathias moaned softly against her mouth. His hands too were roving, burning through the layers of skirt and petticoat covering her thighs, toying with the laces of her bodice. Desire, bright as flame. The gathering outside, the gingerbread, Greta's dowry, the color of her hair, were of little consequence now. She only wanted Mathias's hands upon her. If he did not unlace her bodice and dip his lips to her bare skin, she would surely die.

Then, without warning, he stilled. Raised his head, listening. She strove to catch what he had heard. There was nothing but his breath and hers, ragged, mingling. Then he gave a regretful smile and kissed her brow. Greta, new to kissing, understood nonetheless that it was a farewell.

"No," she whispered. "Don't go. . . ." Her body screamed for him to stay, but he was through the door and gone.

Moments later Hans appeared.

"Greta?" He peered into the gloom. "Did you do it?" His gaze swept over her, breathless on the bench, and the shattered hearts across the floor. "Oh. A bit messy, perhaps. But well done, all the same."

Greta could not answer.

# 16
## Forbidden Fruit

*Hopeful suitors begged to marry Liliane and Rosabell. The viscount refused them all, each time risking alliances, new lands, even war. Some said he waited for the perfect match, for two men worthy of his precious daughters. Others said—in whispers—that Liliane had awakened something unnatural in him and that, selfishly, he could not bear to part with her.*

With the last of the gingerbread gone the gathering soon lost its potency. Lanterns burned low, drums stuttered, and the schäferpfeife wheezed into awkward silence.

"Shall I walk you home?" Mathias was waiting with Greta's shawl and a lantern near the empty table. She nodded, suddenly shy. What had come over her in the storehouse? She had never behaved that way. Had never *considered* behaving that way. She thought of the blood she had added to the dough for herself—*after all, why shouldn't I enjoy the party, too?*—and her cheeks burned.

They joined the guests trickling homeward through the quiet streets. Mathias, too, said little and Greta's unease increased with every step, with every vague and shameful conversation she overheard.

"Did I really eat that much, Klaus?"

"Odd's fish, but my head is pounding!"

"Did you see Herr Hueber? He cast up his accounts in front of us all! That's not something we shall soon forget. . . ."

"It was nothing, Freida—only a kiss! I don't know what came over me—you know I love only you. . . ."

The night watchman frowned down from atop the wall as Greta

and Mathias slipped through the western gate and out onto the road. The lantern lit their steps, but Greta could not shake the darkness from her heart. She wished Mathias would speak. Despite what he had done, and said, in the storehouse, he was distant. Did he regret his actions? It was easy to speak of love at a betrothal. But when the flowers were swept aside . . .

And when the gingerbread was broken . . .

Greta froze in the middle of the road. How could she be so blind? *Of course* Mathias regretted his actions. He had been under the gingerbread's spell, as surely as the men who had grabbed hungrily for her during the dancing. Men who, before tonight, had never regarded her with anything but mistrust or vague curiosity. All changed with a few drops of blood and a secret, seductive spell.

Mathias stopped, too. "Greta? Are you well?"

"Yes." She hurried after him, risked a glance at his face in the lanternlight. Dark brows drawn tight together. Remote. Troubled.

*I take it you know the family history?*

Was he thinking, as she was, of Herr Hueber's warning? It loomed over her, dark as the pines lining the sleepless river. Was he thinking of what had happened in the storehouse—regretting every moment of it, every kiss, every word? *I don't care.* Had he meant it? Or was his acceptance of her, of who she was and what she had done, simply part of the enchantment?

Perhaps—*oh, unhappy thought*—he was thinking regretfully of the Sturmfels, of dusk and ruins, and rabbit cooked over a fire. Had he *wanted* to find her there? Or had the spell been working even then—Greta's blood and the scent of cooling gingerbread calling him to her across the forest, against his will and desire?

Her heart clenched in shame at her selfishness.

They crossed the bridge and walked in heavy silence up the mountain. The house, when it finally appeared, had never looked so dark or lonely.

"Greta." Mathias placed the lantern carefully on a mossy stump and turned to her, his face half-shadowed. "I think it might be best if I spoke to your brother tomorrow."

"You want to speak to Hans? Why?" She knew, though. He believed in Perchta, and the Water of Life. He even knew the truth about the pack. But knowing such things and being willfully manipulated by witchcraft were not the same. He knew about the gingerbread, about what Greta had done to Herr Hueber, to everyone at the gathering. He would go to Hans first, and then he would go to the council. And why shouldn't he? He had every right.

"Is it really a surprise?" He reached for her, gentle. "I thought I made my feelings for you quite clear in the storehouse."

"What?" Realization, cold as stone: he was under her spell, yet. "No, Mathias. You don't have to do this."

"Do what?"

"Say these things. Commit yourself." She forced herself to go on, to speak through her misery. She owed him that, at least. "What happened between us tonight—it wasn't real."

"Wasn't real . . . ?" He looked at her, baffled.

"Answer me truthfully, Mathias: How many gingerbread hearts did you eat?"

"How many?"

"Yes. Or . . ." Burning stars, it was worse than she suspected. ". . . did you lose count?"

He gave her a long look. "Greta, I hope I won't offend you when I say this. But the truth is, I didn't eat any gingerbread."

"You . . . didn't?"

"No. I wanted to, but every time I went for some the tray was empty." He tilted his head, curious. "Can I ask why it matters?"

Greta blushed deeply, and was glad of the dark. "I told you the gingerbread was enchanted. Well, I thought that you must have eaten it, and that was why . . . in the storehouse . . ."

"I see." Mathias grinned. "I wonder what would have happened if I *had* eaten some?"

"For my brother's sake I'm glad you didn't."

He chuckled, low and warm, and she leaned into him, unspeakably relieved. Mathias stroked her hair. The silence of deepest night was all around. The house creaked as it dreamed. A wolf howled distantly, and another answered. Conran and his wolves, roaming the night, watching over the village while it slept.

"Mathias?"

"Hmmm?"

"Are you certain you don't mind? Not just about the gingerbread, I mean. About . . . everything else?"

He drew back, took her hands in his. His fingers were warm, the tips rough. Good, trustworthy hands. "Truthfully?" he said. "You are not the first witch to cross my path. I have met witches who longed for nothing more than to harm and destroy, taking what they will. And I have met others who sought the very opposite. I saw something in you the first time we met. Something nameless and beautiful. There was . . . a light around you. Like mist strewn with gold. The very air tasted of honey." He stepped close, breathed her in. "Other women don't smell as good as you. They don't bake like you, either. So, no. I don't mind."

Not trusting herself to speak, Greta stood on her toes and kissed him. Again and then again, until something of what they had left unfinished in the storehouse returned.

"Greta," Mathias said, pulling back.

Greta was all too aware of the empty house behind them. She wondered recklessly how he might react if she were to draw him inside with her. After all, they were completely alone. No one would know. . . .

A kiss, she found, could work its own kind of magic. It could certainly make a man much larger than she bend to her will. They were at the door when Mathias sensed what she was about. He pulled away, breath ragged. "Greta . . ."

"Surely you do not want to spend another night in the cutter's hut?" she whispered. "It must be cold and lonely there."

"Greta . . ."

She fumbled for her key, for the lock at her back . . . and grasped empty air. She twisted, cold horror rising: the door, locked securely when she left hours before, lay open, exposing a sinister sliver of black.

"Stay here," Mathias murmured, knife already drawn. "There's someone inside."

Greta hissed a refusal, but he was already sliding into the yawning darkness. She seized the lantern, held it high. Its crazed wobbling illuminated the table and half the workbench.

"Mathias?" she whispered.

He dipped into the light, raised a warning hand. *Stay there.* Then he peered upward, into the newly terrifying dark of the loft.

"No, Mathias." A cold sweat of fear. On the ladder he would be exposed—vulnerable—to anyone lurking above. He raised a hand again, calm, firm, and began to climb, disappearing over the edge. Greta's heartbeat was loud in her ears. Ten times it sounded, and still Mathias did not appear. Against her better judgment, his wishes, and each and every one of her instincts she entered the house and raised the lantern.

"Mathias?"

No answer. No sound at all, but for the *thud, thud* of her heart. She waited for some sound or sign. She did not expect a cold, trailing finger to touch the back of her neck. A stranger's breath to ice her skin. A chilling whisper at her ear.

*"Forbidden fruit."*

Greta staggered away, too horrified to scream. The touch came again, feather soft on her cheek, almost loving.

*"Soon."*

She did scream, then. The lantern fell, smashing at her feet. Flames flared, licked at her skirts. She beat at them as Mathias threw himself down from the loft. He stomped at the flames, smothered them with his cloak, and all the while Greta, struggling against a tide of fear so strong it caused her throat to close and her belly to roil sickly in protest, heard two words echoing again and again in her mind.

*Forbidden fruit.*

"There was someone here," she cried. "They were *here*. I felt them! I *heard* them!"

"Are you hurt?"

"No. But . . ."

"I have to go after her."

*Her.* A woman's voice, soft as silk. And familiar, somehow.

"Greta? Lock the door behind me. Do you hear? Open it to no one." Mathias seemed larger than himself. His voice, hoarse and rough, was not his own.

"You cannot think to leave me here alone!" Terror gripped Greta. Someone had been in the house. Someone had watched her, and Mathias, from the shadows. "Mathias?"

He was already at the open door. Greta touched his arm and he rounded on her, his whole body shaking with fury. She ripped her hand away, staggered back. The light of the moon was thin and weak but she would have sworn his eyes had changed. Calm green to a furious, terrifying black.

"Mathias," she whispered. "You are frightening me."

He inhaled slowly, deeply. For a moment, the frightful tension in his bearing eased. "Forgive me."

"What is wrong?"

He went inward, listening to something only he could hear. His shoulders heaved with the rough tide of his breath. Then he turned and—without so much as a glance in Greta's direction—staggered toward the tree line.

"Mathias?"

He was moving like someone drunk, or in unbearable pain. He tried to breathe again, great deep breaths, as though the act would prevent his body from ripping apart. The agony seemed to pass, and he steadied himself against the nearest tree.

"Mathias? What's wrong?"

No reply.

"Mathias?"

He looked up, and his eyes were the color of oak leaves again. "I would never hurt you, Greta. You know that, don't you? I would never, ever hurt you." His face was a bloodless grey, sheened with sweat. The tendons in his neck jumped and quivered.

"I know." She stepped close, but he warded her off with a trembling hand.

"Do not touch me." He sank into himself, gritting his teeth as he began that awful, labored breathing again. For a moment it appeared he had conquered his body: that the pain, the sickness, whatever it was, was passing.

Then his whole body tightened of its own accord, pain rippling through him like water. He lurched forward, throwing himself into the forest.

Greta shoved through ferns and branches, following. "Mathias? What is wrong?"

He made no answer, only stumbled away from her, deeper into the dark. She stopped, uncertain, tears cold on her cheeks.

"Mathias?"

The cruel whispering of the pines, urged on by a night wind that seemed sharp as winter, was the only reply.

When it was clear that he would not return Greta stumbled back to the house. Slammed shut the door and groped at the lock until the key gave a satisfying *click*. Fumbled in the darkness for her tinderbox, a candle. A clumsy strike—hands shaking—and then, mercifully, flame.

The comfort it gave lasted but a moment.

In the center of the table lay an apple, rich and glossy, its perfect skin the hue of fresh-spilled blood.

The crunch and crack of footsteps in fresh snow stirred Greta to wakefulness. Moonlight spilled through the shutters and across her blankets, frosty bright. She padded to the window and opened the shutters. Unlatched the window and leaned out.

The world outside was winter-white, the window frame glittering with ice. Cold burned her face and hung thick and white on her breath. She hardly noticed. A woman stood at the forest's edge, staring up at the house. She was dressed simply, her long red-brown hair bright against the snow.

"Mama," Greta whispered, from somewhere between terror and longing.

Lena's face was waxen, her lips death-blue. She raised one arm and pointed to the forest.

"*See.*"

The whisper was close. As though Lena's shade was in the room with Greta and outside it, all at once.

"*See.*"

Greta choked on a scream and woke, dragged in breath after ragged breath. The memory of the dream-cold was fresh on her skin, despite the blanket over her knees and the steady warmth of the oven.

She looked about, confused—why was she sleeping in a chair? And fully clothed?—until the world aligned.

There had been a woman in Greta's house. A woman who had touched her neck and whispered. *Soon.*

And Mathias had known who she was. Mathias . . . his agony and distress . . . the sadness in his face when he told her he would never hurt her. What had happened to him?

Wide awake now, Greta pushed herself out of the chair and nursed the oven back to a comforting vigilance. She went to the window, looked out. The dream-winter, with its inexplicable dread, was gone.

But her mother was still there. Lena, one pale hand pointing at the forest, her face soft with sorrow.

"*See.*"

Greta gave a low cry and stumbled back from the window, her calves thudding into the chair.

*See.*

There was something out there. Something she had to see.

Greta hesitated. The moon was low, but she had always seen well in the dark. And she knew this ground better than anyone. Every tree, every root and stone. Besides, her mother was with her. She would not lead her own daughter into harm, would she?

She followed Lena into the woods. It had rained while she had slept, and the mountain smelled of damp earth and pine. Deep into the forest she walked, until the moon was all but hidden behind the thick canopy above.

"*See.*"

Greta's steps slowed. She had not been in this part of the forest for a long time. Not since . . .

The shape of a woman in the gloom ahead: one bare arm and a fall of reddish hair.

"*See.*"

The trees parted, revealing a moonlit glade thick with snow. Snowflakes fell gently, just as they had the morning Greta had last come here, fifteen years ago. And, just like then, Lena lay dead, her chest torn open, her heart's blood spreading around her.

But this time her eyes were open. She gazed up at Greta and then along the length of one pale arm stretched out in the snow.

"*See.*"

In her mother's hand was an apple, as rich and glossy red as her blood.

And Greta, waking—truly waking this time, in her own bed, her breath sharp and loud in the dawn-silent house—knew this was more than just the old dream come back to torment her. There *had* been an apple. In the confusion of her screams, in her father's cries as he fell keening at his wife's side, in the rough gentleness of the night watchmen who had helped with the search—*don't look, child, come away*—she had forgotten.

There had been an apple in Lena's hand. An apple identical in every way to the one now sitting on the scuffed table in Greta's kitchen.

Greta paced the house, unable to banish the two apples—one long withered, the other sitting on her table—from her mind. She longed to speak to someone about the day her mother died. But there was no one she could ask. Rob had been away when Lena died. Hans had not seen his mother's body. One of the watchmen might have seen an apple in the snow and wondered. But who? She scarcely knew where to begin.

It hardly mattered. Greta knew—with a grim, unsettling kind of knowing—that it was more than a mere dream. *Someone* had been with her mother the night she died. *Someone* had given her an apple.

And what of her own apple, left behind like some sinister gift? *Soon,* the intruder had whispered. Was it a threat, or a promise—or both? Greta could not banish the echo of the woman's voice from her mind. Who was she? And why had she been in Greta's house? *I have to go after her.* Mathias had known the stranger was a woman. Had known, it now seemed to Greta, exactly who she was.

Was this, then, the woman from Hornberg, who had brought Mathias to Lindenfeld in the first place? The woman who had stolen from him and his family?

Greta turned on her heel, paced. *Perhaps.* But what did *Greta* have to do with it? Why would this woman break into *Greta's* home, and leave an apple for *her?*

None of it made sense.

Only one thing was clear: Mathias knew more than he had shared with her. Much more. She knew his past was an unhappy one; for that reason, she hadn't not pried. But that did not mean she wasn't curious. After all, he hadn't really told her where he went after Herr Auer's hunt. Or where he slept, or what he did, when he was not in the village. Even his reasons for coming to Lindenfeld were vague.

And what had come over him the night before? Was he hurt or sick? Or something worse?

"You are sulky this morning," the book remarked. "I thought you'd be more cheerful, considering. I trust everyone enjoyed themselves last night?"

"They did," Greta admitted. "The gingerbread worked. A little too well, to be honest. But . . ." She chewed at her lip. "I did something terrible. To Herr Hueber."

"Took your revenge, did you?"

Greta nodded.

"Ah! Feels wonderful, does it not?"

"At the time? Yes. But now I feel awful." She wondered what Mira would say if she knew.

"It'll pass. Is that all that's troubling you? I heard what went on between you and Mathias last night in the yard. You can thank me for that, you know. If we hadn't added your blood to the baking he never would have opened your petals."

"That's not true!"

"What's not true? My spell? Or your petals?"

"Both." Greta's cheeks were suddenly hot. She seized a cloth, wiped down the workbench vigorously even though it was already spotless. "He didn't—er—open anything."

"Don't play coy with me, dearie. I know when a rose has been plucked."

"Well, you're wrong. He didn't even eat any gingerbread."

"He didn't? My, my. Impressive."

Greta hid a smile. "You are very talkative this morning. Surprisingly loud, too." She threw the cloth aside and gazed around. The book's voice was coming from the flour garner. She opened it, peered inside. "How did you get in there?"

"You put me here."

"No, I didn't. I put you under the hearth stones before I went to the Sturmfels. I'll toss you in the fire, I swear, if you begin creeping about the house—"

"I can't move, you know that," the book pouted. "And you *did* put me in here. You were all moody and wistful. Pining for Mathias, no doubt. Where is he, anyway? He left in rather a hurry last night."

*Yes, he did.* "He had some . . . things to see to."

"What sort of things?"

"Important things."

The book shifted its pages. "You don't know, do you?"

Another flicker of doubt. Greta pushed it away. "I'm sure he'll explain everything," she said firmly.

"Will he, though? In my experience men can be overfond of secrets."

"What makes you think he has a secret?"

"Poor, sweet child: What makes you think he doesn't?"

Greta went to the window. A pair of squirrels were scampering near the woodpile. She watched as the larger squirrel dipped and disappeared from sight, leaving the other alone. "He wasn't well. That's why he left so suddenly."

"Where is he now, then?" the book asked. "He's young, strong. Surely he has recovered from whatever ailed him last night? If he truly cared for you, as he said, why would he leave so suddenly? Why wouldn't he come back?"

*Why, indeed?*

"Perhaps you should go and find him instead of moping about like a stomped flower."

"Find him? I wouldn't know where to start."

"What about the cutter's hut?"

High in a fir tree, the second squirrel found the first. They raced around each other, blurring into one.

"It won't hurt to check, I suppose." Absently, Greta touched her belt; her knife and tinderbox. She had taken to wearing the fox pelt when she was alone, too, as Mira did. Her fingers brushed against the reddish fur, tingling at the heady thought of change. "I can't say I'm not worried."

"I could come with you?" the book said hopefully. "It's been so long since I've been out. . . ."

"Come along, then." Greta slipped it into her apron pocket. She opened the door, twisted the pelt free and raised it to her shoulders. "See how wrong you are."

But when Greta arrived at the hut and unwound from her fox form, it was she, and not the book, who looked the fool. Words could not do justice to the miserable state of the shelter. The door hung loose, the roof had all but collapsed, and the floor was strewn with leaves so ancient they crumbled beneath Greta's shoes.

"Maybe he meant another hovel?" the book said helpfully. "Surely there are others nearby?"

"There are other huts, yes." Greta thought back to that first night with Jacob and Mathias. What had they said? She had been too distracted with Mathias's presence to listen. "Though I am *sure* Jacob said it was the one near the falls. . . ."

"Mathias is mysterious, I'll give him that," the book mused. "It is the best part of his charm. That, and his forearms. It does make me curious, though. And if I am curious, it must be *killing* you."

"It is not so grim as that."

"Fiddle-faddle. You would be dull as two stones not to be wondering about him. Why he disappeared for all that time after the hunt. Where he sleeps . . ."

"He does not like towns. He is used to traveling, to being alone."

The book snorted. "You had best find out what he is up to when you are not there. After all, a sensible woman always knows where her man is headed."

Greta turned away from the hut, rubbing at the bridge of her nose. The truth always bit hard, and the book had a way of sinking its teeth in so deep and strong it was impossible to shake free. On the long walk back to the house she found herself sifting through every conversation she had had with Jacob, and Rob, and Mathias. Searching for some hint. For anything.

"There is a way to discover the truth," the book said when they were back at the house. It flipped itself open to a page thick with a looping, archaic script. "Do you have a ball of yarn?"

Curious, Greta rummaged in her sewing basket, withdrawing a large ball of undyed yarn.

"Lovely. Now, fetch that knife there."

"Why?"

"You know why. There is always a cost, dearie."

Greta hesitated. "I'm not sure. I did not like the way I felt at the betrothal."

"Don't lie to me," the book said. "You enjoyed every moment."

"Well, yes," Greta admitted. "At the time I suppose I did. But afterward . . ."

"We all feel remorse from time to time. It's best to ignore it. Now, do you want to know what Mathias is truly about or not?"

"Perhaps there is another way?" Greta asked. "Perhaps if we used greenmagic instead . . ."

"*That* insipid pokery folkery? I think not."

"But greenmagic is gentler."

"Weaker, you mean. Though it hardly matters. With practice you will become strong enough to wield whichever you choose."

"I . . . could use both?"

"There is more than one shade of magic, dearie. A true witch knows them all."

*A true witch knows them all.* A sweet little shiver ran down Greta's spine. She wondered why Mira had not mentioned that.

"And right now? For this spell?"

"*This* spell needs but a little to give much."

*Tattermagic gives nothing. It only takes.* Mira's words whispered in the back of Greta's mind. She hesitated.

"It's up to you, of course," the book said. "But listen when I tell you that every man, no matter how pretty, has a deeper, darker self he keeps well hidden. Mathias is no exception. If you can live without knowing, well, good for you. Perhaps it is vanity only that compels other, lesser women to seek the truth."

"It's not that," Greta said quickly. She thought again of the cold, whispering woman, the apple. "I . . . I have to know, that's all."

"Pick up that knife, then," the book said briskly. "A few drops will do."

A few drops was not so much to give. Greta pressed the blade against the soft flesh at the base of her thumb. Pain sparked and then, as the blood began to flow, there came a familiar, delicious hum.

"You see?" the book said. "A little pain for much. Now, hold the yarn beneath the cut. . . . That's right."

Greta guided the yarn to catch the droplets. It warmed in her hand at once, growing rapidly hotter and hotter until she was forced to roll it onto the table.

"There," the book announced. "It's quite cool, now. All you need do is tie it to Mathias's clothing and let it unravel. It will lead you right to him."

Greta eyed the yarn, her apron pressed to the cut. "It does not seem long enough."

"Ah, but that is the charm! It will be as long as you need it to be."

"What if it tangles or gets caught?"

"Fool, it is spelled against such things. As you follow it, say these words: *I wind, I wind, my true love to find.*"

"*I wind, I wind, my true love to find.* That's all?"

"That's all." The book closed itself with a thump. "The back of the cloak works best, I've found. They don't feel the unraveling there."

Greta stared at it. "You've *done* this?"

"Of course not. I'm only a book, after all. But I've seen it done many times."

"How old *are* you?"

"Older than you," it told her. "And old enough to know that womenfolk have little enough power of their own. That is why they must have their charms and their tricks. Their books and their ink and blood. Their eyes, their smiles, their hips; their lace and silk, their ribbons and thread . . . These are your weapons, dearie. You must use them as best you can."

# 17

## I Wind, I Wind

*It came to pass that the viscount, at the insistence of his advisors, took a new wife—a lovely young woman with hair like spun gold. Liliane jealously withdrew from her father's court and took to exploring lonely rooms and half-forgotten towers. It was in such a tower that she came upon her mother's old book of magic.*

"Thank God last night is over," Hans said, slumping at the table. "I think it went rather well, all things considered." Greta, who had just finished making nettle tea, took down an extra cup.

"*And* I'm to have supper with Ingrid's family tonight." He flopped forward, resting his head on his folded arms. "What am I to do, Greta? I can hardly stand to look at her for guilt. She should have been Jacob's wife, not mine. And what if . . ." He raised his head. "What if she should have a *child*?"

"I have no doubt she will," Greta said, pouring.

"Christ, I hope not!"

"You don't mean that." She set two steaming cups on the table and sat beside him. "A child would be a blessing. A wondrous blessing for all of us." She felt a pang of sudden, unexpected longing.

"You don't understand," Hans said quietly. "It's not just Ingrid. I—I never wanted this. I never wanted to be a father. Greta, what if—what if I am like *him*? What if I abandon my child, as he abandoned us?"

Greta did not need to ask of whom Hans spoke. He had never forgiven their father for his treatment of them, despite Peter's efforts to make amends. In that, they *were* alike: Peter had never forgiven himself, either. She had a sudden memory of herself and Hans as

young children, clambering atop a sun-washed log and leaping like
birds into their father's arms. Squealing with laughter as he caught
them, again and again, never once letting them fall.

"Our father did love us, Hans."

"I wish I shared that view," he said. "For I do not see how a man
who loves his children can leave them in the forest to die." His voice
splintered on unshed tears. "What if I am the same?"

He did weep, then. Laid his head upon her shoulder and cried
for Jacob and for himself, and for other things besides. When he
was done, he wiped his eyes with his sleeve, so like the way he used
to when he was a child that Greta suddenly saw him as he *used* to
be, wiry and thin, with tears running tracks through the dirt on his
cheeks, and, unusually, a smear of blood on his brow. She frowned.
Hans had been crying, *bleeding*, right there in the kitchen . . . but
why?

She looked around, seeing the house as it had been, then—
hollow after Lena's death. Cold, comfortless, despite the presence
of a new stepmother. Shards of broken memory glimmered. Peter
was away cutting, and Leisa had been in a fierce temper, blowing
fear and misgiving through the house like a storm. At last she had
smacked Hans so hard he staggered and fell. Greta watched, horrified, as he slid to the floor, his hands raised to his bleeding face.

The fury ebbed out of her stepmother then, as sudden as it had
risen. She crouched at Hans's side. Examined the wound with her
startling eyes, so dark they were almost black, then tested the cut
with her delicate fingers. Hans whimpered.

"Get some clean linen," Leisa snapped at Greta.

Greta ran to obey, almost tripping in her haste. And that was
why she took a moment longer than she should have. That was why,
before she righted herself, she saw her stepmother raise her fingers
to her mouth and lick Hans's blood away.

"There's glass on the floor," Hans said. Greta flinched, fragments
of memory slipping out of reach.

"What?" She looked at him, blinked. "Oh. Yes."

"What happened?"

Those long fingers smeared with blood. "I broke a lantern."

"Tsk, tsk."

Greta sipped her tea, examining Hans's brow surreptitiously. There was a small, round scar above his eyebrow.

"Do you remember when Mother died, Hans?"

A wary glance. "Why?"

"I was wondering if you heard anything . . . unusual . . . about how she was found?"

"More unusual than being killed by a pack of wolves? No. I can't say that I did." He lifted his own tea, took a sip, grimaced. Set it down and looked at her. "Greta, are you serious about the Tyroler?"

Hans's blue eyes could be very sharp when he chose. Greta shifted in her seat. "What do you mean?"

"Exactly that. Are you sure he is what you want? You hardly know him, after all. None of us do."

There was far too much truth in that for Greta's liking. "Rob knows him."

"And what does Rob say?"

*That doesn't mean he's right for you.*

"It doesn't matter what Rob says. It doesn't matter what *anyone* says."

"No, it doesn't," Hans agreed. "This is your decision. I won't try to take it away from you. Not after . . ." He didn't say it. The debacle with Christoph was something neither of them would willingly speak of again. And wasn't Hans about to marry a woman he did not love? "I just want you to be certain."

"Well, I am." The words rang hollow in Greta's ears. Her fingers trailed to her pocket, where the ball of yarn lay.

"There is no denying Herr Schmidt will be able to provide for you, if it should come to that," Hans mused. "I rolled bones with Ernst Bachmann, the merchant, in Hornberg a few nights ago. I won, too."

"I don't want to hear such things, Hans," Greta said tersely.

"No, no, you misunderstand me. I only meant to say that Ernst was unlucky. *Very* unlucky. And look; he paid me with this."

He drew a coin from his coat pocket. It was large and silver, marked with a knight on a towering warhorse. "Impressive, isn't it? I've never seen one like it. Ernst said that Herr Schmidt used it to buy clothes from him in Hornberg last week. He said he had more, too. A purse full of them. Can you imagine?"

Greta flipped the coin, ran her thumb over the eagle she knew she would find there. *Perhaps the white wood woman, Perchta, left you a gift.* Mathias had teased her when she asked him if the money in her shoe belonged to him, swiftly diverting the conversation toward moss folk and kobolds. Why?

Doubt was Greta's companion as she watched Hans leave for the Winters' house, nursing his guilt like a newborn child. *Every man has a deeper, darker self he keeps well hidden.* By the time her brother reached Lindenfeld he would be straight-backed and assured. He would greet Ingrid with a kiss. Share her table and, in a few weeks' time, her bed, as though he were perfectly happy to. Did Ingrid suspect the truth?

Or was she content to love a shadow?

Mathias came back at dusk, a man made of secrets.

"I wanted to apologize for last night, Greta. I know you must be confused. Angry, even—"

"I was worried." She opened the door wide the better to see him. "You were so ill. . . ."

"I am well enough now."

She looked him over. His eyes were their usual color and his breath came easy and slow. There was a narrow tear in his shirt, the brightness of blood beneath the dark laces of his tunic. "You have cut yourself again."

"It is just a scratch."

*Liar.* Three times she had seen that cut in the same place. It was too strange, too precise, to be mere chance.

"Why did you leave like that?" she asked. "If you'd stayed I might have been able to help."

He said nothing.

"Where did you go? To the cutter's hut?" *Go on*, she thought. *Say you went there. Place your foot in the little snare I've laid for you.*

He paused, and for one tantalizing moment Greta thought she had him. Then, "I'm so sorry, Greta."

"You already said that." He had been right: she *was* angry. "Is that all, then? You have nothing more to say to me?"

He jerked back, stung. "No. I . . . I wanted to tell you that I have to leave again."

"Again? Why, Mathias?" She watched him, searching for signs of dishonesty. A cutting away of the glance, a flickering of the eye, a shifting of the feet.

"There's work cutting, near Schiltach . . ."

*Another lie.* She knew it the way she knew the shape of his hands, the curve of his lips, the way his hair brushed against his cloak. And yet, he seemed a stranger to her.

"It's the wrong time of month to cut," she said. "My father never went out after full moon."

"In my country we cut at the dark of the moon. The sap is lower, the wood drier."

So pleasant, so reasonable.

"When will you go?"

"Tomorrow."

"How long will you be gone?"

"I couldn't say."

"And what if I asked you not to go?" she said. "That woman spoke to me, Mathias. *Whispered* to me. She left this on my table." She ducked inside, brought the apple out to him. "Why would she do that?"

"Forbidden fruit," he murmured, taking it from her.

"You know who she is, don't you? You know why she was here!"

A vast, cold space yawned between them, filled with dread and doubt and secrets.

"Please, Mathias. Please tell me." She wanted him to hold her. She wanted him to share her worry. Most of all, she wanted him to tell her the truth.

It was not to be.

"I have to go," Mathias said, turning the apple slowly in his hands. "It's important that I do—more so than ever before. I know you don't understand—I know it's unfair of me to ask—but I *am* asking. Wait for me, Greta. Please. I will come back as soon as I can, and I will tell you everything. I promise."

Doubtless he thought these words would soothe her. As though waiting, alone and powerless and ignorant, would ease anyone's fears.

*Eyes, smiles, hips; lace, silk, ribbons and thread . . . These are your weapons, dearie. You must use them as best you can.*

"Very well," Greta said sweetly. An idea, darkly shining, had formed in her mind. "But come in and have some supper before you go. I can mend your shirt too."

He hesitated, and Greta wondered if her dissembling was as searing-bright as it felt. Then he followed her inside. She left the day's soup to warm on the stove while he removed his cloak, bow and sword belt, laying them over a chair, and shrugged away his tunic so that it fell behind him like one of the sell-swords' plaids. The shirt he peeled off last. At the sight of him in the candlelight, long-limbed and bare, Greta's treacherous heart near forgave him.

"We should take care of that cut, too," she said, dragging her gaze away. He sat obediently in the chair before the oven while she fetched water, linen and honey.

"Always here." She knelt before him and dabbed at the cut, which was deeper than she had first thought, a wicked slice. "It's peculiar, is it not?"

"I suppose it is." He drew a small pouch from the folds of his tunic. "Use this, if you like. Woundwort."

Greta opened the pouch, and was met with the scent of dried yarrow. She cleaned the cut and filled it with the finely chopped plant, then smoothed honey over the top to seal it. She went to rise, but Mathias pulled her close. He nosed at her neck and her hair. Lifted her hand to his lips and kissed the honey from her fingertips.

"I know you're angry with me," he murmured. "Even so I would follow you to the very edge of Hell had I the scent of honey on your skin to lead me."

Oh, sweet treachery. It took all of Greta's will to reclaim her fingers as well as her resolve. "Your soup will be ready," she said. "I'll fetch it."

While Mathias ate, Greta set her sewing box on the table. The yarn was a glowing ember in her apron pocket. Could she do this? *A sensible woman knows where her man is headed.* Yes. Yes, she could. Hans, Rob, her father, and now Mathias. They had all of them kept secrets from her. Well, no more.

She turned her back to Mathias and repaired the shirt with quick, even stitches. Then—after a careful glance over her shoulder—she reached for his cloak. The thick wool at one corner had been torn some time ago, snagged on a low branch, perhaps, or caught on his blade. Slowly, carefully, Greta drew the yarn through the hole and knotted it tight.

*There.*

A moment's triumph, quickly hidden as Mathias's chair scraped against the floor. She watched in silence as he pulled on his shirt.

"You're leaving?"

"The sooner I go the sooner I can come back." He took up his cloak and the yarn hurtled to the floor. She watched, breathless, as it rolled to a gentle stop against his boot.

"I know I've hurt you," Mathias said, taking her hand. "It was not my intention."

"I believe you." That, at least, was true. It was clear that Mathias's dishonesty was not born of cruelty or deliberation. Unlike her own. She glanced at the yarn, guilty of a sudden, and wondered if it wasn't too late to undo it.

"This will all be over soon." He kissed her, aching sweet. "I promise."

And then he was moving away from her, the yarn tumbling after him.

*Too late, too late, to stop it.*

She groped for the ball with clumsy fingers, held it like a live ember as it unspooled in her hands, then seized Mathias's spoon and thrust the handle through. For one panicked moment she wondered if it would tangle and pull—she had given little thought as to how the unraveling might be managed—but the yarn spun smoothly out into the night, tensing and easing with the rhythm of Mathias's long strides.

An age passed. Greta leaned against the open door as the thread rippled out before her, imagining Mathias's inevitable discovery of it, and him turning back in a fury to demand what she was about.

She half wished he would. At least then the truth would be revealed. For there *was* a truth to be revealed. Greta was sure of it. The thought made her angry again. And, since anger is easier to bear than guilt, she held it like a candle in cupped hands. Blowing upon it gently, fueling her resolve.

At last the yarn went still.

Greta dropped the spoon. She threw on her warmest shawl, lit a lantern and looped it over her arm, patted her tinderbox and knife. Then she gathered up the yarn.

"I wind, I wind," she whispered. "My true love to find."

Charmed, the book had said, and Greta saw no reason to doubt it: the yarn was smooth and supple as a spiderweb, glowing with a silvery light. She stretched it between her fingers; it bounced back, taut and true. By its angle she knew Mathias had gone northeast, across the face of the mountain.

"I wind, I wind, my true love to find," she said, stronger. She had begun this, now. Best that she finish it.

Thunder growled distantly and banks of cloud passed across the moon. Only Greta's lantern and the thread's glimmer pierced the night. She made her way through the woods, the yarn spiraling in her hands, until she heard the roar of falling water. The moon peeked between clouds, shining on the falls. Greta followed the thread up the steep bank. When the way became too difficult she set the lantern down and thrust the yarn in her pocket, using her hands to clamber up the slippery path.

"I wind, I wind," she panted. "My true love to find."

Thunder grumbled high above.

The yarn veered suddenly and hung, shimmering, over the river. Beneath it a series of large river stones led to the opposite bank, where a half-fallen pine tree concealed a yawning hole in the side of the mountain.

Not a hole. A cave.

The silver thread shone at its entrance, then disappeared into sudden darkness.

Greta, standing on the river's edge, went very still. She knew this place. Had been here before, with Christoph. And Mathias was close by. There was no need to be afraid. Even so, dread was stealing around her, an icy mantle. She could not go into that cave; she could not. Why would Mathias have done so?

*Because the bear has killed him and—*

No. No. Christoph had been wrong, that was all. This was not the bear's cave after all. And Mathias no doubt had a perfectly good reason for entering it.

A perfectly good reason.

She forced herself to cross the river, skirts lifted away from the dark water frothing around the stepping stones, then paused on the bank, the ball of yarn clutched tight.

"I wind," she whispered. "I wind. My true love to find."

The cave smelled of damp earth and wet stone and animal, and she soon regretted her decision to leave the lantern behind. She pushed on, deep into the suffocating gloom, until she glimpsed light ahead—sweet blessed light—and heard the heartening snap of burning wood. She quickened her steps. The passageway soon opened out into a wide, stone chamber. A fire burned cheerfully at its center, blankets spread beside it. There was a small, scuffed cook pot. Two battered cups, and a hunting horn.

Mathias's things.

*I wind, I wind, my true love to find.*

Greta edged farther into the cave, her feet scuffing the dry, sandy floor. The yarn was harder to see now, but it hardly mattered: Mathias's cloak was before her, hanging neatly on an outcropping of rock. Below it, his bow and sword leaned against the cave's smooth wall.

Against the cave's smooth wall, which bore the unmistakable mark of animal claws, gouging long and deep into the stone. She caught up a tuft of coarse, black fur. This *was* the bear's lair, then. But why were Mathias's belongings there, too? How could a man and a bear inhabit the same space?

Greta wound the last of the yarn and snapped it free of the cloak. Something glinted behind her, catching her eye. Moving toward it she saw a leather purse half open on the blankets, spilling forth a mound of coins that caught the firelight in dazzling silver. On one side, an eagle. On the other, a knight.

*I wind, I wind—*

A ribbon lay beside the purse. A ribbon the color of lavender with vines embroidered delicately along its length.

*—my true love to find.*

Greta's mother's ribbon did not look as though it had spent weeks in the woods. It was just as it had been when she had last seen it, the morning she had baked for Walpurgis and climbed the old beech tree for honey.

The morning she had first seen the black bear.

She rose unsteadily, the ribbon clutched in her hand. *It cannot be. It cannot.* And yet . . . she thought of Mathias's absences, his mistrust of people, his unwillingness to stay in the inn as other travelers did. Christoph, kneeling in the mud beside the bear's enormous prints.

*There are boot prints, too.*

After the gathering—when that woman had been in Greta's house—he had been utterly frightening in a way that was somehow *more* than a man should be. His voice had changed. His eyes, too.

*He is not like other men.*

Mathias did not move through the forest as others did. He was silent, sure-footed. He had found Jacob's body in the woods. When Greta had warned him of the bear before he left for the hunt, he had smiled grimly.

*Do not fear for me. I can take care of myself.*

The bear had licked honey from Greta's fingers that day beneath the beech tree. And just last night, Mathias had—

*No. It cannot be true. It cannot.*

She reeled away, gasping, hot and cold at once. Took it all in once more: the cloak, the bow, the sword. The marks in the stone. The clump of black fur. The cook pot, the hunting horn. The blankets, and the fire. And then, at the height of Greta's distress, when her over-wrought mind was struggling, and failing, to accept what her eyes and heart were telling her, she looked down and found proof.

It came in the form of a letter. Folded tight and half hidden by that fall of silver coin, by the worn leather of Mathias's purse. The paper whispered between Greta's fingers as she opened it. As she took in the words, carefully penned in a hand both ordered and beautiful, captured forever in faded ink.

*To my husband*, it said.

> *I write these words to you so that, wherever you might be, you will know that I am waiting for you. I pray this knowledge brings you comfort.*
>
> *I pray, too, that your journey is swift and that you remain safe. Most of all, I pray that you will find what you seek—an answer to the affliction that has stolen so evilly our family's happiness.*
>
> *Each morning after my prayers I look to the mountains and wonder where you might be. I beg you to remember me fondly, and our son, too. Know that I will keep him safe and teach him well until you can return to us.*
>
> > *From your own,*
> > *Helena.*

Helena. The black ink blurred as tears welled in Greta's eyes, hot and painful. She had not taken a breath for hours, it seemed; her body had frozen, tight with shock. She forced herself to take one and managed nothing more than a shallow, shuddering sigh. The cave seemed too small, too close.

*I pray that you will find what you seek.*

*The affliction that has stolen so evilly our family's happiness.*

*I am waiting for you.*

She looked again at the letter, at the details: a tear at the edge of the page, a smudge that could, perhaps, have been one of Helena's tears. Greta's own writing was rough and untidy. She had learned only what was necessary from Father Markus, crammed into the little church school with the other village children. She would never be able to master the graceful, looping swirl of Mathias's wife's well-formed letters.

Mathias's wife.

His wife, who was waiting for him back in Tyrol. Who was praying, perhaps even now, for her husband to find a cure to the affliction plaguing him and return to her.

Greta was still standing there when Mathias came into the cave, his sleeves rolled up, his arms loaded with firewood. She flinched and then—on guilty instinct—whipped the letter behind her back.

He went very still when he saw her, his face half puzzled, half wary. It was an expression that would have been laughable had things been different.

"Greta . . . ?"

"This is my ribbon," she told him, holding it up. Blood thudded dully in her ears; her voice sounded like it belonged to someone else. "I lost it when I went for honey. When I ran from . . ." *You.* She swallowed. "When I ran from the bear. Why do you have it?"

Thunder knocked against the mountains.

"I wanted to keep it safe for you." He lowered the firewood, straightened slowly as though she were a deer, easily startled.

"How did you know it was mine?"

More thunder, answering.

"That day at the falls," Greta said. "When you found my stays. It wasn't the first time we met, was it?"

He bowed his head, mouth tight. "Greta . . ."

"You're the bear." Her voice trembled. "It's you."

He took a step toward her.

"Don't! Don't come any closer!"

Mathias showed her his palms. "You know I would never hurt you."

"Do I?"

"I never wanted to keep this from you. . . ."

"But you did!" Her voice crashed against stone. "You did! I *knew* there was something wrong. I asked you—and you lied to me!"

"I *never* lied to you."

She burrowed through the words that had passed between them. He *did* move from place to place. He *did* prefer to sleep outdoors. There likely *was* cutting work available near Schiltach. He *hadn't* lost any coins of late. There *was* a cutter's hut near the falls. When he said he could take care of himself, he had meant it: the bear *was* no threat to him. He had been evasive. Brief. He had played with words, spinning them like a jongleur at a fair. But he had never lied.

"You should have told me you were like Rob and the others that night at the Sturmfels." When they had shared supper, and spoken of fire and stars, and she had been so happy in her foolishness.

"That *would* have been a lie. I am not like them."

"But you—you *change*. You become an animal, like they do."

"Yes. *Yes,* but it is not the same. Rob and his men choose when they will change. They were born with their gift. Mine is a curse, Greta. *I* am cursed."

*The terrible affliction . . .*

"It takes all my strength to overpower it," Mathias said. "To regain my body, my voice, my mind. Mira thinks—"

The name was like a punch to Greta's belly. "*Mira* knows?"

He winced.

"Mira knows," she said, slowly. "And Rob, too." Had he wanted to tell her at the betrothal? Or had he, like Mathias, chosen to deceive her? Greta's anger flowered and grew, entwining its limbs about hers until there was no telling where she began and it ended.

"Oh, Mathias. You must think me a worthy fool." She laughed, too loud, the sound off-kilter in the cave's closeness. "For all I know it *was* you who killed Jacob."

"No," he said fervently. "Never think that."

"Why? Don't bears kill people?" Some distant, reasonable part of Greta knew that was unfair. The bear had saved her, after all. He had fought the wolves to protect her. He had—

Lied. He had lied, and he had kept secrets from her. Over and over again.

"You should have told me, Mathias. You knew how angry, how *hurt* I was when I discovered that Rob had kept the truth from me."

"I know."

"And yet you did not think to tell me?"

"Of course I thought of it!" he snapped. "Of course! I have thought of it every moment we've been together."

"And were you thinking of your wife, then, too?" Greta held up the letter. "Were you thinking of *Helena*?"

He edged closer, hands raised again. "Greta. Please listen to me. It's not what you think. My wife—"

"So it's true, then? You have a wife—and a son—waiting for you somewhere?"

"Please, *please* listen—"

"I asked you about your family, Mathias. No home, no family, you told me. And fool that I was, I believed you. Stars above, I even *pitied* you. Perhaps that's what you wanted. Perhaps that's what you planned all along!"

Some men were skilled at turning women's heads. They did it the way a tanner works a skin or a smith a piece of iron. Greta had seen her brother do it many times. Perhaps, for Mathias, what had occurred in the storehouse was commonplace? Perhaps he kissed women, held them close, made them breathless with honeyed words at every village he passed.

"Greta. For God's sake, listen to me." He stepped forward, took hold of her arms. "I wanted to tell you the truth. *All* of it, I swear. But please, put yourself in my position for just a moment. Try to see how difficult it was. How could I tell you?"

"How could you not?" Blossom after blossom of rage. "I shared my heart with you. I told you things—things I have never told anyone. I trusted you—"

"You can trust me, still!"

"How can I trust you now?" she cried, thrusting the letter against his chest. "I can hardly stand to look at you!"

*Wait here,* Peter had said in the forest. *Wait here with Hans. I will return for you both, I promise.* His last words, before he had abandoned his children. His last words, a lie. Hans, in his turn, had deceived Greta, over and over again. Rob had kept the truth from her for years. The three men she loved most, had trusted most, had betrayed her. Now, Mathias was doing the same. And she could not help but hate him for it.

"This," she said, snatching up the ribbon, "belongs to me. Why did you keep it?"

"Because it belongs to you," he said, hollow.

"And why couldn't you tell me the truth?"

They were circling. Coming back, always, to this.

"Because I feared that I would lose you."

"Well in that, at least, you judged rightly." Greta balled the ribbon in her fist and stalked across the cave.

"Don't go," he said, catching her. "Not like this. Give me tonight and I will tell you everything. I will make this right."

She pushed past him. "A thousand nights would not be enough for that."

"At least let me walk with you. It's not safe out there."

She looked back and knew by his face that the bitterness of her loss was written clear upon her own.

"I don't care."

The forest shivered with the first fat drops of rain as Greta crushed through it, heedless of distance or direction. Above her thunder tore at the starless sky. The wind rose. She knew she should seek shelter. But to stop would mean stillness, and to be still would be to face the aching in her heart.

She stumbled on.

The rain came harder, the thunder too, grinding in her ears. She was soon soaked through. The wind buffeted the forest, snagging in her hair and her skirts, whipping at her cruelly. Shelter. She needed shelter.

Lightning ripped the sky, illuminating the trunk of an enormous elder tree. Rough steps in the darkness, the rain in her face, feet slipping. Another flash of light. Her splayed hands, corpse-white against fissured bark.

"Elder Mother, give me of thy shelter. . . ."

She staggered around the tree—more lightning, beating at her bones—until her hands found sudden emptiness: a generous hollow in the tree's side, earthy and dry. She tucked herself inside, shivering. The rain slowed to a quiet pattering, then stopped altogether.

Silence. Stillness. Pain.

Greta wrapped her arms around her knees and lay down, cradling her wounded heart against the earth. No, not earth: pine needles. And she was not alone. A small, thin body was pressed against hers, sharing in her loss.

"He will come back for us," Hans whispered through tears and time. "He will."

They had been lost in the forest for three nights. In the beginning, Hans had kept his terror at bay, staunchly refusing to believe that Peter would not return for them. "It will take Papa some time to find us again," he said bravely as they walked and walked, and the forest loomed and loomed. "We must be patient and brave. God will protect us until we are home again, Greta. We must keep faith." Greta followed her brother, wondering when God would appear. She hoped he would bring bread and flädlessuppe.

And later, "Papa is an excellent tracker. It will not take him long now."

But there, on the third night in the dark, the last of Hans's hope faded.

"He is gone," he whimpered, over and over again. "He isn't coming back. We are all alone."

*He is gone.*

The knowledge was a bitter wound in Greta's heart.

*He isn't coming back.*

The old loss melded with the new. Greta did not hear the storm revive, nor feel the harsh sweep of rain against the tree. Sorrow had taken root inside her, a living thing, bleakly thriving, strangling the fragile remnants of love.

*He is gone, gone.*

*And I am all alone.*

# 18

## My True Love to Find

*Liliane studied the spells and incantations in her mother's book with religious fervor. When her father acquired a magician to entertain his new bride, Liliane watched his every move with a deep and abiding fascination.*

Greta woke to woody darkness. She had fallen asleep, though it could not have been for long; her clothes were still wet, her skin cold. Outside, the storm had passed. The sliver of sky visible through the tree's narrow opening revealed the moon sailing over tattered clouds.

The moon and a small, silvery fox.

A small, silvery fox that unfolded itself and became Mira.

"This is pleasant," the greenwitch observed cheerily. She wafted a hand and warm, soft light filled the hollow. "No sense in staying indoors when there's a storm howling, I always say. May I join you?"

"How did you find me?" Greta shuffled aside so Mira could settle herself beside her.

"The trees whispered to me tonight." Rain and magic lingered in Mira's hair. "They spoke of sorrow and a cave dark with secrets."

Greta nodded miserably.

"You found out, then."

"I . . ." Greta hesitated, unwilling to admit that she had used tattermagic to discover Mathias's secret. "I followed him," she said at last. "We quarreled."

Mira's face was serene. "I'm sorry to hear that." She gazed thoughtfully about. "You know, the trees in this forest are very old. They have watched you walk beneath them and rest within their branches since you were a little girl." Framed by folds of ancient bark, illuminated by the warmth she had created, Mira seemed more sylvan than flesh and bone. "They were with you when you were lost, and when you were found again."

"Lost, and found again," echoed another voice, low and soft as creaking timber in a summer breeze.

"The trees knew your father," Mira said. "Your mother, too. They grieved for her."

"We grieved . . ."

"Grieved . . ."

Another voice, higher, sweeter. And another, different again, like the low, watery *criddup* of a frog. The hollow was suddenly alive with tiny fey creatures, afoot and in the air. Luminous eyes peeked at Greta. Tiny fingers plucked at her hair.

"And now you are lost again," Mira said. "Just as you were when you were a child."

Hans, small and shivering at her back. *We are lost, and will die from cold and hunger soon enough.*

"I'm not lost," Greta said, watching a delicate winged creature flutter above her open hand. "I know where I am."

"But do you know *who* you are? Tell me, why did you quarrel with Mathias?"

The creature lifted, disappearing into the dim heights of the elder's trunk. "Because . . . because he lied to me."

"Did he?"

"Well . . . he was untruthful."

"Hmm. There's a difference, is there not?"

Greta frowned. "What are you saying?"

"I'm saying there is a difference, that's all," Mira said calmly. "Why, I could be angry at you right now, if I wanted. You've certainly given me cause. When I asked how you found out about Mathias, you told me you followed him. That was truth. But you also used tattermagic to do it. Didn't you?"

Greta went cold. "Mira . . ."

"You did not *lie* to me, it's true," Mira said. "And yet you were dishonest. There is, I would say, a difference."

Outside, a smattering of drops as the wind half-heartedly shook the elder, then stilled.

"So tell me," Mira said. "Why were you dishonest with me?"

"Because . . ." Greta shrugged. "Because I did not want you to be angry or disappointed."

"And?"

"Because I was confused. And . . . ashamed, I suppose."

"And?"

"Because I did not want to lose you."

She froze. Mathias's words, in her own mouth.

"I see. Let us talk for a moment of tattermagic," Mira said, as calm as ever. "You've used it twice that I can recall. Once at your brother's betrothal—Rob told me it was *quite* the celebration—and once more tonight. Tell me, how did it go?"

"Badly," Greta said ruefully. "Both times I used it awful things happened." She was still unable to banish the image of Herr Hueber, whining piteously in a puddle of his own filth, from her mind. And Mathias's face as she left the cave . . .

"How did it *feel?*"

"At the time? It felt wonderful. As though I could rule all of Württemberg. But afterward . . ."

"I warned you," Mira said gently. "Tattermagic rends and destroys. It is an imbalance in the flow of things, as all evil is. What *possessed* you to use it?"

"I suppose it was the book," Greta said with a sigh.

"The book?"

"The book that belonged to the woman—to the witch—who stole Hans and me, when we were children. I didn't tell you before, Mira, but . . . I kept it. It helps me bake. It's been helping me since I was a girl. For years I have heard it whispering in my mind, but its voice has grown stronger of late. I can hear it as plain as I hear you. What if . . . what if you were wrong about me? What if I'm *not* a greenwitch?"

*You pushed that old woman into an oven full of fire and burnt her up.*

*Red, the Devil's color.*

*Such wickedness always lingers.*

"Surely you must know?" Greta pressed. "Surely the trees told you? That old woman—I killed her, Mira. I—I burned her alive. What kind of child does that?" These were old thoughts, buried so deep it hurt to draw them into the light. "What kind of child *kills someone?*"

Mira's sigh was the breath of long-ago forests. "You didn't kill anyone, Greta."

"Listen, listen," came a tiny, fae voice. "She does not listen."

"The trees listen to you," Mira said. "They hear you speak. And yet when they answer you do not listen."

"She does not listen," whispered a wood-voice. "She does not see. . . ."

"Time to see," whispered another.

"See."

"Time to see."

*Is it true? Did you really kill her?*

"Time to remember," said Mira.

"Remember . . ."

"See."

Lena's hand, her voice in the dream-dark.

*See.*

*When four weeks had passed the witch tested Hans's finger and screeched with rage.*

*"You are as thin as when you first came to me! How can it be so? Hasn't your sister been feeding you? Have you not enjoyed her beautiful baking?"*

*She stomped around the workbench, muttering. "It will not do. It will not. I found two. One girl, one boy. Two. By right they should both be mine! Mine! And all I get is one skinny, wretched boy. Made an agreement, though, we did. Bitter and binding."* She gripped Greta's arm, her reddish eyes aflame. *"We must bake more, that's all. We must fatten him up. Heat the oven!"*

Greta obeyed. When the oven was good and hot she leaned down for a bag of flour to make the dough. The mouse, sleeping in her apron pocket, slipped out.

*"Agh!"* the witch shrieked. *"Vermin!"* And she plucked the mouse up and tossed it into the flames.

*"No!"* Greta screamed. Outside a wind blew and the fire in the oven leapt and sparked. Greta's rage, boundless and bountiful, matched it.

*"What are you doing?"* the witch cried. *"Stop it! Stop it, I say!"* She ran toward Greta, her bony hands outstretched, but Greta dropped to the earthen floor before the witch could strike her. She was frightened, so frightened, but she could feel the earth's great, strong heart beating against her cheek. Her mother's voice came to her through the rising wind.

You need never be afraid while the forest is near. It will protect you. Just say these words . . .

*"Leaf that's green,"* Greta whispered. *"Earth and air . . ."*

The witch seized her by the hair and dragged her to her feet.

*"Protect me, forest fair."*

The windows shattered as long leafy arms—birch, pine and elder— spilled into the little house. Ivy and bramble followed, snaking around the witch, binding her hands and feet and mouth.

Outside, the trees ripped up their roots. Sunlight flooded into the dank kitchen as oak and white firs bent like old warriors, their woody hands ripping and rending. Birds flew through the ruined roof, pecking at the witch. She screamed through her gag of leaves.

An oak ripped apart Hans's cage. He crawled out and ran desperately for the door, screaming for Greta to follow. She hesitated. The witch's book lay on the bench. Deep, deep in her mind she thought she could hear it screaming, too.

*"Please, dearie, please! Take me with you!"*

She pushed through the tangle and scooped it up, then scrambled from the house, listing now like a broken boat on a wild green river. The last thing Greta saw before she ran after Hans was the oak's enormous roots

*bursting through the floor. The last thing she heard was the witch's chok-*
*ing screams as the roots drew her, struggling and fighting, beneath the*
*earth.*

"Hans was wrong," Greta whispered. "I didn't push her."

It had been a tale, only. Memories scrambled by a little boy's terrified mind: An oven. A tiny body. Flame. Hans had clasped tightly
to the only parts of that day that made any sense.

She had never known which of the villagers had wrung the tale
out of her brother. Father Markus, with the power of God and truth
behind him? Or the baker's wife, sweetening him with sugar cakes?
Whoever it was, they had been richly rewarded with a story of fire
and death. And Lindenfeld had loved it.

"Such wickedness always lingers," she murmured.

"Yet the truth remains." Mira leaned forward. "Greta, you didn't
willingly kill anyone. What you *did* was what any greenwitch would
have done in your place: you called upon the forest to protect you.
You saved not only yourself, but your brother, too. And you were
only seven years old—a child! You didn't even know what greenstrength was." She squeezed Greta's hand. "If that doesn't make you
a greenwitch, then I don't know what does."

"Greenwitch," came a little sylvan voice.

"Wild-wife."

"Moss maid . . ."

"Storm hag."

"Your mother gave you a gift," Mira said. "A precious gift. But you
must *want* to use it. I cannot force you. I cannot make the choice for
you. And there *is* a choice before you, make no mistake. The temptation to use magic for our own desires, for revenge or greed, is always
there. It never goes away. But know that a tatterwitch hurts herself
each and every time she casts. To use another's—or one's own—pain
takes a fearful toll. A few drops of blood might suffice for a time, but
soon she finds that she needs more blood, more pain, until . . ." Mira
looked out at the night. "Until it is no longer safe for anyone."

"I feel as though there is a great darkness coming for me," Greta whispered. "I have felt it for weeks. There have been times I was certain someone was watching me. And I have had terrifying dreams. . . . I saw my mother in the woods. I feel as though she was trying to warn me."

"You need never be afraid while the forest is near," Mira said. "It will protect you. It did so once long ago. It will do so again. You need only ask."

The rain returned, tapping on the forest floor, pattering against the elder's leaves. Despite herself Greta looked at the opening in the tree, at the forest beyond it, where the cave lay.

"I always felt for the man-bear," Mira remarked. "Of all the lost souls who wander the forest, I pity him the most."

"If you must pity someone, pity his wife."

"Wife?" Mira blinked. "You are certain?"

"I found a letter."

"A letter is not a wife," Mira said. "Did he tell you himself he was married? That he loved another?"

"I . . . No."

"I have known Mathias for many years," Mira said thoughtfully. "The trees have known him, too. I never heard them whisper of a wife. Loss, sadness and revenge, yes. But not love."

Despite her wounded heart, her damaged pride, Greta was curious. "Mathias said he was not born to this life like Rob and the wolves. He said he had no choice."

"That is true. The bear's path has ever been a hard one. He walks it alone: caught between two worlds, belonging to neither. It is a tattercurse, of course. No greenwitch would subvert the grace of nature—man or bear—like that."

Shame nibbled at Greta.

*Who are you?* she had asked Mathias at the Sturmfels. *Where have you come from?* Had he wanted to tell her the truth, then? And had she stamped his bravery out like a cinder beneath her boot? Just moments before she had railed against Rob and his dishonesty. Unforgivable, she had called it. How righteous she had been. And tonight, in the cave, Mathias had tried to explain Helena's letter. He had begged her to listen. And she, too hurt, too proud, had refused.

Outside, the rain quickened.

And what of her own deception? Had she not lied to him, too? She had manipulated him, tied a spell to his cloak and used tatter-magic to hunt him down. She had forced his secrets from him, then refused to listen. She had punished him for his differences, even though he had always accepted hers. He had never judged her. Not once.

No wonder he had hidden the truth.

"I'm a fool." She wrapped her arms miserably about her knees, rested her cheek against her damp skirts. "I've been wrong about so many things. And I've hurt Mathias."

"There is time, yet, to go to him."

"You don't understand. I said things. Horrible things."

"Who does not when they are heartsick and angry?"

Greta raised her head. Mira was tranquil as ever, gold-brown eyes warm, yet Greta sensed, deep beneath the surface, the sorrow of a once-wounded heart.

"Rob hurt you," she said. "When he . . . when he met Christoph's mother." Never wife, never lover, Mira had told her of the witch and her wolves. But she had seen the way Rob and Mira looked at each other. And she had not forgotten the tale of Christoph's birth, and the years that followed it. Christoph had been three years old when Rob brought him back to Lindenfeld—the summer of Peter and Leisa's wedding, and Hans and Greta's abandonment. That meant that Rob had been with Christoph's mother when he was still part of the pack.

"Rob never betrayed me," Mira said firmly. "We made no prom-ises; he owed me nothing. He went with Christoph's mother that midsummer because *I* told him to. I had hoped it might free him. Free us *both*." She looked down at her hands, clasped smooth against her skirts. "It is cruel indeed to be bound to someone who can never be yours."

Greta nodded. "Perhaps this"—she gestured at the tree, at Mira, at the storm beyond—"was all for the best. I never expected to be loved. Maybe I was stronger—safer—when I was alone."

"Love is a gift," Mira said. "There is no weakness in relying on someone, when they are the *right* someone. Indeed, there is only strength."

Greta looked out into the night. There was every chance Mathias had changed his shape and taken to the woods, whipped on by her final, cruel words. "He may be gone."

"Oh, he is still there." Mira wafted one hand and the winged wood spirits gathered in a glowing cloud, brighter than any lantern. "Forgiveness, too, is a gift. You need only ask."

Mira had been right: Mathias was hunched by the fire when Greta entered the cave. His clothes were wet, his black hair tangled and dripping as though he, too, had been out in the storm. Blood shone through the fresh tear in his shirt.

"I came back," Greta said needlessly. The slow drip of water from her skirts, the crackle of burning wood, seemed very loud. "I was wrong, Mathias."

He got to his feet. "You were right. About everything."

"No. I was blind. Foolish. I see that now." She moved closer, but he drew away.

"I will never forget that first day beneath the beech tree," he said. "Your hair was like bronze in the sun and there was magic all around you. I smelled it, stronger than the spices, sweeter than the honey on your skin. The air was rife with it. I thought that you might see me—*see* me, for what I truly am—but you did not."

Greta's throat tightened with tears of shame and regret. She was too late. He would not forgive her. "Mathias . . ."

"And then I met you properly. Talked to you. You spoke of the bear, of *me,* with such compassion. You feared the bear and yet you tried to protect it. I had never seen such kindness.

"God help me, I hoped. I hoped, even as I knew I could offer you nothing." He raised a hand, roughly taking in the cave, his possessions. "I tried to keep my feelings for you at bay—I knew it was wrong. I knew I could never be a husband to you, that I could never give you what you deserve. But I belonged to you the moment I met you, Greta. I was bewitched and unmade. I was yours entirely."

Greta stared at him. His speech had torn open her heart and soul, and joy and pain were racking them both in equal measure.

"It was like that for me, too," she said. "How could you not see? How could you not think to trust me—to tell me the truth?"

"I wanted to. I meant to, after I found Jacob's body. I figured you might be more . . . forgiving if I told you I used the bear's senses to find him." Mathias pushed his hair back from his face, paced the sandy floor. "But then you held my hand. In the middle of that crowded marketplace you held my hand and you didn't let go, even when all those faces turned upon us. It was nothing to you, I realize that, but to me . . . It had been so long since another person had touched me. Had trusted me enough to put their hand in mine . . ." He went still, looked across the cave at her. "I could not tell you, after that. Could not bear the thought of you running from me or looking at me with fear. I found I could not go back to how my life had been before that day. I could not undo what we had begun."

He moved again, his hand running down the claw marks razing the wall.

"And then at the Sturmfels, after you learned that Rob had kept his past from you . . . you were so bitter. I was torn. How could I tell you when you were so angry with Rob, determined to never forgive him?"

"I should not have said those things," Greta said quickly. "I did not understand—"

"How could I expect you to love me after that? What right had I to even ask it?" He turned away from her, one shoulder hard against the rough stone as though he would reshape himself upon its edges. "How could I have thought to keep you when I am cursed and . . . broken?"

"You are not broken." Slowly, softly, she took one step, then another, closing the space between them.

"Stolen moments," Mathias said. "That is all I could give you. A life of waiting and uncertainty. Never knowing where your husband is, if he has been shot dead or trapped. Never knowing when he might tire or anger, and turn into a beast." He gave a bitter laugh. "How can such a life be enough? It is not worth the mud on your hem."

At last Greta reached him. She placed her palms and then her cheek upon his back, lightly, as one would gentle a wild creature. His shirt was cool and damp against her skin.

"It is enough," she said.

"You deserve more."

"I do not want more. If it be stolen moments or a life without you, I will choose to steal, Mathias, and gladly."

Slowly, slowly, the tension in his back eased. She slipped beneath his arm and faced him. His eyes were deepest green, hope and uncertainty playing across their depths.

"It is enough." She pressed herself to him, body and soul, calling for him to meet her, believe her. At last he answered. His lips tasted of tears—hers or his, she couldn't say. It soon ceased to matter, for the kisses changed, became something more. She gathered his shirt with clumsy fingers and drew it over his head—he helped her, reaching up—and she felt the cool, bare expanse of him. He kissed her again, his tongue warm and insistent, his hands catching in the wet lengths of her hair. Greta shivered with cold and desire. He unlaced her bodice while she untied her skirts, then peeled away her wet shift. Lifted her against him and carried her to the fire.

Greta thought of all the times she had longed to know his mind. She knew it now, as she knew his body—the long, burnished lengths of it, hard where she was soft. Mathias's mouth moved over her, returning again for kisses that stole away breath and reason. Even so, she knew a moment of fear when he finally stretched himself over her.

"I would never hurt you," he murmured, dark hair falling across his face. "But I will stop if you want me to."

She shook her head. "Don't stop."

He smiled. Leaned down and kissed her again until she felt him at the softest part of her. For a moment, before he began to move, before the long, slow rhythm of him hastened them both to a place she had scarce imagined, Mathias went very still. He whispered her name, and Greta found that she knew him at last, knew his mind and his body and his heart, and it was everything.

# 19

## Snow White, Blood Red

*Unknown to all, the magician was a tattermage of real, and not inconsiderable, power. Here, then, was a meeting of true and darkling minds. Under his discreet tutelage Liliane was soon casting with alarming skill.*

"Father Markus was right," Greta murmured sleepily. Mathias lay beneath her, one arm holding her against him. "He said the bear would ensnare me and take me to a cave where he would perform . . . what was it?"

Mathias shook with mirth. "'All manner of gross and unholy atrocities' were his exact words, I think."

Greta laughed so hard the blanket slipped off her bare shoulder. He drew it back up, settled it over her. "You poor innocent. You did not guard your soul well enough, did you?"

"There was no hope of that. When first we met I thought you were a gift from the forest, a man wrought of wood and moss and earth."

"Not fur and teeth and claws?"

"No. Not that." She ran her hand over his chest, trying to imagine the smooth skin ripping apart, changing. "The forest gave you to me, Mathias. But I fear she hopes always to take you away again, too."

"I can control it, for the most part." His hand ran up and down her bare back, traced gentle rivers in her hair. "But if I am tired, or angry, or wounded it becomes . . . difficult. Even now, after so many years of practice."

"So *many* years?" Greta nestled closer. "The curse has swayed your view of time, Mathias. You are not so much older than I."

The fingers in her hair stilled. "It may look that way, Greta, but it is not so."

She raised herself up on one elbow, looking at him. He was strong and lean, smooth-browed and straight-jawed, his hair rich and dark against the blankets. "How old are you, then?"

He watched her observing him. "I was born two hundred and four years ago. But I have not aged since the day the curse was uttered. I was thirty, then. Each time I come back to myself I find I am exactly as I was the day it happened."

Greta touched his ribs. "That cut . . ."

"Happened moments before."

*Moments before.* One hundred and seventy-four years ago. Greta tried to comprehend such age, such *time*.

"And so your wife," she said. "Your family . . ."

"Have all been dead for more than a century, yes." He said it plainly, without remorse, and yet she sensed a deep and aching loneliness. Everyone he had known, everyone he had loved, had died long ago.

"But the letter . . ." Greta said, carefully. "Helena . . ."

The sensible part of her mind reminded her that well over a hundred years had passed since Mathias had last seen his wife. Helena was long dead, a distant memory. The less reasonable part of her, however, teemed with jealousy. He had loved another before her. Had lain with her like this. Had been her husband and given her a child. "She said that you were going away—that you were going to find a cure to the 'affliction' that had caused you so much pain. She was talking about your curse, wasn't she?"

"No," Mathias said. "No, she was speaking of something else. But I can see how you would have thought that." He looked up at her, frowning. "Greta, there is something else about my marriage you should probably know."

*What more could there possibly be?*

"I did not marry my wife for love."

Greta frowned. "You didn't?"

"No. My father chose my bride, a girl I had never met, because she brought allies and wealth to my family. He was brother to a duke, you see. My mother was the archduke's cousin. She was . . . she was a Habsburg, Greta."

*Habsburg.* The name tolled like a great, rich bell. The House of Habsburg was the most powerful in the Empire. Its sons were kings in their own right, and had served as Holy Roman Emperors for more than two hundred years, ruling a domain that encompassed not only Württemberg, but the Low Countries in the north, the Franche-Comté to the west, Silesia in the east, and Styria to the south.

"I did not love Helena," Mathias was saying. "And I am ashamed to admit I was not a good husband to her."

Greta barely heard him. She was trying to see him as he had been: part of the most powerful family in Europe, sleek and strong and shining like the knight on the back of one of his Tyroler coins. "You're a Habsburg."

"Of some distance."

"You are the emperor's kin."

"A cousin of his forefather's only," he said patiently, "and of a line two hundred years old."

*And I am the daughter of a cutter.* She sat up and covered herself, ashamed suddenly of her nakedness, wishing that his only secret had been that he was cursed. "But you . . . you're *noble.*"

He drew her, gently but firmly, back down against him. "Believe me, I did not behave nobly. I hunted, I drank, I whored. When my father called for it I rode to war and fought for the duke, my mother's cousin. But I did not truly care. Family, duty, honor—those things bored me beyond measure. I was the second son, which meant that, most of the time, I could do as I pleased. I lived for the hunt, be it a beast for my table or a woman for my bed. I had everything a man could wish for: a wife, a son, wealth and a powerful family. I wanted none of it." He smiled wryly. "And that is what I got."

Greta touched his face. He was scarred and stubbled, lean and strong from years spent afoot—nothing like the proud horseman etched upon the silver coins.

"Who did this to you, Mathias?"

He sighed and slid from beneath the blankets. "I don't know what she is," he began, balancing more wood on the fire. "Not truly. She has many names. Some call her Belladonna, or Nightshade, for her beauty and her poison. Others call her Bittersweet or the Heartless One. There are tales—very old tales. Some tell of a witch named Liliane who feasts upon flesh and poisons her victims, holding them helpless in her sway. Others say she was the youngest daughter of a Burgundian viscount, and that a huntsman made her what she is. Sick with desire, he poisoned her with nightshade and cut out her heart."

The fire danced, licking at Mathias's fingers. "Her skin is cold as ice and white as snow. Her hair is black, her lips red as blood. She is ancient—hundreds of years old. And yet, she never ages. Her beauty is her weapon and she uses it to lure her prey. The fragile and the innocent. Men who are lost or weak with sorrow." He paused. "Men like Jacob."

Jacob's face, cracking with hurt and confusion in the light of the Walpurgis fire.

"Are you saying this woman—Liliane—killed Jacob?"

"I am." He slipped beneath the blanket once more. "The cutters and the Bavarian soldiers, too. And that was only the beginning. The people here have no notion of the danger they are in. They do not understand what rules over them from the Hornberg."

Greta stared at him, appalled. "But . . . you cannot mean the *baroness?*"

"The one you know as Elisabeth has gone by many names. Liliane was first. She was Isabelle in Normandy and Elisabetta in Venice. In Flanders she was Lijsbeth, in England, Elizabeth. She was Erzsebet in Hungaria, where she was almost undone by her crimes. For centuries she has moved from place to place, always young, ever fair. The dwarf, Fizcko, travels with her. He is her closest advisor and a powerful mage in his own right. I have hunted them both for a hundred and seventy-four years. When I heard tell of Baron von

Hornberg's bride—black of hair, as fair as the moon—I knew at once that it was Liesbeth."

"Liesbeth?"

"That is what she called herself when I knew her."

"Did she curse you?"

"She could have, I've no doubt. But it was Fizcko who did the casting, on her order."

"Why?"

"To punish me. I would not bow to her whim, you see. It seems I have a stronger mind than most. Or a harder head." He smiled faintly. "Harder than my father's and my brother's, at least. I lost them both to her, as you lost Jacob."

"She traveled through Tyrol?"

"Worse. She married my father."

"My father was besotted with his bride," Mathias said. "Unfortunately, so was my older brother, Friedrich. I blamed Friedrich, at first—I did not yet understand the power Liesbeth had over him—and when I discovered he had lain with her, I beat him. Badly. Even *that* did not help. He was still under her spell when her gaze fell upon me."

He drew a weary hand across his eyes. "I was many things, Greta, and far from faultless—do not believe it of me—but I refused to betray my father. When he sickened, I was desperate to save him."

Mathias could not have known it was *Liesbeth* who was bleeding the strength from his father. She was poisoning him, as surely as the nightshade poisons its victims. The duke grew weak and ill. He endured waking dreams, in which he saw all manner of unspeakable things. Healers were summoned, each more despairing than the last. Finally, in desperation, Mathias decided to seek the Water of Life.

"Do you remember?" he asked Greta.

She nodded. How could she forget that evening atop the Sturmfels, with the moon bright on the distant Alpen, and Mathias's tale of the sacred water that could heal any sickness?

The duke's illness was the affliction Helena had written of, and the Water of Life the cure. Determined to find it and save his father, Mathias made his preparations, including sending his wife and son to his mother's family in Innsbruck. Men, women and children had been found dead in the woods, and he feared for their safety.

On the day he was to set out, he went to take his leave of his father. Liesbeth called him to her first and he obeyed, thinking, despite his dislike for her, to bid her farewell.

"I went to kiss her hand, but she pressed her body close to mine and caught my lips with hers. 'Forbidden fruit,' she whispered."

A knot of unease in Greta's belly.

"For a moment I was tempted—she was so lovely, Greta. But then I smelled the stench of death in her hair. *What are you?* I asked. Her face curdled and she ordered her guards to seize me."

Mathias had fought his way free. He knew every turn of his father's house, and his horse was waiting. He escaped into the mountains and for weeks searched the wildest reaches of Tyrol, to no avail. At last, fearing for his father, he returned. He found his sister first. Dead in the woods she had loved so well.

Liesbeth found him there, as he cradled his sister in his arms. He heard her voice, first. Singing to him softly.

*"Young man came from hunting faint and weary. What does ail my love, my dearie?"*

At first he thought she meant to comfort him. But comfort soon turned to seduction. Her lips, her hands, her body—she used them all against him. He would not be swayed, however, and Liesbeth fell into a fury. She thrashed and tore at him—here Mathias pointed to the ever-present wound beneath his ribs—as though the strength of ten men flowed through her. His father was already dead, she said, and his brother too. Everyone he knew believed that he, too, was dead, lost in the mountains. And all that had been the duke's now belonged to Liesbeth. *Kill me then,* Mathias had spat. *Why do you wait, if you want me dead so badly?* Liesbeth had smiled. *Why, what fun would there be in that?* She called for Fizcko and whispered to him, and they laughed together. Then Liesbeth held Mathias down while Fizcko did his dark work, turning him into a bear.

"Why a bear?" Greta asked.

"In my time, the hunting of a bear meant much in Tyrol. A boy was not considered a man until he took down his first. I was nine when I took mine. I was blessed with considerable skill in such things: tracking, hunting, killing. Indeed, I was renowned for it." His voice hardened. "It was the perfect punishment. The brave and fearless hunter became the hunted. And the pain was . . . formidable. As though my body was tearing apart, my flesh ripping away from my bones."

Greta held him close, longing to protect that long-ago Mathias.

"Liesbeth roused a hunt, promising to marry the man who brought her the black bear's head. Of course, a great gathering of hunters and their dogs was soon upon me. Somehow I escaped. By the time I realized I could control the curse and walk again as a man, Liesbeth had left Tyrol. I swore to find her. And so it has been through all the years since."

"A bear must die, like any creature," Greta murmured. "Why have you lived so long?"

"Fizcko's magic? Liesbeth's spite? She wanted the bear's head; maybe I am still alive because no one ever managed to deliver it to her."

Greta shuddered. "I cannot think of that."

"I have. Often." He stroked her hair absently. "There were times I even considered handing *myself* over to her."

She raised her head, glared at him. "How could you even *say* such a thing?"

"Easily. I have roamed for so long, living apart from the world of men. There were times when my loneliness became too much." He pushed her hair back from face. "I had filled my heart with vengeance and it was vengeance that kept me alive. *Fiat iustitia, et*

*pereat mundus:* Let justice be done, though the world perish. They
are the Habsburg words, and, until now, they are all I have had to
hold to."

"Until now?"

"Now, I have you. And I find I have cause to hope again."

All thought of curses and coins and Habsburgs faded from Greta's
mind. She leaned down and kissed him.

"There must be a way to free you from this curse," Greta murmured,
much later. The fire was burning low and the storm had quickened
again, rain sheeting against the cave's entrance.

"I've been wondering when you would ask me that."

"There is a way, then?"

"Liesbeth was not the only thing I searched for, over the years.
I looked for answers, too. What little I learned came from witches,
though they were few and far between."

"You've met other witches?"

"Only three. Two of them sisters, burned for their ways not long
after I found them. The other lived so deep in the Alpen that she
had all but forgotten her own name. She had one foot firmly in the
forest realm, that one."

"What did they tell you?"

"Very little. The sisters were more interested in taking me to
their bed—as a bear—than in giving me answers."

"Oh." Greta flushed with confusion and embarrassment.

"You are right to blush." He chuckled. "And the other—well, she
said some interesting things, when at last she agreed to speak with
me. She told me of the different kinds of magic and that my curse
was wrought of the kind called tattermagic. She said that there is
only one way to break a tattercurse: kill the one who cast it."

"Fizcko."

"Fizcko."

A ripple of foreboding over Greta's bare skin. "Did the witch say
anything else?"

"No. I put aside my search for knowledge after that and focused instead on finding Liesbeth and Fizcko. A rare beauty and a tiny, bearded mage. I roamed closer to cities and towns and frequented taverns and marketplaces, hoping to hear of them."

"And did you?"

"Once. In Swabia. I found them, too. Unfortunately, Rob and his wolves, fleeing the defeat in Nördlingen, also came across them that day and decided to hunt them down."

Greta thought back to May Day, when Rob and Mathias had met beneath the linden. *Hunting,* they had said, when she had asked them how they knew each other.

"The wolves wanted to kill Liesbeth and Fizcko," Mathias said. "It was their right, I suppose—killing creatures like that was their purpose, their vow. The trouble was, *I* needed to be the one doing the killing. It got thorny. We ended up fighting each other instead of our real enemy. In the confusion, Liesbeth and Fizcko escaped, though he was badly wounded. He acquired that outlandish iron ball, after that. I suppose he thinks it will protect him."

"And now you are here."

"Now I am here. Hunting them both, as I have always done." He tucked a piece of hair behind her ear. "When I have not been with you, that is."

"Have you come close?"

"A few times. Fizcko rarely leaves the Hornberg, and when he does he is always well guarded. But Liesbeth—Elisabeth—likes to ride out and hunt. After all, she must keep up the pretense of being a nobleman's wife. I have caught her scent oftentimes in the forest. Near Hornberg and Lindenfeld, and the other villages too." He frowned. "Greta—"

"I know what you are going to say. She's been near me, too, hasn't she? She poisoned me, somehow, that day in the woods when we first met." The sickness, the burning in her throat, the waking dream of snow and blood. There had been a woman, too, watching her from between the trees. "It was as though I had eaten night-shade."

"I wonder . . ." Mathias mused. "My sister was often ill after my father married Elisabeth. She complained of feeling just as you did in the woods. I think she was more like you than I first realized. I think she may have been a witch, too."

"Greenwitches are connected to all living things," Greta said. "You said Elisabeth was poisoned with nightshade. Perhaps it lingers within her still. And we—your sister and I—are more sensitive to it?"

He nodded uneasily. "That would make sense."

"Elisabeth found me again when I searched for Jacob at the tree house. And last night, after the betrothal, she spoke to me. Forbidden fruit, she told you that day in Tyrol. Mathias, she said the same words to me."

"Did she say anything else?"

"Yes." The woolen blankets were thick and Mathias's body warmed her to the tips of her toes. Even so, there was ice in Greta's blood. "She said *soon*."

Greta woke in the arms of a sleeping bear. Its fur was warm against her back, its front legs wrapped around her. A hand's breadth from her face a set of enormous, curved claws stirred dreamfully.

The fear was sudden, all-consuming, yet she forced every part of herself to be still. Mathias was gone. The curse had stolen him away from her as he slept, binding him in claws of its own. What would happen should the bear wake? Would Mathias open his eyes, or a beast?

The passage leading from the cave was grey with early sunlight. She could hear, beneath the bear's heavy breathing, the distant tumble of water and the sweet trill of a bird. How many steps would it take to reach the river? Twenty? Thirty?

There was only one way to find out.

With agonizing slowness Greta slid out from between the bear's huge paws. Above her it dreamed on, its breath hot on her bare skin. Her heart beat so loud she was sure it would hear it.

*Do not think of it. Do not, do not—*

She was almost free. One twist, a slight wriggle, and she was crawling across the cave's sandy floor, reaching for her shift with one hand. She drew it over her head, shivering, then kept crawling, the shift catching at her knees.

*Keep going. Keep going.*

Movement from behind. A snuffle and a grunt, a heaving of bear-body. Greta reached the wall and turned, cowering, to see the bear pushing itself up on its front paws. Sleepily shaking its head. Sniffing and then stilling.

Dark eyes glinted in the gloom.

"Mathias?" Fear choked his name to a harsh whisper, but he heard it. She was certain. The bear lowered its head and groaned as though a great weight bore down on its shoulders, its heart, its gut. Its fur rippled, the muscles beneath tautening. Then it was staggering across the cave and down the narrow passageway to the river, compelled by some force it could not hope to control. Greta followed. She burst into sudden sunshine, threw an arm over her eyes. Blinked, and saw the bear, cowering at the river's edge, throwing the contents of its belly into the water. The bear . . . but at the same time *not* the bear. Change was coming, swift and relentless, a heaving and roiling of muscle and bone. Some part of Greta worried that Mathias might not want her there to see him sprawled in his own bile, half covered in fur. To hear the sharp, wet sounds of his bones breaking and remaking themselves anew. But she could not look away. Could not leave him to endure it alone.

And then, just as it seemed as though it would never end, it was over. Mathias lay at the water's edge, gasping. He was fully dressed, the hem of his hunting cloak dragging in the water, his sword jarring against the mossy rocks. His jerkin was open; fresh blood welled from the cut beneath his ribs, staining his shirt and the shallows both.

Greta ran to him, fell to her knees. "Is it—is it always like this?"

He nodded. Chest rising, falling.

She stretched out beside him, heedless of the mud and cold. "We have to free you from this."

He threw a heavy arm around her. "I was just . . ." Breath in, breath out. ". . . thinking the same."

Back in the cave, Greta watched Mathias gather his belongings.

"You mean to leave now?" she asked.

"There is no better time."

"Where are we going?"

"*I* am going hunting." He handed her a small loaf of bauernbrot. "And *you* are going back to the house."

"Back to the house?"

"Back to the house," he said firmly. "I lay awake for hours last night, Greta. *Soon*, Elisabeth said. I cannot rid it from my mind. At first I thought she was using you to get to me. To taunt me. But then I remembered the day we met, at the hive. I had been tracking her that day. I thought it mere coincidence that you were there too. When I followed her on May Day and came upon you both near the tree house, I still believed it was chance that had brought the three of us together. But now . . . Greta, I think Elisabeth was already watching you when I arrived in Lindenfeld. I think she was stalking you before you and I ever met. And I think she killed Jacob because he was close to you."

Greta wanted to disagree with him. The cold of dream-snow and three drops of blood on her sleeve—the way the baroness had watched her and Jacob, in the fields before Walpurgis—stopped her.

"But why?" she asked, reaching for her own clothes. "What could she want with me? I'm nothing. No one."

"Not to me. And I fear not to Elisabeth. I cannot stop thinking about the apple she left for you." Mathias rolled the blankets and buckled them neatly, then straightened. "Greta, my sister had one just like it in her hand when she died. It was still there when I found her."

Greta, stepping into her petticoat, stilled. "My mother had the same."

They stared at each other over the dying fire.

"Do you think Elisabeth had something to do with my mother's death?" Greta asked.

"Truthfully? I do not know what to think." He slipped the hunting horn, cooking pot and blankets onto a leather strap, buckled it. "All I know is that I have to finish this. The sooner the better."

Greta drew her skirt over her petticoat and tied it. "Mathias, you don't truly mean to leave me here alone while you hunt the baroness and Fizcko?"

"No. I'm going to leave you here alone while I *kill* the baroness and Fizcko." He threw the leather strap, thick with his gear, over his shoulder. "I had planned to go after the dwarf first. But now, after what you have told me, I think I'll begin with the baroness."

Impossible not to think of Jacob's broken body. Mathias was larger than Jacob had been. Stronger, too. But how many large, strong men—fathers, brothers, sons—had the baroness torn asunder? And she would not be alone. Fizcko, with his dark magic, and the might of the Hornberg would be with her.

"Must you go alone?"

"I've been alone for the best part of two hundred years." He checked his sword, his bow. "What is another week?"

"What of Rob and the wolves?" Greta asked, lacing her bodice. "Surely they would help you. I know you injured Tavey. But if we went to Conran and explained—"

"There is no reasoning with Conran."

"Mira, then."

"Witches have never been much use to me." A hasty sideways grin. "If you'll pardon me for saying."

"Perhaps you've not met the right one." She watched him shoulder what remained of his gear. "Mathias, I saw Mira last night after I left you. We spoke of what I can do. What I *am*. I think I could help you." He was not the only one who could change his shape, after all. She could go with him. Run by the bear's side, sharp of claw, wild of thought.

"No, Greta. It's too dangerous."

"Mira said I'm strong."

"And I believe her, I do. But now is not the time to test that strength." He brought Greta's shawl to her, settled it over her shoulders. "Promise me you won't think of it."

"But what if the baroness should come for me while you are gone?"

"Then I will be right behind her."

"What if you are not?"

"Then Rob will take care of you. His tracks are all over this mountain. He's been watching over you for days."

"He has?" She wondered briefly at that before swerving back to the problem at hand. "But what of you? What if . . ."

"I can take care of myself, remember?" He drew her close. "Just promise me you'll stay at the house where it's safe."

"And if it's not safe?"

"Then go to Rob." He pressed his brow to hers. "Promise me, Greta. I cannot do what needs to be done if I am worried for you."

She nodded. Ran her hands over him, dispelling the tendrils of tattermagic still clinging to his shoulders, his hair. Drawing upon the web and the earth, and whatever gifts her mother had given her, to keep him safe.

"I came here for a reason, Greta. I cannot falter now. For my father and my brother. For my sister." Mathias's voice was hard-edged with promise. "And for you."

# 20
## Hunting

*Dukes were not the only creatures haunting the viscount's roads. Wolves had come to the land, their presence stirring fear among the people. The lord acquired the services of a huntsman and ordered him to rid his forests of the beasts.*

The house seemed grimmer than before. The morning was warm, the sun ruling a sky of storm-washed blue, but the house's heart lay cold and dark. Greta hesitated at the door, peering into the familiar, and yet entirely unfamiliar, dim.

"Back then, my dearie?" The book's voice, too, seemed strange. A prickle of unease went up Greta's back at the sound of it, soft and rasping, in the shadows.

"I suppose I am, yes," she said. "It is, after all, my house."

"That's true." A silence. Then, "Why don't you come in?"

*Tattermagic rends and destroys. It is an imbalance in the flow of things, as all evil is. . . .*

"I am enjoying the sun," Greta said lightly. She could feel the book's power rolling from the open door like fog, reaching for her with ghostly fingers. If only she had listened to Jacob and let him destroy it. She angled herself better to see into the house. The table was empty but the memory of an apple lingered there, red and terrifying.

*Just promise me you'll stay at the house where it's safe,* Mathias had said.

*And if it's not safe?*

*Then go to Rob.*

The stars knew she did not feel safe now. Even so, she forced herself to step across the threshold.

"How did the yarn go, then?" the book asked. Even beneath the hearthstones, its voice was strong and close. "Did you find Mathias?"

"I did, as you knew I would." Greta went straight to her room. The old pack Hans had made her use on May Day was still there. She rolled up her spare skirt, shift, stays, petticoats and bodice and thrust them hurriedly in.

"And what did you find, dearie?"

"You know very well what I found." Comb, stockings, the ribbons Jacob had given her. And, with a gentle caress at odds with the terseness in her voice, her mother's lost ribbon.

The book screeched with laughter. "I told you—every man has his secrets. Every beast, too."

"He is not a beast." Greta whipped aside the curtain.

"What are you doing?" A note of alarm had crept into the book's voice. "Are we going somewhere?"

"*I'm* going somewhere. *You* are . . ." Greta trailed off, fingers brushing the tinderbox at her belt. She had meant to burn the book, had meant to kindle the fire and throw it into the flames now, here, this very morning. She was angry enough to do it—the book had played her as prettily as a zither.

And yet. For all its deceptions and manipulations, for its wickedness and oddities, the book was still the book: her friend, who had been with her every day since the witch's house, who had helped her to bake, kept her alive and—in its own harsh, nettlesome way—loved her.

Her hand fell to her side. She could leave the book behind. She could keep it buried beneath the hearthstones forevermore. But she could not, in truth, bring herself to burn it.

"You're staying here," she said.

"Staying . . . here?"

"Yes." Greta carefully slid the baking molds into the pack, then tightened its strings and threw it over her shoulder.

"But . . . what if you need me, dearie? What if—"

"Don't." She took her cloak from its hook. "I'm not a child anymore. I know what you are, what your magic is. And I want no part of it."

"It's a little late for that, isn't it?" If the book had had a face, it would have sneered. "My magic was good enough for you yesterday!"

"A lot of things were good enough for me yesterday." Greta turned to the door, to the warmth of the morning sun. "But it's a new day, now."

Christoph was driving down the mill road in a cart pulled by Brunhild and Siegfried, his father's workhorses.

"Morning, Täubchen." He drew the horses up, eyeing her pack. "Everything well?"

"I was hoping I could stay at the mill for a few days, Christie." She glanced back at the mountain. "I fear it's not safe at the house."

He nodded. "Da's been worrying for you up there alone. He checks in on you often, you know, when he's out running the woods with the men."

"He does?"

"Of course. It's their job to protect the village, isn't it? It's what the council are paying them for."

"I suppose it is." She patted Siegfried's warm, brown neck. "Where are you three off to?"

"We're going to help Anna-Catherine Casser plant her barley," Christoph said.

"It's late in the season for planting, isn't it?"

Lindenfeld usually split its farming land into three sections—winter planting, spring planting and a third to rest. Ordinarily, the spring crop of barley, beans and oats would have been sown by now. Greta's own small crop of beans was two months in the ground and she and Hans had helped Rob and Christoph with oats and barley in March.

"Yes. But Joseph Casser and his brothers spent the season planting the fields of others. When the tithes were raised they had no choice but to go to the Hornberg."

"They went to pay the Blood Tithe?"

"Of course. They were among the first to go. All the day laborers were."

All the poorer men, he was too polite to say. Greta had seen them herself, climbing into the cart with their wives and children looking on.

"But that was over a week ago, Christie. They should be back by now."

"I'm sure that was the plan, Täubchen. And yet, here we are. Frau Casser is beside herself. I told her I'd help. And Frau Risch and Frau Später, as well."

"Their husbands are at the castle, too?"

"Yes. And Frau Später's son, Nicolaus."

A spool of dread was unwinding itself in Greta's chest, worsening with every word Christoph said.

"I'll come with you."

"Are you sure?"

"Of course. I want to help." Plowing was hard work. She had seen both men and horses stream with sweat as they slogged back and forth across the fields until sunset, churning the earth behind them. Besides, Anna-Catherine was pregnant. Lending a hand was the very least Greta could do.

Christoph helped her up into the cart and clucked to the horses, who plodded sedately on. Greta, settling herself and her pack on the narrow bench seat, noticed several bags of seed resting in the cart beside the plow, sowing baskets and the wide sweep of a brush harrow.

"Frau Casser needed seed, too?"

"In truth, I'm not sure. Joseph *should* have seed enough from last season. But I thought . . . With him away there would have been no money coming in. Anna-Catherine sews and raises goats, but even so it must be hard. She has two little ones to care for, too. . . ."

"Of course." Greta frowned out over the fields, shading her eyes with one hand. Too many had been left unplanted, and those that had were being attacked by countless sparrows, starlings and black-birds. Usually the fields would be scattered with women and children armed with sticks and switches, and boys with rough-made drums. Now, there were only a handful of people trying to stop them. The rhythm of the land, its familiar triple beat, rolling through the seasons for time untold, had faltered.

"Those are Herr Keller's strips, there," Christoph said, pointing across the fields. "He's been at the Hornberg from the first. No one's seen him or had word of him. I helped his wife and son sow beans and barley yesterday."

"It was good of you to help."

He shrugged. "Couldn't just sit by, could I? My father and his friends are always speaking of blood and sons. Firstborn son follows the father, and all the rest of it. But what of the mothers? No one says a word about them. I figure I'm my mother's son, too. She was born in a valley like this one. Her father worked the same fields. Her mother, too, and their parents before them." He brushed the back of one hand across his eyes. "That village is gone now, lost in the war. After it burned the crops failed and the people began to starve. When my father arrived those who were left were packing what remained of their lives and preparing to leave. If things keep on the way they're going here, there'll be no one left to harvest these crops. Lindenfeld will starve, too. I cannot sit by and do nothing."

He was afraid. She could see it in his face. And yet, beneath it, there was resolve.

"You're a good man, Christie." She leaned across, squeezed his hand.

Hundreds of starlings were gathering over the fields. As one they rose against the sky, twisting and funneling in unearthly beauty.

"Must be predators about," Christoph said.

There was a time Greta had wondered at the sight. Now, the flock seemed monstrous and menacing—a shadow swirling and swooping over the empty fields, picking the land's bones.

Joseph Casser's strips were on the sloping land above Lindenfeld. Difficult land, steep and rough, but he had worked hard to clear it. Anna-Catherine Casser was already there, her rounded belly even larger than it had been the last time Greta had seen it, on May Day. Anna-Catherine's father, Johannes Schütz, a wiry old man with a tenacious, gristled strength, stood beside her.

"You really think we can plow all this, just the two of us?" Johannes barked up at Christoph.

"I'm game to try if you are." Christoph hopped lightly from the cart and helped Greta down. "And we have Fräulein Rosenthal, and Siegfried and Brunhild. My father didn't name her Brunhild for nothing."

"Let's put her to the test, then," Johannes said, with a nod at Greta. Behind him, Frau Casser, who was of an age with Greta and had attended school at the same time, smiled uncertainly. Torn, perhaps, between gratitude at having another pair of hands and the memory of that long-ago spelt field.

"Thank you for coming, Greta," she said at last.

They stood back as the men unharnessed the horses, attaching them instead to the plow. The sun was rising, the last of the night's storm clouds disappearing into wide, bright blue.

When the horses were hitched and ready the two men looked at each other.

"The beasts are yours," Johannes said. "You should lead them. But I know these fields . . ."

"And I'm stronger," Christoph said.

"I'll lead them, then, if you think they'll heed me."

"They will. They're good horses, both." He took his place behind the plow and slipped the long rein over one shoulder. "Are you ready? On, Brunhild! On, girl!"

So it began, a steady, relentless dragging of iron and wood and earth, with Johannes guiding the horses back and forth across the ground, while Christoph leaned heavy on the plow behind.

Greta and Anna-Catherine opened the containers of seed— despite Christoph's concern the Cassers had enough of their own—

and poured it into two linen sowing bags. As she worked, movement high on the slope above caught Greta's eye: horses, treading along the tree line. Fine horses, ridden by a group of grand young men, each more richly dressed than the last. A dark-haired woman rode at their head, dressed in a feathered hat and a riding gown of deep blue velvet.

"There's the baroness," Anna-Catherine said, looking up. "Out hunting again. I wonder who that is with her?"

For a moment Greta thought the tall, dark-haired young man beside the baroness was Mathias. But no. This man was younger and dressed almost as richly as Elisabeth.

"I've never seen him before," she said.

"Nor have I. He is not from around these parts, that much is certain." Anna-Catherine watched the group pick their way up the slope and disappear into the trees. "I've half a mind to follow them and kindly ask the lady when I might have my husband back." She shook her head, gazed down at her worn skirts and faded bodice, the seed bag in her rough hands. "Can you imagine?"

Greta watched the trees where the riders had disappeared, wondering who—or what—might be following them. "I would stay away, if I were you." And then, in a whisper: "Protect me, forest fair."

*And protect him, too.*

"Here, then," Anna-Catherine said, shouldering her bag. "The sooner we start, the—" She gasped in surprise and pain, lowering the bag and clutching her belly.

"Anna-Catherine, are you well?" Greta hurried to her side.

"I'm fine." Anna-Catherine nodded, her words harsh through bared teeth. "It's nothing. This baby is rougher than the others, that's all." She exhaled as the pain subsided. "Must be a boy."

"Are you certain?"

Anna-Catherine smiled wearily. "It's kicking now. Here, feel." She pulled Greta's hand over the linen-covered slope of her belly, splaying her fingers wide. Greta went still. Listening, feeling. Then, a sudden rolling beneath her fingers. Two tentative little pokes, followed by a determined jab. She grinned in surprise and delight.

Anna-Catherine, watching her, smiled. "Perhaps it will be your turn next," she said knowingly.

Greta pulled her hand away, blushing. "We should start," she said, reaching for her seed bag. "Are you sure you can manage? I can carry your seed, too. . . ."

"I'll be fine," Anna-Catherine said, wincing slightly as she slid her bag over her shoulder. "Let's go."

The two women walked between the long furrows the plow had made, throwing out handfuls of seed, counting as they went. To help further, Greta took up the strands of the earth, drawing its strength into her fingertips, instilling its bounty into each and every seed. The sun moved across the sky, the rich scent of turned earth lay heavy over the fields. The valley, newly washed after the storm of the night before, was bathed in a soft haze of green, shining with the promise of the coming summer.

The men rested the horses at each turn of the plow, but even so by midday they were soaked with sweat and in need of respite. Greta ate her share of the bread and cheese Christoph offered, and then, while the others caught their breath in the shade, went to the horses.

"There, there," she murmured as they lipped at their feed, heads heavy and low. She stroked their warm, damp necks, willing the strength of the mountains into them, the ease of the breeze that blew down the valley. When she was done they raised their heads and looked at her, eyes wide and bright, bodies rippling with new-found vigor.

"You're welcome," Greta whispered, stroking their velvet noses.

The horses kept her secret, working tirelessly throughout the afternoon, so that the plowing and planting were finished much sooner than anyone expected. The sun was still high when the horses pulled the harrow across the strips, the heavy brush smoothing soil over the newly planted seeds, finishing the day's work.

Johannes, sweat-stained and elated, marveled at the strength of Brunhild and the persistence of Siegfried, while Christoph scratched his head in wonder.

"Even *I'm* impressed," he said. His shirt was wet with sweat, his sleeves rolled, his face smeared with dirt and pride.

Johannes clapped him on the back. "Come, then, Christoph. You and Greta must join us for a drink at the Thorn. I insist!"

"Of course," Christoph said. "If Greta agrees. But we won't stay long, Johannes; the horses need tending."

Anna-Catherine smiled, wide and true. "Thank you, Greta," she said warmly. "We couldn't have done it without you. My Joseph will be so grateful when he returns."

Greta had never been inside the Rose and Thorn. It was darker than she had expected, and over warm. Several councilmen had taken the largest table by the fire, Herr Hueber among them. The rest of the tables were filled with both men and women, some drinking, others eating supper. The she-bear watched over all from its place on the wall. It looked even sadder close up, its dark eyes filled with fear and pain. Greta was glad when Christoph led her to a small table on the opposite side of the room, where, by angling her chair just so, she could avoid its woeful gaze entirely.

Not so easily avoided was Herr Tritten's furious glare. The tavernkeeper had tried, unsuccessfully, to prevent Greta from entering the Thorn. Johannes Schütz had swept him aside good-naturedly, leading Greta inside and ordering tankards of cool beer from the hapless serving girl. Now, Herr Tritten leaned against the long expanse of polished wood where he plied his trade, glowering. In response, Greta took a sip of her beer, smiling beatifically.

"Are you hungry, Täubchen?" Christoph asked. He had barely finished speaking when his belly grumbled so loudly Greta could hear it over the talk rising from the nearest tables.

She laughed. "I think the question is, are *you*?"

He got to his feet. "I'll fetch us something."

Across the room Johannes Schütz was loudly telling Jacob Zimmermann and his wife Maria Dorothea about the wondrous strength of Brunhild and Siegfried, and the way both Greta and

Christoph had helped plow, sow and harrow his son-in-law's fields in less than a day. It was the third table he had regaled with the tale since entering the Thorn.

"You are quite the favorite," Herr Hueber said pleasantly, sliding into Christoph's seat. "I am glad to hear such talk. Fields planted, people helping each other, everybody happy . . ."

Greta looked around for Christoph. He was ordering food, his back to her. She wished that Anna-Catherine had not been too tired to join them.

"There has been quite a lot of talk in this village, of late," Herr Hueber continued. "Most of it not so cheerful, I'm afraid. A fear is gathering over this valley, Margareta. I have heard it said that it is like the war all over again, when people were hunted down like beasts in the forest. The Devil was here, then, too. Indeed, it was He who did the hunting, along with his servants: wolves, bears . . . and witches."

Greta straightened her cup with careful nonchalance. "Did you ever hear more of the Swedish army, Herr Hueber? I trust they received their compensation?"

He leaned forward, eyes narrowing. "Do you know there are some in this village—in this very *room*—who believe that witchery is the cause of our discontent? Indeed, I myself have wondered if it was not witchcraft that caused me to become so very ill at your brother's betrothal. If some of the food at the gathering—the smoked ham, perhaps, or maybe the maultaschen—was bewitched? What say you to that?"

"I say it is a dismal day indeed when people comfort themselves with foolish superstitions."

"Just so, just so. There is, however, the manner of my illness to consider. Many, many people ate of the food that evening. And yet, only I became unwell. It is remarkable, wouldn't you say?"

"There is nothing remarkable about a man overeating."

"It *was* the food, then?"

"I do not know."

"What a terrible liar you are." The feigned pleasantness was gone, now. Herr Hueber leaned across the table, his face twisting with spite. "I know you did something to the gingerbread. I know you made me sick. And if magic really is to blame, then it was *you* who wrought it."

A chill swept over Greta despite the warmth of the tavern. "Herr Hueber, you know me," she said. "You know I would never hurt the people here."

"So you say. But we shall discover the truth. Oh yes, we shall. I have sent word to Offenburg. There is a witchfinder there—a hexenkommissar—named Rupprecht Biermann. Herr Biermann has vast knowledge of the Devil's work. Many a witch has been discovered and punished under his careful investigations."

"Punished?"

"Burned," Herr Hueber said, lingering over the word. "Thou shalt not suffer a witch to live, fräulein. Surely you know this? In any event, Herr Biermann will be here in a matter of days. It is my hope he will find the witch that is surely among us and dispel the ills that plague this valley."

Greta forced herself to stay calm. "Perhaps, then, he will burn those ridiculous boots of yours."

"Greta?" Christoph had returned, his hands loaded with two bowls of steaming flädlessuppe. "Is everything well?"

"Perfectly," Herr Hueber said, rising. "I was just congratulating Margareta on her hard work today."

There was a commotion at the door. Anna-Barbara Wittman and her husband, Klaus, had entered the tavern. Anna-Barbara, who was always generous with gossip, was red-cheeked and wide-eyed, bursting with excitement. At once the room quieted, heads turning to hear what she had to say.

"We have just come from Hornberg," she announced breathlessly. "Oh, such news! The black bear has returned. It attacked the baroness this afternoon while she was out riding. Killed her horse and would have killed her too, had the baron's nephew not intervened."

Blood rushed from Greta's head to her feet, as forceful as the falls.

"The baron's nephew?" Johannes asked.

"Indeed. Lord Frederick, from Heidenheim." Anna-Barbara's round face shone. "They say he is young and very handsome."

"And the best hunter between here and Innsbruck," Klaus Wittman, tall and thin beside his portly wife, added.

"Lucky for the baroness," Herr Hueber said with a smirk. "And even luckier, perhaps, for Lord Frederick. No doubt the lady will be very . . . grateful."

"The baron has not been dead two weeks," Christoph said with a frown. "Surely you're not suggesting that the baroness—"

"I'm suggesting nothing." Herr Hueber shrugged.

"I had it from my sister, who lives in Hornberg," Anna-Barbara said eagerly. "She told me Lord Frederick arrived in Hornberg two days ago with the intention of courting Lady Elisabeth. He met her at his uncle's funeral, of course, and has been sick with love ever since. They say he can hardly take his eyes off her and listens with delight to every word she says. My sister said Lord Frederick and his companions have installed themselves in the castle. There has been feasting and dancing. Masques and entertainments. Can you imagine! And the poor baron hardly cold? It is shameful!"

There were mutters of agreement from around the room.

"What of the bear?" Greta had managed, at last, to get to her feet. She hurried across the room and seized Anna-Barbara's sleeve. "What happened to it?"

Anna-Barbara gave her a curious look. "What an odd woman you are, Greta Rosenthal." She turned to her husband. "She asks after the *bear*!"

"Please," Greta said. "Is it alive?"

"It was, when last it was seen," Klaus said. "Lord Frederick gave it a sturdy poke in the ribs with his hunting sword and it escaped into the forest."

"Much good may *that* do," Anna-Barbara said, "with the young lord bent on hunting it down."

"What do you mean?"

"Exactly what I say. The baroness has asked Lord Frederick to bring the beast to her. Alive."

"Alive?" Christoph was at Greta's elbow. "Whatever for?"

"I asked my sister the same thing. She said the baroness is rather fond of bearbaiting."

"Bearbaiting?" The words were a dry curl of fear in Greta's mouth.

"Never seen it?" Klaus said. "A pack of fighting dogs are set against a bear. The beast is chained, usually. Very entertaining." He touched his wife's arm. "Come, my dear. You have delivered your news. Let me have my supper."

"I can't imagine any creature faring well with such a wound, can you?" Anna-Barbara said gleefully. "The beast will leave a trail of blood in its wake for the lords to follow. Their dogs will soon take up the scent." Her voice hardened. "And then all those poor dead men will be avenged."

Greta watched, wordlessly, as Anna-Barbara followed her husband to a table.

"Come on, Täubchen," Christoph said gently. He nodded farewell to Johannes Schütz and steered Greta to the door. "Let's go home."

# 21
## The Depths of Winter

*The moment the huntsman set his eyes upon Liliane an insufferable hunger burned within him.*

Darkness had fallen by the time Greta and Christoph drove back to the mill. The gentle warmth of the day was gone and the air was cooling rapidly. Greta drew her shawl about her shoulders and then, when the night continued to grow colder and colder, wrapped herself in her cloak.

"Saints preserve our bones, but it's freezing," Christoph said through chattering teeth. A cutting wind had risen and he hunched over the reins, shivering in his shirtsleeves. "Will you pass me my coat, Täubchen? It's in the back."

Greta turned in her seat, fumbling in the cart for the coat, the wind slicing into her face and hands. At last she felt rough wool instead of grainy boards.

"Christ," Christoph muttered, shrugging into the coat. "It's like winter all over again."

"Is that . . ." Greta pointed to a flake of soft whiteness drifting before her as the wind lulled. "Christie . . ."

"It's snowing, Greta!"

They huddled together on the bench as Christoph urged the exhausted horses on. The wind rose, biting and whipping, and the forest bent and tossed above them. At the bridge the horses shied and sidestepped, rocking the cart frighteningly. Greta peered back through the darkness. A handful of low, lean forms flowed out of the storm.

"It's Da," Christoph called over the wind. "Take the reins. I'll walk in with the horses."

He leapt down, the wolves milling about his legs, and fumbled along Siegfried's back and harness until he gripped the horse's bridle. He took firm hold of it, turning the cart for the mill. The wolves surged down the sides of the cart and onto the road ahead. Greta counted four of them through the thickening snow, including the large, grey wolf that was Rob.

The wolves stayed with them until they drew into the mill yard. By then the snow was falling so thick and hard that Greta could barely see. It covered her hood, her lap, her pack, the backs of the frightened horses. At last the house loomed into sight. Christoph pulled up before it, lifting Greta down and bundling her toward the kitchen door. She caught the sudden, vague shapes of men in the snow and knew the wolves had shed their skins. Three of them helped Christoph take the horses to the stable. The fourth, Rob, helped her inside.

"Good God," he said, hauling the door closed against the wind. "Where did *that* come from?"

"From nowhere good," Mira said. She was at the window, looking out at the storm. Behind her Conran lounged in Rob's favorite chair, his attitude one of supreme contentment. The rest of his men sprawled about the kitchen like wolves in a den. Two played dice at the table. One lovingly honed a violent-looking knife on a whetstone. Another, gnawing on a chicken leg, frowned at Mira's words. "Is something astir?"

"Perhaps." Rob helped Greta out of her cloak. "This storm . . . it cannot be natural. I did not smell snow today. I did not feel its coming."

"None of us did," Mira said. "It was summoned."

"By who?" Rob asked.

"I couldn't say. All I know is that it is tattermagic, and that its coming can mean nothing good."

Greta dropped her pack and joined Mira at the window. Beyond it the snow was falling thick and fast. Had the book done this? Abandoned and angry? Or had this brutal weather been sent from the Hornberg? Uneasiness seeped over her like frost upon glass. She shivered.

"Pah," Conran said. "There's nothing stirring. Storms come and go, even in May. Sit down, everyone, and warm yourselves." He noticed Greta, grinned. "Lingonberry! I trust you'll be joining us for supper?"

"I dislike this," Rob said quietly. "Perhaps we should go back out?"

"Yes," Greta agreed at once. "Yes, I think you should go. All of you. Right now."

All eyes turned to her.

"It's Mathias," she said. "He's wounded, and out there somewhere alone. He was in danger *before* the snow began. And now . . ." She looked at Rob. "Please. *Please* go out there and find him."

"You're speaking to the wrong man, Sunrise," Conran said darkly. "*I'm* the one who tells the men when to go and when to stay. And if you think I'm going to skip my supper to help that big black bastard, you are sorely mistook."

A beat of silence, during which the scrape of the knife on its whetstone and the wail of the wind outside were overly loud.

"Conran," Rob said reasonably. "We have a duty to protect the people of this village. The council paid you coin—good coin—to keep them safe."

"The bear is not of this village. He's an outsider. The council won't give a roasted fart if he lives or dies. And nor will I."

"Conran—"

"Rob." Conran slid to his feet and swaggered with deliberate ease across the room, coming to a stop with his face a hand's breadth from Rob's. "Be quiet, now," he murmured. "Or something really *will* be astir."

Greta glanced at the rest of the men. The dice lay forgotten on the table. The knife and the whetstone clung fearfully together. The soldier who had been eating was utterly still, chicken leg half raised to his lips.

"It's not what you're thinking, Conran," Rob said carefully.

"How do you know what I'm thinking?"

"You're thinking I'm deliberately defying you."

"No. I think you're sticking your muzzle in where it's not needed. As usual."

"Mathias is a good man. He needs our help," Rob said. "Let me take Roebuck and Hearn. It won't take long. What harm can it do?"

Conran sighed theatrically. "Christ, but I'm bored. I heartily wish I'd had the good sense to bring my drink with me when I left my chair."

"We have a responsibility," Rob persisted. "To protect those that cannot protect themselves."

"Last time I looked the bear was well able to fend for himself. I won't risk my men because he's afraid of a little snow." Conran shifted his weight, breaking both eye contact with Rob and the tension thickening the room. "You're a good man, miller. You always were. I'll forgive your little rebellion this once, because I genuinely believe you were acting on that tender heart of yours—and because I still need that drink. But question me again, and you'll find I won't be nearly so agreeable."

The door swung open and the remaining sell-swords and Christoph swept inside, bringing a flurry of snow with them.

Conran patted Rob's back. "Now, pour yourself a beer and warm yourself by the fire. Who's for dice?"

Greta managed to get through supper without further provoking Conran. But when the men had finished eating and Rob excused himself to check on the mill, she followed him out into the storm.

"I cannot stand to think of him out there. Alone and hurt, with no one to help him," she said. There was usually a need to raise one's voice in the mill. The clatter and clunk of wood on wood, underscored by the sound of water, were like the inner workings of a great timber beast. Now, the sound of the wind was almost as loud.

"I know," said Rob. His lantern threw shadows across the honey-colored timbers as he checked the wheel, ensuring it was locked firmly in place. Strange, to see it still and silent. Ordinarily, the water wheel was turning, the water itself causing movement and change.

She stepped out of Rob's way as he moved about, touching every surface, every beam. It was his way, she knew, of discovering how the mill was faring—of *feeling* if anything was awry. Water moved through the channel beneath the floury floorboards, its chill seeping into the soles of her shoes. She barely noticed. Her mind was turning, seeking movement. Seeking change.

A striped cat, one of three who inhabited the mill, twined itself against her skirts. She bent to stroke its dusty orange fur. The day's work in the fields was echoing in every part of her body. Her legs were stiff and weary, her back aching. Even so, she could not help but imagine sly and tireless paws, a thick, red coat. "Foxes do not mind the snow," she said. "Perhaps Mira and I could go?"

"Have you lost your wits?" Rob blustered, shocked. "You cannot mean to do something so foolish?"

"What else would you suggest, if *you* will not go after him?"

"You know I would if I could." He rubbed a weary hand across his forehead. "Listen to me, now. It's entirely possible that all this worry is for naught, and that Mathias will be fine. Bears are made to survive, after all."

"They are?"

"Of course. They're very, *very* hard to kill." Rob hung the lantern from a beam and dragged a sack of grain to the foot of the ladder leading to the second floor. "A wounded bear, for instance, does not bleed like you or I. It bleeds into itself—into its fat, into its fur. The blood is quickly absorbed, so it hardly leaves a trail. I have heard of men tracking a wounded bear for miles, only to lose it."

"Really?"

"Truly." Rob hefted the sack onto his shoulder with a grunt and began to climb. One side of each rung was worn thin by years of use: generations of millers, one shoulder weighed down with grain, climbing through time. He reached the top, slid the grain onto the floor above, then climbed down again.

"Almost two hundred years, Mathias has roamed—you think this is the first time he has been hunted? Believe me, Täubchen:

the man will save the bear, and if he does not, the bear will save the man. The best thing we can do is stay out of the way."

*Promise me, Greta. I cannot do what needs to be done if I am worried for you.*

Outside, the wind dropped. Music—sweet, rich—floated across the yard. Greta went to the open door. Through the kitchen window she saw two of Conran's men, one pressing a small, rather battered fiddle to his shoulder, the other blowing into a thin whistle. They played a few strains of something slow and sorrowful, so lovely and so steeped in loss that it stirred Greta's blood. Her eyes filled with tears.

"A lament," Rob said softly, beside her. A third sell-sword joined the whistle and the fiddle, raising a voice that was rich and deep and wise. He sang in a language Greta could not understand, and the others joined him, their rougher voices breaking like waves on a wild and distant shore. It seemed as though the spirit of the world sang with them, rising from the river and the earth, from the mountains and the stars.

"I'm glad you came to stay, Täubchen," Rob said. "I've worried for you these past weeks. There is a darkness hanging over this place. I wish . . ." He hung his head, shook it sadly. "It will seem better when this storm has passed. You'll see."

Greta nodded. Back at the house she went to the small room beside Rob's, where Mira had made up a second pallet. She stripped down to her shift and crawled into bed. Outside, the whiteness of the storm filled the window. It was cold, and she drew the blankets up around her shoulders, listening as the mercenaries played below. Many of the songs were of loss and sadness. Some spoke of love. Others longed for home. They sang of a maiden who was like a red, red rose, as fair as the spring, and of a man who was in love with her. He would love her, they sang, till all the seas ran dry and the rocks melted with the sun.

Her worry for Mathias became a sudden, tangible thing, so strong that it set an aching in her heart. On the other side of that white night Mathias was alone. She tried to imagine the space that lay between them, the vast and rolling forest, thick with snow. At last, exhaustion overcame her. She fell asleep listening to the sell-sword's song:

> *And fare thee well, my only love,*
> *And fare thee well a while,*
> *And I will come again, my love,*
> *Though it were ten thousand mile.*

The storm continued throughout the night. When at last the weather was spent, blue skies and glittering sunlight revealed a blanket of winter over the land. The fields, rooftops and mountains were covered in snow, the river running icy clear between perfect white banks. There was a frosty stillness to everything, as though the world had withdrawn into itself. White and still, it waited.

The sell-swords, Rob with them, had left early to go into the village. "We'd best show those fools on the council that we're still earning our keep," Conran had said with a wink before leading the men out into the snow-bright morning. Christoph, whose hopes of planting more fields had been firmly put to rest, was working in the storehouse, securing seeds and tools. And so Greta was alone when a figure appeared at the end of the road. She thought, at first, that it was Mathias—an entire day and night had passed since the bear had been wounded by the baroness's suitor, and she was desperate for news of how it fared—but as the figure drew near, she saw it was small, and decidedly feminine, with wings of silver-gold hair peeping from beneath a thick woollen cap. It was Ingrid Winter.

Hans's betrothed had always seemed otherworldly, an ice maiden from a fairy story. Now, sitting awkwardly at Rob's table, she seemed no different from any other young woman: her cheeks were red with cold, her skirts tangled with snow.

"I saw Herr Mueller in the village," she said. "He told me you were here."

Greta forced herself to focus on her guest. She had slept poorly, disturbed by the storm's wrath and her constant worry for Mathias. Even now she imagined him hunched in a cave or bloodstained hollow, sleepless with pain. Hunted, hounded.

"I'm sorry to disturb you like this. It's just . . ." Ingrid toyed with a bunch of heartsease Mira had left on Rob's table. She bit her lip, then spoke in a great rush. "I know we have not always been friends. I know that I have not always treated you fairly, or kindly. But we are to be sisters. And, knowing that, I could not just sit by when . . . especially with Hans away . . ." She looked up, her beautiful eyes wide. "How could he forgive me if I said nothing?"

Greta blinked. "Whatever are you talking about, Ingrid? What do you mean, Hans is away?"

Ingrid tilted her head, puzzled. "I thought you knew. He said he told you. . . ."

"Told me what?"

"About the Blood Tithe. He left two days ago, in the cart. I admit I was very sad to see him go, but the baroness is so generous, allowing us to pay the summer tithes with labor instead of coin, don't you think?"

*She will watch over you all.*

"Ingrid, why would Hans do that?"

Ingrid's confusion deepened. "I thought you knew about this, Greta. Hans told me he discussed it all with you. He said it was *you* who suggested it. Times being what they are . . ."

"Why would he do this?" Greta whispered to herself in horror. She had more than enough to pay the summer tithes; Mathias had ensured it. He had admitted everything to her, before they parted at the cave. He had left the silver coins in Greta's shoe after hearing— with the bear's powerful ears—Herr Hueber's threats the first time he had bullied her at the house. He had wanted her to have the money. He wanted her to have it still. She touched her pocket, where even now the coins lay.

"Greta?" Ingrid, clearly concerned, touched Greta's arm. Her fingers were soft and cold. "Hans said it was his turn to pay the tithes. That it was time for him to share the load, instead of always relying on you . . ."

*Oh my God.*

"I told him my father would give him the money. That he would be happy to. But he refused. He said something about your friend Jacob and a debt being owed. He said that it was time to make things right. Greta? Are you quite well?"

"Of course," Greta lied, forcing a weak smile. "We *did* discuss it; I remember now. I did not think he would go so soon, that's all."

"He said he wanted to go sooner and be home in time for the wedding. He said he wanted to make a fresh start. Be a good brother as well as a good husband." She ducked her head, blushing. "And, God willing, a good father."

Greta grasped once more at her pocket, tied at her waist beneath the layers of her skirts. More money than she had ever owned in her life, right there in her hands. Utterly useless, now.

"Greta, there is something else I wanted to talk to you about." Ingrid was playing with the heartsease again, pressing the leaves nervously between her fingers. "I wish I did not have to say this, but I fear I must. You should take care. The people are frightened. The bear and the wolves, those poor dead men in the forest . . . They're blaming witches."

An icy finger trailed its way down Greta's back.

"I'm only telling you this because . . . well, because your name has been mentioned."

"*My* name?"

"In whispers only," Ingrid said hastily. "I do not think anything will come of it."

"What are they saying?"

"Well, there are the old stories about you, of course," Ingrid said reluctantly.

"And?"

"You've been seen several times with Herr Schmidt—it is well known he is a Catholic, and, well . . . you know what they say about Papists."

"Yes," Greta said faintly.

"And then, of course, there's this dreadful weather. It only came about after *you* helped Anna-Catherine Casser plant her spring crops. It will damage all the crops, of course, but Herr Casser's fields have been the worst affected. The whole mountainside above it collapsed under the weight of the snow. Trees, rocks, earth . . . the fields have been destroyed. But it gets even worse. Last night, when the storm began, Anna-Catherine went into labor. It was too early, of course . . . she was only six months gone. She . . . she lost her baby, Greta, and what's worse is that I have heard more than one person suggest it was because of you."

"That's not true," Greta whispered. She thought of those sturdy little kicks, the life they had promised. "I . . . would *never* . . . I *helped* Anna-Catherine. . . ."

"I believe it. And I will defend you if such things are said in my presence," Ingrid said, squeezing Greta's hand. "I do not wish to alarm you. I just . . . thought it best you knew."

Greta nodded numbly. "Of course. Thank you."

Ingrid got to her feet. "I should go. This snow is so deep, it will take me an age to walk back to the village."

Greta glanced uneasily at the strange, silent winter beyond the window. "I could ask Christoph to walk with you. . . ."

"I'll be fine," Ingrid said, drawing on her gloves. "Did you not hear? The bear has been captured."

"Captured?" One word, to steal Greta's breath and stop her heart.

"Yes! It all happened early this morning." Ingrid took in Greta's expression. "Are you not happy? The threat is over. And your friend, the one who was killed—what was his name?"

"Jacob."

"That's right." Ingrid smiled her beautiful smile. "Jacob will be avenged."

Greta gripped the edge of the table, her knuckles bone-white. "Where is the bear now, Ingrid? Was it taken alive, as the baroness wished?"

Ingrid frowned. "Are you sure you're not unwell?"

"The bear, Ingrid. Where is he now?"

"Lord Frederick and his men brought it into Lindenfeld this morning. They found it not far from here." Ingrid shuddered. "Can you imagine? Such a creature lurking so close to where you and I are sitting right now?"

*Stars above.* Had he been trying for Rob's land? Had he needed help? Had he been struggling, wounded and alone in the storm, to reach her?

"You look as though you might faint," Ingrid said worriedly, getting to her feet. "Shall I fetch you some water?"

Greta seized her hand, pinning it against the table. "You're sure they didn't kill it?"

"They wanted it alive, they were very specific about that." Ingrid glanced at her trapped hand. "They trussed it and heaved it onto the back of the watchman's cart for the journey back to Hornberg." She gently peeled back Greta's fingers, extricating herself. "Of course, they stopped at the Rose and Thorn to celebrate, first. They'll be pickled when they leave again, no doubt."

"They're still there?"

"They were when I left the village. Greta, are you *sure* you're not unwell?"

"I'm fine," Greta murmured. Her thoughts were ablaze, her heart roiling.

"Be comforted," Ingrid said soothingly. "There were some who thought the black bear was a witch, or even the Devil himself in disguise. With it gone people will be comforted, and perhaps think of witchcraft no more. You'll be safe again. I'm certain of it."

When Ingrid had gone Greta paced the house and then the yard, and then—when neither had relieved the aching in her heart—threw herself out into the snow-covered fields. She began to run, her boots crunching, her lungs burning, the pocket full of silver clanging dully against her thigh. She ran until she could run no more and stopped, sides heaving, the winter air cold in her throat. In the far distance she could see the highest towers and rooftops of the Hornberg, perched atop its mountain. At the sight, her frustration and her fear came roaring in, so that the valley, silent and white, seemed filled with it. She wanted to scream into the emptiness. She wanted to fall to her knees and weep.

Movement, across the fields. Rob and the men were returning to the mill, their weapons clattering softly.

She ran toward them.

# 22
## A Darker Shade of Magic

*It was not unknown to the huntsman, this hunger, nor was the even blacker act of sating it. He kept a chest in his quarters, locked and hidden. In it were thirteen human hearts, each belonging to a girl more beautiful than the last, each of whom had fallen under his knife. Liliane, however, was fairest of them all. Confident in his skills and in his cunning, and set most ardently on his desire, he promised himself that he would have her.*

Hello, Rosehip," Conran said as Greta stumbled to a halt in Rob's yard. "To what do we owe the pleasure?"

"The baroness has captured Mathias."

"So we heard." He picked at a scrap between his teeth, spat it out.

"My brother is in the Hornberg, too," she said. Rob, a little apart from the others, opened his mouth, glanced at Conran, and closed it again. "My brother, and countless others who have paid the Blood Tithe. I want you to help them."

"*Help* them?"

"Yes." Greta looked into each of their faces. "You and your men are soldiers. You have weapons. Skills. I want you to find a way into the Hornberg and bring Mathias, my brother, and anyone else who is imprisoned there out."

"*Do* you, now?" Conran's face was unreadable. "And just why would we do that?"

"Because the council is paying you to protect this village—"

"Wrong," Conran barked.

Greta, knocked off rhythm, faltered. "What do you mean?"

"As of this morning, we're no longer employed by your council to do a damned thing. The bear's been caught. The people of Lindenfeld are safe once more. *Our* services"—he gave an exaggerated shrug—"are no longer required. We've just come from the Rathaus, where we heard it from the honorable bürgermeister himself."

"Then *I'll* pay you," Greta said, slipping her pocket out of her skirt and brandishing it like a sword. "Silver. It's yours if you'll help them."

She loosed the pocket's strings and a tantalizing silveriness spilled into her palm. Conran stroked one of the coins with a large, scarred finger.

"Pretty, I'll admit," he said. "But not enough to make a difference."

"You don't care about what happens to all those people?"

"Honestly? Not really. But I *do* care about my men. And I'll tell you this, Candles: I'd gladly watch a hundred peasants die—your brother included—before I'd lift a single finger to help that steaming pile of bear-shit."

"Why do you hate him so?" Greta lowered the coins. "What did he ever do to you?"

"Tavey," Conran said sharply. "Do you think we should help the bear?" He did not wait for the young man's answer. "Remember Tavey's ribs? He's lucky he can breathe. Your bear did that."

"Because you were hunting me," Greta said, stung. "Mathias only wanted to protect me!"

"Of course he did. But what about the others?"

"The others?"

"It was years ago now, so my memory *could* be somewhat tarnished—but I'm *sure* I lost three of my best men to him in Swabia. Almost killed me, too, not that I much care to admit it, the fucker."

Rob tensed. "Conran—"

"Settle, Rob. I'm telling her how it is, that's all." He sliced his fierce, dark gaze back to Greta. "Their names were Struan, Alasdair and Donan. Struan had it the worst—his arm was torn clean off. All three of them died in the mud on a lonely road in Swabia. Terrible place to die, Swabia. But my men did just that, thanks to your fucking bear."

Soft footsteps in the snow. Mira, taking in the scene.

"Mathias only attacked you because you were going to kill the baroness," Greta said. "She was there, in Swabia. Fizcko, too. I'm sorry for your men, but he had no choice—had you killed them he would have lost any chance of breaking his curse."

"You think I give a fart for his curse? We should have killed him then. Would have, too, if not for the miller, there." Conran smirked at Rob. "He stepped between us. Made a great show of it, too. Pity, honor and all the rest of it. Bloody fool. I suppose I should be grateful to him, really. And the bear. If not for them, I wouldn't be leading this fine operation."

Greta looked to Rob, her eyes wide. "Is that true?"

Rob nudged at the snowy ground with the tip of his boot. "When I would not allow the men to kill Mathias, Conran challenged my leadership," he said. "I suppose I should have fought. But I was tired of fighting. So tired. So instead of defending what was mine, I took your father and Mathias"—Rob's gaze fell, as it so often did, on Mira—"and traveled south. Mathias did not stay with us long but your father and I made it here. You were the first person we saw. *Look at my little dove*, Peter said. *My heart's peace.*"

Greta knew this part of the story, though she could never have imagined what it had cost Rob to bring her father home—or that his was not the only life he had saved.

"A heartwarming tale, to be sure," Conran sneered. "But the moral is clear: Wolves don't run with bears. They never have and they never will."

One of the men grunted, though whether in agreement or defiance Greta could not be sure.

"And what of mercenaries?" she demanded. "They don't much care who they run with, do they, so long as the price is right?" She thrust the coins at Conran. "You cannot tell me you don't want this. Here. Take it!"

"I don't want *his* money." Conran made to move past Greta. She caught his arm.

"They're going to bait him," she said. "They'll bring dogs, and . . ."

There must be some part of you that can pity a man—any man—who must face such a thing." She sought the gaze of each of the mercenaries. "Please. *Please* don't leave him to die."

The wind soughed over the icy river, the willows. Greta shivered but did not let go of Conran's arm.

"This is a bad business," the ginger-haired mercenary muttered. His large open face, usually the merriest with its bright set of whiskers, was troubled.

"I agree," said one of his companions. "It would be easy enough to climb up to the Hornberg at night. The forest is thick at the back; it grows right up to the wall."

Hope roused itself in Greta's heart.

"Might be a postern we could wriggle our way into," mused the roundest of the men. "What would there be—one guard? Two? Half asleep, most like. We have faced worse odds—much worse—and lived to tell the tale."

"I'm bored," added the surliest of the group, stroking the imposing knife that hung at his side. "I'd kill for someone to kill."

"Besides, are we not all shape-strong?" the sell-sword nearest to Greta demanded. "What's done is done. I, for one, will be sorry if we do not help the bear."

"You will be sorrier if you *do*," Conran snarled, shaking Greta roughly away. "In case you lot have forgotten, *I* say who kills who here. I say where they do it, and I say fucking when. Anyone has a problem with that, they can face me. Is that clear?"

The tension that followed was the kind that came before men bared their fists outside the Rose and Thorn. One wrong word at such a time, and it would all turn to savagery.

"*Is that clear?*"

They were still as carvings, eyes on the ground, shoulders bowed.

Greta's fingers were clenched so hard her nails dug into her palms. "And what of your vows? Your purpose?"

"I know my purpose well enough." There was a nasty glint in Conran's eye.

"What of Ashildr?"

"What about her?"

"Didn't she say her wolves must protect the weak? Fight for those who cannot fight for themselves? Hate Mathias all you want but think of the people in that castle. They need you."

Conran touched the end of Greta's long red plait. "Compelling, aren't you? Quite the enchantress. But witch or no, it does not mean I'll answer to you."

"But Ashildr—"

"Fuck Ashildr. Any wench can crush herbs and whisper pretty words. Ashildr's strength came from the men who ran beside her. Without them she was nothing. Just another mewling whore-daughter."

"Watch your tongue," Rob warned.

"Easy now, miller," Conran said, rounding on him. "Anyone would think you are trying to tell me what to do."

The air—already dense with man and wolf and rage—thickened as the two men chested close.

"Like that, is it?" Conran murmured.

"Enough." Mira pushed between them. "You insult me as well as Greta when you speak thus, Conran. Rob spoke rightly."

Conran narrowed his eyes. "Did he now?"

A fearful silence.

"Tavey's chest is still healing," Mira said at last. "This cold will be hard on him. We'd best get him indoors if you want him to be strong enough to travel."

"You're leaving?" Greta's dwindling faith in the wolves diminished even further.

"Our work here is done," Conran told her. "We came for the pup and got the father instead. No matter; he's worth three of the boy. And our contract with Lindenfeld is ended. We won't stay anywhere that's not worth our time."

"Where will you go?"

"West. France is at war with the Spaniards *and* with itself." He chuckled. "An enterprising sort of man could do quite well there."

"When?" Rob asked quietly.

"In a day or two. Gather your weeds and potions, Mira." Conran turned to the house, throwing a mocking salute at Rob. "And you, miller—best farewell that son of yours. We've a journey ahead."

"Is that it, then?" Greta demanded, when Conran and the rest of the men had gone inside. "You'll do nothing to help them? To help *me*?"

Rob winced. "Täubchen . . ."

"Don't call me that. I'm not a child." Her voice was rising, cracking and wavering, not hers at all. "You told me Mathias would be fine. Bears do not bleed out, you said. Bears are strong. Stay here. Wait. Do nothing. Had I acted sooner I might have prevented this. I might have done something to help him!"

"There is nothing you could have done. . . ."

"He was here, Rob! They found him *here*. He was trying to get to us. He needed our help!"

"You cannot know that for certain—"

"It doesn't matter, now. *I* will go to the Hornberg. I will find Mathias and my brother and set them free *myself*!"

"You'll do no such thing!" Rob roared.

"There is another way." Mira's voice was barely audible above the cold murmur of the mill race. "One that will save Mathias *and* restore the natural order of things." She looked at Rob. "The men would follow you again, Rob. You know they would."

"Have you lost your mind?" he hissed, gesturing at the house. "Talking that way, where anyone might hear?"

"There is only the three of us," Mira said calmly. "Besides, the men would agree with me. They are tired of fighting without cause. If you were to lead them again . . ."

"No honorable man would challenge his captain!"

"The time for honor is over. A man's life is at stake. And the lives of many others, besides. You don't truly mean to sit by and do nothing?"

The light shifted as the sun began its long slide behind the mountains. High in the lindens a redstart trilled.

"I swore my allegiance to Conran," Rob said. "And I mean to honor it."

"That's what you want, then?" Greta demanded. "To do what Conran says? To follow him to France and leave Mathias and Hans, leave *everyone*, to die?"

"Of course not!"

"But that is what you're going to do," Greta persisted. "You're going to go. Just as—just as you did when I was a child. You left then, too, when we needed you most. When my mother died and my father lost himself in despair, when he . . ." She swallowed. "He abandoned us. And so did you."

The color drained from Rob's face. "No, Täubchen—"

"You call yourself my father's truest friend. Brothers, you said. You saved his life. But you could not save him from himself. How could you, when you weren't there?"

"Believe me, I did not go lightly!"

"And yet you went all the same. And now you mean to do it again, when I—when *Hans*—need you most!"

Rob turned away. An old millstone lay near the barn, half sunk in the snow. He brushed flakes from its grooves. "It's true. I failed your father, and you and Hans. But I have done everything I could to make up for my mistake. I have protected you every day since I returned."

Mira was watching him, a pool of stillness. "Why did you go?"

"To search for something I had lost."

Understanding dawned in Mira. "You came back for me."

Rob shrugged. "I figured there was more to be said."

"There was," Mira agreed. "Much more."

"I searched for you and the pack all through the winter. Until I came to the village where Christoph was born. I could not leave him there to starve. . . . So I gave up looking for you and brought him here instead." He turned to Greta, imploring. "By the time I came back your mother was dead and your father had married again. You and Hans were lost in the forest—"

"Not lost," Greta said coldly. "Abandoned. And if you think that

I am going to abandon my brother again now, you are very much mistaken." She turned from him and strode into the house, emerging moments later with her pack.

Rob hurried after her. "Greta, please. You *cannot* think of going to the Hornberg."

"I cannot think of going anywhere else." A plan was blooming in her mind, spreading like drops of blood on a linen sleeve.

"*No*," Rob said fiercely. "I won't let you do this. The baroness—"

"I *know* what the baroness is!"

"Listen to me, Greta, I'm begging you." He caught her arm, drawing her up short. "There are things you do not know—"

"Robert the Miller!" Conran bellowed from the house. "Mira! You're needed!"

"You should go," Greta told Rob. "You should both go."

"Greta," Mira said anxiously. "Remember what I told you. There is a cost when a witch is tempted by the dark. But the forest—the forest will protect you. You have only to ask."

"I need more than just protection," Greta told her bitterly, wrenching herself out of Rob's grasp.

"Wait," he said desperately. He had stopped following her, prevented from taking another step by the oath he had sworn to Conran. "Please!"

Greta looked back at him, standing there in the yard. Expecting her to nod meekly and do as he bid. Expecting her to do nothing.

But she was tired, so tired, of nodding meekly and doing as she was bid. So tired of doing nothing.

She kept walking.

It was dusk by the time Greta lit the fire and arranged everything on the workbench. Ginger, cinnamon, flour, cloves, nutmeg, cardamom, honey. The house was dark and silent, lit only by the oven's faint light. Strange shadows stalked its corners. Outside, the forest seemed to shiver and press close, fearful, expectant. A single, despairing howl rose from the valley below.

She drew the book from its hiding place and bent over the ancient pages, searching for the familiar recipe.

"I knew you'd come back to me."

A woman's low voice, startling in the quiet. Greta gripped her knife.

"Who's there?"

Nothing but dusk and shadows. The windows prickling with black pines. Then a woman emerged. She was of Greta's own age, her hair unbound, her dark dress old-fashioned in its making.

"Who are you?" Greta whispered.

"Who *am* I? What a question!" There were markings on the woman's skin—words and swirls, as though a quill was scrawling furiously over her face and arms, her wrists and collarbones. No sooner had they appeared than the words began to fade, to be replaced by others.

*. . . I conjure you . . .*

*. . . take the gall of a dog and rotten sally wood . . .*

*. . . crack the tooth from a dead man's skull . . .*

"Book?" Greta whispered. "Is that *you*?"

"You've grown stronger, dearie," the woman-book said with a smile. Her voice was younger, smoother, than before; soft as a breath over ancient pages. "Strong enough to *see* me. Fiercer, too. I gather you've grown tired of playing in the dirt with that old ditch witch and are ready for some *real* magic?"

"I need your help."

"Ah." The woman-book made a smooth, silent circuit of the table, inky words floating across her papery skin.

*. . . whoever shall taste of this apple shall greatly be inflamed with love toward me . . .*

"Mathias is in the Hornberg," Greta said. "He was captured by the baroness. My brother is a prisoner there, too."

"Let me guess: you intend to save them?"

"I intend to try."

*. . . grind the clawes of a goat into powder and . . .*

"With gingerbread?"

"What else?"

*. . . I bind them by the sun and the moon, and by the stars of Heaven . . .*

"You want my help," said the woman-book with a sigh. "This time I do not think I will give it."

The real book closed itself with a thump, pinching Greta's fingertips.

"Surely that is no way to speak to a friend," she ventured.

"Friend? Ha! When have you ever cared for me?"

"I saved you, remember? All those years ago? I carried you from the witch's house."

*. . . and in the night thou shalt dreame . . .*

"That is true," the woman-book said. "That is true."

"We're better together, you and I," Greta went on, recognizing, with an uneasy pang, that she was sounding very much like the book itself. "I've taken care of you for all these years—"

"As I have taken care of you! And what do I get for it? Shut away! Forgotten!"

"I'm sorry I've neglected you."

"It hardly matters." The woman-book sniffed. "I am just a book, after all."

"It is clear to me you are much more than that."

A long, measuring glance from those inky eyes.

"I am sorry. Truly," Greta said. "Please say you'll help me."

The woman-book sighed. "Very well. But you must do something for me, too. It's only fair."

*. . . understand my words . . .*

"What would you have me do?" Greta asked, uneasy of a sudden.

"No need to be nervous, dearie. All I ask is that you take me to the Hornberg with you."

"To the Hornberg?" Greta frowned. "Why?"

Dark lashes against a paper-pale cheek. "A lady is allowed a secret or two."

"And if I refuse?"

"You'll go alone." The book held out her hand. Words spiraled along her forearm.

*. . . fulfill my command and desire . . .*

"Do we have an agreement or not?"

"We do." Pushing aside her misgivings, Greta reached for the book's hand. Her fingers passed through it uselessly, like smoke.

"Not strong enough, yet. You can hear and see. But it takes true power to touch. You'll get there with *my* help." Smirking, the woman-book turned to the workbench. "We'd best get started. See to the oven, won't you? And perhaps this time we could capture a little bird, or maybe a squirrel . . . ?"

"No," Greta said firmly. "I'll hurt no one but myself."

"Very well," the woman-book grumbled. "Make the cut nice and deep, then."

They worked together as the night darkened, the woman-book hissing instructions over Greta's shoulder. When at last the hearts were ready—there were a dozen in all—the scent of them almost took Greta's breath away. Already light-headed—she had added far more blood to the mixture this time—and tense with worry, she slid the tray from the oven and sat heavily in a chair, willing herself not to faint.

"Good, dearie," the woman-book purred. "Very good. But we can do better."

"Better?" Greta brushed the sweat from her brow with her forearm.

"More blood, I think."

"But—"

"There's no need to start from scratch. A few drops on these finished pieces should do the trick. Have you the knife? Do it quickly, while they're still warm."

"I don't think I can," Greta said. Her arm was throbbing from the knife's earlier bite. "I think we took too much."

"Nonsense. Do you want to save Mathias or not? What are a few more drops when his very life is at stake?"

Greta pushed herself to her feet. Why was it so hot? She twisted her sticky hair back from her face and raised both arms over the workbench, the knife clasped in one slippery hand. Pressing the tip of the blade to the tender flesh of her forearm she winced, then pushed down harder. Blood hissed and glimmered on the first heart, then sank into the rich cake as though it had never been.

"There," the woman-book said happily. "That wasn't so difficult, was it? Now for the rest."

Greta managed a faint nod. She was moving her bleeding arm slowly across the remaining gingerbread when the sound of booted feet and wary voices came from the yard. There was a terrific crash as the door flew inward. A swarm of black-garbed night watchmen surged into the house, pikes raised.

"Witchery," Axel Lutz said, eyes wide with horror as he took in the knife, the blood and the twelve perfect, potent gingerbread hearts. Between them, crimson drops were startling and sinful against drifts of flour. "Look! Look at that book! And that knife! Is that—?"

"By the blood of Christ," breathed Jan Karsten. "How could you, Greta?"

Greta lowered the knife. "Please, listen. I wasn't going to hurt anybody—"

"Don't move, witch," Dieter Abendroth spat, raising his gleaming pike. "Stay where you are!"

Herr Hueber strolled into the room. "It is as I feared," he announced, examining the blood-spattered workbench. "She has indeed been poisoning us with her baking."

"And don't forget the storm!" added Jan. "Our crops, ruined. And Joseph Casser's poor child . . ."

"She's cursed us!" another watchman, Peter Riegal, shouted. "It's because of her that ill luck has come to this valley!"

"No!" Greta cried. "I had nothing to do with any of that!"

"We shall see." A grand-looking man dressed all in black with a plumed hat atop his silver hair swept into the room. "Rupprecht Biermann, Hexenkommissar, at your service." His hard gaze flicked over the workbench, the knife, the book and Greta, her long red hair loose and wild in the firelight. "And not a moment too soon, I see."

# 23

## The Wolf's Jaws

*Liliane had taken a particular dislike to her father's golden-haired wife, which was not helped by the proclamation of a drunken courtier that the new viscountess, and not Liliane, was the loveliest at court. With the magician's help she concocted a charm that caused the viscountess's laces to tighten so violently she lost breath and fainted.*

The entire village came to the trial. They squeezed themselves onto the benches filling the great room in the Rathaus, rustled and creaked in the gallery above, and spilled out the open doors into the snowy Marktplatz. The councilmen were there, Herr Hueber among them, and Father Markus.

Greta had spent a fearful, sleepless night in the dungeon beneath the Rathaus. Even now terror was coursing through her so hard her cuffed hands shook. She stood on a raised platform above the enormous room, eyes carefully down, avoiding the sea of eager, upturned faces. A waist-high railing surrounded her on four sides like a cage.

The hexenkommissar, imposing in rich black robes, was a few paces away from her. Before him, on a table spread with documents, ink quill and Bible, sat the book as well as the twelve bloodstained gingerbread hearts.

"The Devil is in Lindenfeld," Herr Biermann announced. A hush descended over the room. "I have come here in the hope of restoring the light of God. Know that I am His warrior and do His work. You are all in His keeping, now."

Greta watched him warily. Herr Biermann's voice was deep and strong, gilded with authority, but he was unsettling, too, in his dark, flowing robes. He was also vaguely familiar.

"Margareta Rosenthal," Herr Biermann continued, turning to her. "You stand here today accused of bringing ill luck and sorrow to this village by way of witchcraft: of communicating with the Devil, of meeting with him in the shape of a bear. Of bewitching the people with your baking and poisoning them. Of summoning the weather—that is, of causing a storm which froze the precious crops in the ground and caused a landslip to ruin Herr Casser's fields. You are accused, also, of touching his wife's belly, of *breathing* on her and killing her unborn son." He paused, allowing his words to sink in. "What say you to these charges?"

"I say that falsehood and misfortune have led me here," Greta said. "I am innocent."

She risked a glance at the crowd below and saw Christoph. He threw her a reassuring smile. *Take heart, Täubchen.*

"Indeed. Then I would like to call upon our first witness: Herr Tritten of the Rose and Thorn."

Herr Tritten came forward, smoothing his coat and slicking his wig importantly. He had spoken ill of Greta before and appeared to be delighted at the prospect of doing so again.

"That woman," he said, pointing at Greta, "is ill luck. We've always known it. When she was a child, Kommissar, she went into the woods and did not come out again for a month. Killed an old woman, we heard. Pushed the poor wretch into her own oven and roasted her alive."

There were shocked mutterings from the onlookers at this and Greta looked away, disgusted. They had all of them heard the tale before. Their reaction was for the kommissar's benefit only. *God knows it is not for mine.*

"My wife has always said that Greta Rosenthal has the touch of the Devil on her," Herr Tritten continued. "Her mother Lena Rosenthal was the same."

A grave covered in windflowers and a single, hateful word. HEXE. Greta was certain then that Herr Tritten's hand had carved it.

"She knows of such things, my wife," Herr Tritten said rather proudly. "She was born in Bamberg, you see, and was there for the trials."

"Indeed," Herr Biermann said. "Go on."

"Well, one only has to look at Greta Rosenthal to know she's a witch. She's poison-pated. Red hair is a sign of the Devil, and no mistake."

"That is true," Herr Biermann mused, with a glance at the tangled lengths of Greta's hair. "Red *is* the Devil's favorite hue."

There was a stirring at the Rathaus doors. A figure clad in brightly colored velvet—rose and blue and forest green—had entered the great room, surrounded by scarlet-cloaked men-at-arms of the Hornberg. Fizcko was free of his cage, the danger to his person presumably over now that Mathias had been captured. He waited patiently while one of his guards commandeered a chair then took a seat, smiling up at Greta all the while.

"And then there was that business with old Frau Elma," Herr Tritten was saying. He had found his rhythm now, the words flowing like good wine after harvest. "You might remember her, sir, seeing as you were here for the trial."

A wave of faintness passed over Greta. *Of course.* This was the man who had sentenced Frau Elma to burn, almost five years before. She closed her eyes and clutched tight to the rail before her.

"Didn't Fräulein Rosenthal wail when the old witch was set alight? Didn't she beg for her life? Why would she do that, if not to save one of her conspirators? I tell you Greta Rosenthal was a witch five years ago and she is a witch still. She called down a storm that same year and ruined our harvest. She cursed Herr Drescher's spelt so it withered and died. Not two days ago she helped Frau Casser plant her fields. That very night an ungodly storm came to this valley. It ruined our crops and destroyed Frau Casser's fields—the very fields Fräulein Rosenthal had worked that day!"

Herr Tritten stepped down, and another took his place, then another. They spoke of Greta's baking, how it caused the villagers to crave it, *dream* of it, until they were forced to sate their gluttonous desires by parting with their precious pfennigs. They spoke of the bear, how Greta had tried to hide its presence, and how sad she had seemed when the hunt had gone out to kill it. She had seemed troubled, too, when news of the beast's capture was revealed to her in the Rose and Thorn. Indeed, was it not that very moment that the wind began to rise and the storm to blow?

Herr Hueber himself spoke of Hans and Ingrid's betrothal, when he had succumbed to a strange and gruesome sickness. Frau Casser described the damage to her fields, the bitter cold that lingered, even now. She spoke tearfully of her baby, born amid the storm, tiny and malformed.

"Greta Rosenthal touched my belly," Anna-Catherine said. "She breathed her poison into me and killed my child."

On and on it went, until Greta understood she would not escape. The villagers' hatred was too strong, the kommissar too practiced. He weaved their tales together, fashioning a rope that grew longer and longer, binding her tightly to the witches' pyre. He had, she remembered, done the same with Frau Elma.

Another disturbance at the Rathaus doors: Rob strode toward the dais, flanked by Conran's band of sell-swords. His face was dark with fury. For a moment Greta thought he might leap onto the dais and take Herr Biermann by the throat. But Dieter Abendroth and the other watchmen leapt forward, barring Rob's way. He stood, mute with rage, glowering up at Herr Biermann through a cluster of raised pikes.

"Tell me about this book of yours," Herr Biermann asked Greta, when the room had settled. "It is a grimoire, is it not? A witch's book," he added, for the benefit of his audience, "containing all manner of spells and enchantments. Who gave it to you?"

Greta said nothing.

"Who gave it to you, fräulein? Was it the Devil?"

"No."

"Was it his gift to you, when he took the form of a black bear and you met with him in the woods? When he caressed your naked body with his claws and spilled his cold seed inside you—"

"That is enough!" Rob Mueller's roar shattered the rapt silence. "I have stood by and let this farce endure. But by this light, I can do so no longer! *You will not speak to her so!*"

The kommissar stared at Rob. "Herr Mueller, I presume," he said at last. "I have it on good account that you were once friend to the accused's father. And that you are a decent man. Even so, if you do not desist I will have you forcibly removed from this hall."

"Can no one here speak but you?" Rob demanded. "Can no one defend her?"

"You wish to defend her?"

"I do."

"You understand it is evidence of witchery to speak in favor of a witch?"

"I do," Rob said. "And yet I could not forgive myself if I did not seek to help her." He glared around the hall. "And what of the rest of you cowards? You who call yourselves good, God-fearing folk? You have turned against one of your own and thrown her to this crow, who has grown sleek and fat by gorging on the misfortunes of others. Who dares to call himself a soldier of God—"

The room erupted. Men rose up and shouted, defending their honor and their piety. The kommissar ordered the watchmen to seize Rob. Rob in his turn raised his fists and goaded them *all* on, before the sell-swords dragged him, struggling and cursing, outside.

"The bear is the unholiest of God's creatures," the kommissar said thoughtfully when peace had returned. "He is dark as the Devil and clothed in the colors of Hell. He walks on two legs, a mockery of man, of God himself. For this reason he is the Devil's favorite guise." He gazed around the room. "But there is no need to fear. For does the Bible not tell us, too, of young David, and how he killed the beasts threatening his father's sheep? Bravely did he vanquish the bear, saving the innocent flock—"

A third distraction at the open doors. Panicked screams and agitation as the crowd seethed and parted, leaping up from benches, stumbling over skirts, pushing and crushing each other as they scrambled to get away from eight long, low shapes arrowing through the Rathaus.

Wolves.

Many things happened at once, then, and though they happened fast it seemed to Greta that they moved as slowly as a dream.

Swaths of people scrambled for the double doors, even as the night watchmen stationed outside struggled to get *in*, pushing against the press of terrified bodies. The wolves came on, heads low, aiming for the platform at the head of the room where Greta and the hexenkommissar stood. Everywhere was chaos, people screaming, flailing, falling.

"These are the Devil's own hounds!" Herr Biermann shouted. "Kill them! Kill them, I say!"

The night watchmen guarding Greta leapt forward, pikes and muskets ready. Axel Lutz ran for the large reddish wolf, his pike raised. The wolf turned on him, snarling and leaping, pushing him down. There was a high, gurgling scream, and Axel went still.

More watchmen flowed into the room. They were joined by Fizcko's men, a wall of red and black breaking through the crush of fleeing villagers.

The roar of the watchmen's muskets, the acrid smell of gunpowder. Smoke filled the room, drifting over the carved walls and high ceiling. Through the haze Greta glimpsed Fizcko moving to the doors under the protection of his guards.

The wolves pushed on. Rob reached the dais first, while three more wolves snarled at the watchmen who tried to protect the hexenkommissar. The Devil's own hounds, the kommissar had said, and they looked the part.

"Kill them!" he shrieked, in terror and rage. "Kill them!"

Rob leapt at him, jaws wide, eyes yellow and wild. They crashed into the table, spilling ink and gingerbread. Herr Biermann went down, screaming, sputtering, beneath the wolf's fury. In moments he was naught but a mound of fine black brocade, twitching gently. Rob flowed up the polished stairs to Greta, briefly pressed his head against her side. The warm, wolfish weight of him was a wonderful comfort.

At the foot of the platform, a grey wolf snarled at a Hornberg man-at-arms and received a blow in the muzzle from a musket stock. Blood and cracking bone. Two more wolves took down the man, teeth sinking into his fine red cloak. More shots, more screams.

"Time to go, Täubchen." In the smoke and confusion Rob had flicked off his pelt. He crouched at Greta's side, half-hidden by the railing separating her from the rest of the room. With a deft twist of his knife he broke the lock on her wrist cuffs, yanking on the chains and freeing her.

"Put this on," he grunted, thrusting something coppery into her hands. It was her fox pelt, glistening with remnants of magic and shape-salve.

"You cannot leave me here!" the book cried. "They'll burn me! Destroy me!"

Greta glanced at Rob. His gaze was fixed on the melee unfurling in the heart of the Rathaus. He had not heard the book. Its voice was for Greta and Greta alone.

"Please, dearie. Please!"

She hesitated. Both the book and the gingerbread hearts were within reach, on the floor beside the broken table, the fallen kommissar.

"*Please!*"

There would be time later to decide if saving the book was right. For now Greta lunged across the platform, scooped up the book and as much of the gingerbread as she was able, and tucked it all into her apron pocket.

"Any time, now," Rob muttered, throwing on his pelt.

"Sorry." Greta settled the fox pelt over her shoulders. Magic rippled across her back, her hair, her skin.

*Sharp of claw, wild of thought.*

*Follow me,* came Rob's voice in her mind. He leapt down the dais steps, the-fox-who-was-Greta close behind. The other wolves saw them and came too, their sleek forms twisting through the melee until they burst as one into the snow-covered square. Greta blinked in the harsh sunlight. The Marktplatz was a maelstrom of panic and fear, crowded with people—some running from the Rathaus in terror, slipping and sliding in the slush and snow, others moving toward it, charging headlong at the steps with muskets, pikes and spears. Herr Auer was among them, clutching his boar spear.

*Christ,* one of the wolves muttered in Greta's head. There was a confused wash of oaths and questions and directions. Rob, it seemed, was in control. The others deferred to him, quietening as he told them what to do. Greta looked around, searching for Conran. There was no sign of the black wolf.

*Greta,* Rob said. *Run to the east gate and out to the forest now. Mira will be waiting. We'll meet you both there.*

There was no time to question Rob's command; the men of the watch and the baroness's guard were coming, bursting from the Rathaus, streaming across the square, while all around the villagers closed in. Greta threw herself forward, ducking and weaving, relying more on the fox's instincts than her own, now desperate to escape. Around her screaming and growling, the explosion of muskets and the ringing scrape of blades. A watchman thrust his pike at her and an iron-grey wolf leapt at him from the side, bearing him, shrieking and flailing, to the snowy cobbles. Greta shivered as the wolf spat out a mouthful of glistening flesh.

*Go,* it snarled at her and she obeyed, twisting through the forest of boots and breeches, her paws slipping on the cobbles, until she was at the eastern side of the Marktplatz. She was about to slide down an alley that would take her to the eastern gate when a furious howl tore across the square. Turning, she saw the black wolf—Conran—tearing through the battle. For a heartbeat she was relieved—here was help for the outnumbered wolves. Then she saw that Conran was running not at the men, but at *Rob*. He snarled, lips curling in fury, and threw himself at the lighter wolf. Rob, who

had been avoiding Herr Auer's boar spear, went down hard, and the
two wolves tumbled and slid in the snow, scrabbling and growling.
Greta watched, horrified, as they battled, heedless of the fighting
going on around them.

*Run, Täubchen,* Rob threw at her, before he fell, struggling, beneath Conran's jaws.

Greta waited until he had regained his feet and plunged bravely
against the black wolf, then ran on. The sounds of screaming and
musket shots followed her. She kept moving, heart bursting, breath
rasping. She did not see the horse, not until the flat edge of a sword
had already struck her, sending her tumbling along the snowy road, a
mess of magic and fox and woman. She came up hard against a wall,
dazed and winded, the pelt a puddle of red on the slippery cobbles.

The scarlet cloak of the horseman who had hit her blurred against
the sky. There was a rumbling sound and the clop of many hooves.
A shadow blocked the sun: a gleaming carriage. The door creaked
open to velvet darkness.

"Hello, Rose-Red," said Fizcko pleasantly. He kicked the pelt
away from Greta's reaching fingers and leaned in close. "Leave that;
I never did like foxes much."

He signaled to his men and they closed in. The last thing Greta
heard before she was bundled into the carriage was the high, desperate whining of a wounded wolf, rising over the square, then falling into terrible silence.

"So serious," Fizcko said, when the carriage was rocking gently out
of the village. "Anyone would think this was a tragic moment, instead of a happy one."

Greta flinched as a long, low howl rose from the Marktplatz.
It was joined by another, and then another, until it seemed that
the entire pack was howling as one. Whether it was in grief, or in
triumph, she could not say. Her only means of knowing—the fox
skin—remained on the cobbles in Lindenfeld. She pushed at the
carriage window, at the shining handle on the door, but both were

locked fast. No way to look back. No way to see if Rob was the wolf who howled in victory, or Conran.

"Be still, now," Fizcko said lazily, sinking back into the cushions. "You are as flighty as a strumpet on Monday."

"Where are you taking me?"

"You know where."

This close Greta could see that the magician was younger than she had first thought; the skin about his eyes was smooth and youthful, an odd contrast to the whiteness of his brows and long, thick beard. In his splendid velvets he was jeweled and glossy as a king.

"Isn't it nice to be free of that cursed dungeon?" he asked. "Those tiresome peasants? Never liked witch trials much, myself, but needs must and all that."

"What do you mean?"

"It was the only way we could get to you," Fizcko said with a shrug. He stroked one finger along the polished paneling beside him. "What with that meddling bear and those pesky wolves . . ."

The terror that had taken hold of Greta when his men had seized her had settled, to be replaced by a cold dread. Mathias had been right: the baroness and Fizcko *did* want her. Now the question remained: Why?

"It was you and the baroness," she said slowly. "You summoned the weather and froze the crops."

"How kind of you to notice."

"You caused the landslip!"

"Indeed, although I cannot take *all* the credit." He leaned in conspiratorially. "Did you like my storm?"

"That was *you*?"

"Who else would it be?"

"I thought the baroness . . ."

"No." His face darkened. "My poor Lili has not cast for years. Not since . . ." He shook his head. "It hardly matters, now. All will be as it should, soon enough."

"You—" Greta swallowed, forced herself to speak. "You killed Anna-Catherine's baby."

Fizcko shrugged. "I told you, dear Rose: needs must."

"But why?" she demanded. "What do you want with me?"

"Well, that *is* the question, isn't it?" Fizcko slid from his seat and pulled himself up on the cushions beside Greta. She caught the scent of expensive soap and spices. "My. You *are* a pretty red fox, aren't you? A rose indeed."

*Rose.* Why did he keep calling her that? She shrank away as he touched her hair, rubbed the strands between his fingers. She itched to beat against the door, to escape his keen eyes and keener magic. Curses and trickery, greediness and cruelty rolled off him like oil. But she needed answers, and soon. With every passing moment the carriage was drawing closer to the Hornberg, and she had no idea what she would find when it arrived. Her life, and the lives of Hans and Mathias, might very well depend upon what Fizcko told her now.

"Perhaps you and I will have a little *celebration* of our own tonight, when the festivities are over." Fizcko smiled in a way that reminded Greta of Herr Hueber.

"The festivities?"

"Oh, yes. It'll be quite the evening. Lili has it all planned. Feasting and dancing. Perhaps a little bearbaiting. And you, of course, will be our special guest."

The rhythm of the carriage changed as the rough road became cobbles once more. Greta looked out the window and saw the familiar streets of Hornberg, the houses rising grandly, their rooftops and window frames covered in snow. High above, Schloss Hornberg reared into view, its towers glowering through banks of lingering cloud. The half-timbered turrets were painted a fresh white, the patterned curves of the timberwork a merry red. Blood against snow.

The driver flicked his whip and the horses lowered their heads, pulling their heavy load around the forested hips of the mountain. The wintery rooftops of Hornberg were soon lost behind a wall of misty, snow-clad pines.

Fizcko swore as the horses stumbled on the slippery road, jolting the carriage. Greta would have been thrown against the window had he not steadied her. He moved with surprising speed, his arms and chest thick with unexpected muscle.

"Surprised?" He winked at her. "You should see the rest of me."

She pulled away from him, but he held her fast.

"You smell like cinnamon, you know, beneath all that blood and fear," Fizcko told her, inhaling. "Cinnamon . . . and honey. I will so enjoy becoming better acquainted with you."

And then as abruptly as he had left his seat he returned to it, settling back into the cushions. "You should rest now, dear one. You've had quite the day, and you will need your strength tonight." He closed his eyes, giving every appearance of drifting into an easy doze.

Up and up they went, winding back and forth along the mountain's face, the horses straining in their traces. With each turn the Hornberg was lost to sight, only to appear above the pines again.

*. . . when we get there, they'll lock you away so you can't escape*, the book whispered in Greta's mind. *You must find something you can use. Pain. Sorrow. Anything.*

The winter forest opened up at last, revealing the Hornberg. The castle loomed at the end of a long, cobbled causeway, its stone haunches straddling the mountain, its turrets folded like wings against the sky. The quaintness of the half-timbered towers did little to soften the castle's formidable appearance: here was a fortress, more beast than building, which had stood long centuries atop its mountaintop weathering armies and storms alike, and never fallen.

A crowd had gathered at the gates, the people shouting and shaking their fists against the portcullis.

"Where is my son?"

"And my daughter?"

"My niece came to serve Her Ladyship and never returned. . . ."

They were pushed roughly back by men-at-arms as the cart approached.

"They don't come back."

A scrawny old man stared up at the carriage window with one piercing blue eye, a filthy rag concealing the hole where his other should be. "They don't come back, the ones who go in there."

A burly guard caught sight of him, headed his way.

"It's not too late to run," the old man told Greta, through the glass. "Run, for the love of God—"

The guard struck him down with a sickening thud and two more dragged him limply away. Greta glimpsed the soles of his filthy feet, the curve of his sunken belly beneath his tattered shirt, before the portcullis lifted and the carriage rumbled slowly through. Iron teeth set in gums of weathered stone floated above. Then they were under and the heavy grating was rolling down behind them with grim and terrifying finality.

# 24

## Gingerstruck

*Soon after, Liliane contrived to destroy the lady's long, blond locks
by poisoning her favorite hair comb—a wedding gift from the viscount. All but one vital element was assembled—a single blossom
from a moon apple tree.*

The carriage passed beneath another, smaller gate and entered
a large, busy courtyard. Stone buildings peppered with neat,
red-framed windows rose sharply on all sides, so close and steep the
sky above seemed distant as the moon. Turrets topped with crimson-
and-white woodwork sailed above.

One of the buildings was larger and grander than the rest.
Graceful half-rooms with beautiful, curved turret roofs floated
among trimmings of scalloped granite and windows of colored
glass. Broad stairs led to a set of imposing doors flanked by scarlet
banners bearing the Hornberg coat of arms. Snow lay on the stone-
work and window frames, the rooftops and turrets, covering the
castle in winter.

*. . . stop gaping like a peasant and look,* the book hissed. *Is there
anything you can use?*

There were people everywhere, hurrying to and fro: stable boys
and chambermaids, grooms and even musicians, their instruments
held carefully above the slush and muck of the yard. Two gleaming
horses clopped by, led by a scruffy boy, his face pinched with cold.
A woman swung behind them, a basket brimming with cabbages
balanced on her hip. The carriage slowed. Greta heard voices on the
other side of the carriage door; the clink of weapons, the scuff of
boots on snow.

*. . . there is sorrow and pain everywhere,* the book said urgently.
*Find it!*

A young man entered the courtyard with two of the largest, most terrifying-looking dogs Greta had ever seen. Heavyset and fierce, the dogs were covered in scratches and wounds, some still bleeding. They were also proving difficult to handle, snarling and struggling against their restraints. She rested a fingertip on the glass, pointing.

*. . . ah,* the book murmured. *Bandogs. Yes, they'll do.*

"Bandogs?" Greta's voice was the barest edge of a whisper.

*. . . fighting dogs. They'll fight each other, or anything else their master sets them to. See their wounds? I'd say they've been busy of late. A good thing, too; their pain will be our power.*

Greta's belly gave a sick twist.

*. . . focus,* the book said. *Draw their pain, their suffering, into yourself.*

She did as the book instructed, reaching for the dogs' pain as though it were filaments of the earth's web and drawing it into her heart, her mind. Power thrummed through her, crackling in her hair, nipping at her toes. She steadied herself against the window.

*. . . get ready.*

The carriage slid to a halt and Fizcko's eyes fluttered open. "Home at last," he sighed, releasing the door with a deft flick of his wrist. He winked at Greta and jumped lightly down from his seat.

The carriage door opened, revealing a wash of red cloaks and stern faces. Fizcko alighted first, delivering clipped orders to the men-at-arms. The nearest of them leaned into the carriage, gauntleted hand set to close on Greta's arm. At that moment the bandogs in the courtyard turned on each other, barking and snarling. Someone swore with eye-watering proficiency. The horses shied and the carriage lurched violently forward. The man-at-arms was knocked off his feet by the heavy swing of the carriage door, his cumbersome, cloaked body, prickling with pike and sword and breastplate, crashing into his companions. Several men went down hard onto the snowy cobbles, boots splaying, pikes skittering, grunting and swearing. The carriage rolled onward, almost trampling the woman and her basket of cabbages. Round, green vegetables rolled everywhere: under the carriage wheels, beneath the boots of the men-at-arms struggling to right themselves, through the greyish slush accumulating at the bottom of those wide, grand stairs. All the while, the vicious battle between the two bandogs raged on. Their leather leashes slipped from their unfortunate handler's fingers and the animals exploded into the crowded yard. Screams and curses bounced off the Hornberg's high stone walls as the stable boys and chambermaids, the grooms and musicians descended from swift and ordered precision into spectacular, ear-wrenching chaos.

It was easy enough to slip free of the guards. Greta fled through one door then another, quickly losing herself in a web of dim corridors. She passed a slow-moving serving maid, her arms loaded with clean linens, and a yawning kitchen hand. If they had heard the commotion in the courtyard they gave no sign. Neither spared her so much as the briefest of glances.

Unheeded, Greta moved rapidly through the Hornberg, taking its measure. She passed the kitchen and the pantry, the scullery and the bakehouse, the brewhouse and the chapel and the well. She passed through the kitchen garden, its mingled scents of herbs and flowers a fleeting haven. At last she climbed a set of stairs that opened out onto a startling breezeway. Gaps in the wall revealed a heart-stopping vista of endless, rolling mountains. Below the steep wall, the forest clung to the side of the snowy mountain, winter-bare. Farther out, at the edges of the valley, the trees shaded into autumn, their leaves red and orange-gold. In the distance, beyond the baroness's domain, the mountains were springtime green in the last of the light.

"Now what?" the book asked. It had taken its ink-clad-woman shape again, dark hair lifting gently in the breeze.

"Now we find Hans and Mathias." Greta touched her own hair, cursing its bright color for an entirely different reason. "Although I'm not sure how we shall move around this place without being seen."

The book chuckled. "I am invisible to all but you. And as for *you . . ."* One ink-scrawled hand pointed to a depression in the stone walkway, where melting snow had pooled. "Behold the kitchen maid."

Greta leaned over the pool and found someone else's reflection looking back. Her hair was no longer red but an unremarkable brown, neatly coiled and covered by a demure linen coif. Her eyes, too, were brown. The clothes she had worn in the dungeon were gone, replaced with a fresh shift and neat woollen bodice, a clean skirt and snowy apron. She touched the apron's pocket and felt the reassuring shapes of the book and the bloodstained hearts.

"How did you . . . ?"

"Those dogs had suffering to spare."

Greta tried and failed to avoid thinking of who had caused that suffering. Or what they had given him in return.

"Come on," she said, turning away from her un-reflection. "We need to keep moving."

The watchtower had two curved openings in its sturdy stone-work, allowing anyone walking atop the castle wall to pass cleanly through. It also—and this was most unfortunate for whomever was posted there—allowed the weather to do the same.

The spindly guard stationed there that strange and wintery evening was feeling the tower's design most sorely. When Greta came upon him he was huddled in his scarlet cloak, scrawny hands stretched over a mean little brazier. Beside him a rickety table was spread with a set of scarred knucklebones, a half-eaten crust and some miserable-looking cheese.

"The Blood Tithes, you say?" he said, through mouthfuls of gingerbread. He held what was left of the heart out and narrowed his eyes. "By God, this is good. Added something to it, have you?"

"Just ginger," Greta said sweetly.

"It's wonderful. Warming me up good and proper, just as you promised."

Greta hid a smile. Axel Lutz had had every right to be wary of the enchanted hearts on the night of her arrest. They were easily the most potent she had ever made.

"We were speaking of the people who came to pay the Blood Tithe," she said, tapping the guard's forearm to keep him focused. "Where would I find them?"

"What? Oh. I don't know much about that, if I'm honest. . . ."

"Anything you can tell me would be most helpful." She fished another heart from her apron pocket and placed it on the table before him.

"Well . . . I *do* hear the kitchen hands talking about it, from time to time. They say the people who come up in the carts are taken to the rooms beneath the kitchen. I don't know why; there's naught but storage for powder and cannon down there; a few cells for prisoners, too."

"Do you ever see them? The people beneath the kitchen, I mean."

"No, now that you mention it." The guard had finished the first heart and bit into the second, closing his eyes as he chewed in bliss.

"I have heard there is a bear here in the Hornberg," Greta said. "Is that true?"

He ceased his chewing and eyed her suspiciously. "The bear? Why would you care where that hellish creature is?"

"I have a younger brother," Greta lied. "He wants nothing more than to see one."

"He's never seen a *bear?*"

"Not one like this. He'll never forgive me if I don't describe every detail."

The guard's eyes narrowed further. "Are you new here? I don't recollect seeing you before."

"I arrived just this week to help in the kitchen." She tilted her head modestly toward the gingerbread. "I'm a baker."

"And a damned fine one, too, if I may say so." Appeased, he stuffed what remained of the second heart into his mouth and got to his feet. "Come on, then."

He bundled his cloak around himself and started along the covered walkway atop the wall. Greta hurried after him, shivering as the wind bit into her bare neck and thin linen sleeves. The day was drawing to an end now, the Hornberg's walls falling dizzily away to the darkening forest below.

"I'll show you the great bailey, quick enough." The guard passed through another tower and emerged on a stretch of wall that was made of older, rougher stone. To her left Greta could see the back of the keep. Beneath it, the mountaintop flattened. Lawns, gardens, a small orchard and a scattering of outbuildings, some shadowed by the watchtowers dotting the wall, huddled together beneath the snow. Encircling it all was the defensive wall which narrowed in the north toward the arrow's tip. And there, near-hidden in the wall's rough stonework, lay an unassuming little door.

"What's that?" Greta asked, pointing.

"Postern," the guard said. "Opens onto the mountainside. In case we're ever attacked and need to make a sortie," he added importantly.

Two enormous linden trees rose above the central bailey, their green leaves frozen by Fizcko's unnatural winter.

"They keep the beast over there," he said, pointing to the farthest linden. "Near the kennels. Those stairs will take you into the bailey."

Greta thanked him and darted down the stairs, keeping close to a long, low outbuilding. A dog whined from within its depth. The kennels, then. She rounded the corner, breath tight in her throat, shoes quiet in the snow.

Three linden trees had once grown in the bailey. One had been recently felled, its branches torn away, its trunk sheared off. The snow around the stump had melted and in its place was a wide circle of sawdust stained with rusty smatterings that could only be dried blood.

A heavy chain was secured to the linden's bare trunk.

And at the end of the chain was the black bear.

It slumped in the sawdust, eyes closed, unmoving. Its fur was matted with blood and sawdust. Gashes scored its hide, its chest, its face, exposing the delicate, pinkish skin beneath.

"What are you doing there? Keep away!"

Greta recognized the young handler who had struggled with the bandogs in the courtyard. She ignored him, running heedlessly through the bloody sawdust.

"You there!"

The bear raised its head.

"Stop!"

Got to its feet.

"*Stay back!*"

Charged.

*If I am tired, or angry, or wounded it becomes . . . difficult.*

Too late, Greta skidded to a stop. The bear pounded on, devouring the space between them. Its paws shook the earth. Its eyes were cold as two black stones.

She threw herself to the ground, cringing away, tensed for the strike.

It never came. The chain snapped to its full length with a sickening jolt and the bear was caught up short, enormous paws spraying sawdust, heavy haunches grinding in place as it tumbled backward with the force of its own assault. It bawled, its teeth bared, dripping with spittle and blood.

Arms closed around Greta, pulling her back.

"Are you mad?" The handler was terrified and indignant beside her. "Do you know what that beast *is*?"

At this distance she could see that the air around the bear was murky with tattermagic. It was everywhere, staining the very ground with its unnaturalness. She could see, too, the leather collar binding the bear to the felled tree. The leather collar, and the heavy silver lock securing it in place.

"Soft in the head or something, are you?" The handler had a round face, pocked with faded scars. "That bear's a demon. You could have been killed!" He stalked toward the kennels.

"Please." Greta followed him. "I'm sorry. I did not think . . ."

"That's abundantly clear!"

More men were at the building's entrance, seated around an old board balanced atop two stools to form a makeshift table. Behind them, countless eyes glittered wolfishly in the shadows.

"What happened?" one of the men asked, throwing a pair of ancient bones. He had fair hair tied back in a greasy tail.

"Some cracked piece wanted to pat the bear," said the first man. He noticed Greta behind him, winced. "Brace yourselves. She's followed me back."

As one the men looked up from their gaming and focused on Greta.

"Loosen the top of your bodice," the woman-book whispered.

*Eyes, smiles, hips; lace, silk, ribbons, thread . . . these are your weapons.*

"I'm sorry if I frightened you," Greta said, fumbling at her laces. Her whole body was trembling. "I only wanted to see the bear."

"Did you hear that? 'I only wanted to see the bear!'" One of the men gave a mocking rendition of Greta's voice and the others laughed.

"The bear's to be kept away from people," said a third man, older than the rest with a broad scar running down one side of his face. His gaze flickered over Greta's chest before returning to the bones. "It's the baroness's orders."

"That's a shame." She drew out a handful of hearts and waved them enticingly. "And I brought you some of my very best baking, too."

"Baking?"

"Hm-hmm." She spread the hearts on the table, leaned in. "Try some."

The greasy blond took the first bite. "Heavens. It's as good as—"

"Here, give me one."

"And me!"

One by one they snatched up the hearts until all were crunching rapturously.

It was wonderful.

"Ease up, lads!" the young handler complained. Crumbs spilled down the front of his shirt. "I've only had one. . . ."

"That's not true, Bernd," said the scarred man sternly. "You've had at least three."

"That fool," the woman-book remarked, "is glazed as a butter cake."

"He's gingerstruck," Greta murmured. "They all are." She leaned over the handler. He stopped eating at once, sniffing at her hair. "My, but you smell good."

"I was hoping you might help me with something." She drew back and he followed, getting to his feet so fast his chair crashed over. The others laughed.

"What would you have me do?" He was like a puppy, eager and sniffing.

"Have a care," the woman-book muttered. "At any moment he might lick you or soil himself. It's difficult to know which."

"I want you to give me something," Greta said.

"Anything."

"I want the key to the bear's collar."

He went still. "The key?"

"You don't have to tell the others." She pressed close. "It will be our secret."

"Our secret?" He all but whined the word.

The woman-book snickered.

"Just one little key." Greta tapped his nose with her finger. "That's not so hard, is it?"

"Oh, but it *is*," he moaned. "I wish I could, believe me—but I can't."

"Why not?"

"Because I do not have it. Only one man keeps the keys in the Hornberg." He sniffed. "If man he can be called."

"Who?"

"The baroness's imp. Lord Fizcko."

There were marvels everywhere. A cistern caught rainwater from the rooftops, so there was no need to haul fresh water up from the river. Forty fireplaces—*forty of them!*—many set within lavish bed-chambers. Tapestries so large and rich that a tall man could not reach the top. They glimmered with scenes of noble hunts and deep forests filled with fantastical beasts. There were chalices and candle-sticks wrought of gold, and private chapels lined with glass windows stained in blue, yellow and red. Beneath them, the last of the day's sunlight fell across the polished floor like jewels. All these wonders, and yet it seemed to Greta that God was nowhere near the Horn-berg. There was a coldness to the castle despite its rich furnishings; a pervasive, malevolent air.

The last of the gingerbread hearts had gained her access to Fizcko's chamber. She hesitated at the door, listening.

"He's not here," the woman-book whispered.

Still Greta lingered, unwilling to admit, even to the book, how much the man unsettled her. She thought of Hans, locked away somewhere below, and Mathias, and all that he endured. *Would* endure, if she did not act. She set her shoulders and stepped inside.

The walls shone with weavings of gold and silver and the bed was thick with cushions and furs. Jeweled caskets crouched on gleaming cabinets. Clothing chests billowed with coats and shirts and hose. A beautiful, costly room. Even so a shiver of unease passed over her.

"Best hurry," the woman-book whispered. "I cannot promise he won't recognize you. Or, at least, recognize the spell."

Greta looked helplessly around. The room was immense. There were half a hundred places where a man might stow a key. "Where should I begin?"

"It hardly matters. Just hurry."

She moved about the room, opening and closing, lifting and looking. She stopped, however, when she saw the iron cage, empty now, its intricacies catching the last of the sun though the shutters.

"Have you found the key?" the woman-book asked, coming to Greta's side.

The ball was cold to the touch. A portion of its ironwork was hinged, forming a door small enough for Fizcko to clamber through. A heavy iron lock held the door in place.

Greta hefted the lock in her fingers, considering. Despite his power, despite his magic, Fizcko feared the bear. The knowledge was oddly comforting. A matching key lay in a carved box on a table nearby. She slipped it into the lock. Twisted. The door swung smoothly open.

*Well, then.*

"What do you do there?" A harried-looking woman bustled into the chamber, a pitcher of hot water in one hand, a linen sheet in the other. She was followed by two young chambermaids bearing a large tub.

"Tell her you were sent here to help," the woman-book hissed.

"I've come to help," Greta blurted.

"Oh?" The woman looked her over. "I've not seen you before."

"I came this morning. With the Blood Tithes."

"Blood Tithes?" The woman frowned. "Why aren't you with the rest of them?"

"Lie," the woman-book whispered.

"They told me to come here."

"Hmm." The woman gestured impatiently to the chambermaids. "No, no. Put it by the fire. And start bringing up the water." She looked at Greta. "I could certainly use you. There's too much work, what with the young lord come back to stay. I take it you can sweep a floor? Set a fire? Clean a hearth and tend a flame?"

Greta nodded.

"Very good. I'm Frau Pieters. I oversee Lady Elisabeth's household." As she spoke Frau Pieters laid the linen sheet into the tub and poured the pitcher of hot water over it. "You'll answer to me, for as long as you're here. What is your name?"

". . . Lena."

"Take this, Lena"—she handed Greta the empty pitcher—"and help the others fetch hot water."

"Hot water?"

"For Lord Fizcko's bath. Off with you, now!"

The sun was setting when the bath was filled. The other chambermaids promptly scurried off, leaving Greta alone with her empty pitcher.

"What are you doing there?"

Greta whirled. Fizcko himself lounged in the doorway, a goblet in one hand.

"Readying your bath, Mein Herr."

"*Readying your bath, Mein Herr*," he mimicked, high and cruel. "Well, ready it and get out!"

Greta nodded.

"Wait."

She went still.

"I've not seen you before."

His gaze crawled over her new face, her new clothes.

*. . . calm, be calm*, the book breathed. Its womanly form had disappeared at the magician's approach. *I cannot mask your scent. That oil there for the bath, see? Spill it.*

"I arrived this morning," Greta said in her new voice. She felt surreptitiously for the carved oil pot on the table behind her, unscrewed the lid.

He came closer. "Come to work your tithes away, have you?"

"Yes." She kept her eyes downcast. "My mother could not afford them after my father died, so— Oh, no! I'm so sorry, Mein Herr!"

The lidless oil pot lay on its side, a stream of oil oozing across the table and onto the carpet below. The scent of lemons and spiced oranges filled the room, warm and fragrant.

"Fool!" Fizcko cried, hurrying to right the bottle. "Do you know how much this cost?" He tried to scoop the oil back into the pot, and instead smeared it all over his sleeve. "Curse it! Here, take my coat. You'd better pray it's not ruined."

Greta did as he bid, sliding the rich fabric from his shoulders and settling it over a beautifully carved chair.

"Bah, there's oil everywhere," Fizcko lamented. He had done what he could with the oil, and stood, slick hands raised helplessly. Oil splodged his fine shirt and breeches.

"Foolish girl. Don't just stand there—help me undress!"

"I'm so sorry. . . ."

"No, you're not. But you will be, I promise you. Here, help me with my shirt. You'll have to kneel."

"Mein Herr . . ."

"*Kneel.*"

On her knees Greta was of a height with him. She grasped the hem of his shirt and lifted it carefully over his head. His skin was smooth, the muscles of his chest and arms beautifully defined.

"Now the buckle," he spat.

Greta hesitated; the buckle in question belonged to Fizcko's fine leather belt. She opened her mouth to protest, then closed it again. Hanging from that fine leather belt was an iron ring bristling with keys of every shape and size. Somewhere amid that mess of metal must lie the keys to both the bear's collar and the cells. She forced herself to reach for him. Forced her fingers to slide the buckle free.

Fizcko was watching her. "You've undressed a man before," he said. His anger was waning and a new gleam had come to his eyes. "What was your name again?"

"Lena." Greta drew away from him and laid the belt—and its cargo of keys—beside the coat.

"Come closer, Lena."

Greta, still on her knees, edged toward him.

"Perhaps there is another way you can make your clumsiness up to me." Fizcko stroked the top of her breast, leaving a shining trail of lemon and orange. "After all, it would be such a shame to waste this oil. It came all the way from Spain, you know."

"*Where is my hot water?*" The voice floating along the corridor was furious and feminine. "*And why has my fire not been tended?*"

Footsteps in the corridor and the maidservants scuttled by. One looked in, her eyes wide with fear. "Frau Pieters says you're to help us fill Lady Elisabeth's bath," she told Greta, with a brief curtsy in Fizcko's direction.

"You'd best go," he said regretfully. "As much as I'd love you to wash my back, my lady needs you more."

Greta got to her feet and hurried from the room, taking her pitcher with her. At the end of the corridor another door lay open, revealing a chamber of such startling loveliness that she slid to a stop.

Clusters of buttery candles glowed upon creamy walls painted in exquisite detail: trees, vines, flowers and leaves. The ceiling, heavy rafters and enormous hearth were the same, twining and weaving in greens and crimsons and pinks, so the room became one large and glorious work of art. Huge timber pillars stretched from the floor to the ceiling, oak-broad, their tops outstretched like the boughs of ancient trees. It was as if the forest had come indoors, bringing with it all its beauty. There was untold luxury, too: glossy furniture, vases of fresh flowers, silken cushions, rich carpets, and a washstand with a golden basin surrounded by lotions, creams and powders in china pots and wooden boxes. A young woman stood before a shining mirror, her back to Greta, her long black hair unbound. Beyond her, Greta glimpsed a sumptuous canopied bed, set atop a high platform with intricately carved steps.

"Well? Do you intend to stand there and stare all night, girl?"

Greta flinched, expecting that sharpness to be directed at her, then stilled as she realized that the lady was addressing the second chambermaid, who was hurrying across the room, a pitcher of steaming water in her hands.

The chambermaid's hands shook as she emptied the water into the golden basin. Water sloshed onto the glossy table, splashing the gown of crimson satin thrown over the chair. Greta winced as the baroness's fist cracked against the girl's jaw, her heavy rings splitting skin. The girl stumbled out, clutching at her bleeding face. Greta followed her, but not before she glimpsed the tip of the baroness's perfect nose and one fine, black brow as she licked the girl's blood from her fingers.

# 25
## Baiting

*Moon apple trees flower only in winter and are exceedingly rare, for they do not start from a seed as other trees do. For a moon apple tree to exist, a wild apple tree must first grow in a place where the moon shines upon it. It must also—and here is the heart of the matter— grow beside a bittersweet nightshade. This potent little plant must twist and climb all over the apple tree, overpowering it, so the poison in its small, red berries turns the apple's leaves and branches black, and its fruit a poisonous crimson.*

Night fell over the Hornberg. Greta, who had no intention of helping the chambermaids fill the baroness's bath, hurried through the keep, the pitcher clutched to her chest. She passed the baroness's sweetheart, Lord Frederick, and his companions, each one of them sleek and supple as a warhorse, all of them resplendent in jackets embroidered with silver and gold thread. Frederick wore silver hose that showed his shapely calves and breeches adorned with countless silken bows. She would have laughed at the sight— such riches, such waste—were she not so frightened. It had been easy to slide Fizcko's keys from his belt as she passed that lovely chair; to clutch them tight against her skirts to stop their rattling as she hurried from the room. Now, they burned against her skin.

She wound through corridors and across breezeways, hardly knowing which way to turn. To the kitchen, and the dungeons below it? Or to the bear? She had no doubt that Fizcko would miss his keys the moment he climbed from his bath. And when he did, his men would come looking. They would rip the keys from her and bear her away.

*Lili has it all planned. Feasting and dancing. Perhaps a little bear-baiting. And you, of course, will be our special guest.*

"Lena! Good." Frau Pieters hurried toward her and Greta thrust the keys in her apron pocket. "My lady has ordered that supper be served outside tonight, in the bailey. Though how she can eat while they're tormenting that poor beast, I'll never know."

She took Greta's pitcher and led her farther into the depths of the keep until they came to a huge, whitewashed room topped with arching stone pillars. Copper pots gleamed in the light from the massive hearth and rows of smoked meats and wurst hung from hooks beside baskets of onions and cabbages. Pots of oils and spices, honey and goose fat sat in neat rows on heavy-timbered shelves. Cooks and kitchen maids hurried to and fro, shouting and ordering, stirring and pouring. Greta's stomach clenched in hunger. She had not eaten since the evening before, when Axel Lutz had pushed a bowl of watery soup between the bars of her cell beneath the Rathaus.

"We'll need you to help serve," Frau Pieters said, gesturing at a platter.

Greta's heart sank. She had hoped to find a way down into the rooms beneath the kitchen. Instead, she found herself joining the ranks of servants filing across the kitchen garden and down into the bailey, their arms loaded with platters of salted meats and candied fruits, whole roasted birds and joints of meat. She walked with them, belly grumbling, trying not to look at her platter of soft bread, delicate cheese and olives.

The bailey looked vastly different, now.

Two long tables had been arranged beneath the row of linden trees, draped with heavy white cloths. Chairs lined them, best placed to watch the bear pit. Torches flickered everywhere, brighter than the rising stars. They burned in a bright ring around the pit itself. And in the center of it all, the bear. Huge, and savage, its great dark head resting on its paws.

Greta joined the other servants at the tables, sliding her platter onto the expanse of snowy white fabric. Her heart was pounding, her hands trembling. Her longing to get to the bear, to free him from what was coming, was palpable. Ten steps. Ten steps, perhaps one or two more, and she would be at his side.

At his side. The last time she was there the bear had leapt at her as though he would kill her, as though *she,* and not the dogs, were his enemy. If not for the chain binding him to the stump, he would have killed her. Whatever remained of Mathias was gone, swallowed by fear and pain.

Back and forth Greta went, between bailey and kitchen, between determination to free the bear and fear of what he might do to her when she tried. When temptation became too much she stole food from the platters, cramming bread and meat and olives into her mouth, hardly pausing to chew. More than once she attempted to slip away and search for Hans, but each time there was something else to fetch or carry. She was in the bailey, setting yet another mouthwatering platter upon the table, when the servants around her began to draw fearfully back into the shadows beneath the lindens. Greta went with them, her gaze following theirs to the top of the bailey steps. The baroness had arrived. In a crimson gown, her dark hair curling, her fair skin glowing, Elisabeth glimmered like rubies and snow on black glass. Frederick took her hand as she descended the steps. Even from a distance the handsome young lord's affections were painfully clear. He could hardly keep his eyes off her.

Greta searched for Fizcko and saw with relief that he was not yet there. Even so, she was not willing to risk crossing the bailey and being seen by the baroness. She ducked her head, melting into the mass of servants, touching the nearest linden as she passed.

*Leaf that's green, earth and air . . .*

Rough steps led upward. Greta took them quickly, skirts bunched in her hands, until she emerged on top of the wall. Torchlight rose against the Hornberg's vast walls and flickered against its windows. The mountains were a rolling darkness; far below, the lights of Hornberg twinkled. She leaned on the parapet, the night breeze cooling her sweaty brow, the evening star comforting her with its steady light. Worthless, both, when the barking and snarling began. When the harsh growls of a wounded bear rose from the pit below.

It is one thing to think of a bearbaiting. To imagine the bear, chained and muzzled, and the dogs dancing around it, snarling.

It is quite another thing to see it.

To begin with, there is blood. Lots and lots of it. Blood from the dogs, blood from the bear. Blood from scratches and bites, maulings and broken teeth, from the dog handler's whip. There is skin and spittle and slather, too; the sawdust is soon soaked with it, and flecked with chunks of gore.

There is the baiting itself—the eagerness of the dogs, their nimbleness, their patience as they wait for their advantage. They lunge for the bear's throat, and leap upon it, biting everywhere so the bear is forced to claw and twist and tumble to wind itself free. There is but a brief moment of respite before fresh dogs are released into the ring to replace the ones that are exhausted or wounded or dead. More dogs and more, a relentless tide, crashing again and again against the staggering bear, worrying and snaring until its sides heave and its skin hangs in tatters and its mouth foams.

And then there is the sound of it. The yapping, the crack of a broken neck, the whine of a dog as its tongue is ripped out or its scalp clawed away. Whimpering. The screams and jeers of the crowds. The huffing and blowing of the bear, the wet slap as it shakes the blood from its fur. And the smell? The copper and salt tang of blood, the smoke from a hundred torches, the reek and sweat of the watching nobility, so fine in their velvets and satins, their jewels and hose and shining boots. The cloying sweetness of wine spilled on silk and sawdust.

Greta turned away, too sickened to watch further. She stumbled along the wall, ears ringing with the sound of high-bloodedness and cruelty. Faster she ran, until her hands found cool stone and night air and silence. Too late; nausea washed over her, hot and fast. She leaned over the wall and heaved until there was nothing to give up but bile and hopelessness.

Distantly, she heard the crowd's appreciative howls.

"How long can a bear survive such treatment?" the woman-book, elbows leaning on the parapet, mused.

"I hardly know." Greta slumped against the wall, the stone beautifully cold on her skin. Before the baroness's arrival she had planned to go back to the kitchen and search for Hans in the chambers below. When her brother was safe, she would return to the bailey and wait in the shadows until the feasting was over and the bear was alone once more. Instead, she was trapped atop the wall, with the baroness between her and her brother. And Mathias . . .

"Rob said bears are hard to kill. He must hold on," she said. "He *must.*"

In a bid to distract herself she fumbled in her apron and drew out Fizcko's keys.

"Which one is it?" the woman-book asked.

Which indeed? Greta held the bristling ring up against the cold sky. Starlight caught at a key that was smaller than the rest. Dull and unassuming as it was, something about it called to her.

"That's the one," the woman-book agreed.

Greta slid the little key from the bunch, then hesitated. Beside it was a key that was larger and shinier than the rest. As large and shiny as the one that had opened Fizcko's beautiful cage. She held it up against the stars. A perfect match. She slipped it, too, from the ring, tucked them both into her bodice and pushed the ring back into her apron.

"There!" The clatter of boots, the scrape of steel. "There she is!"

It seemed Fizcko had emerged from his bath.

"Run," the woman-book hissed, needlessly; Greta was already on her feet. She dashed along the wall, shoes slipping on snow-patched stone. Through one watchtower, then another, the men-at-arms clamoring and clanking behind. The keep gloomed above, its turrets and towers menacing against the stars. A stairway loomed out of the darkness. Greta scrambled down it, landing in the cool sweetness of the kitchen garden. Rosemary and lavender stained the air.

Shouts and curses behind her. She ran for the closest doorway, slipped inside. Darkness. Then, as her eyes adjusted, a faint light far below. A stairwell, winding steeply down.

"What is this place?"

"Who cares? They're coming. Down we go."

Greta edged down the stairs, one hand braced on the rough wall. The steps were narrow, uneven. They curled tightly about one another, a deathly spiral, tightening and tightening. Torches hovered in wall brackets, illuminating the downward curve of the stairs, shiny-wet in the dim, fading into darkness.

"I don't like this," she whispered.

"You think I do? Keep going."

The smell, when it came, near buckled her over. She clung to the wall, gasping. The torches had become fewer the farther down they went, and the dark—and the stench—rose steadily.

"Like the privy, the tanners and the slaughter yard, combined," the book-woman gasped.

Fear took tight hold of Greta. Panic squeezed. The stifling air, the stench, the weight of the stone walls seemed about to crush her. Somewhere below, the source of that smell was waiting.

"I can't go down there."

"You have to. They're still looking for us. Can you not hear them?" Faint voices, from above. Boots on stone. Cursing.

Greta swallowed, squared her shoulders. Took down a torch from a bracket in the wall and held it high. One step, two. Three steps, four. Down, down, around and down until the stairs pushed her into open space: a forest of stone pillars webbed with iron. More torches revealed cages. Cages everywhere, and inside them, people.

The light from Greta's torch shone on glazed and sunken eyes. Tangled limbs, many bare and filthy. Some poor souls stared at her. Others did not.

"Keep moving," the woman-book hissed.

Something touched her arm and she skittered away, stifling a scream. A dead man leaned against the bars of his prison, a mess of jumbled limbs poking through the bars. Greta knew his face. Herr Weber had helped in Rob's fields at harvests and bought gingerbread for his children. Now, his eyes were open and sightless, his lips a mottled grey. Greta almost dropped the torch. Almost turned and fled back up the stairs.

Then, in the cage beside Herr Weber's, another face she knew.

"It's Hans," she whispered, to the book. "Change me back, quickly."

"That would be foolish," the woman-book warned.

"I don't care. Change me back!"

She felt the magic lift, a peculiar prickling over her face and head and body, before she ran to her brother.

"*Hans!*" She fell to her knees, gripped his hands as he reached weakly for her through the bars. "Thank the stars I've found you. Are you hurt?"

"Greta! Is it really you?"

Hans seemed to have aged years in just a few days. His eyes were huge and dark, his face wasted. His clothes were smeared with dirt and rusty rings of dried blood.

"Hans?" Her voice trembled. "What has happened to you?"

"They came for him three days ago." In the cage beside her brother Greta made out the features of Gertrud Werner, who owned the inn in Wolfach, and a dozen more faces she recognized from Lindenfeld and Hornberg. Gertrud's lined face was haggard, her eyes bright with fear. "They said they needed his pain."

"Who?" But Greta already knew the answer.

"The baroness and that white-haired man. They took your brother, and they . . . tortured him. We could hear them. It went on for hours and hours. We thought he would surely die."

"They said they needed it to snow," Hans said weakly.

"Oh my God." That unnatural storm, the snow that had fallen and fallen, coating the valley. Every moment of it Hans had suffered.

"Greta, they spoke of you," he rasped. "They made the storm because they wanted you to come here. Why did you come? You should have stayed away." His hands were thin, his fingers like bones. Greta clutched them tight.

"I came for you," she said. "Do you think I would leave you here to die?" She raised her head. "I came for all of you."

"Bless your heart, Greta Rosenthal," Gertrud said. "But I do not think you will manage it. Blood Tithe, they call us. Never was there a truer name. You see those poor people chained, there?"

Greta turned. Behind her, more people, though these poor souls were strung up on great hooks and hanging like pigs at Martinmas. Each and every one had had their chests cut open. Blood spilled down their bellies, pooled on the stone floor.

"They tortured them like they tortured your poor brother, and then they took their hearts and livers, their lungs and their blood," Gertrud said. "Cut them up and drained them like animals. We're like pigs and goats to them, nothing more. Every day they come for more of us."

*They don't come back, the ones who go in there.*

*It's not too late to run. Run, for the love of God—*

"You should go, Greta," Hans said. "Get out. Before they catch you, too."

"No, Hans. I'm getting you out of here." She drew the keys, a bristling mass, from her pocket. "I have the keys, see?"

There was a stirring among the prisoners, a wave of surprise and hope.

"She has the keys," someone muttered.

"Look! She has *his* keys!"

Then, from the stairs Greta had descended only moments before, the sound of footsteps and voices. Wavering torchlight.

"They're coming, Greta," Hans said. "You must go."

"Take us with you!" A chorus of terrified pleas. "Please, don't leave us!"

Greta could have sobbed. Could have pressed her face against the bars and cried till her shoulders heaved and her throat was hoarse. Instead, she pushed herself to her feet.

"There are more stairs," Hans murmured, pointing. "That way."

"I'll come back," she promised, squeezing his hands. "I'll come back for you all, I swear."

She turned and ran, past the cages and the chained bodies, to where a second set of stairs rose. Greta hurried up them, heedless of what might lie at their end, until, breath rushing, legs burning, she burst into whitewashed splendor.

The kitchen.

It was empty, now. Somewhere nearby the clank of cups and the scraping of spoons. Weary voices. The kitchen workers, taking their own supper while they could, before the clearing and washing and cleaning began. Greta threw herself among a heap of vegetable-filled sacks and baskets, pulling them close about her, burrowing beneath their earthy mass. She listened, heart pounding, as the men-at-arms clattered into the kitchen. Most of them kept moving on into the keep, but two lingered.

"Why do we need her again?" said one close by. Through the basket's weavings Greta saw him prod half-heartedly at a pile of cabbages.

"The goblin wants her," his companion replied, peering into a barrel.

"Hsst! Don't *call* him that! Lord Fizcko hears all, you know. Every whisper. Every *thought!*"

"Hogwash."

"It's true! Isn't he a magician? I've heard—"

"I care not a shit for what you've heard," the second man hissed. "His Grace the Goblin has asked for the new cinder-garbler, and we're to deliver her to him. That's all you need worry about."

They moved off after the rest of the guards, their voices fading.

Silence.

"Is this what we're reduced to?" the woman-book asked snidely. "Hiding among the cabbages like rats?"

Greta pushed the baskets aside, clambered to her feet. Shouts floated up from the bailey, and then the bear's sudden groan, fearful, pained.

She was in danger, it was clear. But Mathias needed her desperately. And, below her very feet, her brother and half a hundred other people were confined like animals before slaughter.

"I don't know what to do." The enormity of the task before her, the danger, was overwhelming.

"Could be there's a way to save yourself *and* the bear *and* the peasants," the book said. It had once again assumed its woman shape. The light from the hearth glowed through its inky form. "And all without leaving this kitchen."

"What do you mean?"

"So much pain," the woman-book murmured enticingly. "So much loss and fear. Can you not feel it? It's everywhere."

Greta *could* feel it. Suffering cloaked the world like the night sky: vast and dark. The bear's distress, and her own. And, even stronger, the terror of the people below.

"Their pain is your salvation," the woman-book said. "Your weapon. Draw upon it, Greta. Use it. Why, in such a place a tatterwitch could kill every one of those guards with a snap of her fingers. She could free the bear with a glance."

"I'm not a tatterwitch."

"Aren't you?"

"Adding blood to some gingerbread hardly counts."

"You've been tattercasting for much longer than that. Think of all the baking we've done together, over the years."

"But I never cut myself then," Greta objected. "I didn't use blood—"

"Not all pain can be seen," the woman-book said. "We used your suffering. Your grief, your loneliness, your heartache. The Devil knows you had enough to spare."

She moved about the kitchen, her papery skin illuminated by the fire. Behind her, pots of spices sat neatly labeled on the shelves.

*. . . hang it on a tree that never bore fruit, and she shall bear of a surety . . .*

*. . . if you would be loved . . .*

*. . . to punish and torment . . .*

"The people below are ripe for the picking," the woman-book said. "They will give you what you need. Fear. Pain. Loss. The air is thick with it. You could save the bear, and free yourself, so easily." She held out her arm, where words glimmered like wet ink, freshly scriven.

*. . . to kill a man . . .*

"No," Greta said, backing away. "No."

And yet . . .

*Yes. Grief, suffering, heartache. Haven't I given enough?* She could *feel* the anguish of the prisoners below, their pain. And something else.

Power.

"You value the lives of those peasants over your brother? Over Mathias?"

"No." Greta's voice trembled. Magic seeped through the stone floor, the soles of her feet, swirling around her, dark and delicious. It was as addictive as the rush that came with drinking a heady wine, the breathlessness that followed a lover's dance. What would it be to wield such power? To destroy the baroness, the Hornberg itself? Stone and ruin, and Hans and Mathias safe. So easy. So very, very easy.

"We cannot," she said thickly. The dark was gentle as a lover against her skin, insistent, persuasive. She shivered. "We cannot . . . harm others to save them."

"Not harming. Just *using* what is already there."

Greta shook her head, clenched her hands into fists; her fingers itched to take and take and take.

"A little," the woman-book purred, "for *so* much."

She was there: at the edge of a great precipice, her entire body begging, *screaming,* to throw itself over, into the intoxicating shadows below. No more pain. No more guilt. Just freedom. Just bliss.

Greta took a step. Then another. One hand opened, coils of inky magic spiraling at her wrist and fingertips, eager to do her will.

"Yes," the woman-book breathed.

Another step, and still another.

One more step.

She leaned up, plucked something small from a kitchen shelf, and slipped it into her pocket.

"What—what are you *doing?*" the woman-book gasped.

Greta did not answer. It was taking all her resolve to push what remained of the darkness aside and return.

"You were there! You were so close!"

"I was *too* close," Greta managed. "It will not happen again."

"*What?*"

Greta turned to the stairs. The dark was ebbing, her strength returning.

"Where are you going?" the woman-book demanded.

"To free my brother."

When the last of the cages was unlocked Greta helped Hans up the winding stairs and into the courtyard, where the rest of the prisoners were emerging from the gloom. The noise of the baiting had ceased. She heard raised voices, the clink of glasses, drunken laughter as Elisabeth and her guests returned to the castle. From somewhere inside musicians were playing, sweet notes skimming the night.

"Must be time for the dancing," Greta muttered. She turned to the other villagers. "Come on. We must get to the postern. Stay in the shadows if you can." It was the only way she could think of to get them out safely. The way would be steep and rough and dark, but they would manage. They had to.

"We should find weapons first," hissed a young man Greta recognized. It was Joseph Casser, Anna-Catherine's husband. "Or, at the least, something to defend ourselves with. If they try to lock us up again I intend to fight my way free."

"I, too," Joseph's brother, Peter, agreed.

"Joseph is right."

"Joseph *is* right," came a familiar voice. "There's a guardroom at the base of the tower across the court. You'll find weapons there."

Greta swung around. Rob Mueller leaned against a shadowy wall, arms crossed, completely at ease. "Although, my men and I would be more than happy to do any fighting for you."

They flowed out into the night, a frightened flock with only wolves to guard them. Rob's men moved among the villagers, assisting the wounded, edging them steadily on, or ran along the battlements above, keeping watch. Rob led the way, one arm supporting Hans, the other tight about his musket. They kept to the shadows, moving fast, avoiding the larger courtyards where the baroness and her guests were strolling back to the keep, their laugher and pleasantries drifting on the night.

"Conran isn't with you," Greta said quietly to Rob. She was on Hans's other side, helping Rob, coaxing her brother on.

"No. Turns out I wasn't as tired of fighting as I thought." He glanced at her over Hans's curly head, resting on his shoulder. "A good thing, too, as it turns out."

She swallowed. "Did you . . . ?"

"I did what I had to do."

There was a faint scuffle from the wall above, a muffled cry. A Hornberg man-at-arms fell from the top of the wall, landing with a thump. A sell-sword leaned over the battlement, his wolfish grin flickering before he disappeared again.

"And the village?"

"Will not forget what happened for a very, very long time. I'm sorry to tell you, Täubchen, that you won't be able to return there. You were seen . . ." He slowed his steps, shifted his musket to the crook of his arm and drew her fox pelt from within his coat. "*This* was seen. If anyone believed you to be innocent, they do not believe it now. I'm so sorry."

"Do not be." She reached across Hans and took the pelt. "You did what you had to do."

"Is that . . . a fox skin?" Hans muttered thickly.

"I'll tell you everything," Greta promised him as Rob took her brother's weight once more and urged him forward. "Just keep moving."

Northward through the long, night-dark bailey they went, past the kennels and the mews, the snow-covered gardens and orchard, until they came to the loneliest corner of the castle, the tip of the spearpoint with its secret door.

Greta watched her brother worriedly. He had managed the long walk to the postern but was clearly flagging, his face pallid and drawn. "Will you manage it?"

Hans threw her a pained smile. "To be free of this place? I would happily crawl through Hell." He broke away from her, leaned heavily against the wall. "But first a moment's rest . . ."

They stood together watching as Rob unlocked the postern, creaked it slowly open. The first of the villagers stepped through, moving slowly into the steep darkness on the other side. Beyond them, stretching away into the night, was the tantalizing freedom of the forest.

"I wanted to thank you, Greta." Hans was looking at her, the bones of his narrow face sharp. "You saved me. Again. I fear I do not deserve it."

"Of course you do," she said, throat tight. "Now, go."

She nudged him toward the postern, watching from the shadows beneath the wall as he walked slowly painfully through. When he was gone she fell back. Farther and farther, until the last of the villagers had passed ahead of her. The sell-swords were all at the postern now, helping the villagers ease themselves down the steep, snowy mountainside. Greta tucked herself hard into the curve of a watchtower. Rob, his hair shining silver in the starlight, was the last to go. He checked briefly for stragglers and ducked through the doorway. It closed behind him with a rusty click.

"You," the woman-book hissed from the shadows, "are a bigger fool than I gave you credit for."

"It's fine," Greta assured her. "It's fine. We'll be right behind them." She laid the fox pelt over her shoulders and became another shadow in the snow, moving fast and light, unseen.

# 26
## The Truth of Things

*Rosabell tried to reason with her sister—to treat their stepmother so was not only cruel, but dangerous. She knew too well how virulent moon apple trees could be. They grew against the very tide of nature: fruiting in the winter and blooming strange, silvery flowers in the autumn. They were rare, difficult to find. In all her ramblings Rosabell had seen just one, as deep in the forest as she had ever allowed herself to go. Despite her sister's pleas Liliane would not be dissuaded. She set out one winter's morning, a basket over her arm and a cloak of crimson wool warming her against the snow. Rosabell, of course, went with her.*

The first time Greta had met Mathias his eyes were utterly dark. His huge, black body had loomed like a boundary stone marking the path to Hell. He had licked honey from her fingertips, and she had thought she might die of fear.

It had been nothing compared to how she felt now.

The bear's eyes were open. Glinting in the starlight. Watching her. No sign of recognition. No telling what beast-dark thoughts stalked its mind.

*I will never forget that first day beneath the beech tree. There was magic all around you. I smelled it, stronger than the spices, sweeter than the honey on your skin. The air was rife with it.*

It seemed to Greta now that they had come to it: the moment when Mathias's fate would be decided, and the strands that bound her life to his would either tighten or fray. She slipped out of the fox skin, straightened in the snow.

The woman-book cleared her throat, pointing to Greta's apron where the real book lay. "Perhaps you should leave me on that nice stone wall there, while you . . ."

"You're frightened."

"Never. But I would rather not be torn to shreds, should your little plan fail."

"That makes two of us." But she removed the book from her apron and laid it carefully upon the wall. Then she drew the smaller of the remaining keys from her bodice, opened the little jar she had stolen from the kitchen, and smeared its contents over her hands, collarbones, and throat.

All was ready.

"*That's* your plan?" The woman-book, who had removed herself to a careful distance, shook her head in disgust. "You turned down my magic to dabble with *bee piss?*"

"It's not—" Distracted, Greta went to argue then shook her head. *No time.* She faced the bear and took a deep, snow-cold breath. Willed her feet forward into the sawdust. The scent of blood assailed her, and a memory: Mathias's bare chest in the firelight, the scents of yarrow and blood and honey.

*I would follow you to the very edge of Hell had I the scent of honey on your skin to lead me.*

She pushed her honeyed palms out before her, forced herself to keep moving. One step and then another. Her heart was beating so hard she was sure the bear would hear it. Part of her hoped it would. Perhaps it would recognize the sound and remember her.

Closer and closer.

The bear raised its head. Heaved itself to its feet.

*To the very edge of Hell . . .*

Paces away, now. She could barely think for fear.

"Mathias," she breathed, crouching slowly, stretching out her arms. "Come back to me."

The bear shuffled forward. It nosed her outstretched palms, sniffed at the sticky sweetness there. It reeked of blood and violence, the wounds on its face glistening. And yet its tongue was gentle as a dog's.

"That's right," Greta murmured. "That's right."

The bear nosed at her face, her neck, licking at the honey there. Her fingers smoothed its thick, matted fur, fumbled against its collar. She found the lock, slipped the key inside, twisted.

The heavy collar slid free.

"Come back, Mathias," she said. "Please. I need you to come back."

The bear's fur trembled beneath her fingers. It lowered its heavy head, stumbled and groaned, just as it had in the cave. She stepped back, waiting.

A hand closed around her wrist, iron tight. Fizcko, leering up at her, his fingers digging into her skin. She tried to pull away. Turned, struggling, to find a dozen red-cloaked guards assembled on the snow-covered wall above, their muskets raised.

"You are a tricksy fox, aren't you?" Fizcko said. "Stealing my keys, changing your face. But no more." His grip on Greta's wrist tightened, twisting. Pain, white and blinding. She gasped, fell to her knees in the snow.

The bear gave a furious roar and plunged toward her. A musket fired, then another. Musket balls peppered the sawdust.

"Don't shoot him!" Greta cried.

Fizcko raised a hand. The shooting stopped. Greta, hearing the *tap, tap, tap* of powder horns on metal, the hiss of lit match cords, knew that it would soon begin again.

*"Mathias, run!"*

The bear wavered, caught between reason and instinct, man and beast. Then it pivoted on its haunches and ran, ripping through the bloody sawdust, scattering snow in its wake.

"My lady would have the beast's head," Fizcko called to his men. "There's a bag of gold to the man who brings it to her!" At once all but two of the men-at-arms set off in pursuit. When the sound of their footsteps in the snow had faded, he gave Greta a charming smile. "'Bearbaiting' is such a strange term, isn't it? I have always wondered—is the bear the bait, or the dogs? In this instance Mathias has proven himself worthy bait, indeed. And you took it, my sweetling. Oh yes, you did. And now I'd like my keys back, if you don't mind."

He squeezed her wrist again and pain shot up Greta's arm. Fizcko gathered it to him like a rope, throwing it about her, binding her completely. Pinned into place, unable to move, she could only watch as he patted at her skirts, whistling a merry little tune. The men-at-arms looked on, impassive.

"Aha! Here they are!" Fizcko held the keys aloft, triumphant. Then, smile fading as rapidly as it had appeared, he leaned close, so close that Greta thought that he might kiss her. Just before his lips were upon hers, he whispered a single word.

"Sleep."

And Greta slept.

She woke to light and warmth. Distant music and voices raised in merriment. She was on her feet, a hard surface stretching behind her from her head to her heels. Her arms were raised above her head, her wrists bound. Panicking, she tried to move; the ropes held firm.

Her eyes were blurring, useless. She blinked, tried to clear them. Pale walls swirling with traceries of green that could have been painted leaves and flowers rose around her.

The baroness's chamber.

More ropes stretched around Greta's chest and thighs, holding her in place. Moving her fingers she felt timber above her head and knew she was tied to one of the thick, oaken pillars supporting the enormous beams in the chamber's high ceiling.

Arms upraised, helpless.

She closed her eyes, searched for the strength of the earth, the waters, the stars. There was nothing but the vaguest stirring of green. The baroness's chamber lay at the edge of the keep, high in a tower of stone. The earth and its power lay far below.

"There, now," came a woman's voice. "You're awake! Don't struggle; the poison will fade soon enough."

Familiar, that voice. Greta blinked and blinked again, but the world remained resolutely liquid, vague shapes beyond a rain-soaked window. She turned her head, caught the edges of an oval face framed by smudges of dark hair, the hazy gleam of some rich, red fabric.

"It's been quite the day for you, hasn't it?" the baroness said, sympathetically. "First the trial, then your adventures here in the Hornberg. I trust you enjoyed the bearbaiting?"

"Where is he?" Greta rasped.

"Oh, he's about somewhere." She wafted a long, fair hand. "I really should have killed him myself after the baiting. But this is a new gown. Venetian lace, you know. Besides, my men will find him soon enough."

"Why do you hate him so?"

"*Hate* him? Dear one, I don't hate him. In fact I'm rather grateful to him. Rob, too. If not for them both I would never have found you."

"Found me?"

"Rob never told you? Why, it was because of him—and Mathias—that I came to Lindenfeld at all."

Greta shook her head, willing her eyes to clear and the baroness's poison to leave her body. "I don't know what you're talking about."

"You don't remember? I suppose it must seem a very long time ago to you."

"I've never met you." But Greta heard the uncertainty in her own voice. The more she listened to Elisabeth, the more she believed she knew her. Knew her beyond the whisper-cold presence in her house after Hans's betrothal and in the woods.

"Once upon a time in Swabia, your uncle Rob and his wolves attacked Fizcko and me as we were crossing the mountains. They wounded me, but they near killed my dear Fizcko. If Mathias had not stopped them . . . It was only good fortune that an abbey lay nearby. I left Fizcko there to recover and went after the wolves myself. Such violence, you understand, could not go unanswered." The baroness paused, sipped from a goblet-shaped haze of gold. "I found

Conran first. The wolves' new leader, as it turned out. He was quick to tell me so—quick to blame Rob for the attack in Swabia. And quick to strike a bargain with me, too. He told me where I could find Rob. One word, he gave me, in exchange for gold. *Lindenfeld*."

A river of ice flowed across Greta's skin.

"And what do you think I found there?" Elisabeth asked. "Not your uncle, no. Just one pathetic wolf . . . and his wife. A beautiful witch with hair like fire. She was perfect. She was everything I had been searching for."

"You . . . knew my mother?"

The baroness chuckled. "Think back, my dear. Remember."

*See.*

Slowly, slowly, the veil of sickness and pain that had fallen over Greta lifted. She saw the exquisite detail in the painted walls above: flower, leaf and vine. She saw the rich canopy covering the baroness's beautiful bed, embroidered with golden thread. And, closer, the deep red satin of the lady's gown. The candlelight shining on the long, deep plane of the pointed stomacher, the wide, billowing sleeves. The creamy lace edging her bare shoulders. The pearls hanging at her ears and in ropes across her dark curls. The velvet patch, shaped like a star, at the outer corner of her eye. Even so, Greta saw another young woman beneath the finery. A young woman who, the last time they had met, had been dressed in coarse linen, her bodice much mended, her black hair dull beneath a greasy coif. Greta had been a child herself, then, but she would have recognized those large black eyes anywhere.

"*Stepmother?*"

Her mind stumbled and slid over the connection.

*It cannot be. It cannot.*

And yet, it was.

Standing before her was the woman who had married Mathias's father, two hundred years before. Who had stolen his life and that of his children. Who had caused Mathias to be cursed and taken everything from him. But here too was the woman who had enchanted Greta's grieving father and taken her mother's place so quickly. The woman who had held Greta's hair up to the sun, exclaiming over its rare color and beauty. Whose cool touch had made her skin crawl. Who had whispered to Peter of starvation and mercy when she thought Hans and Greta lay sleeping, and convinced him to leave his children to die in the woods.

Leisa. Liesbeth. Elisabeth.

They were all one woman.

The baroness-stepmother's skin was winter-white, her hair as black as sorrow. "There will be no more interruptions, now. No bears, no wolves or uncles. Just the two of us. I told you it would be so, didn't I?"

*Soon.*

She stroked Greta's face lovingly.

"'Margareta' means pearl, did you know that? And what a treasure you are. So like her. Perfect."

"So like who?" Greta whispered.

"Why, my dear sister, of course. Rosabell. You are very much like her. Your hair, your face . . . You are the *exact* age we both were when . . . when I lost her. Twenty-two."

Greta shrank away from that cold touch. "You remember how old I am?"

"Dear one, I remember everything!" The baroness's long fingers ran over the items assembled on the table beside her: the golden, gleaming washbasin Greta had glimpsed through the open door. A matching pitcher and embroidered towels. A hairbrush. A green silken dress, neatly folded, and underclothes foaming with lace and expense. A beautiful, heart-shaped box, its edges chased in silver.

An apple.

The book.

And the most terrifying knife Greta had ever seen.

Elisabeth-Leisa touched each of the items reverently, like a pastor readying his altar on Sunday morning, or a hunter checking his kit.

Like a butcher preparing for slaughter.

"If you and Rosabell were the same age, you must have been twins," Greta said. Her blood was thrumming in her ears, all but smothering the snatches of laughter rising from below. The clatter of a plate, and clank of a dropped cup. The Hornberg's guests, feasting in the hall, oblivious to what was unfolding above them. She tore her gaze away from that knife, the cruel twist of its blade, and searched the room. The long chamber had two doors, one at either end. Could she free herself and reach one?

"Yes. Rose was the oldest. By a few moments, only, but even so . . . she loved to tease me about it." Elisabeth's smile was real. Warm and beautiful. "She was sweeter than I, too. A greenwitch, like you. While I . . . I was always drawn to a darker kind of spellwork. We were two halves of one whole."

"What happened to her?" Greta worked her fingers surreptitiously against the ropes binding her to the beam.

"She died." Elisabeth's smile had disappeared. "And I died with her. I came back, but . . . she . . . I could not . . . My ability to cast had gone. We were always stronger together." She shook herself. "But none of that matters now. Everything that was done will be undone. Everything that was lost will be found." She touched Greta's hair. "Rose had hair just like yours. Red. Wonderful. It curled at the ends, too. I used to brush it for her, and she mine. It is the first thing I will do when she is with me again. I have the brush ready, see?"

"But . . . you told me Rose was dead." Greta, who had been intent on freeing her wrists, stilled.

"Yes." Elisabeth twirled the end of one long red strand around her finger and let it spring back. "The brush is for you. For *your* hair."

"But . . . *I* am not Rose."

"No." Twirl, spring. "But you will be, soon."

*Soon.*

Greta looked at the knife, the brush, the dress laid out as carefully as a bride's. Panic seized her. She pulled desperately against the ropes.

"You're distressed." Elisabeth's dark eyes glittered. "I felt the same way when I first saw this blade. But all will be well in the end, I promise you."

"Please let me go," Greta said, struggling. "*Please.*" She glanced at the book on the table, begging it silently to concoct another of its sizzling, biting spells and save them both. But it was quiet. Still.

"Let you go?" Elisabeth echoed. "After all these years waiting for you to grow up and be ready? This, right now, is your moment. Your destiny. I knew it as soon as I saw you. You were so young, then. Too young. What use had I for a child? The crone in the woods, though—*she* knew how to care for children."

Greta ceased her struggling.

"That's why I left you with her. I promised her that if she kept you safe, trained you well, I would return for you when you were grown and reward her richly for her service. I even allowed her to keep your brother as a token of my goodwill. She disliked being robbed of two children, of course. She believed she'd found you herself—finders keepers, you know—but I told her, one child can easily be fattened into two. You were both rather thin, after all."

Hans's small fingers, clutching the chicken bone. And Greta, watching the witch bake, feeling, through her fear, the power that thrummed in every crumb, every curl of perfect icing. When the witch began to teach her—how to knead and press and measure— she had wondered why. Why she was to be spared, while Hans was in the cage? It was her stepmother's plan all along. A crazed, and terrifying, design.

"If it was truly *me* you wanted," Greta said, glancing at the golden candlesticks and cushions, the richly painted walls, "why did you marry my father? He couldn't offer you wealth or power."

"Why, I told you, dearest. For revenge. It was Rob I truly wanted—but he was gone. So I made your father pay in his stead. He was broken and grieving . . . it was easy to make him love me. Easy to steal his soul. I knew he would not be strong enough to raise you, my precious child—the world is a dangerous place for witches. And besides, I wanted him to hurt as I had hurt. So, I asked him to leave you in the woods where the crone would find you. . . ."

Greta's vision wavered as it had in the beech tree and the tree house, until she saw not the baroness's chamber, but her parents' loft in the dark of some long-ago night.

"How can you ask this of me?" Peter demanded, flinching away from his new wife. "How could you bring your heart to leave my children all alone in the wood? The wild beasts will tear them to pieces!"

Leisa slid closer in their bed, coiling her limbs about his. "Then you had better plane the coffins for us all," she whispered, pressing her lips, a treacherous red, against him so that Peter gasped and arched his back.

The next morning he packed the last of the bread and led Hans and Greta deep into the woods. When they finally stopped the sun was low in the sky and Greta's legs were trembling with weariness. Peter built a fire and bade the children sit down together.

"Wait here," he said. The braid of red hair at his wrist shimmered in the light of the fire. "I will return for you both, I promise."

And then he left them there.

The baroness laughed cruelly, jarring Greta out of the past. "It was perfect," she said. "And the most beautiful part? Your father blamed himself. He thought it was *his* decision to forsake you!"

Greta barely heard her. All these years, she and Hans had doubted their father and his love.

*What if—what if I am like him, Greta? What if I abandon my child as he abandoned us?*

She saw two children playing in the sunny woods, leaping from a fallen tree as their father caught them, his arms strong and sure. He swung the little girl high then placed her, dizzy and giggling, back on the log. The little boy threw himself fearlessly into his father's arms, his smile as brilliant as his curls.

"You made him leave us!" Tears burned Greta's throat. "How could you?" Her heart broke anew for her father, who had died thinking he had abandoned his children.

"*To punish him, of course!*" Elisabeth shrieked. Her eyes blazed. "Didn't he and his cursed wolves all but kill my darling Fizcko? My only true friend in all the world? Your fool of a father loved you so—his anguish was a joy to behold!"

"And what about *me?*" The book, on the table between the apple and the knife, fluttered its pages as the woman-book appeared once more, standing shade-like before the enormous hearth, her inky eyes large and furious. "What about *my* anguish?"

"*Your* anguish?" Elisabeth demanded. She was glaring at the woman-book, not in surprise or fear, but in impatience. An accustomed, well-worn kind of impatience, the kind that comes with long years of familiarity.

"Wasn't *I* your true friend, too?" the woman-book grated. "When poor Rosabell died, didn't *I* comfort you?" The inky scrawlings on her skin moved faster, and faster as her anger rose.

. . . *write these words upon a paper* . . .
. . . *and in the night thou shalt dream* . . .
. . . *to break a tattercurse* . . .

"And what thanks did I get?" the woman-book shrieked. "You left me with that stinking crone in the middle of the woods, and then, when *she* killed her"—an angry gesture at Greta—"you disappeared. Fifteen years I've been languishing in this valley! Abandoned! Forgotten!"

. . . *gingerbread to make the heart sing* . . .
. . . *cardamom, cinnamon, honey* . . .
. . . *shatter the one who cast it* . . .

"And when you finally *did* return, you did not come for me. You left me with *her,* again! I have done everything I could to get back to you. Why if not for me Greta would not even *be here!*"

Greta gasped, stung by the book's words, by its betrayal. By the knowledge that it had been part of the baroness's design all along, its years with Greta little more than petals in a vast and poisonous bloom. She thought of the night of Hans and Ingrid's betrothal. Elisabeth had been in the house, then. She had left the apple behind. And the following day the book had not been where Greta had left it beneath the hearthstones. Greta had swallowed its lies, but she wondered now what the two of them had whispered in the quiet darkness of her kitchen. The two of them with their secrets and their wickedness.

"And now," the woman-book was saying, "I hear that I am *nothing* to you? What would your mother say if she were alive to hear this? I was her most precious possession. I taught her *everything she knew!*"

"Of course you are dear to me," Elisabeth crooned. "I trusted you above all others to care for Greta, and teach her, when the crone could not. Why else do you think I left you with her?"

"*I* think you left me there because you had no other choice," the woman-book said. "*I* think the miller came back before you'd finished off Greta's father, and discovered what you had done. *I* think he all but killed you. Dead stepmother indeed!"

The baroness went still. "Hush now, dear one."

"It's true, isn't it?" the woman-book crowed. "He *did* almost kill you! Oh, I wish I could have seen it, dearie! Surely the memory would have sustained me throughout these long and woeful years!"

"Enough. We are wasting time." The baroness rustled to the table and lifted the silver box's lid. "Here, Greta, see? Rosabell's heart. *Your* heart."

It lay on a bed of velvet, as delicate as a dried rose or the frilled fungi that grew in the dankest parts of the forest. Paper-frail, its sunken chambers dusty and dry. Waiting for the warm rush of fresh blood.

"Is it not beautiful?" Elisabeth sighed. "We covered it with salt and kept it in this leaden box. My dear Rose. It is all I have of her." She tore her dark eyes from the heart and fixed them on Greta. "*You* will become Rose. Her heart will beat within your chest. We shall be two sisters together again. And everything we lost shall be returned to us."

"So you say," the woman-book said wryly. "What will this be, your third attempt?"

The baroness gave a warning hiss, but the woman-book ignored her. "One can only hope that Greta will be wiser than her
mother," it muttered. "Between you and me, I don't hold much
hope."

# 27

## Snow, Apple, Blood

*Liliane and Rosabell sang as they walked, their voices rising sweet.*

> *"Young man came from hunting faint and weary.*
> *'What doth ail my lord, my dearie?'*
> *'Oh, Mother dear let my bed be made*
> *For I feel the gripe of the woody nightshade.'"*

*On and on the sisters went, deep into the snowy forest.*
*The huntsman followed.*

W hat did you say about my mother?" Greta was no longer afraid. She glanced at the apple, red and luscious on the baroness's table. Exactly like the one on her own worn table after the betrothal. Exactly like the one beside her mother in the snow.

"It is nothing," Elisabeth said dismissively. "The book is rambling again."

*Lies.* Greta could smell them, as cloying and sweet as old blood.

"You killed her, didn't you?" she said. "There was an apple in her hand just like that one. Just like the one you left for *me.*"

Not wolves. Never wolves. She forced herself to look at that glimmering knife, its twisted blade.

*"What did you do to her?"*

Elisabeth gave a bored little shrug. "Your mother was a fool," she said. "I came to her one winter night. She was shin-deep in snow, looking for her lost children. I offered her what I am offering you. Youth, beauty and strength unending. A body that would never weaken, never age or die. Riches she could scarce dream of. All she had to do was bite the moon apple and give me her heart. All she had to do was let me make her Rosabell. As my sister she would have wanted for nothing, needed for nothing.

"She refused me. Ran from me, into the forest." Elisabeth laughed. "Much good it did her. I tracked her through the trees. She called the forest to protect her. She wasn't as strong as you, Greta, or my Rosabell, but still, she used what she had and it worked—for a time. But when she began to tire I found her. Cowering in the snow like a rabbit."

Greta closed her eyes.

"I gave her the moon apple," the baroness said. "I begged her to bite it. She spat it back in my face. She fought me then—how she loved you brats and her worthless life in your father's dismal little hovel. She said she'd rather die than leave you." A little half shrug, one milky shoulder raised. "And so . . ."

"You killed her," Greta whispered.

"She killed herself. It was her choice." Elisabeth took the apple, held it up. "It is up to you to do your part, now. It won't be quick, I'm sorry to say. And it will hurt before the end. But it is the only way."

The door opened and Fizcko entered, encased in his iron ball. He rolled across the flagged floor as smoothly as a performer at a fair, coming to a halt at Greta's feet.

"About to bite the apple, I see. I'm just in time." He grinned up at her. "Not so clever now, are we?"

"Fizcko," the baroness said, smiling indulgently. "Where are your manners?"

"I lost them some time ago, as you well know." An uneasy glance at the corridor. "You'd best hurry, Lili; I cannot rest when that beast is nearby."

His words, his cage, stirred Greta to hope once more. She tugged downward on the ropes holding her wrists with renewed strength.

The baroness smiled, her lips as red as murder. "Poor fool. You think he loves you, that he will come to save you. *You*, a scrawny peasant with rough hands and bare feet. Mathias is a son of kings. Of emperors! How could he possibly want you?"

Greta tried not to listen. She struggled against the ropes, the skin at her wrists burning.

"But if you bite the apple—if you join me—you will change. You will be stronger, faster, more beautiful than you can imagine. You will have Mathias. You will have *anyone* you desire." She swooped on Greta suddenly, squeezing her throat with one dainty hand and raising the apple with the other. "Bite the apple, dear one. Bite deep into its flesh. Let the poison do its work."

"But don't swallow!" Fizcko warned with a smirk.

"No." The twisted knife glinted in Elisabeth's hand. "No. You must choke, as I did."

*Forbidden fruit.*

"Bite," the baroness commanded. She raised the apple to Greta's lips. *"Bite it now!"*

Greta struggled desperately against her bonds, against the baroness's crushing grip, against the smooth, cool skin of the apple being forced against her closed mouth. She could not, *could not*, allow that poisoned flesh to pass between her lips. Fingers pinched her nose, cutting off her breath. She twisted and writhed, her fingers tearing at the ropes binding her to the wooden pillar. And then, as the drowning panic rose to overtake her—she must, she *must* open her mouth and breathe—she felt other hands alongside hers, helping her. Her mother's hands, and her voice, too, as clear as if she stood at Greta's side.

*The forest will protect you. All you need do is ask.*

Mira, too, seemed to be there with Greta, her voice hushed and calm as though they were still safe within the warm, woody heart of the elder tree.

*You need never be afraid while the forest is near. It will protect you. It did so once, long ago. It will do so again.*

Greta closed her eyes. Reached, with the last of the breath remaining to her, for the strands of the web. Implored the ancient oak tree at her back to awaken.

And then, wondrously, it did. The pillar moved. Groaned softly, low and woody and deep. A fallen forest queen, roused from her

long and deathly slumber. Around the chamber, creakings and stirrings as centuries-old timber remembered itself and woke.

*Darkness, devil, death and fear.*

*Get thee gone from here.*

The room trembled. The painted vines covering the walls
throbbed with sudden life, rising from the plaster, peeling away.
Flowers which had been daubed in dye suddenly bloomed, their
scents filling the chamber. The tops of the oaken pillars grew leaves,
spread their boughs in a glorious canopy. Vines slid down to Greta.
Fine green tendrils tugged at her ropes, twisting them free. Her
arms dropped to her sides, bloodless, aching.

More vines came, growing and growing, falling from the now-
bare ceiling and walls in a heaving mass. They snaked toward Elisabeth, twisting about her wide skirts, coiling around the rosettes
on her satin shoes. She kicked and struggled in vain. The apple fell
from her hand and rolled across the floor, halting at Greta's feet.

"Stop this, Fizcko!" she cried. "Stop *her*!"

Fizcko, however, was distracted. He was muttering, low and
venomous, hands raised, warding off the greenery as it sought to
entangle itself in the bars of his cage.

"The knife, Fizcko! Give it to me!"

He managed to grasp it through the bars of his cage and toss it
toward her. Elisabeth scooped it up, slashing at the vines in a bid to
free herself from their grip. It was useless; as one vine fell beneath
her blade, more came to take its place until she was all but encased
in a writhing, sweet-scented cocoon.

Greta, untouched by the forest swirling relentlessly around the
baroness and the magician, seized the apple. Ignoring Elisabeth's
cry of rage she stepped easily across the room—a tangle of tree
roots, blooming flowers and undergrowth made a path for her—
and tossed it into the fire. The flames turned black as they devoured
the fruit. The core blazed, and then a scattering of seeds, poison-
bright.

"I should have let you die years ago," the woman-book said, beside her. "You are worthless, dearie. *Beyond* worthless." The fire flickered and snarled through her lucent, scrawling skin.

Greta gripped her by the shoulders. "Look at that," she said. "I can touch you, after all."

And then she pushed.

The woman-book screamed as the fire engulfed her. The book, still in its place on the table, burst into flames. A heavy silence followed, broken by the scrape and sigh of growing things, the sizzle of burning paper. Then Fizcko drew a sharp, horrified breath. Elisabeth made a sound that might have been a whimper.

Greta turned.

Something loomed in the chamber's doorway. Something impossibly large and black. Something that watched the baroness and the white-bearded man in patient, brutal silence.

"*Guards!*" Fizcko screeched. "In here! *In here!*"

Greta wondered how much of Mathias remained in the black bear. Whether it was more man or more beast regarding the magician so darkly. Then the bear padded inside and nosed the door closed.

More man, then.

"Lili!" Fizcko cried in terror. "Lili, help me!"

"You sound frightened, Fizcko," Greta observed. She had not failed to notice what the woman-book had revealed during her tirade against Elisabeth, when rage had caused heedless words to scrawl across her skin.

*. . . to break a tattercurse . . .*

*. . . shatter the one who cast it . . .*

"The witch in the forest was right, Mathias," she told the bear. "You must kill *him* first."

The bear snarled, the sound terrifying in the confines of the chamber.

"No!" Fizcko tore at the greenery tangling in his cage, stamping his boots. The flags beneath him began to crack. He laughed wildly, crushing the stone with his boots as though he meant to burrow his way free. Greta clenched her fist and the stone closed back over, catching the end of his white beard. *Hair and stone, stone and hair.* Pinned. Immovable.

Fizcko howled.

"You smell like lemons and oranges," Greta told him sweetly, crouching beside the cage. "Lemons, oranges . . . and fear."

"I'm not afraid! This cage of mine is made to withstand that brute!"

"In a moment or two you won't be in your cage."

"No?"

"No."

She reached into her bodice and removed the silver key.

"Fucking thief," he spat. "Not content to steal from me just the once, eh?"

"It is far less than what you stole from him." Greta seized the lock. "And what you would have stolen from me."

"No!" Fizcko squashed his face piteously against the bars. "You can't! You mustn't! I will give you anything you want! Coins, jewels, priceless gowns—I will teach you how to spin straw into gold!"

There was a rich click as the lock sprang free. Greta threw open the door to the tiny fortress and seized Fizcko by his velvet coat. His beard, stuck fast in the stone floor, ripped free and he screeched in pain. At the sound, she knew a moment of doubt.

"You stupid whore!" he spat, seizing on her hesitation. "He'll die! Don't you see? Kill me and you'll kill him too. He should have died years ago. Only my magic has kept him alive. Take it away and he'll be nothing more than a pile of stinking beast dust!"

There was an unearthly cry. Greta whirled. Elisabeth had cut herself free from her green prison and was charging at her, knife raised. Before she could reach her the bear leapt between. He seized the baroness in his jaws and bit down, rending and shaking. Greta heard the crunch of teeth against bone, the reluctant snap of breaking limbs, before the bear flung the baroness away. She hit the wall and slid to the floor, limp.

"Let me go." Fizcko was hoarse with horror. "Please, let me go!"

Greta wondered if she ought to run. It was clear to her that more of the bear ruled Mathias than she had first suspected, and that he was reveling in its savagery.

Then he raised his head, jaws dripping, and looked at her.

*Let justice be done, though the world perish.*

One hundred and seventy-four years. Alone, hunted and wandering, his family lost. In her hands lay his revenge. In her hands lay his happiness, and her own.

She drew the magician, kicking and screaming, from his gleaming sanctum.

He fought for his life, in the end. Clung to the ironwork and kicked at her in a fury. He screamed as Greta dragged him across the flagstones and Mathias fixed him with those unsettling eyes. The bear reared up onto its back legs—to its full, appalling height. It roared and Greta heard in it the absolute depth of Mathias's despair, the relentless grieving, the years of empty forest, empty days and empty nights.

She gripped Fizcko in both hands and pushed him toward the bear.

The bear raised one paw, ready to strike.

Greta turned away at the last, unable to watch, and saw that the chamber was empty.

Elisabeth had gone.

Drops of blood shone like a trail on the smooth stone of the Hornberg's corridors. Greta followed them, drop by drop, until she came to the kitchen garden. Beyond it, through a snow-covered archway, lay the orchard.

Drop by drop, dark against the snow.

A deep cold had settled over the castle. She heard distant shouts, the clatter of armed men. High above, the moon bloomed.

The blood on the snow thickened. Greta hurried through the sleeping orchard until she came to an ancient apple tree. At least it *had* been an apple tree, once. Now its gnarled branches were black and dripping with ruby-red fruit. Bittersweet nightshade grew in a tangle around its trunk, squeezing it in a poisonous embrace.

"Moon apples," Greta whispered. The tree shivered miserably. She understood then that it was suffering. That Elisabeth had planted the nightshade and forced it to grow around its tender trunk.

Elisabeth, too, was suffering. She slumped in the snow beneath the tree, blood from her wounds pooling on her pallid skin, on her torn gown, on the silver box she cradled in her lap. One arm hung at an odd angle and the bear's bite marred her lovely neck like a savage string of pearls. Her hair straggled over her shoulders. A familiar, wicked blade glittered in one frail hand. In the other, an apple.

And suddenly it was not the Hornberg's snowy orchard that Greta stood in, but a wide, snowbound clearing in the midst of a faraway forest. The coldness she felt was not born of ill-gotten magic, but the deep, pure power of midwinter. There was a moon apple tree in this clearing, too. It was magnificent, its trunk proudly festooned with ropes of bittersweet nightshade, the apples adorning its stark branches an explosion of crimson against the winter landscape: ebony black and snow white. And there, at its base, sat Elisabeth. She was not wounded and bleeding, now. She was alive, her skin creamy and rose-tinged, her dark hair shining. A basket of freshly picked moon apples sat beside her in the snow. She was singing, her voice young and sweet.

"Young man came from hunting faint and weary . . ."

A man stalked from the forest, broad and tall, dressed in the colorless garb of a huntsman. He pounced upon Elisabeth, pressing his blade, a wicked, twisted thing, against her neck.

She screamed. The basket overturned, spilling apples into the snow. The huntsman shoved her to the ground and pushed an apple between her teeth, holding it down, silencing her. A piece of apple broke away, lodging cruelly in her throat. She coughed and retched, fighting for breath, her body arching beneath his gloved hands.

Movement in the tree above. A young, red-haired woman was watching from the tree's dark branches. Rosabell peered down, eyes wide and fearful. She raised her hands and the apple tree shuddered, its roots tearing from the wintery ground, its branches clawing angrily at the huntsman. He slashed at the tree with his knife and Rosabell leapt bravely down, plunging her own small blade into the distracted huntsman's back. He turned with a roar, struck out with one gloved hand, knocking her to the ground. He wrapped his hands in her red hair and lifted her head, dispatching her with one slice of his knife against her throat. Easily and efficiently, as he would a deer or a fox.

Elisabeth rolled over, coughing, struggling, reaching for her sister as she bled into the snow. The huntsman threw her back down—the piece of apple caught once more in her throat—and cut away her fine red cloak, her silken dress, stitch by delicate stitch. She twisted and bucked in terror as he pressed himself upon her. As the dark rhythm of his desire took him, she began to choke in earnest.

When it was over the huntsman drew away from his prize and saw that she was wan and cold as death. He ran his hands through her black hair and kissed her rosy lips. And then he took his knife and cut out her heart.

Three drops of blood, a deep and startling crimson, fell onto the snow.

A cold wind rose and the black trees whispered. The huntsman shuddered as the heart began to beat of its own accord, thudding against his palm.

Once.

Twice.

Thrice.

He cried out in fear, dropping the heart. It fell back into Elisabeth's broken body with a gentle slurp. Beat and beat again, stronger and stronger, until . . . Blood ebbed, flowing back from whence it came. Tattered flesh grew together again. Bones straightened. Ribs soared. Skin pooled and smoothed itself like perfect, pale silk, until

Elisabeth lay as though sleeping. White as snow, red as blood, black as ebony; she was more beautiful than ever.

The huntsman whimpered.

Elisabeth opened her eyes. Sat up. Coughed and reached into her mouth, drawing out the piece of moon apple. She laced what was left of her gown and pulled her cloak around her shoulders. The movement should have been graceful. And it was. But something slow and scheming, some newly gained strength in those slender hands, hinted at more. And then she looked at him, and he understood.

He was hunter no more.

When the huntsman lay dead, the piece of apple burning in his throat, Elisabeth ran to Rosabell. She unlaced her sister's dress, lifted the huntsman's knife and thrust it deep into her chest. She cut out her heart and held it high, as the huntsman had held hers. She let it drop into Rosabell's empty chest. Knelt in the snow, her bloody hands not feeling the cold. Waiting for her sister to wake.

Hours passed and the weak winter sun tracked a path across the sky.

Dusk came with its sorrows and shadows.

And still Rosabell lay silent and cold.

At last Elisabeth clutched her sister to her, screaming her anguish. Three drops of blood, as red as Rosabell's hair, dripped on the snow beside her.

"I'm so sorry," Greta said as Rosabell and the huntsman faded and that long-ago glade became the orchard once more. "You have suffered so."

"We have both suffered," Elisabeth rasped. She tried to stand and sagged against the tree. "But we can still help each other. Give me your heart. Let me have my sister again."

"Your sister is gone," Greta said gently. "No spell, no magic, can bring her back. Just as nothing can bring my mother back."

"It is not too late for us. You can still join me. Help me grow strong again. In return I shall give you whatever you wish. Gold, treasures, lands. Life beyond life. Whatever you wish, it shall be yours."

The moon apple beckoned in her palm, rich and red with promise.

"Or perhaps it really *is* Mathias you want," Elisabeth said. "I know you care for him. Indeed, you have risked much for him. But you are a fool if you believe he loves you in return. No sooner has he had his fill of you than he will cast you aside. And where will you be, then? Alone, abandoned, just as you were when you were a child. Bite the apple. Bind him to your will. You will never feel loss or loneliness again!"

"I'm sorry you have felt such loneliness," Greta told her. "But you are wrong. Mathias won't leave me." Her voice hardened. "And I was *never* abandoned."

Moon apple trees flower only in winter and are exceedingly rare. They are known for their fierce magic; their potency and malevolence. But, like all trees they have roots that go deep into the earth. They have need of the sky and the rain. Berry, blossom, resin and root. They suffer, as all living things suffer.

And they will heed a greenwitch's will.

The tree rippled and spread, throwing off its mantle of nightshade, coiling its roots around Elisabeth's waist and throat and wrists. The black trunk cleaved back upon itself, exposing its dark heart, yawning like a tomb. As Elisabeth struggled the roots and branches tightened until they enfolded her completely, dragging her inside.

When she was gone the tree righted itself. Its trunk closed seamlessly. Its groaning roots returned to the earth. It shook off its choking burden of bittersweet, its clusters of poisonous fruit and stretched its branches toward the moon.

Three drops of blood, a deep and startling crimson, fell upon the snow.

# 28
## Home

When the apple tree had sighed its last and silence fell over the orchard, exhaustion took hold of Greta. She fell back in the snow, weightless in the cushioning cold. The apple tree shivered above her, shedding clumps of melting snow. The stars exhaled.

Rapid footsteps crunched toward her.

"Greta!" Mathias was at her side. "Greta? Are you hurt?"

"I'm fine." And she was. A warm breeze wove across her skin, her hair, her soul. The unnatural winter, lifting.

"Where is Liesbeth?"

"Gone."

He took in the apple tree, the blood. One gloriously heeled shoe, its scarlet satin vivid in the snow. "You did that?"

"I suppose witches have their uses, after all." She caught his cloak, pulled him down with her. Hardly daring to believe he was there, safe and whole.

"I suppose they do." He lifted his arm, scooped her close. "I should have listened to you when you told me you could help. I won't doubt you next time."

"Next time? How many curses do you expect us to break?"

Mathias laughed at that, the sound bright as summer in the winter night. Greta realized she had never truly heard him laugh. Until now, she had never really seen him smile. She laughed too and drew his face down to hers. There was nothing but joy, then. Pure. Strong.

And brief.

"As much as I don't want to," Mathias said, "we really do need to move."

"Do we have to? I'm so tired." And, oh, but the stars were beau-

tiful. She could lie there and watch them all night. Or sleep, whichever came first.

"Would that we could." He kissed her quickly then got to his
feet, lifting her with him. She shivered as the cool air hit her wet
clothes, and she heard what he already could: dogs barking and
guards moving. Shout after shout—Elisabeth's name echoing emp-
tily against stone and tower.

"This way," she said.

They staggered together along the fortress wall, the magicked
snow melting rapidly around them. At their backs the Hornberg
glowered and twitched as all within searched for a mistress that
would never be found. The sound of Elisabeth's name faded as they
reached the farthest corner of the battlements and passed through
the portcullis. Beyond it, the forest waited.

A pair of redstarts woke Greta before dawn. She blinked into earthy
darkness, listening to the birds' sweet song. A crease of greyish light
revealed the edges of the hollow, the intricate knotting of root and
dirt and tree that curved above, a secret place known only to the
wild things of the wood. When Mathias had found it the night
before—after they had stumbled down the steep mountainside beneath the Hornberg—she had barely been able to stand. Cold, and
all that her body had endured, had caught up with her. The hollow,
hidden beneath an enormous bank of pine trees and protected from
the worst of Fizcko's snows, had seemed unspeakably appealing. It
had taken all of Greta's strength to crawl inside. In moments she
had been asleep.

Daylight was coming. Beyond the hollow's entrance she glimpsed
patches of snow and pine trees. She closed her eyes against the sight,
willing herself back to sleep. Here, nestled on a bed of dry pine needles, with Mathias's cloak over her and his long body curled warmly
around hers, the Hornberg and its horrors, the world above, the
future—and all the accompanying unknowns—seemed far away.

"Are you awake?" His voice was soft with sleep.

"No."

He chuckled, his arm tightening around her, and she thought of another morning in another cave when she had woken with a bear beside her, its paw heavy on her waist. She smiled into the darkness, twined her fingers through his.

"The redstarts are awake and planning their day," Mathias murmured, not without reluctance. "We should do the same."

Greta had given no thought to what would come after the Hornberg, only that she must get there, free Hans and Mathias, and stay alive. Now that it was done there was no avoiding that which she had tried her best to forget: Lindenfeld.

*If anyone believed you to be innocent, they do not believe it now.*

Mathias listened in silence as she told him of her arrest, of the trial and her escape. When she had finished he was quiet for so long that she wondered if he had fallen asleep again.

"Mathias?" she said, uncertain.

"I'm considering paying the good people of Lindenfeld a visit." He did not sound sleepy now. "Maybe burning their Rathaus while I'm there, seeing as they enjoy fires so much."

"I think we've had enough vengeance for one night," she said carefully. "Besides, Rob and his men made rather a thorough job of it."

"I suppose that will have to be enough." He sighed regretfully. "Well, this certainly makes things simpler. I had thought to speak to your brother, see about finding work. Settling here, if that's what you wanted. But I see now that that cannot be. We'll have to leave Lindenfeld, Greta. Today. Now."

She nodded miserably. She was not such a fool as to think she could stay in the village. They had not burned her in the Marktplatz, but they might as well have—Greta would never again walk its cobbles or fill a market board with gingerbread. She had known it would be this way since the very moment of her arrest, before the trial had even begun.

She could hide from it no longer.

"The watchmen could be looking for you even now." Mathias was up, gathering his things, edging toward the light. She crawled after him, almost bumping into him when he halted suddenly in the low entrance.

"What is it?"

Mathias pointed and Greta peered out into the gloom. The sun had not yet risen but she could clearly see the grey wolf and the silver fox curled together and sleeping at the base of a pine.

"It's Rob," she said with a smile. "And Mira."

They watched as the wolf shook itself, sat up. Glanced at the fox and moved guiltily away.

"Brace yourself," Greta whispered, before they slipped free of the hollow. "When Rob left the Hornberg with Hans and the others I stayed behind to find you. I doubt he'll be happy about it."

Rob wasted no time in proving her right.

"What in God's name were you thinking, Täubchen?" he all but shouted when he had removed his wolf skin. "We were almost at the village before we realized you weren't with us! Mira and I went back for you. Worried sick, we were, until we found your trail. We've been here for hours—"

"I can see that," Greta said with a meaningful glance at Mira, who was stretching gracefully out of sleep and into her human form. "That must have been awful for you."

Rob went to say more, stuttered into silence and turned angrily to Mathias.

"She freed you?"

"She did."

"The baroness is dead," Greta said. "Fizcko, too."

"And the curse is broken," Mira added, smiling approvingly at Mathias.

"Well, then," Rob blustered. He looked as though he would have very much liked to be angry at someone, but was not sure whom. "Well."

Mira drifted to Greta's side. "It seems you've achieved all that you wished to," she said. "Only one question remains. What will you do now?"

The light of the rising sun was touching the eastern mountains.

A robin had joined the redstarts, their songs mingling. The day was coming and with it, the future.

Rob cleared his throat. "Täubchen, I've spoken to the men—Mira too, of course—and we think you should leave with us. I don't know where we'll go. But you'd be welcome. And safe."

Greta glanced at Mira. There was knowledge in the witch's eyes. And, deeper, a farewell.

"I hadn't given much thought to what I would do, or where I would go," she said slowly. She looked at Mathias. "What did you dream, through all those years? Where did you long to go?"

"Home," he said at once. "To Tyrol."

He had not said as much in the hollow. He had spoken only of Lindenfeld. At Greta's word he would have forsaken all that he had lost so long ago. He would have settled among people who had never trusted him, never accepted him, who had *hunted* him, simply because it was where she wanted to be.

*Home.*

Greta thought of the Alpen, the tantalizing glimmer of white on the far horizon. The promise of snow, of distance. Places so high and wild that there was magic in the water.

She took Mathias's hand.

"Thank you for your offer, Rob," she said. "But Mathias and I are going to Tyrol."

Rob's face crushed with understanding and grief. Greta stepped quickly into his arms, pressed her cheek against his shirt, the comforting linseed and leather scent of him. "I hope one day you will find us there."

The silky-cold dark of the morning was lifting when they arrived at the little house at the edge of the forest. The sight of it nestled in its clearing, the old apple tree foaming with blossoms, tore at Greta's heart.

"I'll wait here," Mathias murmured. "Remember, you must be quick. The farther we get before sunrise the better."

Greta nodded slowly. Unwilling, now that they had come to it, to do what must be done: pack her things and say goodbye to the only home she had ever known.

She paused on the threshold, one hand pressed to the rough timber. Had her mother laid her hand in this very place? Her father? She felt them with her as she stepped inside, looked over her mother's woven rugs, the workbench her father had made, the scarred table where they had eaten too few meals together. The heart of the house, the oven, where she had spent so many hours. And her father's favorite chair. Slumped in it, his boots propped atop the oven in the way he knew Greta hated, his head lolling in exhausted sleep, was Hans.

Greta's throat tightened painfully at the sight of her brother. Unwilling to wake him, she went to her pack, which was exactly where she had left it—half open, a petticoat tumbling free where she had ripped out the baking molds—before her arrest. She rewrapped the molds carefully, including the bloodstained heart, and stuffed them inside the bag. Then—quietly, quietly—she went to her room.

The sun was rising, the tops of the trees beyond the small window lit with early gold. Greta packed the rest of her clothing, her stockings and coifs, her linens and her scrap of mirror. She rolled the blanket from her bed and secured it neatly, wrapped her shawl around her shoulders, tucked her cloak into her pack. Stood a moment, looking. There was nothing left.

Nothing but her brother.

Hans's skin was ashen, his clothes damp and dirty, stained with the blood he had shed in the Hornberg. He shivered in his sleep and Greta, dropping her pack, knelt beside the oven. She remade the fire, blowing gently on the embers until new flames awoke. When it was burning well she closed the little door and straightened.

Hans was watching her. Staring as though he feared she was a dream, and would soon disappear.

"Greta?"

"It's me."

He threw himself from the chair and caught her hard against him.

"I thought—"

"I know. I'm sorry."

"You were not with us when we arrived at the village!"

"I went back to the Hornberg."

"*Why?*"

"Because we left someone behind." She pulled herself free, gestured to the open door and beyond it, Mathias. The rising sun caught on his hunting sword and bow, the buckles on his gear.

Hans swallowed. He glanced at Greta's pack. Her shawl, tucked neatly into her belt beside her knife, her tinderbox, and the fox pelt.

"And now you're leaving," he said. "Together."

"You know I cannot stay." The words caught in her throat.

"Yes." Hans nodded rapidly. "Yes, Rob told me what happened at the Rathaus. They found you with the book, didn't they? Jacob was right after all." He swallowed again, looked away, but not before Greta saw his pain. "And the Tyroler—Mathias—will take care of you, won't he? So that's good. You'll be safe and far from here. Yes, that's very good." He kept nodding, too fast, until his face crumpled. "But how shall I bear it without you?"

Greta pulled him close. She was crying. Or were they his tears? It hardly mattered.

"Hans, whatever happens, I need you to know . . . our father did not abandon us. He loved us. He did. It was not his choice to leave us in the woods."

Two children leaping from a fallen tree, the sun slanting gold upon the forest floor. Their father reaching up to catch them again and again. Never letting them fall.

"What? How do you know that?"

Would that she could stay and tell him everything. But there wasn't time. Sunlight was angling through the open door, catching on his golden curls. "Ask Rob. He knows."

She held her brother tight, molding all her love and protection into him, pressing him close so her heart might remember his shape. "Our father loved you. *I* love you. And one day you'll be a wonderful father too."

Mathias came to the door, his voice gentle. "Greta. We should go."

"Yes," Hans said, releasing her and wiping his face. "Yes. Go." He clasped Mathias's hand and arm, as a brother would. "Is there anything you need? Have you enough coin?"

Mathias dipped his head. "We have all we need." He took Greta's pack, slung it over his shoulder.

One last embrace, a final glimpse of her brother, his cheeks wet with his tears and her own, and then she was walking: her hand in Mathias's, her feet soft on moss and earth, into the forest.

# EPILOGUE

There is a very great difference between working a market board on the night of summer solstice and simply enjoying the festivities; between working for days at oven and bench—mixing, rolling and pressing—and savoring the sweet anticipation of a night of revels. Sweating in the dull heat of a kitchen when the world without is fresh and green and summering—birds singing, wildflowers blooming, their faces turned to the sun—is very different from being *part* of the summer, with time to learn the many paths winding through a rich green valley, or to lose oneself in the shadows of mountains so mighty that snow shines white on their jagged peaks, oblivious to summer's reign.

To find new forests, new trees, and to have time to listen to them breathe.

It is a joy indeed to wander without hurry through market boards heavy with countless delicious scents, the sounds of children summerwarm and bright with excitement, your hand in his. There are cheese dumplings and apple wheels to be tasted, kiachl pastries and delicate strauben to be savored and wine to be sipped. Close by an old woman is telling even older stories, forgotten tales of heroes, love and magic. Of men who become beasts and walk between two worlds, and brave women who break curses.

There are secret smiles to be shared.

There is music too, different from the music you know, but with a rhythm you recognize. There are steps to be danced and then, when the sun begins to sink behind the mountains, there are fires to be lit and jumped over. People to laugh and clap, and a breathless kiss—and relief—when you find your skirts aren't singed. An old woman, the storyteller, to smile knowingly and whisper, "You and your man jumped well; you are surely blessed."

And perhaps you are blessed, with the sun going down and the snow on the peaks bright in the last of the day's light. With a full belly and a home of your own, and someone to share it with.

The dusk finally comes, soft and silver-grey, and more fires are lit—great bonfires as high as three men—until showers of sparks lift above the village. The people clap and cheer. They gather around the fires, turn their faces to the mountains. Waiting. The music softens and the air is heavy with expectation, ancient and deep: something is coming, something wild and sacred and rare.

He takes your hand and draws you away from the crowds, past the church, along a path that rises steeply behind the village and into the forest above. Up, he leads you. Up and up. The air is cold, but he has your shawl—and your heart—and so you are warm.

The jagged line of the Alpen bruises the evening sky. Below, in the village, the expectation builds. You can feel it, a live thing, carried in the air and the water. You watch the mountains as you go, eager for the sun to sink, for the darkness to come. Up, he leads you. Up and up, until you leave the darkening forest and reach the open mountainside, a single, bold pine watching over the long sweep of the valley. He settles himself against its trunk and draws you down against him.

It is cold. Early stars sprinkle the sky like scattered coins.

To keep the demons and witches away, he told you once on a mountaintop far from here. But you know that's not true. For here you are, drawn to this, to these mountains, to the promise of fire, with something you cannot name. Alight, soul-bright.

Time has slowed with the setting sun, heavy with anticipation. You try to make out the tiny shapes of the men you know are crouched upon those distant peaks and see only dusk or snow.

And then, on the highest peak, a delicate flicker of flame.

A distant cheer rises from the village below. You hold your

breath as fire after fire shimmers into life, blazing across the mountaintops. Heaven and earth meeting, burning away the darkness of the world, its losses and its sorrows.

A hundred fires burning like stars.

# ACKNOWLEDGMENTS

E. L. Doctorow once said, "Writing a novel is like driving a car at night. You can see only as far as your headlights, but you can make the whole trip that way." Since I don't like driving much, day or night, and since I'm the kind of person who spends a good portion of their time wishing they were a mermaid or a hedge witch, I'd probably describe it like this: "Writing a novel is like walking alone through a vast, dark forest. You can only see as far as your lantern's light, but you can make the whole journey that way."

I added the word "alone" because the journey is, by its very nature, often lonely. Long, too. But all journeys in dark forests worth their salt include meetings—be it with wolves, magicians, witches, fairies, grandmothers, or beasts—and mine is no exception.

The first person I happened upon on my writing journey was Kate Forsyth. Wise witch, teacher, and mentor, she offered unfailing support, kindness, honesty, and knowledge. Kate has stayed with me every step of the way, from editing my terrible early drafts to celebrating my publishing news over strawberry cocktails. I hope we enjoy many more (but not all at once).

Thank you, too, to the Australian Society of Authors, whose Emerging Writers and Illustrators Mentorship program made a mentorship with Kate possible.

My agent, Julie Crisp, was next. Warrior, guide, and answerer of silly questions, she carved a safe path through the woods and kept me on course. Julie, I cannot thank you enough for loving my witchy gingerbread book enough to become its champion.

It was Julie who led me to Tor Books—let's make them a castle on top of a misty mountain. Rachel Bass, Will Hinton, Oliver Dougherty, and the rest of the team at Tor: thank you! My worn and much-loved copies of *Daughter of the Forest* by Juliet Marillier and *The Ill-Made Mute* by Cecilia Dart-Thornton both bear the Tor logo—it is because of them that I have dreamed of being published by Tor my entire adult life. I still can't believe it's happened.

To nature guide Monica Wurtz of Schiltach, Baden-Württemberg, who showed me the forest and put up with my terrible German; the Schwarzwälder Freilichtmuseum Vogtsbauernhof in Gutach; and the bears, wolves, and humans of the Alternativer Wolf-Und Baren-park Schwarzwald in Oberwolfach: danke schön. I saw so many beautiful bears at this sanctuary but was warned that I wouldn't see the wolves—they had been keeping to themselves for two weeks and hadn't been sighted by anyone. Standing alone in the misty rain when the rest of the visitors retreated to the warm, dry café and feeling a hush descend over the dripping forest as three wolves padded silently from the trees a few meters from where I stood—one of them looking directly at me—is one of my most precious memories.

Closer to home—thank you to the Australian Writers' Centre and Writing NSW for offering such wonderful writing courses, and to Allison Tait for her excellent advice and friendship, and for reminding me that a book only gets written when one actually sits down and writes.

Thanks, too, to my library colleagues for their support, especially Ursula for her tireless patience with my requests for help with German and my fairy godmother Kristin (and her partner, Paul) whose unconditional support and belief saw me through many moments of doubt.

Lauren Chater and Carla James are always willing to walk the blackest parts of the forest with me. Writing, structure, life, fairy tales, feminism, history, social media, mothering, trauma, love, loss, and endings—thank you, dark hearts, for dissecting it all.

To my sister, the rose to my snow, who has never stopped believing in magic (and who I hope never will)—thank you.

To my mum for reading me fairy tales, and my dad for always believing I could write them, too—and for a lifetime of love and support and good times and great music—thank you.

To my husband and my hobbits, who gave me the space and time I needed to write, who brought me tea and food, gave me hugs and gracefully accepted having a wife/mother whose mind is often away in the woods—thank you. Everything's better when we're together.

And back to that lonely forest path—to everyone along the way who asked me how my writing was going, who supported me and encouraged me, thank you. It meant more than you can know.

Turn the page for a sneak peek at
Kell Woods's next novel

# Upon a Starlit Tide

Available Winter 2025 from Tor Books

# 1

## Wrecked

May 1758
Clos-Poulet, Bretagne

S he thought him dead at first.

A man was draped lifeless upon a wedge of broken hull, cheek pressed against the timber as tenderly as a lover's as he rose gently up, gently down with the exhausted breath of the sea. The storm had raged all night, howling and hurling itself against the shore, rattling the windows so hard that it had taken all of Luce's will not to fling them open and feel its cold, wondrous breath on her face. Only the chintz drapes, her mother's great pride, had stopped her. Papa had brought the fabric all the way from India, and there was no telling how Gratienne would react had Luce allowed the weather to spoil them. And so she had kept the window closed, watching the storm as it battered the gardens and orchard and pried at the roof of the dovecote as though it would rip it free and toss it, rolling and bouncing, down the sweep of rain-soaked fields and into the furious waves.

It had been the kind of weather that stilled the world and sent folk hurrying indoors, that closed shutters and caused ships to fly before it into the harbor at Saint-Malo. One ship, at least, had not been fast enough.

Its remains dotted the gray water. Shards of decking, a slab of hull, tangles of rigging. Luce narrowed her eyes against the glare of the early morning sun, her boots nudging the water's edge. She had seen the sea's victims before, of course. Many times. Could not avoid it, with the storms that blew in from the northwest, tearing down the Manche, leaving ruined ships and their dead strewn across the beaches of Clos-Poulet like flowers after a wedding feast. Faded petals across the sand. This man's face, however, lacked the telltale pallor of death. And did he cling to the timber? She had seen men who had lashed themselves to ships as they broke apart, only to wash ashore, drowned, their fingers open and empty. No rope bound this man to his floating sanctuary.

Not dead, then.

A quick glance down the curved, rocky cove. There were folk from Saint-Coulomb about; she had seen them as she had climbed the steep path down from the cliffs. Men in their low boats and shawled women, heads bowed as, like Luce, they combed the sand for treasure in the storm's wake. Brandy and waxed packets of silk; coins and tea and candles. The men, however, had pushed out into deeper water, sails cutting the gray horizon, and the women had rounded the rocky point separating the cove from the next beach, where, farther along the shore, the path to the village lay.

But for a scattering of foam and weed, the beach was empty.

Decided, Luce tossed her boots, stockings, and garters to the sand and shrugged out of the heavy men's coat. She wore it like a shell, that coat; a briny leather casing that hid the soft, female truth of her. Her long, dark hair had been tucked safely within its collar; it unraveled around her shoulders as she bent to unlace her woolen caraco, then unbuttoned her breeches, sliding them down her bare legs. A final glance along the beach and her battered black tricorn joined the motley mound of clothing upon the sand. Clad in her chemise and stays, Luce limped to the water's edge.

One, two, three steps and she was shin deep. Four, five, six and the fine cotton of her chemise was dragging at her thighs. Luce's skin prickled. It was May, and the Manche had not lost its wintery bite. Seven, eight, nine and she was pushing off the sandy bottom with her toes, diving clean and strong into the first rush of sea and salt. She opened her arms and scooped them back, gliding toward the man.

A feeling of dread as she neared him. What if she was wrong? What if he was tangled, not clinging? Dead instead of living? Would he roll languidly to greet her, already bloating, eyes glazed and sightless?

Too late now. She had to know. A few strokes more and she was at his side: a man from the waist up, clinging to the surface while his legs fell into shadow. His eyes—to her relief—were closed, his skin pale against his dark hair, but when Luce touched his wrist she felt the fluttering of his heart. A tattered sail and rigging trailed about him. She grasped the rope and turned for shore, swimming hard, towing the cumbersome load behind her.

The tide was coming in. Papa always said that Saint-Malo's tides were the most powerful in Europe and that, together with the city's position, surrounded by the Manche on three sides with a happy proximity to the trade routes between Spain, Portugal, England, and the Netherlands—its treacherous necklace of reefs and islands that caused even the staunchest of navigators to falter—and the legendary, protective storm-stone forming its mighty walls and ballasting the hulls of its ships, was what gave it its enviable strength. Luce let the water help her, let it push broken man and ship both toward land. When the hull scraped against sand, she drew away the rigging holding him to the timber. He sank beneath the surface as though he were made of marble and not flesh. Panicked, Luce dived after him, wrapping her arms about him as the Manche dragged him hungrily down. How heavy he was! She opened her eyes—the familiar salty sting—and checked to see if the ropes that had saved him were now conspiring to drag him to his death. They were not. Yet still he sank, arms trailing slowly upward, dark hair wafting like weed. She kicked harder. Felt, through the water around her, the rumble of distant thunder.

Storm-stone.

Sailors on stricken ships sometimes helped themselves to its storm-stone ballast, hoping the stones' power might save their hides. Luce plunged her hands into the pockets of the man's breeches, scooping the fist-sized ballast stones free. They grumbled as they fell, tiny granite storm clouds heavy with magic. Lightened of his burden, the sailor lifted easily in Luce's arms. She pulled him to the surface and on toward the shore, his head lolling against her shoulder, his fingertips trailing in her wake.

He was taller than she, and strong, but she managed to drag him clumsily onto the beach, her chemise twisting around her thighs, her feet screaming in protest. His own feet—bare, perfect—were hardly clear of the water's grip when she lowered him onto the sand and sank down beside him, gasping. The Manche hissed regretfully, stroking at his bare toes, the cuffs of his breeches.

*Be still,* Luce told it silently. *You have had your fill of sailors today. You shall not have this one, too.*

The sun slid above the storm clouds tattering the horizon, washing the water in weak spring sunshine. It drifted over the near-drowned man, catching at his face. He groaned a little and frowned, closed eyes scrunching tight as though he feared the day.

Luce could not blame him for that. His ship, his crew, were gone, the former heaving and rocking itself into death in the deeps of the night, dragging the latter down with it. It seemed that only he had survived.

The strike of a ship's bell drifted faintly from the clifftop above. Eight strikes; eight of the morning. Luce pushed herself to her knees.

He lay on his back, eyes closed, his hair—as dark as Luce's own—fanning across his brow. Long black lashes were startling against his skin, his eyelids the faint mauve of a mussel shell. Beads of water glimmered silver on his skin.

Luce shifted closer, heedless of the cold sand, her exposed skin, the open beach. Took in his generous lips, the stubble on his jaw, the column of his neck. His forearms, tanned to smoothness. The lean and clinging shape of him beneath his shirt. Luce swallowed, exhaustion forgotten. He was waterlogged and soaking, near-death— and yet he was as beautiful as the dusk.

Her heart panged hard against her ribs as the young man's eyes flickered open.

Dark eyes they were, like a moonless night. He blinked twice, rapid. Frowned. His gaze settled on Luce's face. The frown deepened, then smoothed away, to be replaced by something else. Fear? Wonder? And then, before Luce knew what he was about, he raised himself up on one elbow, reached out with his other hand, and cupped her cheek in his palm.

Strong he was, deceptively so, and Luce knew a flutter of anxiety as he drew her face toward his. Then he was kissing her, the rush and the shock of it, the taste of his mouth, salt water and the stale, almost-death of him. There was life, too—warmth and wanting, and Luce found herself kissing him back, pushing her body against his, wrapping her cold, bare arms about his neck. She was soaking wet, shivering, water breaking jealously over her hips, yet nothing, nothing mattered but the two of them, his arms locked about her, her legs and hair and soul twined about him.

*No,* she thought to the sea. *No. You shall not have him.*

# ABOUT THE AUTHOR

Follow the Sun Photography

KELL WOODS is an Australian historical fantasy author. She lives near the sea with her husband, two sons, and the most beautiful black cat in the realm. Woods studied English literature, creative writing, and librarianship, so she could always be surrounded by stories. She has worked in libraries for the past twelve years, all the while writing about made-up (and not-so-made-up) places, people, and things you might remember from the fairy tales you read as a child.

kellwoods.com.au
Instagram: @kellinthewoods
Twitter: @kellinthewoods